THE
DARKEST HOUR

MAYA BANKS

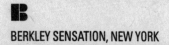

BERKLEY SENSATION, NEW YORK

THE BERKLEY PUBLISHING GROUP
Published by the Penguin Group
Penguin Group (USA) Inc.
375 Hudson Street, New York, New York 10014, USA
Penguin Group (Canada), 90 Eglinton Avenue East, Suite 700, Toronto, Ontario M4P 2Y3, Canada
(a division of Pearson Penguin Canada Inc.)
Penguin Books Ltd., 80 Strand, London WC2R 0RL, England
Penguin Group Ireland, 25 St. Stephen's Green, Dublin 2, Ireland (a division of Penguin Books Ltd.)
Penguin Group (Australia), 250 Camberwell Road, Camberwell, Victoria 3124, Australia
(a division of Pearson Australia Group Pty. Ltd.)
Penguin Books India Pvt. Ltd., 11 Community Centre, Panchsheel Park, New Delhi—110 017, India
Penguin Group (NZ), 67 Apollo Drive, Rosedale, Auckland 0632, New Zealand
(a division of Pearson New Zealand Ltd.)
Penguin Books (South Africa) (Pty.) Ltd., 24 Sturdee Avenue, Rosebank, Johannesburg 2196,
South Africa

Penguin Books Ltd., Registered Offices: 80 Strand, London WC2R 0RL, England

THE DARKEST HOUR

A Berkley Sensation Book / published by arrangement with the author

PRINTING HISTORY
Berkley Sensation mass-market edition / September 2010

ISBN: 978-0-425-22794-7

To Stephanie Tyler, Jaci Burton, Karin Tabke,
Sylvia Day and Lorelei James.

Good friends are the sweetest pleasures in life.
Thank you for being mine.

CHAPTER 1

HE'D hoped if he drank enough the night before he'd sleep right through today. Instead his eyes popped open at eight A.M., and sunlight promptly fried his retinas.

Ethan Kelly threw an arm over his face and lay there as the reality of the day hit him square in the gut.

June 16.

He could say something incredibly corny like . . . June 16, the day his world irrevocably changed. June 16, the day everything went to hell. Truth was, it had done that long before.

The phone rang shrilly from the nightstand, and he quelled the urge to smash it. Instead he listened as each ring pierced his skull like an ice pick.

When it didn't quit in a reasonable length of time, he reached over and yanked the cord from the wall. It could only be one of his well-meaning family members, and the last thing Ethan wanted today was sympathy.

If it was his dad, he'd give Ethan a lecture about how Rachel wouldn't like the man he'd become. No, Rachel hadn't liked the man he'd *been*. Huge difference there. *He* hadn't liked the man he'd been.

Frank Kelly would go on about how it was time to get on with his life. Move on. He'd grieved long enough.

If it was one of his brothers calling, they'd ride his ass about when he was coming to work for KGI.

Try never.

Knowing there was no chance of him going back to sleep with a head that was split apart at the seams, he struggled to the edge of the bed and planted his feet on the floor.

He'd sought oblivion, but all he had to show for the alcohol binge was cotton mouth and a stomach that felt like he'd ingested lead.

And he still had to face today.

Eyes closed, he pressed his fingers into his temples and then covered his face with his hands. His palms dug into his eye sockets, and he massaged as if he could wipe away the cloud hovering in his vision.

Rachel.

Her name whispered through his tired mind, conjuring memories of his laughing, smiling, *beautiful* wife. They floated there like butterflies.

Just as quickly they shriveled and turned black as if someone had held the wings to fire.

Rachel was gone.

She was dead.

She wasn't coming home.

He pushed himself up from the bed and staggered toward the bathroom. His reflection didn't shock him, and he didn't spare a moment to splash his face with water or wash out his mouth. He took a piss and stumbled back out, his tongue rasping over the roof of his mouth.

He needed a drink. Preferably something that wasn't going to make him puke.

Mechanically, he walked barefooted across the wood floors into the living room. Everything was just as she'd left it. The room reflected her personality. Classy, elegant, and uncluttered.

He was a rough-around-the-edges slob.

With a heavy sigh, he wandered into the kitchen to make himself a cup of coffee. Maybe his dad was right. Maybe it was time to put the past behind him. Get on with his sorry life. But he wasn't sure he could ever forgive himself for pushing her away.

He stood by the coffeemaker, waiting for it to quit gurgling.

He could sell the house and move to something smaller. It didn't make sense to keep it since it was just him now.

He needed to move somewhere he wasn't reminded of her at every turn, but then this was part of his penance. She didn't deserve to be forgotten and discarded even if that's what he'd done.

He thrust his cup forward and poured the steaming coffee from the pot. Then he ambled over to the glass table that overlooked the back deck. He sat and stared out over the landscape that had suffered over the last year. Rachel and his mom had painstakingly planned every detail, putting in long hours planting and weeding. Ethan had helped—when he was home.

He'd often been gone for weeks on end, the assignments always out of the blue, classified. He left Rachel with her never knowing where he was going or if he'd return. It was no way for them to live.

He'd resigned his commission after Rachel had miscarried their child. During the two years they were married, he'd failed her a lot, and he'd sworn he wouldn't do it again. But he had.

He rubbed his eyes then let his hand rest lingeringly on the three days' worth of stubble that resided on his jaw. He was a wreck.

A flash of peach caught his eye. He zeroed in on the vase of roses he'd bought yesterday. They were her favorite. Not quite orange, not quite pink, she'd always say. A perfect shade of peach. He should take them to her grave, but he wasn't sure he could bear to stand over that cold slab of marble and tell her for the fortieth time he was sorry.

As quickly as the thought seared through his mind, he curled his lip in disgust. He'd go. It was the least he could do. In the weeks leading up to the one-year anniversary of her death, he'd avoided the cemetery. It shouldn't surprise him that he was all too willing to shirk his responsibility. He'd made a practice of it.

He shoved the cup of coffee across the table, sloshing liquid over the rim. Ignoring the mess, he went back into the bedroom and pulled on a pair of jeans and a T-shirt. He needed a shower and a shave, but he wasn't taking the time to do either. If his appearance put people off, all the better. Making small talk and exchanging pleasantries wasn't on his agenda.

Back in the kitchen, he paused in front of the vase of roses.

With shaking fingers, he touched one of the soft petals. He hadn't bought Rachel flowers in a long time. Not since the first year of their marriage. What did it say about him that he bought them now?

Regret was hard enough for a man to swallow, but to swallow the knowledge that he could never do anything to right the wrongs was more than he could bear.

He gripped the vase, his self-disgust making him more nauseous than the sour alcohol swirling around his belly. He grabbed for his keys and stalked toward the front door, determined to go to her grave, face the past and make his peace with the day.

As he opened the door, he came face-to-face with a FedEx deliveryman. He wasn't sure who was more surprised, him or the FedEx guy, but judging by the way the man backed up a step, Ethan guessed he didn't look too welcoming.

"Are you Ethan Kelly?" the guy asked nervously.

"Yeah."

"Have a package for you."

"Just leave it," Ethan said, gesturing toward the rocker on the porch. He was impatient to be gone, and he looked pretty damn stupid standing there clutching a vase of flowers.

"I, uh, need your signature."

Ethan caught the snarl before it escaped and set the flowers down on the porch railing. He gestured impatiently for the stylus and scribbled his electronic signature on the handheld unit.

"Thanks. And here's your package."

The guy thrust a thick envelope into Ethan's hand and hastily backed down the steps. With a wave, he got into his delivery van and roared off down the drive.

Ethan glanced down at the envelope but didn't immediately see any identifying information. He leaned back into the house and tossed it on the small table in the foyer. Then he slammed the door and reached for the vase.

When he arrived at the small church his family had attended for decades, his gut tightened. It was old, whitewashed and situated off a gravel road well off the beaten path. The cemetery was adjacent to the church, and it was where his ancestors had been buried since the late 1800s.

He got out of his truck, swallowed and then made his way down the worn path to the fenced-in plot of land that made up the cemetery.

The roses shook in his grasp, several petals falling and then catching in the breeze. They swirled crazily and blew across the collection of marble headstones.

His mom had been here. Probably this morning. There were fresh flowers and Rachel's headstone gleamed in the mid-morning sun.

Rachel Kelly. Beloved wife, sister and daughter.

They'd loved her. His whole family adored her. His brothers used to tease him, tell him if he wasn't careful they'd lure Rachel away from him.

His gut churned. Acid rose, burning a path through his chest. Why had he thought he could return to the place where he'd said good-bye to his wife? His family had gathered round him that day, his mother's hand on his arm, his father standing to the side, looking for all the world like he'd break down and cry any moment.

He hated this place.

He leaned down and placed the roses next to her headstone. Tears burned his eyes, and he clenched his jaw, determined not to allow his emotions free rein. He hadn't cried. Not since he'd received her wedding bands in the mail. The only personal effects recovered from the crash. A crash that had taken the lives of the small group of relief workers flying home from South America.

No, he wouldn't cry again. If he started, he'd never stop, and he might well lose his tenuous grip on sanity after all. Coldness suited him much better. He knew his family thought he was unfeeling. He'd never allowed anyone to see how profoundly affected he was by Rachel's death. The truth was he couldn't bring himself to share her memory with anyone.

He stood there, hands shoved into his pockets, staring at the place where Rachel rested. Overhead the sun rose higher, beating relentlessly down on him. But he felt frozen.

"I'm sorry," he whispered. "If I could take it all back I would. If I just had one more chance. I'd never let a day go by that I didn't show you how much I love you."

The knowledge that he'd never *have* another chance crippled him. The fact that he'd fucked up the best thing in his life . . . he didn't have the words to describe the agony.

Unable to stand it another minute, he turned away and walked stiffly back to his truck. The drive home was quiet. He blocked out everything but the road in front of him. Numbness he could deal with.

He walked back into his house, absorbing yet more quiet as he shut the door. The FedEx package lay to the side, but he walked by it, his only desire right now to get a shower and rid himself of the smell of stale booze.

Twenty minutes later, he sat on the edge of the bed and hung his head as he tried to settle his roiling stomach. The shower had helped. Some. But it hadn't rid him of the aching head and sick gut.

If it hadn't meant facing his mom, he'd have gone over to get some of her soup. She didn't deserve to see him hungover and looking like shit, though. It would upset her and make her and his dad worry more than they did already.

He flopped back onto the mattress and closed his eyes. Peace. He just wanted peace.

WHEN Ethan next cracked his eyes open, the room was dark. He sucked in a breath through his nose and tested the steadiness of his stomach. He didn't immediately suffer the urge to puke, so he counted that as a victory.

He glanced over at the window to see that night had fallen. Somehow he'd managed to sleep the entire afternoon. Not that he was complaining. It meant he was that much closer to putting June 16 behind him.

His muscles protested when he crawled out of bed. He stretched and rolled his shoulders as he padded into the kitchen. His stomach growled, another thing he took as a positive sign.

He threw together a sandwich, poured himself a glass of water and made his way into the living room. Not bothering to turn on the light, he sat on the couch and ate in the dark.

He briefly considered finishing off the liquor he'd purchased the day before, but it would mean he'd start all over tomorrow and eventually his family would get tired of his avoidance and they'd come for him.

He'd shoved the last bite of his sandwich into his mouth when his gaze found the FedEx envelope hanging halfway off the table in the small foyer. He frowned as he remembered the encounter with the delivery guy.

Setting his glass on the coffee table, he walked over to

retrieve the heavy envelope. As he returned to the couch, he ripped at the seal. He reached over to flip on the lamp, then flopped onto the sofa and slid his hand inside the sturdy Tyvek envelope.

He dragged out a stack of papers in varying sizes and shapes. Some were legal-sized documents while others were half pieces of paper. There were charts and stuff that looked like satellite imagery and GPS coordinates.

Had he gotten KGI stuff by mistake? Surely his brothers wouldn't have made an error like that. No one they knew should even have his address, but this stuff looked official. It looked military.

There were photos. Several spilled over his lap and onto the couch. When he picked one up, his heart stuttered and all the breath left his chest in a painful rush.

It was a photo of a woman, obviously a prisoner in some shithole jungle camp. If Ethan had to guess, he'd place odds on South America or maybe Asia. Some fuckhole like Cambodia.

Two men flanked the woman in the photo and both carried guns. One had a grip on her arm, and she looked scared out of her mind.

That wasn't what blazed through his mind like a buzz saw.

The woman looked remarkably like Rachel. His wife Rachel. Rachel who was dead. Rachel who he'd just visited in the fucking cemetery.

What kind of twisted joke was this?

He rifled through the stack of paperwork looking for something that made sense. Maybe some haha note from some sick fuck looking for kicks.

When he came across the short handwritten note, he froze. All the blood left his face at the four simple words.

Your wife is alive.

It was a kick right to the balls. Rage surged through his veins like bubbling lava. He crumpled the note in his fist and threw it across the room. It skittered along the floor and landed under the television.

Who the hell would pull a stunt like this and why?

He snatched up the photo again and then another. He gathered them all, his hands shaking so bad the pictures scattered like a deck of cards.

Cursing, he got down on his knees to collect the photos from underneath the coffee table. Some had slid under the couch, and still more were wedged between the cushions.

Papers had also scattered everywhere. Charts, maps, a whole host of crap that made no sense to him.

Get a grip. Don't let this asshole get to you.

Even though he told himself it was all some morbid prank, he couldn't control the rush of anger. Hope. Fear. Rage. Helpless fury. Hope. Against his fucking will. *Hope.*

He curled his fingers around the papers, wrinkling them with the force of his grip. The pictures stared back at him, mocking him. They were Rachel. All were Rachel.

Thinner, haunted. Her hair was shorter, her eyes duller. But it was Rachel. A face and body he was intimately familiar with.

Who would do this? Why would someone set up such an elaborate hoax just to fuck with him on the one-year anniversary of her death? What could they possibly hope to gain?

He forced himself to look away from the scared, fragile woman in the picture because if he continued to stare and if he gave any thought to it being Rachel—his *wife*—he was going to vomit.

The other documents blurred in his vision, and he wiped angrily at his eyes so he could make sense of what he was holding. He forced calm he didn't feel. It took everything he had, but he switched off his emotions and studied the documents with the detached coldness necessary to remain objective.

He hastily spread everything out on the coffee table, positioning what he could fit, and then he lined the rest out on the couch.

The map pointed him to a remote area of Colombia about fifty miles from the Venezuelan border. The satellite photos showed dense jungle surrounding the tiny village—if you could call it a village. It was nothing more than a dozen huts constructed of bamboo and banana leaves.

Special attention was given to the guard towers and to the two areas where arms were stockpiled. What the hell would a shithole like that need with guard towers and enough ammo to support a small army?

Drug cartel.

He glanced again at the photo of the woman.

Rachel.

Her name floated insidiously through his mind.

It looked like her. Made sense it could be her. If it weren't for the fact that her remains had been shipped home along with her wedding rings.

No DNA testing had been done.

Nausea surged in his belly until he physically gagged.

No. No way in hell he'd blindly accepted his wife's death while she was being held, enduring God knows what by men who had no compunction about terrorizing an innocent woman.

She'd been identified only by the personal effects supposedly recovered with her remains. The fire had made even dental record identification a moot point. The explosion had incinerated everything in its path. Everything but the bent, misshapen rings and the charred remains of her suitcase. Half of a melted passport had been found in the wreckage. Her passport. It was the flight she'd taken and there had been no survivors. Ethan had never thought to question it.

Jesus, he hadn't questioned his wife's death.

He shook his head angrily. Boy was he getting carried away. There had to be some other explanation. Someone was messing with him. He didn't know why. He didn't care.

He scanned the rest of the papers. Guard post schedule. Drug drop schedule. What the hell? It certainly looked like someone wanted them to be able to waltz right in. It screamed setup.

GPS coordinates. Satellite photos. Topo maps. Whoever had sent it was thorough.

If this was for real, this information made these jokers sitting ducks. The Boy Scouts could mount an assault on the camp that would take it down inside of five minutes.

Your wife is alive.

He glanced at the shadow of the small, balled-up piece of paper lying underneath the television.

Four words. Just four simple words.

He hated the hope that sprung to life within him. His heart thumped like a jackhammer inside his chest. His pulse raced so fast he felt light-headed, almost like the night before when he'd obliterated any rational thoughts with really cheap liquor.

Only tonight he was stone cold sober.

No. No fucking way. He wouldn't allow himself the small glimmer of hope that was battling its way through a year of grief. This shit didn't happen in real life. People didn't get handed second chances on a fucking platter.

He'd prayed for a miracle more times than he cared to admit, but his prayers had gone unanswered. Or had they?

"You're losing it," he muttered.

Finally he was losing the last shreds of sanity. Was this what it felt like at the end of the road? Was all that was left was for him to start barking at the moon?

He rubbed his hands over his face and then over the back of his neck. Then he stared down at the information spread out before him like a road map. A map to his wife.

He wanted to believe it. He'd be the worst sort of dumbass to give this any sort of credibility. But could he afford to dismiss it without even talking to his brothers about it?

Hell, they ran KGI. They kicked asses for a living. There wasn't a military operation they couldn't mount. They found people who didn't want to be found. They rescued people from impossible situations. They freed hostages. They blew shit up. Surely some rinky-dink cartel outpost in the middle of Bum Fuck, Colombia, would be a walk in the park for an organization like KGI.

Oh God, they'd think he'd finally lost his mind. They'd have him committed.

But what if this isn't a joke?

The thought took him by the throat. It had teeth. It wouldn't let go.

He spent the entire night rifling through the material, document after document, mentally compiling the image in his head until it was so ingrained he could see the compound in his sleep. He knew it intimately, knew where every hut stood, where the guard towers were positioned. He knew when they changed guard, knew their drug drop schedule. Even when they took their prisoner and moved her to a different hut.

He had to be prepared. His brothers might think he was nuts. He couldn't really blame them if they did. One thing he knew for certain. With or without them he was going in after his wife.

If she was there . . . if she was alive . . . he was bringing her home.

CHAPTER 2

THERE weren't scripts for moments like this. Nothing in his years in the military had prepared him for this bizarre turn of events. Even as he tried to beat down the hope pulsating in his chest, it lived and breathed inside his skin.

Ethan parked his truck in the driveway of his brother Sam's lake house then reached down onto the seat to grip the envelope containing all the information on Rachel's whereabouts.

They'd be surprised to see him. In fact, Sam, Garrett and Donovan were probably inside planning their raid on Ethan's house. They'd been after him for months to join their special ops group, KGI. All in their plan to shove him firmly back into the land of the living.

A FedEx package had done what his brothers couldn't do.

For the first time, he felt something other than guilt or grief. He was angry. Very, very angry.

He harnessed that rage and kept it close, needing it for the impending confrontation. His brothers were going to think he'd lost his mind. They were his only hope, though, so he had to convince them that Rachel was alive.

He got out of his truck and glanced toward the adjacent lot where the war room was located. Built next to Sam's rustic log cabin that was nestled on the bank of Kentucky Lake, the

state-of-the-art, completely decked-out, two-thousand-square-
foot building housed the offices of Kelly Group International.

It was where Sam, Garrett and Donovan, Ethan's older
brothers, practically lived. They slept in the war room more
often than they did the house.

Ethan headed there first. Last he'd heard, one of the KGI
teams was doing a recon mission, which meant that his brothers
wouldn't venture far from the communications room.

The facility was impenetrable thanks to a high-tech security system. The location was benign and seemingly innocent,
which was why Sam liked it so much. No one would suspect
that military operations were planned and carried out in rural
Stewart County.

Ethan stopped at the keypad and had to think hard to remember the security code. The last thing he wanted to do was get it
wrong and get his ass laid out by his brothers.

After he'd punched in a series of codes, the door opened
and he walked inside. Sam and Garrett were sprawled on the
couches in the middle of the room, while predictably, Donovan
was manning the computer system referred to as Hoss.

Ethan strode forward, a determined set to his mouth. There
was nothing to be gained by coming across as some weak pansy.
Sam looked up when he heard Ethan, and his eyes widened in
surprise. He kicked at Garrett's leg that rested on the coffee
table and gestured in Ethan's direction.

"'Bout time you dragged your carcass out of that house,"
Sam drawled.

Donovan swiveled in his chair, and his surprised gaze met
Ethan's. "Hey, man, it's good to see you."

"You look like shit," Garrett said bluntly. "When was the
last time you slept?"

Ethan ignored the pleasantries and Garrett's observations.
"I need your help."

Sam's brows drew together, and he stared intently at Ethan.
His gaze swept up and down, taking in every detail of his
appearance. When he spoke, it was in a quiet, but firm voice.
"You know all you have to do is ask."

Ethan licked his lips and swallowed back the urge to blurt
out everything in a rush. "I need KGI's help."

Garrett's feet hit the floor and he surged upward. "What's
wrong? Are you in some kind of trouble?"

Trust Garrett to immediately bristle. Sam might be the oldest, but Garrett was an overprotective bear when it came to family. He'd lose his mind when he learned about Rachel. Especially since he had been so close to her.

Ethan looked down at the thick envelope in his hand, doubt clouding his mind. This was insane. How could he convince his brothers when he couldn't quite bring himself to believe it? But if it was true . . . if there was even the slimmest chance she was alive, he had to move heaven and earth to find out. There simply wasn't an alternative.

The knot in his stomach grew larger, and he finally thrust the envelope in Garrett's direction. Sam shot up from the couch and took it before Garrett could. Donovan and Garrett crowded behind Sam to look over his shoulder as Sam started pulling stuff out.

"What the hell is all of this?" Sam demanded as he shuffled through the charts, maps and GPS coordinates. When he reached the photos of Rachel, Garrett's and Donovan's expressions froze. Sam's frown grew fierce, and he stared back up at Ethan. "Where did you get this?"

"It was delivered yesterday along with a note telling me Rachel is alive." Ethan pointed to the stack of papers and photos Sam held. "That was the proof."

He marveled at how calm he sounded. How composed. As if hearing that the woman he'd thought dead was alive was a common occurrence.

Garrett cursed viciously, and Donovan . . . he looked at Ethan with sad, understanding eyes. Ethan hated that look. It was one beat off patting him on the head and recommending a good therapist.

Sam was still studying the photos, his brow furrowed in concentration.

"This looks like Rachel," he said slowly, as if it pained him to say it, to admit that maybe Ethan wasn't certifiable.

"It *is* Rachel," Ethan said, impatience simmering through his veins. "Believe me, I've been through it all. I've been up the entire night going through all of this, telling myself this is some sick joke. But what if it isn't? Can I afford to blow it off and pretend I never got this? My God, if she's alive . . . if she's been over in some hellhole for a year . . ."

He broke off, his chest heaving as he tried to regain control of himself. He curled and uncurled his fingers as the horror of that thought played over and over in his head. Rachel. Alive. Held prisoner and subjected to God knows what.

"Sam, you have to help me. I need KGI for this. Who else am I going to go to? No one else is going to believe me. You've been wanting me to come to work with you forever. Do this for me—help me—and I'm yours."

Sam swore and shook his head. Garrett scowled. Donovan's face screwed up like he'd just sucked a lemon.

"This isn't about you coming to work with us, man," Sam began. "I wouldn't manipulate you like that. Shit, I'm trying to get my mind wrapped around this. Do you know how far-fetched it sounds for Rachel to be alive after all this time? You know that, right, Ethan? You haven't convinced yourself that she's alive, have you?"

Ethan fought to keep his expression neutral. He wanted to snarl, he wanted to rage, and goddamn it, he wanted action. He wanted it now. He wanted to crawl right out of his skin. How could his brothers stand in front of him so calm, so *rational* when they should be planning Rachel's rescue?

"Christ, you have," Garrett muttered.

"Ethan," Donovan began in his quiet voice. "You have to know, this is probably just a hoax. Some sick joke. It might even be someone with a grudge against KGI. What better way to get us in the line of fire with our balls hanging out than to dangle Rachel in front of us like that?"

Sam nodded grimly. "We certainly have to treat it as a possible threat."

Ethan exploded in rage. He slammed into Sam, grabbed handfuls of his shirt and got into his face. "That's my *wife* down there in some shithole. We aren't talking about some nameless hostage or some political pawn who doesn't matter. This is Rachel. With or without your help, I'm going in to get her."

"Take your hands off me, Ethan," Sam said calmly. He stared back at Ethan, his expression unreadable. There wasn't anger or judgment in his eyes, and maybe that bothered Ethan the most.

Ethan slowly uncurled his fingers then shoved Sam back with a sound of disgust. He started to walk away, but found himself in a headlock. Garrett's arm tightened around his neck, and he muscled Ethan back across the room. He loosened his hold and shoved Ethan onto the couch.

Ethan stumbled and sprawled onto the cushions. He would have come up swinging, but Donovan promptly sat on him.

"Goddamn it, get off me!" He wanted to hit something—someone. Let loose the rage that was fast erupting, that he was losing control over with each passing second.

He blinked when Sam's face came into focus, their noses just centimeters apart.

"Listen up, little brother. If you think we're going to leave Rachel in that shithole, think again. But I'm not going to risk my team—my brothers—by going off half-cocked without any intel or backup, you got it?"

Ethan closed his eyes. He wasn't stupid. Desperate, yes. Stupid, no. He knew they couldn't stomp down to some South American jungle, guns blazing, and start a fucking war, no matter that his wife was being held captive by a bunch of assholes.

He nodded and felt Sam move away. Donovan eased off Ethan, and Ethan rolled off the couch and onto the floor, the carpet soft under his knees.

"I'll get Steele on it," Garrett said. "He and his team are finishing up a recon in South America. I can get satellite imagery based on the coordinates you have in that packet. If those guys so much as take a piss outside a hut, we'll be able to tell their dick size."

Sam nodded. "We need photos. We need numbers. We need to confirm every single piece of that information. We don't go until I'm convinced we're not walking headlong into an ambush."

Ethan remained there, on his knees, watching as his brothers calmly did what they did best—plan a military operation. Only this time they weren't rescuing a nameless hostage or recovering a fugitive.

Numbness gripped him. Everything moved around him in slow motion. A firm hand gripped his shoulder, and Ethan slowly turned his face upward until he met Garrett's hard gaze.

"If she's there, we'll get her out. You know that, man."

"Yeah, I know," Ethan said in a voice just above a whisper. Then he stood, irritated by his paralysis. "What can I do?" he demanded. He needed to do something or he would go crazy.

Sam eyed him, his demeanor calm, but his eyes betrayed him. There was a harsh gleam. Anger. Something Ethan could relate to. "We need an extrication plan. Why don't you get with

Van, pull out some maps and learn everything you can about the lay of the land. Download satellite imagery from Hoss while I get on the horn to some of my contacts. I've got a guy with the DEA who should be able to tell me if we're stepping in the middle of a drug war."

Ethan's lips twitched and he glanced sideways at Donovan. "You mean I get to touch Hoss?" He relaxed the slightest bit. He had every faith in Sam and KGI. They employed some of the brightest military minds in the world. They could do this. Soon. Rachel would be home. Soon.

Donovan grunted. "No. I'll do the touching. You just sit and watch. I don't want you fucking with my computer."

"That's as close as he gets to a love affair," Sam muttered. "I think he came in his pants when we got the thing."

"Ha ha. You're such a comedian," Donovan said as he flipped Sam off. He motioned for Ethan. "Come on, little brother. I'll show you the real brains behind KGI. Peckerhead over there couldn't wipe his ass without me to tell him when and how."

Action. Something to do. Something to keep his mind off the fact that right now, at this very moment, Rachel was terrified and alone. And worse, she thought he wasn't ever coming for her.

THREE days later, the war room looked precisely like its name-sake. There were blown-up satellite images and maps covering all surfaces and even some spread out on the floor. Donovan sat at the computer, his brow creased in concentration while Sam spoke in low tones to Steele over the satellite link.

Garrett stood across the elevated planning table from Ethan while the two of them studied the picture of the encampment they'd put together with satellite images as well as photographs taken by their man on the ground.

Ethan looked up when Sam walked back over. "What's up? Have they made a positive ID yet?"

Sam stood next to Garrett and picked up one of the photos. "Things are quiet there. Too quiet. Steele got there two days ago and has been pulling round-the-clock surveillance with his team. They've seen the woman in question twice."

Ethan surged forward, putting his palms down on the table. "So she *is* there. She's alive."

Sam hesitated. "That's not what I'm saying, man. We don't know that it's her."

"Bullshit. You're telling me Rachel has some goddamn twin in the exact same place she went on her mercy mission a year ago?"

Garrett and Sam exchanged glances. "I just don't want you to get your hopes up, Ethan," Sam said. "We agree that whoever the woman is, it's obvious she's not there by choice, and the fact that she strongly resembles Rachel is enough for us to go in for the extrication."

Ethan's shoulders sank in relief. "When?" he asked. They'd already spent three days—three agonizingly long days—waiting for information, data, satellite photos, and Steele's recon.

And then another thought hit him. "You're not leaving me out of this." It wasn't a question. There *was* no question. He wasn't staying here while KGI went in after Rachel.

"To be honest we thought about it," Garrett admitted. "But I also know if it was my wife, no way in hell would anyone keep me off the mission. So yeah, you're going, but you're going to keep your head on straight. You've been out of action for a while, and you have a personal stake in this."

Ethan nodded, adrenaline stirring in his veins. "When?" he asked again.

"As soon as we can be assured we know exactly what we're getting into," Sam said. "Steele's on the ground with his team. He's positioning them so we have a tight circumference around the encampment. As soon as I can get a chopper lined up for the extrication, we'll gear up and fly down on the jet to Mexico. We take the helicopter into Colombia and drop into the jungle. It'll be a bitch, but it's doable."

Garrett's jaw tightened. "Hell yeah it's doable."

"Just got an email from Beavis and Butt-Head," Donovan called over his shoulder. "Are we telling them what's going on?"

Ethan grimaced. The youngest two Kelly brothers, Nathan and Joe, were still active military and currently deployed to Afghanistan. Ethan was sure Sam and the others probably kept the twins updated on the goings-on at KGI, but the last thing he needed was for his brothers to be worried and distracted when they were fighting in a hot zone.

"No," he and Sam said at the same time.

Sam glanced over at Ethan and nodded. "No reason to get anyone's hopes up until we know for sure that Rachel is alive."

"So what are we telling Dad?" Garrett asked.

Donovan turned around in his seat to tune in more to the conversation.

"I'll tell him it's a classified mission," Sam said with a shrug. "Not like we haven't had a dozen of those."

"Yeah, but what are you going to tell him when he notices that our holdout isn't holding out anymore?" Donovan asked with a jerk of his thumb in Ethan's direction.

Ethan shifted uncomfortably when all three of his brothers focused their gazes on him.

"Just that he's not holding out anymore," Garrett said. "Dad will be glad to hear it. He's worried about Ethan."

Donovan nodded and turned back to the computer. The satellite link beeped and Sam walked back over to the receiver.

"Do we have any backup?" Ethan asked Garrett in a low voice. As much as he wanted Rachel back, safe and in his arms, he didn't want to risk his brothers' lives with a dangerous extrication. Things could and did go wrong all the time.

Garrett grunted. "I won't lie to you, man. This kind of operation usually takes a hell of a lot more planning. We don't have the backing and manpower of the government for this. It's not as easy as picking up the phone and asking for shit like when we're contracting for Uncle Sam. If we start a goddamn war with fucking Colombia, our asses are in a sling and there ain't no one there to bail us out."

"I know I shouldn't have asked," Ethan said as he stared back at his brother. "But I *had* to. I can't leave her down there."

Garrett's eyes grew cold. "Hell no, we're not leaving her down there. We'll get her back, Ethan. No one fucks with the Kellys."

Ethan cracked a smile then reached out to bump his fist against Garrett's.

"All right, we have a go time," Sam said as he returned.

Donovan swiveled in his chair again. "I'm downloading the local maps into our GPS's along with the digital images Steele captured. I'm done on my end."

Ethan leaned forward. "When?"

Garrett and Donovan also looked to Sam for the answer.

"We rendezvous with the guy getting us a chopper in Mexico

in forty-eight hours. From there we fly into Colombia, do the drop, get Rachel, then get the hell out. Rio and his team are still over in Asia, but he's heading to South America as fast as he can get there. He'll be our backup if we need him."

"How many will we have on the ground?" Ethan asked.

"Steele and his team . . . and us," Garrett said. "More than enough to take out these assholes."

Ethan sat back and blew out his breath in frustration. Forty-eight hours. It was a lifetime and not enough time all at once.

Fear for the danger he'd placed his brothers in gnawed at his gut, but at the same time, he'd do anything to bring Rachel back.

"You're not wimping out on us, are you?" Garrett asked Ethan.

Ethan yanked his gaze to his brother in surprise. There was a gleam in Garrett's eyes. A calculated gleam that bordered on challenge.

He met Garrett's stare with resolve. KGI was the best at what they did. He had every confidence in their ability to head up the mission to rescue Rachel. His brothers had all served time in the military, and there wasn't another badass out there who could hold a candle to his brothers.

"Hooyah," Ethan said softly.

Sam rolled his eyes. "Don't start that navy shit with me, frog boy."

"Oohrah," Garrett said with a smirk.

Donovan laughed and echoed with an oohrah of his own.

Sam shook his head. "Why is it Nathan and Joe showed the only good sense among my brothers and followed my example of joining the army?"

"They're the dumb ones," Ethan said.

"Yeah well, what's your excuse?" Garrett demanded. "Donovan and I set such a good example for you with the marines. But no, you had to go be a navy boy. Although you look damn pretty in the little sailor suit."

Donovan snickered, and Ethan reached out to slug Garrett in the gut. Garrett doubled over as a laugh escaped.

"It's good to have you back, Ethan," Sam said, his tone growing serious.

Ethan glanced up at Sam. "I just want *her* back, man."

"Yeah, I know, and we'll get her. I promise."

CHAPTER 3

THE jungle around them was alive with hundreds of critters. The air was so heavy and concentrated that it swam in lines in front of Ethan's eyes. Breathing was damn near impossible. The heat was so oppressive that it weighed down on them like two tons of concrete.

Seamlessly, the men—and the lone woman—moved stealthily through the jungle, closing in on their target.

P.J. Rutherford, their best sniper, took position and trained her rifle on the distant guard towers. She held up two fingers to signal there were two men in each of the two western posts.

David Coletrane, or just Cole, was half a mile directly in front of P.J., poised to take out the two east towers. Steele, P.J. and Cole's team leader, held up a fist and signaled his ready.

Donovan and Garrett disappeared from sight as they maneuvered to the south. Their job was to set explosives, provide distraction, and take out anyone in their path.

Steele and the rest of his team would take the north.

Sam and Ethan surveyed the ragtag camp in front of them, taking in each of the straw-thatched huts. Sam held up his finger and motioned toward the three to the north and then he pointed at Ethan and gestured toward the four huts on the southern perimeter. Ethan nodded and hunkered down to wait for the fireworks to begin.

It took every ounce of his training to sit there and not charge into the camp, gun blazing, throwing grenades and leveling everything in his path. It was still his preference. These bastards didn't deserve any mercy. If it weren't for the fact they weren't sure where Rachel was being housed and that she might get caught in the cross fire, Ethan would say fuck the plan and decimate the village.

Sam checked his watch and then signaled Ethan that they had two minutes to go time.

Ethan's gaze drifted through the leaves and tangle of vines, but the only person other than Sam he could see was P.J. At one minute to go time she'd take out the guards and then she and Cole would pick off anyone in the way of Ethan and Sam.

She was an interesting character. When Sam had told Ethan about her, he'd assumed she'd be a doggish-looking woman, stocky in build with a manly haircut and tattoos. Instead she was delicate looking and utterly feminine. That she was a highly skilled assassin was incongruous with the image she projected.

Her hair was pulled back in a ponytail, and her face was painted camo. She was hunched over her rifle, her expression one of intense concentration as she found her target.

At one minute to go, only the slight shift of her body told Ethan that she'd taken the first shot. Within two seconds she'd taken the second and then she swung her rifle over to aim at the other guard tower.

She took two more quick shots then held up her hand to signal her success.

Twenty seconds to go time.

P.J. repositioned so she'd have Sam and Ethan's path within her rifle sights. Five seconds to go-time and she was on her belly, her rifle up and steady.

A thunderous explosion shook the ground. Multiple fireballs lifted through the jungle canopy, lighting an eerie path into the sky.

Ethan lunged forward, his gun up as he ran through the tangle of jungle growth and into the cleared area of the camp.

Machine gun fire erupted on both sides of Ethan as he made

his way toward the first hut. He hadn't checked Sam's progress, and he just hoped the sharpshooters did their jobs.

SHE huddled in the darkness, hugging her knees to her chest. She rocked back and forth, a constant motion as she rubbed her hands up and down her legs.

Her medicine. She needed her medicine. Where were they? Had they forgotten? Had she done something bad? Was she being punished? She needed her medicine. The pain crawled over her flesh, leaving a burning trail over her body.

She closed her eyes and rocked harder. Sweat bathed her shoulders, and she shook uncontrollably. The dirt floor felt hard and cold. Despite the oppressive heat and humidity, coldness seeped into her bones. Chill bumps broke out on the surface of her skin.

Rachel. Rachel. Rachel.

She said the name, a litany on her lips. If she didn't say it, she was sure she would forget, and she had already forgotten so much.

My name is Rachel.

Some of the panic subsided as she managed to hold on to that one vital piece of information. Pain and nausea welled in her stomach, twisting it around in knots.

She sucked in deep breaths and tried to focus her thoughts. She closed her eyes again to conjure the image that had brought her comfort in the long months she had lived here.

Rachel couldn't remember *his* name. She didn't even know if he was *real*, but as long as she could see him, she could believe there was still hope.

Her guardian angel. He hovered on the fringes of her shattered mind. Big, strong, a warrior. Her protector.

Where was he?

How many days had she sat here wondering if he would come? She had lost count long ago, the scratches on the wall to mark the passing time a long-forgotten diversion.

Oh God, she was going to die. They weren't bringing her medicine. She needed it. She couldn't take the pain. Fear lodged in her throat, and she tried in vain to breathe around it. Her chest burned with the effort.

She rocked faster.

A huge explosion echoed like a million thunderclaps. The ground shook beneath her and she threw her arms over her head. The sound of gunfire rang sharply in her ears, and fear clutched her with dead fingers.

The lock on the door of her hut rattled impatiently, and then another gunshot, much closer, pierced her hearing. She glanced up just as the door flew open. Sunlight blinded her, and she ducked away. When she looked back, silhouetted against the odd orange glow behind him, stood a man.

He was big and menacing, his features drawn and made ghoulish by the fire and smoke and more sunlight than she'd seen in days. His rifle swept the room before he focused all his attention on her.

Oh God, he was going to kill her. The day had finally come. The one they had taunted her with.

She whimpered deep in her throat and wrapped her arms protectively around herself.

"Jesus," the man swore. "Rachel, honey, we've come to help you. Everything's going to be okay."

She flinched. They had never used her name. In her darker moments, she wondered if she had made the name up.

The man turned his head sideways and spoke into some kind of a receiver he was wearing. "I've got her. Hut three. North. We'll need cover."

He looked back at her and started forward.

She threw her arms over her head and shrank as small as she could. She closed her eyes so she couldn't see what was to come.

Above her the man swore softly, but he stopped. She could no longer hear him move. She chanced a peek from under her arms and saw him standing sideways to the door. He was looking out, his profile illuminated by fire.

A few seconds later, another man burst through the door, a gun cradled in his arms. His gaze settled immediately on her.

The second man ripped off his helmet, and her mouth dropped open in shock. She knew this man. She'd seen him so many times in her mind. But he wasn't real, was he?

He knelt cautiously in front of her and extended his hand. "Rachel, it's me, Ethan. I've come to take you home."

He knew her name. Her guardian angel knew her name.

She began to shake harder, her teeth chattering loudly in her head. Pain gnawed incessantly at her. She needed her medicine.

"Medicine," she croaked out. It hurt to speak. She hadn't spoken aloud in a long time. "I need my medicine."

Ethan frowned and looked back at the other man. Then he reached out and gently took her arm. The first man moved from the doorway so that the light shone more fully in, and she flinched away from the glare. Ethan turned her wrist over until the inside of her arm was exposed.

He let out a hiss of anger.

She yanked her arm away and shrank from the power emanating from him.

"Shit, Sam," Ethan murmured.

The man he called Sam echoed the curse and then jerked his thumb over his shoulder. "We have to move. Now. It's three miles back to the chopper and we're still taking fire from all sides."

She stared between the two men, mystified by what was transpiring. Where were they taking her?

Ethan touched her cheek and then scrambled up, pulling her with him. Pain wracked her body and she was bathed in heavy sweat. Yet she'd never felt so cold in her entire life.

"Trust me, baby," Ethan said softly. "I'm going to get you out of here, but I need you to do as I say."

She barely had time to nod before he picked her up and threw her over his shoulder in a fireman's carry. He fumbled with his rifle with his free hand and then charged out the door behind Sam.

The ground spun dizzily underneath her and his shoulder dug painfully into her belly until bile rose and ate at her throat. Around her the world had gone mad. Fire blazed a path across the village and beyond. Gunfire peppered the ground and trees around her, and she was sure she would die. Now, when rescue was imminent, it would all be for nothing. They would never let her go. They'd told her as much.

Suddenly she went flying through the air. Her back hit the ground with such force that all the air was forced out of her lungs. She lay there, one muscled arm banded tight around her waist as she tried to breathe. Pain, so constant, exploded in her head until dark spots danced in her vision.

She tried to turn when the nausea finally overwhelmed her, but she was trapped. Panicked, she kicked and flailed but his grip only tightened on her.

"Shhh, baby. I'm here. It's okay."

His voice comforted her, and she stilled beneath him. Ethan pulled her to her feet, and she blinked as she adjusted to the constant stream of sunlight.

As suddenly as he hauled her up, he shoved her back down, covering her head with his big arms.

"Son of a bitch! Where's the cover?"

Ethan lay there, sprawled over Rachel as he quickly scanned the area. Goddamn it, Sam was pinned down several yards away. Ethan looked again in the direction he knew P.J. to be and where Garrett and Donovan would be rendezvousing.

He couldn't leave Sam, but he had to protect Rachel. Hell of a choice. His brother or his wife.

He pushed Rachel's hair from her face and took in the stark terror in her eyes.

"Listen to me, Rachel. I need you to do exactly as I tell you. See that slight path into the jungle?"

He pointed and waited for her to turn her head. When he was satisfied she was locked on, he motioned again.

"When I say go, I want you to run like hell. Straight down that path. Get into the jungle and hide. I have people there. They'll find you."

She stared at him in horror, and he wondered if she'd even absorbed his directions.

"Come on, Rachel, say something. Tell me you understand. I have to help Sam."

Slowly she nodded. He let go of her and she scrambled to her knees, looking warily at her surroundings.

Ethan pulled the mic to his mouth. "I need cover. Sam's in trouble. I'm sending Rachel to you, P.J."

In response, a heavy line of fire peppered the area beyond Ethan. He shoved Rachel forward. "Go! Run!"

She didn't hesitate. Like a colt getting its legs under it for the first time, she stumbled erratically and lunged toward the heavier growth of the jungle.

She looked back, and he raised himself enough that he could see her. Fire seared across his scalp, and he smelled the unmistakable scent of scorched hair and blood.

Rachel stared at him in horror about the time he felt the warm slide of blood down his neck.

"Go!" he barked.

He dropped down and ran his hand over the area above his right ear. It came away stained with blood. He still had most of his hair and he wasn't missing any body parts, so it obviously wasn't serious.

He waited only long enough for her to disappear into the greenery before he turned to find his brother.

He crawled over and Sam shot him a disgruntled look.

"Save it," Ethan said shortly. "I'm not leaving you."

"You should be taking care of your wife," Sam bit out. "Not babysitting my ass."

Another round of fire peppered the metal barrels they'd taken cover behind.

"Goddamn sons of bitches," Sam said. "Where the fuck are Van and Garrett with all the goddamn explosives?"

An explosion shook the ground, and both men covered their heads with their arms as debris rained down all around them.

Ethan grinned. "Right there I'd say."

Another boom rocked the area, and Ethan and Sam took advantage of the chaos to bolt from their cover. The earpiece fell from Ethan's ear, and in front of him, Sam cursed a blue streak as they dove behind a stack of boxes.

"Cole's been hit. Some fucking lucky ricochet. Steele's on his way to get him. Dolphin and Renshaw are providing cover."

"What about Rachel?" Ethan demanded. "Have Garrett and Van gotten to her yet? Where the hell is P.J.?"

He hadn't realized he was yelling into the mic until Sam winced.

"P.J. says to tell you she's busy saving your ass. No sign of Rachel. Van and Garrett are looking. What the hell happened to your earpiece?"

"Lost it."

"Shit, Ethan, you're hit. You're bleeding like a stuck pig."

Ethan glanced up at his brother and curled his lip. "What are you, a pussy? Your years out of the army turned you into a girl? Since when do you worry over anything less than a missing limb?"

Sam shook his head and then gestured over his shoulder.

"P.J. taken them out yet? I'm getting damn tired of lying here in the dirt."

Ethan rose up on his elbows and swept his viewing area with his rifle. Just when one of the assholes popped his head over a barrel, P.J. put a bullet between his eyes. Damn the woman was good.

"I've got to get to Rachel," Ethan said.

Sam nodded. "On my count."

Ethan rolled, coming up on his knees.

"One."

"Two."

"Three."

The two men dove from behind the crates, and ducked and ran for the jungle.

The world around them went eerily quiet when they reached the area where P.J. was positioned. It made Ethan uneasy.

Moments later, Steele, Renshaw, and Baker staggered through the growth dragging Cole between them. Ethan glanced around to see Sam holding his hand over his ear as he listened intently to traffic. He looked up at Ethan, his expression grim.

"What?" Ethan demanded. "What the hell is going on? Where are Van, Garrett, and Rachel?"

Sam motioned for the others to gather, and the knot in Ethan's stomach grew bigger.

"Goddamn it, Sam, talk."

Sam motioned for quiet. "Okay, this has to be quick. Garrett and Van are looking for Rachel. They haven't turned anything up yet. Renshaw, you and Baker get Cole and get the hell back to the chopper. The rest of you fan out. Let's find Rachel and get the hell out of here."

CHAPTER 4

MARLENE Kelly stepped out of the bathroom and padded across the bedroom floor toward the bed where her husband was sitting up reading. As she neared, he lowered the book and took off his glasses.

"You look worried," he observed.

She managed a faint smile, amused by the fact that after all these years, he still had a knack for stating the obvious. He couldn't exactly be called intuitive when she'd moped around the house the entire day.

She pulled back the covers and slid under the sheets. As she settled against the pillows, she crossed her arms over her chest and sighed. "I am worried."

Frank turned on his side and propped his head in the palm of his hand. "About?"

"Ethan."

He blew out his breath. "I thought we agreed that it was good that he finally joined his brothers? Does a man no good to stay locked up in that house with all her things."

"I just worry that he wasn't ready," she said unhappily. "Rachel's death affected him badly."

"Our boys will take good care of him. You know that. Sam wouldn't let him go out if he wasn't confident in Ethan's abilities."

"You're right, I know. I just worry. I want him to be happy again."

Frank touched her cheek, his calloused fingers tracing the faint wrinkles at her temple. "He will be. It'll take time."

She frowned when she heard a sound downstairs. She sat up, Frank's hand sliding from her skin. Then she turned to her husband. "Did you hear that?"

"Hear what?"

She huffed in exasperation. "That sound. It came from the kitchen."

He stiffened and put a hand on her arm when she started to get up. "You stay here. I'll go down."

"We should just call the police," she hissed.

He gave her a look of annoyance as he headed toward the closet. "It's probably just a mouse. No need to get Sean over here for nothing."

He disappeared into the closet and returned seconds later with a shotgun.

"Frank, don't you dare mess up my kitchen!"

He waved her off and walked out the door. Marlene reached for the phone. Typical Kelly man. All things could be solved with firearms. Not that she had anything against them, but she didn't want a hole in her newly done walls.

She gripped the phone, determined that if she so much as heard a peep she was calling Sean, and she didn't give a damn if he had to get out of bed or not.

"What the—Hey, you come back here!" Frank roared.

Marlene winced when a crash sounded. Her fingers were pounding the phone keypad when she heard Frank again.

"Marlene, get down here," he yelled.

She flew out of bed, the phone to her ear. When she hit the bottom of the stairs and then rounded the corner into the kitchen, she skidded to a halt, staring at the bizarre scene in front of her.

"Get off of me!"

Marlene stared down at the screeching girl lying facedown while Frank sat on her in the middle of the kitchen floor. Frank was rubbing his hand and cursing with every breath.

"Frank! What on earth is going on?"

Frank glowered up at her. "What does it look like? I caught this little hellcat raiding the fridge. She threw the cookie jar at my head and tried to run. Call Sean and have him come over."

Marlene stared hard at the still-struggling girl. "Girl" was an appropriate description. Why, she couldn't have been more than sixteen if she was a day. Stick thin, she looked like a toothpick under a boulder. All Marlene could easily see was a bunch of pink hair sticking out in forty directions.

"Frank, get off her," she chided as she hurried forward.

"What? Get off her? The hell I will. Crazy woman tried to kill me."

"You're killing her," she pointed out. "A man your size sitting on her. I doubt she can breathe."

Frank glared at her then shoved the butt of the shotgun down so he could get up. He kept his free hand square in the middle of the girl's back while he rose. "Don't you be getting any ideas, girly. I have no compunction about filling your hide full of buckshot."

Marlene rolled her eyes then shoved her husband aside.

"Don't get too close to her, Marlene, damn it," Frank protested. He tried to get between her and the girl, but Marlene stepped around him.

"You can get up now," Marlene said pointedly. "But I'd do so slowly if I were you. Frank is just dying to use that shotgun."

The girl slowly turned over and she quickly masked the fear in her eyes. Replacing it was sullen defiance. She was pretty enough, but skinny as a rail. She had enough shadows under her eyes for Marlene to realize she hadn't slept in probably as long as she'd gone without eating.

Her clothes, if you could call them that, hung off her, and her hair was probably pretty under all the pink dye.

Her heart went out to this girl. It was obvious she wasn't some hardened criminal. Of course Frank would laugh at her and say that she was way too softhearted for her own good. Her boys would growl and say that she took in too many strays, and she did, but usually they were of the animal variety.

"Are you hungry?" Marlene asked.

The girl's eyes narrowed. "No, I was breaking into your fridge for some ice."

Marlene nearly laughed at her bravado. "No need to get snotty with me, missy. I can assure you that in my years as a teacher I've faced bigger and badder than you, and if you don't mind me saying, there isn't much of you to be intimidating so much as a flea."

The girl scowled at her, but Marlene remained firm, hands on her hips as she stared her back down.

"Now, we can do this two ways. You can sit down like you have some manners while I fix you something to eat, or we can call the sheriff and you can spend the night in jail. Completely up to you."

The flicker of hope in the girl's eyes nearly broke Marlene's heart. Then she cast a cautious glance at Frank, who stood a few feet away, his expression belligerent.

"Don't pay him any mind," Marlene said in exasperation. "His bark is way worse than his bite. Now, do you want something to eat or not?"

Slowly she nodded.

"That's settled then. Sit down at the bar while I figure out what kind of leftovers we have. And Frank, you quit scaring the life out of her. She won't be able to swallow for you scowling at her that way."

Frank sighed but put the gun down and attempted to drop the frown. It would be difficult, because all her men did love to scowl when they were put out. One thing the boys got from their father for sure.

The girl maneuvered onto one of the bar stools, her gaze never leaving Marlene and Frank. She looked as though she'd take flight at the least provocation.

"Now, what's your name?" Marlene asked as she went to the fridge.

"Rusty," she said in a voice that Marlene had to strain to understand.

"How the hell did you get past my security system?" Frank demanded. "My boys installed it three months ago."

Rusty gave him a triumphant smirk. "It was easy."

"Well goddamn," Frank muttered. "That's a fine waste of money."

Rusty shook her head. "Not for most intruders. I just happen to know my way around electronics is all."

"And why were you intruding here?" Frank demanded suspiciously.

Rusty shifted uncomfortably and looked away. "I was hungry," she muttered. "Looked as though you could afford it if I took a little."

"I'll have you know I've worked damn hard for everything

I've got." He shook a finger in her direction. "That's the problem with today's youth—"

"Frank, please. Don't get started," Marlene interjected. "You'll give her indigestion."

She pulled out several containers and plunked them on the table.

"Do you want something too, dear?"

He just glared at her in response.

Marlene turned her attention to Rusty as she threw together sandwiches. "Do you have a place to stay, Rusty?"

Rusty froze, and fear returned to her eyes. "Yeah, of course I do. I'm not homeless or anything."

"You just don't have food at this place to stay?" Marlene asked gently.

Rusty's lips came together in a firm line. Marlene put two sandwiches in front of her and then reached up into the cabinet for a glass.

"Get her some ice, dear," she instructed Frank.

Frank looked annoyed, but he did as she asked, returning a second later with the glass. The ice crackled and popped when Marlene poured the tea, and she pushed the glass across the table to Rusty, who was already devouring one of the sandwiches.

Marlene exchanged unhappy glances with Frank, who looked as moved by the sight as she felt.

"Why don't you stay here tonight?" Marlene offered.

She wasn't sure who was more shocked, Rusty or Frank. She silenced Frank with a look, then directed her gaze back to Rusty.

"Well?"

"Why do you want me to stay?" Rusty asked warily. "I tried to steal from you. You two aren't into any freaky shit, are you?"

Marlene blinked in surprise, and then her heart broke as she realized what Rusty must be thinking.

"No, honey," she said gently. "I'm just offering you a place to sleep and a good breakfast in the morning."

"But why?" Rusty blurted.

She looked as though she wanted to cry, as if she had no idea how to deal with kindness dealt to her. Which told Marlene she'd seen far too little of it.

"Because you look like you could use some rest and another good meal."

The yearning in Rusty's eyes hit Marlene like a hammer. Lord, but she hurt for this child.

"And what happens tomorrow? Are you going to call the police?"

Marlene shook her head. "No, Rusty. No police. Unless you try to steal from us again. You do that, and I'll call Sean myself. But you're welcome to stay. And as for what happens tomorrow, why don't we discuss that over a hot breakfast in the morning? You'll have to pardon me for saying so, but you look dead on your feet."

"Uh yeah, sure, okay," Rusty said around a mouthful of bread.

"Don't think I won't be watching you," Frank warned.

Rusty's nostrils flared, but she didn't respond.

"Go on and finish your meal, then I'll show you to your room. You can take a bath and change into some of Rachel's clothes I still have."

"Who's Rachel?" Rusty asked.

Marlene paused, sadness creeping into her soul. "She was my daughter-in-law," she said quietly.

Rusty must have sensed her misstep because she didn't press the issue further. Instead she wolfed down the remaining bite and chased it down noisily with the tea. Afterward, she wiped at her mouth with the back of her sleeve.

Marlene's eyes narrowed, and Frank actually grinned. If there was one thing she didn't tolerate, it was poor table manners. Every one of her boys had been subject to her ire at some point over the years, and as a result, they all had impeccable manners, even if they didn't always choose to use them.

Still, she didn't comment. The poor little chick probably hadn't ever had too many decent meals, so table manners weren't a priority.

"Come on then. Let's get you upstairs. I'll get you some clean sheets while you're in the shower."

CHAPTER 5

RACHEL. Her name was Rachel. She had proof now. The strange man who'd appeared so suddenly in her hut had called her Rachel, and then her guardian angel, the one she'd feared was a figment of her imagination, had arrived to save her. Finally.

Only she didn't feel saved. She was scared mindless, and everywhere she looked, there was only jungle. She was hopelessly lost and alone.

Alone. Not in captivity.

The idea gave her fierce pleasure as the realization settled over her. She was free.

She fell to her knees, nearly crying out when her stomach revolted and lurched. Her palms planted in the damp soil, she braced herself as she dry-heaved.

In the distance she heard movement, and she immediately stilled, holding her breath. Were they coming to take her back? It was tempting just to stay there and let them find her. At least then she'd get her medicine and the horrible pain would go away.

Angry tears burned her eyelids. She wouldn't go back there. She'd die first. Ethan had been shot trying to rescue her. The thought made her stomach heave all over again.

She had to get away. The idea of going deeper into the jungle, into the unknown where any number of creatures stalked for prey, scared her to death. But staying frightened her more.

She pushed herself to her feet. She took one step. And then another. The ground felt warm and alive under her bare feet. She picked up speed until finally she ran.

Pain. Fear. She couldn't tell which was winning. They both overwhelmed her. Rachel stopped to rest, leaning against a tree for support. She weaved and bobbed as nausea welled in her stomach.

Every nerve ending felt like it was firing in random succession. An endless staccato of agony barreled through her veins. Her skin itched, and it took every ounce of her will not to claw raggedly at her flesh.

Sucking air through her nose, her nostrils flaring with the effort, she looked around at the dense jungle cover. Helpless panic ripped over her until tears gathered in her eyes. She had no idea where she was going or how she'd survive.

A vicious chill wracked her body even as she registered the oppressive humidity. She was cold on the inside though. A sound behind her startled her into motion. She spun around, unsure of which direction to go. Which way had she come from?

Fatigue made her eyes droop, but she blinked and forced herself forward. Slime and God knows what else sucked at her toes. She jerked her foot up when something slithered across her ankle.

Ready to scream in panic, frustration and fear, she dove into a dense area of plant growth. A twinge in her shoulder, and then pain erupted like fire through the protesting muscles. Had she pulled her shoulder out? She lay there panting as agony ripped through her body.

She had to get farther out of sight.

The leaves were moist and brushed across her cheek, leaving a cool trail. Holding her injured arm tightly to her chest, she slapped the ground with her other hand and crawled forward until the ground cover engulfed her.

Her knees bumped over several gnarled tree roots, and she hastily scooted against the trunk, huddling for warmth and to try to still her thundering pulse.

Quiet, she had to be quiet. Her breathing sounded like a roar in her ears even amid the cacophony of the jungle around her.

Carefully she pulled her legs up, sandwiching her injured
arm between her knees and her chest. She kept herself as still
as possible.

Her muscles quivered and jumped. Her skin rippled, and she
fought the urge to scratch and rub, to wipe at the millions of
things crawling over her body. She kept her eyes open, knowing
she couldn't see anything crawling there, but her body refused
to believe what her mind knew.

She caught movement out of the corner of her eye, and she
froze. Her eyes slowly moved to her left, scanning the area. And
then she saw him.

Her breath caught in her throat. He was the one who'd been
with Ethan. Sam. He was big and mean and carried a rifle. His
gaze swept the area, his expression fierce and concentrating.

Oh God, oh God. What should she do? He scared the life out
of her. She didn't know him. Didn't trust him. He knew her
name, though. Would he take her back to the hut now that Ethan
was dead? Would he help her or want to be rid of her?

Then to her right she caught another flash. At first she
thought she'd imagined it, but when she looked again, she saw
men moving into the area. They were barely discernible, their
camouflage clothing melting into the dense cover.

No matter how frightened she was of Sam, she had more
to fear from these men. She knew all of their faces well, had
seen them on a daily basis for what seemed an eternity. Bile
rose in her throat, and she shook so bad that her teeth chattered
loudly.

She was taking a gamble. With Ethan gone, this Sam person
might not care what happened to her. But he hadn't tried to
harm her, and she couldn't say the same for her captors.

Desperate fear nearly paralyzed her, but she rose on shaky
feet anyway. She had to warn him—had Sam seen the threat?

"Sam, behind you!"

He dropped like a stone. Gunfire erupted. She saw one of the
men fall. A sense of savage satisfaction gripped her. Then more
gunfire, this time from behind her.

She dove to the ground, throwing her arms over her head,
her mind screaming endlessly. Desperate to protect herself in
some way as the jungle erupted into a war zone, she curled into
a tight ball, trying to make herself as invisible as possible.

And then she realized the stupidity of curling into a ball. She needed to get away. She'd given away her hiding spot already. It was only a matter of time before they came for her.

Terror lending her strength, she pushed herself up and started crawling as fast as she could. She flinched when a bullet hit the tree just over her head, and she threw herself down once more.

When no other bullets smacked the ground around her, she started forward again, praying with every inch she gained. The gunfire stopped, but instead of reassuring her, it inspired gut-wrenching panic. No longer distracted, they'd be after her.

She crawled faster, her breath ripping painfully from her chest. Sweat rolled down her face, or was it tears?

She ran into the body before she saw it. She was too stunned to scream or even process that the man was dead. Blood was everywhere and the rifle he'd carried was still firmly in his grip.

She knew this man. She hated him. She spared no sympathy for his death. With more strength than she thought she possessed, she ripped the rifle from his grasp and crawled beyond him.

They wouldn't take her back. She'd kill them—all of them.

When she'd crawled as far from the body as possible, she stopped to catch her breath. Her sides ached, her shoulder burned, and her vision was blurred by tears.

A sob caught in her throat and she swallowed rapidly. Afraid of betraying herself, she lowered her head, burying her face in her free hand. She just needed a moment to rest.

Several long minutes passed, or maybe it was seconds. It seemed an eternity. And then she heard her name. The softest whisper, carried on a breeze. *Rachel.*

She flinched but refused to look up. They never called her by name.

"Rachel."

Too close this time.

Her head came up, and she grabbed for her rifle. She rolled over, jamming the gun in the direction of the voice. A strange man stared back at her, his expression blank. His ice blue eyes were unreadable as he surveyed her calmly. He didn't seem bothered by the fact she was pointing a gun at him.

She tried to scoot away, but she was tangled in ground cover. She thrust the gun forward, trying to at least keep her finger on the trigger.

From behind the man, another man appeared. Sam. He said nothing as he put himself between her and the other guy.

"Back off, Steele," he murmured.

Sam put one placating hand forward, his other loosely holding his own rifle, though he made no effort to point it at her. "Rachel, listen to me. I won't hurt you. I swear it. You need to put down the gun and come with me so I can take you back to Ethan."

Tears immediately swirled. A knot formed in her throat, and no amount of swallowing would make it go away.

He couldn't be trusted. He was lying to her. Ethan was dead. She'd seen the blood. Seen him fall right after he'd yelled hoarsely for her to go.

Holding back the grimace of pain, she got awkwardly to her feet. Sam relaxed and held out a hand to her, but instead of moving forward, she backed away, her gaze never leaving him or the man still standing just a few feet away.

Her hands shaking, she leveled the gun at an area between them, hoping they would just go away. Sam's brows came together for a moment and then he stepped forward.

"No," she choked out, as she stabbed the gun in his direction.

His hand moved upward and he stepped back, his expression guarded.

"Rachel," he said soothingly. "Honey, I'm here to help you. It's time for you to go back home. To the people who love you. Your family."

Her heart seized. Family? She couldn't remember a family. All she could remember was Ethan, and even those images were vague. When had she forgotten? All she could remember was endless pain and fear. The haziness brought on by injections thrust upon her and the crawling need when they waited too long to give her another dose.

For a brief moment she hesitated, drawn to the idea of family. A home. People who loved her. But then she remembered. Ethan was dead. He was all she had, all she could remember. Surely she would remember if there were others. Would she have forgotten her family?

You can barely remember who you are.

The thought drifted through the twisted pathways of her mind, taunting and reminding her of her tenuous grasp on her sanity.

She caught movement in her periphery and yanked her head to the side to see another man stalk toward Sam and Steele. He wore a ferocious scowl as his gaze homed in on her. He was bigger and meaner looking than Sam, and he should have put the fear of God in her, but there was something familiar, something oddly comforting about him.

Was she losing her mind?

He stopped at Sam's side, and she still stared as images flashed erratically in her mind.

"What the hell is going on, Sam?" he asked in a low growl. "We don't have time to be fucking around. Let's get her and go."

"Tell her that," Sam murmured as he stared at the gun she held. "I'd say she doesn't want to go."

Like flashes of lightning in a black sky, pictures shot randomly through her shattered mind. Memories? The man standing beside Sam, only he was smiling, almost tenderly. Water. A dock. He lifted her and then tossed her into the lake. He stood laughing as she came up sputtering, and she was laughing too. *Happy*. She'd been happy.

Another memory, haunting and sweet. A church. Her gliding down the center aisle. Ethan waiting . . . and this man in front of her . . . he'd escorted her. Her hand clutched tight over his arm. He whispered low for her not to worry, that she was the most beautiful bride in the world and that his brother was the luckiest man on earth.

Garrett. Ethan's brother?

"Garrett?" she whispered.

His face immediately softened. The scowl disappeared and something that looked like joy flashed in his eyes for just a moment.

"Yes, Rachel. It's me, Garrett."

Making an instant decision, she flew to his side, careful to put him between her and the other two men. He stiffened in surprise but put an arm around her. She tucked herself into his side and leveled a guarded look at Sam.

"Let me have the gun, sweet pea," Garrett murmured as he gently pried it from her fingers.

She flinched when it glanced off her injured shoulder, and her breathing sped up. Sam frowned and made a move toward her, but she hastily backed away, her feet tangling in the undergrowth. She went down on her backside, landing painfully.

Garrett was down beside her instantly, his hand going to her arm. Sam stood back, his brows furrowed.

"Are you okay, Rachel? Where are you hurt?" Garrett asked.

"My shoulder," she said. "I can't move my arm. Hurts too much."

"Probably dislocated," Sam said grimly. "The angle is crooked, and she's favoring it awfully bad."

She scooted back as Sam moved forward again. He cursed and halted.

"She doesn't remember you," Garrett said.

"Yeah, I noticed," Sam muttered. "I'm not surprised she remembers you, though. Thank God for that at least."

"He lied," Rachel whispered.

Garrett's eyes narrowed. "Who lied?"

"Sam."

Sam's head rocked back in surprise. "Me?"

Garrett's hand came out to smooth her hair from her face. "What did he lie about, sweet pea?"

Tears welled, and she bit her lip to keep the moan of despair from escaping. "He said he'd take me back to Ethan, but Ethan's dead."

Both Garrett's and Sam's eyes widened in shock. Sam blew out his breath then squatted beside her, ignoring her efforts to move away.

"Why on earth do you think Ethan's dead?"

"I saw him fall. He was shot. He told me to go and then he went down. I saw him."

Sam smiled. "He's not dead, Rachel. It would take a hell of a lot more than that to kill that ornery bastard. It was just a graze. He bled like a stuck pig, but he's fine. I swear it."

Her gaze flew to Garrett for confirmation, hope beating relentlessly against her chest. Garrett gave a short nod.

"Is he okay now?" she asked in a shaky voice. "Where is he?"

"I'll take you to him," Sam said. "But we have to hurry."

Fear leapt into her throat, and she began to shake. "Don't let them take me back. Please."

Garrett's face darkened, and she shivered at the raw violence on his face. From behind Sam, the other man stepped out. For a moment, his cool eyes bore into her and then he crouched down beside her. He didn't press into her space. He just squatted there staring intently at her.

"You don't know me, Rachel," he said in an even voice. "You have no reason to believe me. But there's one thing I can guarantee you. I won't allow those bastards to take you back. I'm going to get you and Ethan back home where you belong. Do you understand?"

There was rock-hard assurance in his voice. An unwavering confidence that, despite her fear and anxiety, calmed her.

Slowly she nodded. Steele nodded back and then rose, putting several feet of distance between them.

"This might hurt," Garrett said. He reached down and tucked one arm underneath her knees. His other arm slid along her back, and he carefully picked her up, trying not to jostle her hurt shoulder.

She snuck a cautious look at Sam, studying him from the safety of Garrett's hold. He didn't look like Ethan. Garrett did, and maybe that's why she remembered him. While Ethan and Garrett were big, black-haired men with hard bodies and hard faces, Sam was leaner but no less muscled. His hair was light brown, but his jaw was square and had a determined set that unnerved her. His eyes were a cold blue. A lot like Steele's. Impenetrable ice.

As if sensing her perusal, he glanced up. Like magic, those hard eyes softened and became warm. He offered her a tentative smile.

"I don't remember you," she said softly. "I'm sorry."

He reached out and tucked a strand of hair over her ear. "That's all right, sweetheart. You will. What's important is that we get you back to Ethan and then home, where we can all fuss over you and get you well."

Garrett started out, jostling her slightly as he navigated the tangled jungle floor. Sam moved swiftly ahead, his gun up as he scouted the area in quick, methodical sweeps. Steele brought up the rear.

"Who is 'all'?" she asked Garrett in a low voice.

"Shhh, not now," Garrett said, though his voice was even and unscolding. "I promise to tell you all about it when we're out of hot water."

She tucked her head underneath his chin and rested her cheek against his broad chest. And then as she settled, need, harsh and relentless, hit her. She began to shake. She was simultaneously hot then cold. Sweat broke out over her skin, and she shivered in continuous spasms.

Garrett's arms tightened around her until pain shot down her arm. She gasped, and he immediately loosened his grip.

"Medicine," she gasped. "Please, I have to have it. I'm going to die."

"You're not going to die," Garrett whispered against her hair. "I'm not going to let you. I know it hurts, honey, but you have to fight it. Don't let them win. Think about Ethan. You'll be back with him soon."

She closed her eyes as a thousand insects crawled over her body. Over her skin, burrowing underneath her clothing. It was all she could do not to scream and throw herself down to swipe at them, to scrub them from her flesh.

"Goddamn it, Sam, do you have a sedative in your bag?" Garrett said.

He stopped walking and shifted her in his arms. A few seconds later, she felt a sharp stick in her arm. She yanked her head up in surprise and stared wordlessly at Garrett.

"It's okay, baby girl," he said in a thick voice. "Close your eyes. It'll get better, I promise."

His face blurred in her vision. "Ethan," she whispered. "You promised."

"When you wake up, he'll be here," Sam said beside her. "Relax and don't fight it."

For a moment, she continued to fight, too immersed in the wave after wave of pain and vicious hunger to simply let go. The world faded around her and her eyes fluttered, but she hung on tenaciously.

A warm hand stroked her cheek and then her hair. With a yearning sigh, she leaned into the touch, drawn to the comfort it offered. Lethargy flooded her body, and she went limp.

Ethan.

CHAPTER 6

MARLENE was up early as was her habit. Too many years of herding kids where they needed to be and then off early to her own job as a schoolteacher. Frank wasn't any different. He'd run the only hardware store in their small town for the last thirty years, and he opened up at seven A.M. six days a week, rain or shine.

She peeked in on Rusty, half-expecting to find her already gone, but what she found was a sound-asleep little girl, the covers pulled up to her nose. Marlene's expression softened as she watched from the door. Whatever the girl's situation, it wasn't a happy one.

Quietly, she backed out of the bedroom and eased the door shut behind her. Then she headed downstairs to get a start on breakfast. She put the biscuits in the oven then started the bacon to frying and set the grits on to boil. One by one she cracked eggs and dropped them into a bowl.

It was strange not to have at least one of her boys sticking his head in on a Sunday morning. They were perpetually hungry, and Sundays were big breakfast days at the Kellys'. These days they stayed gone more than they were at home. Nathan and Joe were deployed overseas, and Sam, Garrett and Donovan always seemed to be off on some classified mission for KGI.

Ethan was the only one routinely at home. Until now. She sighed as she beat the eggs a little too vigorously. Ethan led such a quiet life after Rachel's death. He withdrew from his family. The only time Frank saw him was when he showed up at the hardware store to help out, but even then he was reserved.

And now suddenly he was off on some mission with Sam? Something wasn't right with that picture. "And don't think I won't find out what," she muttered.

Those boys always thought they could pull one over on her, but not a one had ever managed to hide anything for long.

She looked up when she heard a sound at the stairs. Rusty stood there in Rachel's jeans and T-shirt, her hair in disarray and a guarded expression on her face.

"Well good morning," Marlene said cheerfully. "You hungry?"

Still eyeing Marlene cautiously, Rusty edged her way over to the bar. "I could eat."

"Well good. Frank'll be down shortly and we'll have a nice meal."

Rusty perched on the edge of a bar stool and watched as Marlene poured the eggs into a skillet. She turned the bacon and turned the heat down on the grits to let them simmer.

"I don't like eggs."

"I hate to hear that since that's what I'm cooking. I expect you'll eat them or go hungry."

"Don't you want to know when I'm leaving?" Rusty said in a belligerent tone.

"Since I haven't asked you to leave, no."

Rusty frowned and fidgeted on the stool. "So you don't care if I stay?"

"I'm concerned that there are people worried about you. Seems to me you ought to let your folks know where you are at least."

Rusty's eyes iced over and her entire body stiffened. "I don't have any folks. None that give a damn anyway."

Marlene had figured as much, but she didn't want to take this girl in if she had a family worried about her somewhere.

Just then Frank ambled down the stairs and into the kitchen. He stopped to drop a kiss on Marlene's cheek before he turned to the bar. He eyed Rusty warily but took a seat without comment. Rusty didn't exactly roll out the welcome mat for him either.

They squared off like two cagey animals, each watching the other for any unexpected moves.

"So are you saying you want to stay?" Marlene asked casually.

Rusty scowled. "I didn't say that."

Marlene turned as she picked up the skillet and shoveled the eggs onto a plate. "Frank, will you get the biscuits please?"

She arranged the bacon next to the eggs and then scooped the grits into a large bowl. After everything was set on the bar, she took a seat across from Frank and Rusty and gestured for them to dig in.

"Will you be going after breakfast then?" Marlene asked as she buttered a biscuit.

Rusty's lip curled derisively. "You want me to go, don't you?"

"If I wanted you to go, I'd say so. I'm not one to mince words."

"Got that right," Frank muttered.

She shot him a quelling look. Something that resembled a smile skirted Rusty's mouth.

"I'd like for you to stay if that's what you want," Marlene said to Rusty. "But if you accept my offer, you're going to have to be honest with me. About everything. And there are rules."

Frank snorted and Marlene glared at him again.

"Don't get her started on the rules," Frank said with a resigned sigh. "Just nod your head and say yes ma'am."

Marlene leveled a stare at Rusty. "Does that sound like something you can live with?"

Rusty squirmed under Marlene's scrutiny. She picked at her food and toyed with a piece of bacon with her fork. "What if you change your mind?"

Marlene willed herself not to react to the fear and insecurity in the child's voice. And she was a child. A child trying very hard to be an adult, but a baby nonetheless.

"I won't change my mind, Rusty. As long as you abide by my rules and respect my house, then we'll get along just fine."

For a long moment Rusty stared at Marlene as if she couldn't believe what she was hearing. Then she glanced sideways at Frank.

"Then I'll stay. For now," she added hastily.

CHAPTER 7

THANKS to losing his goddamn earpiece, Ethan was paired with Donovan as they searched the heavy undergrowth. Ahead, Donovan stopped and held a hand to his ear.

"Say again, Sam, you're breaking up."

Donovan turned to Ethan as he listened intently.

"Roger that. We're on our way."

Donovan fiddled with his GPS unit, stared down intently and then looked up as if determining the direction to go.

"What the hell did he say?" Ethan demanded.

"They found Rachel. Garrett's carrying her back. They'll meet us at the chopper."

P.J. broke through a snarl of leaves, her rifle seemingly too big for her small frame.

"Let's make tracks," she said. "Chopper is two and a half miles over that ridge. Going to be a bitch on our current trajectory."

"You got an easier way?" Donovan asked.

"Nope."

Ethan strode ahead, not waiting for them to hash out the best route.

"Wait up, man," Donovan called. "Since I'm the one with the GPS, you might want to let me take the lead. Otherwise you're going to end up in Venezuela."

"Then go already," Ethan snarled. "We've had enough delays already."

They stalked through the jungle in silence, eyes and ears alert to any noise or movement. Though they'd crippled the small village with their surprise attack, they were still outnumbered, and when the enemy had time to regroup, they'd be on KGI's asses.

Ethan wanted to be the hell out of Colombia with his wife well before that happened.

All the breath left his chest, leaving him deflated. His pace slowed as the events of the day caught up to him. He hadn't even been able to revel in the discovery of Rachel—alive—before all hell had broken loose. Even now she was with his brothers, and he was dependent on them to get her safely to the helicopter. Not that he didn't trust them. He trusted them with his life—and Rachel's. But he ached to be the one with her, offering her reassurance.

He picked up his step when Donovan gained distance on him. He couldn't afford to mentally wander off like that. It could get him and his teammates killed.

He glanced over at P.J. She'd kept up with no problem, and she looked unruffled by the fight.

"Thanks for the cover," he said.

She looked startled by the thank-you. Her ponytail swung as she glanced sideways at him. "No problem. It's my job."

"It's a job you're good at," he said sincerely.

"For a woman you mean."

"I didn't say that."

He looked over to see a smile nudging the corners of her mouth.

"You're doing that on purpose to make me feel like a slime bucket," he accused.

She shrugged. "You're a SEAL. You're not used to going into combat with women. It stands to reason you'd be impressed. I doubt you're as impressed by Cole, and his job is the same as mine."

She had him there.

"Okay, busted. You're right. I'm impressed because you're a woman. A really small woman."

Donovan snickered in front of them. "Quit while you're ahead, little brother. She's kicked people's asses for saying less than that."

P.J. rolled her eyes at Donovan's back.

"Got an ETA, nerd boy?"

"Ouch," Donovan said. "You hurt me with your insults. Half mile more." He pointed at the slope ahead. "Just over that ridge and we'll be looking down at the helicopter."

"Then what do you say we walk more and talk less," she said as she surged ahead.

And again, summarily dismissed like an errant schoolboy. The woman had a way of making a man feel about an inch tall.

Donovan and Ethan exchanged amused glances and picked up the pace.

They were dirty, sweat-drenched, and Ethan had dried blood caked on his neck and shirt, when they topped the rise. Below, the helicopter sat covered in a camouflage net.

Donovan spoke quietly into his mic, and slowly, the men surrounding the chopper came into view.

Ethan, Donovan and P.J. hurried down and were met by Dolphin.

"Give me a report on Cole," Donovan said briskly.

"He's in the chopper. Gave him a shot to ease the pain. Ricochet. Bullet's still in the leg. We'll have to stop over in Costa Rica and let Maren look him over and hope we can refuel there."

Donovan nodded and then looked over to where Baker and Renshaw stood, their gazes wary as they stood guard. "You guys okay? Any other injuries?"

"Just Dolphin," Renshaw said, jerking a thumb in Dolphin's direction.

"What the hell happened to you?" Ethan demanded.

Dolphin grimaced. "No big deal. I may have busted a few ribs. Got too close to one of the blasts."

"That'll do it," P.J. murmured.

"Sam, Garrett and Steele are coming in with Rachel," Donovan said as his hand left his ear. "Get the cover off the chopper. It's time to roll."

The team burst into a flurry of activity. Ethan dove in to help, though his mind screamed at him to go meet the others. He forced himself to contain the excitement building inside.

Rachel. His wife. He was taking her home.

"Ethan," P.J. murmured beside him.

He turned when she nudged him, and she gestured to a point in the distance. He followed her stare and saw Garrett striding toward the chopper, Rachel in his arms.

He forgot everything else. Uncaring of how it looked, he broke into a run, ignoring the ache in his head and the soreness of his muscles. All that mattered was that he get to her.

Garrett stopped and waited for Ethan to come to him. Sam and Steele passed and Sam put a hand on Ethan's shoulder.

"Get her and come on," Sam murmured before he walked on by.

"Is she okay?" Ethan asked around the catch in his throat.

"Sam sedated her. It was pretty bad," Garrett said after a pause.

Ethan took her from Garrett, marveling at the feel of her in his arms again after so long. This time he absorbed the sensation, where before he'd thrown her over his shoulder so they could move quickly.

"Come on, let's get her in the chopper," Garrett said.

Ethan cradled her in his arms and walked over to get into the helicopter as they were pulling the net from the tail rotor. He sat as the others took their seats and Donovan climbed into the cockpit.

Ethan stared down at Rachel's delicate face and took his first long look at his wife since he'd burst into her hut.

Her clothes were ratty, the shorts thin and threadbare. Her T-shirt had numerous holes and was matted with dirt. She wore no shoes, and her hair hung limply on her head. But to him, she had never looked more beautiful.

Emotion overcame him, his throat swelled and tears burned his eyelids. Unable to think, to react, he simply pressed his lips to her forehead and held on to her as tightly as he could.

"I have to admit, I was skeptical," Sam said as he slid onto the floor beside Garrett and in front of Ethan.

Ethan looked up to see sorrow and regret burning brightly in his brother's eyes.

"I'm damn glad we got her out."

Ethan nodded. "I owe you one, man. I owe you all."

"Bullshit. You don't owe us anything. I'm mad as hell we couldn't have been here sooner," Garrett growled

"I don't understand," Ethan ground out. "Why? Why her?" He buried his head in her hair. "What did she ever do to deserve any of this?"

He sucked in several steadying breaths. He felt close to going completely insane with anger, grief and guilt. How could he have not known she was alive? He should have demanded more proof. Instead, he'd blindly accepted the proclamation that his wife wasn't ever coming back home.

Sam leaned forward to allow Steele to step over him. "The important thing is you have her back."

Yes. He had her back, and he'd kill any son of a bitch who ever tried to take her from him again.

"She okay?" Steele asked as he took position on the other side of Sam.

Ethan noticed the blood on Steele's arm and the way he grimaced when he sat down. Ethan looked over at Sam, who shook his head. It wasn't serious, but Steele looked none too happy with the injury.

Ethan swallowed and answered Steele's question. "I don't know yet. I think they have her hooked on drugs."

Anger tightened Steele's jaw, and his blue eyes flashed. "We should have just dropped a bunch of C-4 and been done with the assholes."

P.J. slid in next to Ethan, while Baker, Renshaw and Dolphin climbed in the back to be near Cole, who was out like a light. Dolphin stretched out and let out a moan. He put his hand over his ribs.

"Man, I think I'm getting too old for this shit."

Ethan felt some of the tension leave him. He began to shake as reality set in.

"Want me to take her?" Sam asked.

Ethan shook his head, tightening his grip on her. She still wasn't conscious, thank God. The sedative had done its job.

"Thank you," Ethan said loud enough for the others to hear.

"You would have done the same for one of us," Steele said with a shrug. The action made him wince again, and he held his hand to his shoulder. Ethan could see blood seep between his fingers. "And truth is, when you told me what had happened to Rachel, I was itching to kick some cartel ass. I'm just glad she's okay."

Was she okay? That was the million-dollar question. She was alive, but who really knew how she was. The bastards had shot her up with drugs for God knows how long. Certainly long enough to get her addicted. She had been in the throes of withdrawal when Sam found her. Ethan didn't even want to dwell on what else they might have done to her.

He needed to get her to a doctor fast. But first they had to get the hell out of here. Alive.

The whir of the blades and the roar of the engine cut off anything else Ethan might have said. Within seconds, Donovan lifted off the ground and skimmed along the trees. In the distance, smoke could be seen floating skyward in a black stream. Ethan's nostrils flared. He wished they'd done exactly as Steele had said and dropped a load of C-4 and been done with it.

Ethan leaned back and shifted Rachel so that she was even closer to him. It didn't matter that they were both dirty, they stunk, and they had more dirt and mud caked on them than a hog. She was his. She was a miracle.

He closed his eyes and buried his face in her hair. The slow rise and fall of her chest, the slight movement against his body gave him much needed reassurance.

He kissed her and kept his lips pressed to her head. No matter what, this time he wouldn't make the same mistakes he'd made before. He'd cherish each day with her.

He only hoped she'd forgive him their past.

CHAPTER 8

"I think we should have had Sean come with us," Frank grumbled. "And what were you thinking leaving Rusty alone in our house? We'll be lucky to have a house when we get back. She probably sent us on a wild-goose chase. How do we know she was telling us the truth?"

Marlene's mouth tightened as they turned off the rural county road onto a dirt path that was barely wide enough for the truck. "It's important that I show her trust."

Frank snorted. "Trust? You just met the girl last night. Trust is earned, Marlene. You need to get your head out of the clouds."

She sighed as they came to a stop in front of a dilapidated trailer overgrown with weeds and grass that hadn't been cut in years.

"You should have at least let me bring the shotgun. Does it look to you like these folks want company?"

"Frank, stop. Look at this place. Rusty doesn't belong here. Is it any wonder she ran away?"

Her heart ached for the hurt and distrust in the young girl's eyes. Eyes that were way older than the rest of her.

"Let's get this over with," Frank grumbled. "And I want you to stay behind me until I know it's safe, okay?"

Marlene nodded and they both got out of the truck. Before she could close her door, a man stepped from the screen door that only hung by one hinge.

"Whatever you're selling, we don't want any," he called in a belligerent tone. At least now Marlene knew where Rusty got it.

She stepped away from the truck and called back. "We're here to talk to you about Rusty."

"What's that fool done this time? I don't have any money to bail her out of trouble, so you might as well go on now. She's on her own."

"That much is evident," Marlene said under her breath.

Frank stepped in front of her and held his hand back for her to remain still. And quiet.

"Are you her father?" Frank asked.

"Don't see that it's any of your business."

"Well we need to speak to whoever her guardian is."

The man stared for a long time, and then he shoved his hands into his tattered jeans and thrust out his chest. "She ain't any kin to me. She and her mama were living here with me, but her mama done took off again. No telling when or if she'll be back. Girl's following in her footsteps. Been gone for a week."

Marlene closed her eyes against sudden tears. A week. A week on her own with no food, scared out of her mind and no place to go back to. Rusty hadn't lied about that.

She reached for Frank's hand and squeezed urgently. He caught her fingers and gave a tug in return.

"So you aren't her legal guardian."

"Hell no. That would be her no-good mama. I've washed my hands of both of them. Good riddance, I say."

"Thank you," Frank said. He turned and gestured for Marlene to get back in the truck.

"Who'd you say you were again?" the man called. "And what's happened to Rusty?"

Frank walked back around to his side and paused at his door to look at the man. "I didn't say. Thank you for your time."

He got in and started the engine. They were two miles from the trailer before he said a word. And then he only spoke to swear a blue streak.

"Man ought to be shot," Frank growled.

Marlene battled to keep the smile from her lips. She knew

Frank well. He may have put up a good front, his bark was always worse than his bite, but deep down, he had a heart as soft, if not softer than, her own.

"So I guess you won't mind if she stays."

"She'll need some decent clothes. Maybe you could take her shopping over in Clarksville. Can't have her running around in Rachel's castoffs forever."

Marlene reached over and tucked her hand into his.

RUSTY was sitting on the same bar stool she'd been perched on when Marlene and Frank left an hour earlier. Her posture was tense, her expression ill at ease. She glanced up when they walked in, but ducked her head, refusing to meet their gaze.

Marlene wanted desperately to hug her. The child probably hadn't had too many of those, but she wasn't sure Rusty would tolerate it. Her body language screamed back off, don't touch.

Instead she walked around the bar and set her purse down on the counter. Frank hovered in the background as if he wanted to say something, but then he blew out his breath and walked away, leaving the two women alone.

As if she couldn't take the silence any longer, Rusty clenched her fists and looked up at Marlene, her eyes screaming defiance. She wore her best *I don't give a shit* snarl.

"Well, did you talk to Carl?"

Marlene nodded. "We did."

Rusty shrugged. "Then I guess he told you that Sheila ran off and that he doesn't give a damn about me."

"First rule. Watch your mouth. I don't take that kind of language from my boys, and I won't tolerate it from you."

Her lips curled into a sneer, but she didn't say anything further.

"I won't lie to you, Rusty. Carl said exactly what you expected him to say, but I needed to hear it with my own ears. I had to make sure that we weren't getting into a legal mess by offering you a place to stay."

"Yeah, well, only way Carl would say he cared was if there was something in it for him. If he thought you had money, he'd use me to get it."

Marlene sighed. "You don't have to worry about Carl any longer. I promise you that. There's still the issue of your mother, but we'll cross that bridge when and if we come to it. For now, you're staying here. First thing we're going to do is go shopping for some decent clothes."

Rusty looked suspiciously at her, but Marlene ignored her and went on.

"There's also the matter of school. I'll expect you to attend and finish your education when it starts in August."

"School's boring," she said with a roll of her eyes.

"For a smart girl like you, I don't doubt it, but it doesn't make it any less necessary. You'll never get into college if you don't finish high school."

"College?" She laughed, and it sounded bitter and derisive. "What's a girl like me going to do at college? I can't afford it and I'd never get in anyway with my record."

"Record?"

"Yeah," she mumbled. "Nothing major. Got sent to Juvie once."

"What for?"

Her chin came up, and fire blazed in her eyes. "Solicitation."

Marlene closed her eyes and willed herself not to break down in front of this child. When she opened them again, she saw anger reflected in Rusty's face. She didn't appreciate Marlene's pity.

"Well, what's done is done. We can't change the past, but we can darn sure change your future. You're going to school, and you're going to work hard. No excuses."

There was a slight shift and Rusty seemed to wilt a little on her stool. Marlene leaned on the counter and took a chance as she covered Rusty's hands with her own.

"I don't doubt you've had a hard life and that a lot of people have let you down. You can wallow in that misery and remain a victim, or you can take charge of your destiny and turn it all around. The choice is up to you. I can't make you do it, and I won't. Frank and I will provide you with the opportunity, but you have to want better."

Rusty looked down at Marlene's hands, her eyes glistening with what looked to be hard fought tears. "Why are you doing this? What's in it for you?"

"Not everyone does something for what's in it for them," Marlene said gently. "Besides, seeing you graduate and go on to college and make something of yourself will be what I get out of it."

"So I can stay?" she asked hopefully.

"You can stay."

Marlene picked up her purse again and fished for her car keys. She walked toward the garage door and then turned and pinned Rusty with a stare.

"Well, don't just sit there, come on."

Rusty scrambled off the stool and rubbed her hands nervously down her pant legs. "Where we going?"

"To buy you some clothes and shoes. Maybe do something with that hair while we're at it."

Rusty frowned and ran her hand defensively over the long strands. "What's wrong with my hair?"

"Nothing if you don't mind looking like a pink rooster," Marlene said dryly. "I know kids these days get strange ideas about fashion, but trust me, that look is never a good idea."

IT was dark when they pulled back into the drive. Frank met them at the door and took the bags they carried. He did a double take when he caught sight of Rusty.

Marlene beamed and turned to Rusty. "Didn't I tell you he wouldn't recognize you?"

Rusty ducked her head self-consciously and looked like she wanted the floor to swallow her up. Her confidence was in the gutter, but if Marlene had her way, she'd build it back up.

"You look nice," Frank said gruffly. "Like a young lady instead of some punk."

Rusty actually grinned at the backhanded compliment.

"There's more bags in the trunk," Marlene said as they walked on into the kitchen.

"You buy the store out?" Frank huffed.

"Almost. I haven't had that much fun shopping since Rachel and I used to go."

Her mouth trembled as the words slipped past her before she thought better. Frank squeezed her arm on his way out the door.

"What happened to Rachel?" Rusty asked. "You mentioned her before."

Marlene sighed. "She was married to my son Ethan."

"They get a divorce?"

"No. She died a year ago," she returned softly.

Rusty shifted uncomfortably. "Sorry."

Marlene smiled. "Don't be. I tell Ethan all the time that it's time to go on with life and then I don't heed my own advice."

"You loved her a lot."

It wasn't a question, but a matter-of-fact statement.

"Yes, I did."

Frank bustled back in with the rest of the bags, and Marlene turned to Rusty.

"Well young lady, you've got a lot of unpacking to do. Better get on upstairs and get all your things settled. The bathroom on the end will serve as yours. With all the makeup and hair stuff we bought, you'll be arranging clothes and cosmetics until bedtime."

For a moment Rusty didn't move. She fidgeted uncomfortably, shifting from one foot to the other. Then she glanced at Frank and finally Marlene.

"Thanks. Uh, I mean . . . well thanks."

Marlene patted her on the arm. "You're quite welcome."

CHAPTER 9

AS Donovan set the helicopter down on the bare patch of soil next to the nondescript stone building, a woman in a white lab coat hurried out, shielding her face with her hand.

Ethan gathered Rachel closer as Sam hopped out and ran ducking toward the woman. Dr. Maren Scofield. He'd heard of her from his brothers. KGI had rescued her during an intense hostage crisis. She'd been the only survivor. Afterward she'd left Africa and set up her clinic in a poor, rural area of Costa Rica.

Sam returned with Dr. Scofield a moment later, and she poked her head inside the helicopter to survey the injured. She pointed to Cole.

"Get him in first. Front exam room." Her gaze glanced over Rachel and then Dolphin and on to Steele. She pointed first at Steele. "Second exam room." Then she gestured to Dolphin. "Take him into the back. I have a portable X-ray. I'll see if he's broken any ribs."

Cole grunted and shook his head. Dolphin also remained still.

"See to Rachel first," Steele said in a firm voice.

Dr. Scofield looked at Rachel in surprise then back at the men as if gauging their determination. "I really think that gunshot wounds should be looked at first."

Cole held up his hand, pain evident in the crease of his brow. "Rachel comes first."

Dr. Scofield shrugged and looked at Ethan. "Bring her in." She turned to Sam. "Get your men in the exam rooms or they're not going to have any limbs left. If they rot off, it's not my fault. The rest of you can shower in the back while you wait."

Sam grinned and motioned for Ethan to get out. "We'll get them inside, Maren. Don't get your panties in a knot."

Dr. Scofield scowled at Sam, but Ethan could see the affection twinkling in her eyes.

Ethan stepped down, holding Rachel tightly. Dr. Scofield leaned over as they walked toward the clinic and then looked up at Ethan. "How long has she been unconscious?"

"We gave her a sedative," Ethan said. "It was easier that way."

Dr. Scofield led the way into one of the tiny rooms then motioned for Ethan to lay Rachel down on the exam table. As she brought the stethoscope up, the doctor peered at Ethan over her glasses.

"I need you to give me a rundown of her situation. Then you can go shower with the others while I finish up."

Ethan hesitated. He didn't want to leave Rachel here alone. What if she woke up and panicked?

Dr. Scofield's expression softened. "I won't be long, and then you can come back in. She probably won't even wake up."

Reluctantly, Ethan told her everything he knew about Rachel's condition. Which wasn't much. When he was done, Dr. Scofield nodded and motioned for him to go.

He left the room and found Sam in the hallway talking to his other team leader, Rio.

"Ethan," Rio said with a nod when Ethan approached. "Good to see you."

Ethan shook his hand. "What the hell are you doing here?"

"I was just asking the same thing," Sam said dryly.

Rio flashed a grin. "Brought you fellows a present. A new helicopter. That one out there is going to get you attention you don't want with all the bullet holes. Not to mention the fact that the Colombian government has issued a statement saying such a helicopter is an item of interest in national security."

Sam swore. "I was afraid this would happen. Our departure was too messy."

Rio shrugged. "Bound to happen when you only have three days to plan a mission and you're low on manpower. You should have waited for me and my team to get in. It would have only meant one more day."

"We couldn't wait one more day," Ethan broke in. "They had my wife."

Rio stared at Ethan for a moment and then nodded. "I understand. Still, we need to ditch the helicopter. No way someone won't notice even in this shithole little village in the Costa Rican jungle. I'll take care of it."

Without another word, he turned and strode away, disappearing as quickly as he'd appeared.

Sam shook his head then turned to Ethan. "Rachel settled?"

"Dr. Scofield is looking her over."

"Let's go grab a shower then. We both smell like goats."

They went to the back of the clinic where the small room housed two open showers. There wasn't much in the way of hot water, but even the lukewarm felt good to Ethan. He washed away the dried blood and felt along his scalp for the wound. He was damn lucky he wasn't dead.

"Rio's men go with him?" Ethan asked after they'd showered and dried off.

"Yeah. Where Rio goes, so does his team. They're a cagey, antisocial bunch to the core. They probably resented like hell having to come out of their caves even briefly."

"Sounds like my kind of crowd," Ethan said with a brief smile.

Sam looked at him in astonishment. "Well I'll be goddamned. You cracked a joke. What on earth is the world coming to?"

Ethan popped him with a towel. "Cut the smart-ass attitude, big brother. I can still kick your scrawny ass."

Sam actually smiled. Then without warning he grabbed Ethan in a big bear hug and pounded him on the back. "It's damn good to have you back, little brother."

"Cut the mushy shit out," Ethan grumbled as he pulled away.

"You girls having a love fest back here?" Donovan asked.

Ethan and Sam turned to see Donovan and Garrett standing in the doorway, amused grins plastered on their faces.

Sam flipped them both off. "Get cleaned up before Maren

tosses your smelly carcasses out of her clinic. Ethan and I will check in on the others while we're waiting for Maren to finish with Rachel."

Ethan stepped into Cole's room to find his teammate lying awkwardly on the too-small table, his eyes closed and forehead creased with tension.

"Hey man," Ethan said quietly.

Cole opened his eyes and stared back at him. "Rachel?"

"Nothing yet. Dr. Scofield is examining her. Wanted to see how you were feeling."

"I've been better. I've been worse. Nothing I won't get over with the help of some good drugs," he offered wryly.

Ethan hesitated and swallowed uncomfortably.

"Something wrong?" Cole asked.

"I just wanted to say thanks. You risked your life to save Rachel. I can't ever repay that. Having her back . . . Just thanks. I appreciate it."

Cole made a rude noise. "Just don't holler that Semper Fi shit and we'll call it even."

Ethan gave him a mock look of horror. "Hooyah, baby. Hooyah."

Cole grinned. "Right on, brother. Right on."

Then he lay back and groaned. "If those fuckheads had better aim, this would have been a clean through-and-through."

"Yeah, well, if they had better aim, your brains would be splattered over the Colombian jungle," Ethan said dryly.

Cole closed his eyes wearily. "There is that."

"I'm going to get out of here. I'll go look in on Dolphin and Steele."

Cole opened his eyes again and lifted his head. "Save your breath with Steele, man. And for God's sake don't thank him. It'll just piss him off."

Ethan chuckled. "I'll remember that. Try and get some rest. Doc'll be in shortly."

"You take care of that girl of yours. You're a damn lucky man. Not everyone gets a second chance."

"Yeah," Ethan said soberly. "I am lucky."

He turned and walked out, his shoulders tight, his chest even tighter. A door down, he poked his head into Dolphin's room, only to see Baker and Renshaw crowded in. He nodded at Dolphin and continued on.

Steele sat up on the exam table, his expression brooding. He connected glances with Ethan and gave a quick, dismissive nod. Ethan took the hint and walked on to the small reception area where Sam sat. He slouched into one of the tiny, uncomfortable chairs and closed his eyes.

The next thing he knew, Sam nudged him awake. He blinked rapidly as Dr. Scofield's face came into view.

"Ethan," she said softly. "Can you come with me?"

He scrambled up, scrubbing the sleep from his eyes as he followed the doctor toward the exam room. Anxiety made him jumpy, and he rubbed damp palms down his fatigues. When they bypassed Rachel's room, he shot an inquiring look at the doctor.

"I thought we'd talk in my office," she said as she opened the door and stepped inside. "Such as it is." Her arm swept over the room that more resembled a closet.

Papers were piled on every exposed surface and boxes lined the walls on either side of her desk.

She shoved a pile of envelopes off the chair in front and extended a hand for him to sit. Then she walked around to the other side and sat down.

No longer able to stand the suspense, he blurted, "How is she?"

"She's okay physically. There is some bruising around her shoulder, but it wasn't dislocated. It'll be sore and stiff for a few days, but she should regain full use of it."

She took off her glasses and ran a hand through her shoulder-length blond hair. "There's a lot you're going to have to deal with. I won't candy-coat that for you. She's undernourished and fighting off infection. In short, she's run down and is going to need a while to recover properly."

"Did they hurt her?" Ethan asked quietly. "I mean physically?"

Her face twisted in sympathy. "I didn't find any recent evidence of sexual trauma. She was in captivity a long time, so it's impossible to say what she may have endured early on. I drew blood, and I'll test for STDs."

Ethan swallowed and then swallowed again. He wanted to vomit at the thought of what those dirty bastards could have done to her. She'd been their prisoner, helpless, while he'd been a world away.

"It won't do any good to torture yourself," Dr. Scofield said gently. "And as I said, there isn't any recent evidence of sexual assault. My gravest concern is the evidence of drug abuse."

"They forced those on her," Ethan said fiercely.

"I know. My concern is in not knowing what they gave her. The educated guess would obviously be cocaine given its accessibility in the geographic region where she was held captive. And indeed some of her withdrawal symptoms match those of cocaine withdrawal. However, as odd as it may sound, there's evidence that she was injected routinely with heroin."

Ethan closed his eyes against the sudden rush of rage and pain.

"Many of the symptoms she's exhibited are indicative of heroin withdrawal. On a positive note, heroin withdrawal isn't as long or as far-reaching as cocaine withdrawal. It's nasty while it lasts, but is thankfully over in days as opposed to the extended cravings cocaine addicts have for months, and sometimes even longer."

"And her memory? Is her memory damaged irreparably?" Ethan asked.

"I can't say with medical certainty. The human brain is such a fascinating thing. Unpredictable. The drugs could have done damage to her brain. Whether it's permanent, I can't say. It could simply be a matter of the cobwebs not having time to clear yet. The longer she's off the drugs, the better chance she has of the past coming back to her."

"So what do I do?"

Dr. Scofield offered him an encouraging smile. "You take her home and get her feeling better. She has some weight to gain. But most important is her mental health. This isn't going to be easy, Ethan. I'd suggest you contact a therapist as soon as you get home, as well as have her health monitored by a physician. You're going to have to be patient and understanding even when you're at your limit. She could very well shatter."

He blew out his breath, startled at the sheen of tears that blurred his vision.

"And remember that you'll need help too," she said softly. "Don't be afraid to lean on your family. I'd suggest you consult with a therapist as well. You can't do it all."

"I'll do whatever it takes to make her better."

Dr. Scofield nodded. "She's sleeping right now. She came

around briefly, and once I assured her that she was safe and that you were nearby, she slipped back under. She's visibly in withdrawal. Even in sleep she shakes and has muscle tremors."

Ethan shifted in his chair and then leaned forward. "When can I take her home?"

She tapped the desk with her pen for a moment. "She can't go home as she is. Withdrawal isn't something you can wave a magic wand at or give her a few days of IV fluids, good nutrition, and she'll feel better. Normally I'd recommend she stay in a rehab clinic until the worst of her withdrawal is over, but I recognize that this situation is different and you don't want to draw attention to yourselves in a foreign country. The next best thing is for her to remain here where I can monitor her withdrawal and make sure she regains some of her strength. Going home will be traumatic for her, so she shouldn't be pushed into going too soon."

Ethan shook his head in confusion. "Traumatic?"

"Well, yes. Overwhelming is a better word, I suppose. I think your brothers should go ahead and smooth things out for her homecoming. Keep it as low-key as possible. She's in a very delicate state right now and you don't want to push her too hard."

"So we stay here," Ethan said slowly. "Is that a good idea? I mean for you?"

"Talk it over with Sam. I'm sure once he understands the situation he'll agree. As for me, I'll be fine. After the shit in Africa, not much scares me anymore. The government putzes around here leave me alone to treat the villagers. I'm not seen as a threat."

"That could change with our arrival," Ethan pointed out. He liked the doctor. She had a no-nonsense air about her that was appealing. Or maybe it was because she hadn't sugarcoated things when it came to Rachel. He needed honesty and bluntness because he was at a complete loss for the first time in his life. Even when he'd been wrong in the past, he'd been decisive. Blunt and quick to make a decision. Most of the time to his detriment.

This time he was going to take it slow and put the needs of Rachel before his own. Something he hadn't been willing to do in the past.

"It's a risk I'm willing to take. KGI risked a lot for me. It's the least I can do." She smiled. "Now if you'll excuse me, I have other patients to see.."

Ethan rose. "Thank you, Dr. Scofield. For everything."

"Call me Maren, please."

"Thank you, Maren."

"My pleasure."

She walked out of her office and ducked into Cole's exam room, leaving Ethan standing in front of her desk, his heart beating a little faster than before.

CHAPTER 10

RACHEL opened her eyes, blinking to adjust to the dim light. After a moment she could see clearly. Things had changed since the last time she'd woken up. No longer was she on a narrow table in a room so small that she'd immediately broken out in a sweat. Instead she was in a bigger, more comfortable bed.

She glanced down to see an IV line running from her arm to a bag dangling from a pole beside her bed. For a moment she just lay there in the quiet and stillness, absorbing the first sense of peace she'd experienced in longer than her shattered mind could comprehend.

There was no hunger. No overwhelming need for the poison that pricked her skin and crawled insidiously through her veins. For the space of few moments there was no pain. Only sweet silence.

A movement to her right startled her, and she let out a gasp. The shadow moved and soft light flooded her eyes.

"Rachel, it's me, Ethan. Sorry if I frightened you."

He came into view, standing at her side. She took the opportunity to study him with borrowed clarity. He was large, much larger than the men who haunted her nightmares, and yet she knew instinctively that he wouldn't hurt her, that she was safe with him.

Sleek, black hair worn short. *Military.* The word floated through her mind unsummoned. Startling blue eyes, serious and brooding. Another image flashed, those eyes sparkling with laughter as he spun her round and round. She closed her eyes, wanting more of the memory, but just as quickly as it came, it was gone.

"Are you hurting?"

Ethan's urgent voice crashed through the pleasantness of her dreams. Her eyes fluttered open again, and this time, he was leaning close, his fingers reaching tentatively for her cheek.

Instead of responding, she reached up and caught his fingers. They were so warm and strong around hers. He rubbed his thumb across the top of her hand and then brought it up to his lips in a gesture so tender that it deeply moved her.

"Hey," he murmured in a voice that cracked. "How are you doing?"

"Ethan."

"Yes, baby, it's me, Ethan. You're safe now. Do you understand that?"

She nodded, her throat too constricted to say anything.

He leaned down and pressed his lips to her forehead, and then he withdrew and carefully pushed her hair back with his fingers.

"Got room for me to sit?" he asked.

She looked down at where his hip leaned against her bed and then hastily scooted against the rail on the other side.

He settled onto the bed, his thigh pressed to hers.

"How are you feeling?"

She thought for a moment. How could she explain how she felt?

"Free," she finally said.

He reached for her hands and pulled them into his grasp. "I'm going to take you home soon. Dr. Scofield wants to watch you for a few days and make sure you're okay to leave before we go home. But I'll be with you the entire time."

More images haunted her memory. Smoky, hanging on the edge of her recall. This time she saw Ethan's face drawn in anger. He shouted and she recoiled from the dark feeling that swept over her.

"Rachel?"

She yanked her gaze to his and tried to control her rapid breathing.

"What's wrong, honey?"

She shook her head, unable to explain the brief flash that had unsettled her so.

For a long moment, he simply stared at her, his gaze caressing her face as surely as if he were stroking her with his fingers. She absorbed it greedily, wanting this contact, the feeling of security he instilled just with his presence. For the first time in so long, she wasn't eaten alive with fear and pain.

Again he brought her hands to his lips and held them there, his mouth pressed to her knuckles. He trembled against her fingers as he kissed them.

"I just need to touch you," he said. "To have you here. To see you. To feel you again." Emotion clogged his voice, making it strained and raw. "I thought you were dead. They told me you were dead. I buried you, mourned for you, tried to get on with my life without you. And now here you are. It's more than I ever hoped or dreamed."

Her breath caught and hiccupped roughly from her chest. Her insides twisted and squeezed. Tears burned like acid.

"I waited for you," she whispered. "Over time I thought I'd imagined you. When I forgot everything but my name, I thought maybe I'd made you up and that hope was forbidden to me. I knew you'd come when I knew nothing else."

He bowed his head, lowering until his forehead touched hers. "I love you, Rachel. So damn much. I know we have a lot to get through, but you aren't alone anymore. You won't ever be alone again."

She closed her eyes, savoring his promise. She was afraid to believe, to hope that after so long her nightmare was over.

"There's a lot I don't remember," she said hesitantly. Would it anger him that she could only remember bits and pieces of their life together? Not only that, but she could barely remember *her*.

As if sensing her turmoil, he pulled away. He stared down at her, his eyes suddenly troubled. Almost guilty. Her eyes narrowed in puzzlement. What would he have to feel guilty over?

"It'll be okay, baby," he soothed. "It'll come back in time, and we'll face it together. The important thing is that I have you back."

"What did she give me? The doctor. I feel . . ."

"Are you in pain? Do you want me to get her?"

She shook her head. "No. I feel . . ." She mentally examined her physical state. "Quiet. My mind is quiet. My skin isn't crawling and yet I know it's there, waiting to come back."

He gently touched her face, his fingertips sliding over her cheekbone and to her lips. "We'll beat this."

She closed her eyes as grief settled, thick and suffocating. "What did they do to me? Why?"

Ethan's hands stilled on her face. "I don't know why." Anger tightened his voice. She opened her eyes to see fury reflected in his. "I won't let it happen again. I protect what's mine."

A peculiar prickle shivered up her spine, leaving a warm glow in its wake. Her chest fluttered, and something inside her long dead awakened and unfurled.

She belonged to this man. He'd keep her safe.

"Tell me about us," she whispered.

He smiled then, and it transformed his face. Gone was the serious, gruff man, replaced by boyish charm. It was a marvelous thing to behold.

"We were married three years ago."

Her brow wrinkled. "Oh, not long then."

His eyes lost some of their shine. "No, not long."

If she concentrated hard, she could summon distant memories. It was odd. Though she could remember them, it was as if they belonged to someone else. The connection to her hadn't been forged in her tattered mind.

"Did Garrett give me away at our wedding?"

Ethan stilled and then slowly nodded.

"I remember that. He told me I was the most beautiful bride in the world."

"And you were."

"I remember seeing you, waiting for me."

Ethan hesitated for a moment. "What else do you remember?"

She sighed. "It's sort of a mess. I mean I remember lots of random things, but I don't have a clear chronological list of events. It's like someone's shooting out-of-order pictures at me."

"Don't rush it. You've been through a lot. When I get you home, and you feel safe again, you'll remember."

She cocked her head to the side for a moment. "How many brothers do you have? I only remember Garrett. Sam . . . he scares me. And there's another here. Donovan?"

Ethan smiled. "Garrett is usually the one who scares people. Sam is the oldest, but you'd think Garrett was."

"Garrett wouldn't hurt me."

"Neither would Sam," he said gently. "To answer your question, there are six of us in all. Nathan and Joe are twins and they're deployed to Afghanistan."

"Do I have any family? It seems odd that I would remember Garrett but not my own family."

He shook his head. "You were an only child, and your parents died in a car accident several years ago."

"Oh." She couldn't help the disappointment that accompanied his statement.

"You were very close to my mom, though. She and Dad both loved you like a daughter. You were a part of the family long before I married you."

She relaxed and smiled. Then her forehead furrowed as she remembered one detail. "They think I'm dead. Like you did."

Ethan sighed and rubbed a hand through his hair.

"How did you know? I mean how did you find me?"

She trembled as she spoke, and already she could feel the slow crawl of need creep over her skin.

"It's a long story, baby, and right now it isn't important. What is important is that I found you. You're a miracle to us all. Mom and Dad are going to be so thrilled. I don't know yet how I'm going to tell them. They'll think I'm crazy."

"I'm hungry," she blurted. She rubbed her hand over her arm, trying to make the itch go away. Hunger beat at her, but she wasn't sure which was more prevalent: the hunger for food or the hunger for the needle.

She could *feel* the needle sinking into her flesh, welcomed it, wanted the horrible ache to go away.

Ethan's hand closed warmly over hers. "I'll be right back."

He eased from the bed and left the room after a quick look back at Rachel. Whatever Maren had given her was wearing off, and she was becoming agitated again.

He stuck his head in the doorway of Cole's room to see him passed out cold. From there he passed Steele's room, only to find it empty, not that it surprised him. He nearly bumped into Maren as she came out of Dolphin's room.

"Is there a place we can get some food?" Ethan asked. "Rachel's hungry."

"That's good. She needs to eat. But take it easy. Don't give her too much too quickly. I have a small kitchen in the back where we can nuke some soup."

She turned, and Ethan followed her past the shower area to a kitchenette that had a two-burner stove, a small fridge and a microwave.

"All the comforts of home," she said ruefully.

"You don't live here, do you?"

"Yes and no. When I'm busy or have patients I crash in the back room here, but no, I have a cottage a half a mile from the clinic. Not much, but it's dry and keeps the rain out."

"Where is everyone?" he asked as he watched her take a bowl out of the refrigerator.

"I sent them down to the cottage. They can crash, eat and generally stay out of my hair there. Sam said to tell you he'd be back in a few. Why don't you go back to Rachel? I'll heat this up and bring it down in a few minutes."

"Thanks. I appreciate it, Maren."

She smiled and made a shooing motion with her hand. Ethan turned and walked back down the hall. He was nearly to Rachel's door when he heard a crash.

He broke into a run and burst through the door to see Rachel standing by her bed, the IV pole knocked over. She yanked frantically at the line at her wrist, and before he could react, she pulled the line free of the catheter. Blood spilled from the catheter still inserted into her arm onto the floor and her gown.

She ignored it, rubbing and hitting frantically at her arms, her chest and her legs. Blood flew in all directions as she batted at invisible objects.

He vaulted over the bed and grabbed her to him. He reached for her wrist to try to stop the flow of blood, but she fought relentlessly. She wasn't even aware of his presence.

"Rachel! Stop. Baby, stop!"

"Get them off!" she cried. "God, get them off me!"

He held her tightly, subduing her flailing arms and all the while trying to get his hand over the IV lock to stop the blood. Finally he held her, helpless in his arms, her body locked to his, but still she twitched and cried out in anguish.

"Maren!" he yelled. "I need you in here!"

Rachel screamed again, a high-pitched sound of terror. She arched her body, bowing against him with surprising strength.

"Rachel, honey, I've got you. You're okay, I swear."

"They're all over me," she wailed. "Get them off!"

"Get what off? There's nothing there."

Maren burst into the room, her lab coat flying in her wake. She took one look and went into action.

"On the bed," she ordered. "I need to get that IV hooked back up."

Ethan hauled her onto the bed and held her down as she kicked and bucked endlessly. Her eyes were wild with fear, the pupils fixed and dilated. Sweat bathed her face and hair, and her cheeks were chalky white.

"Hallucination," Maren said grimly. She deftly reattached the IV and then yanked a bottle of medication out of her pocket. With sure hands, she filled a syringe and then bent to inject it into the port.

When she was done, she put her hand over Rachel's forehead and gently wiped away the sweat and tangled hair. "Listen to me, Rachel. It's not real. Whatever you're seeing, it's not real. Look at me."

Rachel's wild eyes focused on Maren, her mouth open in a silent scream.

"That's it. Now listen to me. You're safe. It's a hallucination. Ethan's here. I'm here. We're not going to let anything happen to you. You'll feel better in a minute, I promise."

Rachel crumbled, her eyes filling with tears. Harsh, ragged sobs came deep from her chest and shook her entire body as they spilled from her lips. How she'd held it together this long, Ethan didn't know.

As soon as Maren backed off, he gathered Rachel in his arms, holding her tight as she cried. He stroked her hair, her back, every part of her body he could touch.

Something inside of him broke. He wanted to hit a wall. He wanted to cry with her. For her. For all she'd endured.

What had those bastards done to her? She could remember almost nothing and was suffering endlessly in withdrawal. What if the drugs had permanently destroyed her mind?

He shook his head. No, he wouldn't accept that his Rachel was gone. She'd come back to him. She had to. Only he had to make sure that when she did, when she remembered the past, he managed to convince her that he'd been wrong. He loved her.

Asking for a divorce had been the worst mistake of his life, and something he'd regret to his dying day.

He shut his eyes and held on, his body shaking almost as badly as hers.

"I'm so sorry, baby," he whispered, his voice choked with emotion. "I'm so sorry I let you down."

For several long minutes he knelt on the bed, his arms wrapped around her until finally he realized that she'd quieted. As he pulled away, her head lolled to the side. Carefully he cupped her face and then lowered her back to the pillow. Her eyelashes fluttered delicately against her cheeks as she settled into oblivion.

"Most of the blood is on the floor and her clothes," Maren said in a low voice. "We can change the sheets later. Let her rest. I'll clean up what's on the floor, and when she comes around again, I'll get her a fresh set of clothes."

"Can I stay with her?" he asked, though he had no intention of leaving her, even for a minute.

"Of course. I'll be out of your way in just a second. I left the soup on the table, but she'll probably be out for a few hours. When she wakes, be sure she eats. I'll be staying in my office tonight to monitor Cole and Dolphin. Steele told me to fuck off and he left," she added with an amused glitter to her eyes.

"Don't take it personally. He likes everyone pretty much the same."

Maren shrugged. "I don't care if he likes me. I did what I could. The rest is up to him."

Five minutes later, Maren finished mopping the spilled blood and then she quietly left the room, leaving Ethan alone with Rachel.

Ethan relaxed on the pillow as much as the awkward position would allow. He'd never been so bone weary in his life, nor had he ever felt so goddamn helpless. Or angry.

He wanted to be able to fix what was wrong, but he couldn't. All he could do was stand by while Rachel tried to put the tattered pieces of herself back together.

"I love you."

The words blew quietly across her forehead, ruffling a tendril of hair.

"This time I won't quit on us," he vowed.

CHAPTER 11

"HOLA," Rio said as he burst into Maren's cottage. His dark eyes swept the interior where Sam and the others were sprawled haphazardly on the floor and furniture.

Sam rose to greet his team leader, extending an arm. Rio grasped it and gave it a firm shake.

"How are Cole and Dolphin?" he asked. Steele was notably absent from Rio's concern.

"Dolphin has busted ribs, Cole took a bullet to the leg and Steele took a bullet in that last exchange."

"Christ. What a clusterfuck."

"You get the chopper? Where are your men?"

Rio grinned, his white teeth flashing. "They're with the chopper. I stashed it a few miles away then doubled back on foot. Good way to learn the terrain and find out what we're up against."

"Reconnecting with your people, amigo?" Steele drawled as he walked over to join Rio and Sam.

"Fuck you," Rio said. His gaze swept over Steele's bandaged and bound arm and he offered a mocking smile. "Hurt yourself?"

Sam shook his head. It was a running source of irritation between Rio and Steele. Rio hated the gross generalization of lumping all people of Latin heritage into the same pot. Rio was Brazilian and Sam didn't even know his real name. He had always been called Rio, short for his home city.

Steele smiled, but it was more of a grimace. His teeth clicked as he stared eye to eye with the other team leader. "At least I was there and not off on some pussy mission to Asia, which if I'm not mistaken is where you should still be?"

"Just saving your ass. Ain't nothing new about that," Rio said easily.

Before things could escalate further, Sam stepped between them. "I'd like to speak to both of you outside."

He glanced back at Garrett and Donovan, who raised their eyebrows in question, but Sam shook his head and then motioned for Steele and Rio to follow him outside. This wasn't something he wanted his brothers involved in.

"What's up?" Steele asked in his impatient voice. He adjusted his arm, only a flicker in his eyes to betray the pain he must be feeling.

"I'm sending you home with our injured," Sam said to Steele.

Steele's lips tightened. "You're taking me out of action?"

"Dude, you've been shot," Rio said. "That's what normally happens."

Sam held up his hand. Then he turned to Rio. "What I'm asking you to do is off the books. You'll get paid just like always, but this isn't official, and you don't have to agree."

Both Steele and Rio went silent as they stared back at Sam.

"Okay," Rio said slowly. "What are we talking about here?"

"I want you and your men to go back into Colombia. Deep cover and surveillance. Chances are the village will move since we know their location. I want their every movement closely monitored. It will require patience. I want reports, but I don't want you to move—yet."

Rio nodded. "Okay, we can do that. What's the big hairy deal? You act like this is high treason or something."

Sam's jaw tightened as he tried to control the surge of anger. "This isn't a mission, Rio. It isn't business. This is personal. I want these bastards. I want them to pay for what they did to my family. I want information, and I don't care what we have to do to get it."

Steele and Rio went still and Sam could see they were finally understanding where he was coming from.

"I want to know why they kept Rachel alive. Why the big hoax. Why would they make us believe she died and then keep her alive all this time?"

"I understand," Rio said evenly. "I'll get your information for you."

"Not just you, Rio. Me. I can't—won't—ask you to do something like this without me. I'm going home with my family. They need me right now. When I get everything settled, I'll meet up with you in Colombia and we'll go in."

"You're not doing this without me," Steele cut in.

Sam shook his head. "No. You're going back with your team. They're your responsibility. Cole and Dolphin need the downtime. You know the rules. We work as a team. We live as a team. The team is everything."

Steele swore under his breath. "I don't like it, Sam. You have too much of a personal stake in this. If you don't want me going, fine. Let Rio lead his team in."

Sam slowly shook his head. "I can't ask someone else to do what I want done."

"I don't like it," Rio said. "If you want the job done, fine. I'll take my team and we'll round up the riffraff. We'll make them talk. But I think you should go home with the others. Your family needs you right now."

"I'll take care of my family," Sam said quietly. "But then I'm going back in. I want their blood. I can't ask you or anyone else to do my dirty work for me."

"Bullshit," Steele snorted. "Think about this, Sam. Use your damn head. You're as emotionally involved as Ethan is. You take this shit personally. Someone fucked with your family and you want revenge. Do you honestly think Garrett is going to quietly go home while you race back into the jungle? Do you think Ethan is going to just say okay while you go avenge his wife? What you need to do is go home and take your brothers with you. You know it's the right thing to do or you wouldn't be sneaking outside your brothers' hearing and trying to slide one by them."

"That's a load of crap about you not asking us to do something," Rio cut in. "We're beyond that shit. This isn't the U.S. fucking Army. I'll take my team back in. Steele can fly his home and you take your family home. They're going to need you. I'll find your answers."

Sam hesitated, torn between his need for vengeance and the knowledge that Rio and Steele were right. Ethan needed him. The next weeks were going to be hard on his family. But at the same time, getting answers was all important. He needed to know why Rachel had been taken. Why his family had been lied to. Why the grand deception? None of it made sense.

"Leave it to us," Steele said bluntly. "I know it slays the control freak in you, but this is one mission you need to stay away from. I'll get my men settled and the rest of my team will provide ground support for Rio and his team."

Rio raised one brow. "Wow. The mighty Steele is going to act in a support role." He clutched his chest and staggered backward.

Steele pinned him with the full force of his glare.

"And you wonder why I have such a hard time turning things over to you guys," Sam muttered. He ran a hand through his hair. "Look, I appreciate the concern. But tell me this. If it was your family. If this was someone you loved we were rescuing. Would you be willing to let someone go back for vengeance?"

Rio blew out his breath. "No. I wouldn't."

Steele nodded his agreement.

"Okay then it's settled." He broke off and glanced back toward the cottage where his brothers were resting. "This needs to stay between us for obvious reasons."

"You're the boss," Rio said.

Sam wiped a tired hand over his face. "You guys get some rest. I want to check in with Ethan and Rachel one more time."

"You coming in?" Steele asked Rio as he turned in the direction of the house.

"Nah, I'll head back to the chopper. I'll check back with you guys in a few hours."

Steele shrugged. "Suit yourself."

A hand closed around Ethan's shoulder and gently shook him awake. Beside him, Rachel lay curled in his arms. He turned his head to see Sam standing over him.

"What the hell happened?" Sam demanded in a whisper.

It took Ethan a few minutes to process that Sam was looking at Rachel's blood-spattered clothes.

Carefully, Ethan eased away from Rachel and awkwardly

got up from the bed. Every muscle in his body protested, and
he had a monster crick in his neck from sleeping in such a
cramped position.

"Get much sleep?" Sam asked.

"Not much. Rachel's in pretty bad shape."

Sam put a hand on Ethan's shoulder. "We'll get her home.
She's going to be fine. She's a fighter. How else would she have
survived this last year?"

"She shouldn't have had to. I should have been here for
her."

"Bullshit."

Ethan remained silent. Only he knew the depths of his failure when it came to Rachel. He didn't want Sam to know. Ever.
He couldn't stand the disappointment in his older brother's
eyes. Their father had always drilled a sense of honor into them.
Do right by your woman. His thirty-plus years married to their
mother was a testament that he lived by his word.

Not only had Ethan not done right by Rachel, but he'd ducked
responsibility, and he'd laid the blame for his own unhappiness
at her feet.

"You can't live in the past, man," Sam said in a voice barely
above a whisper. "Rachel needs you. Get over your guilt and be
strong for her. You've got some tough days ahead of you."

Ethan nodded, though he doubted Sam could see him in
the darkness. Sam was right. For whatever reason, he'd been
granted a precious second chance. No, he didn't deserve it, but
he wasn't going to turn his back on it.

"Maren doesn't think Rachel should go home just yet, and
after what happened earlier, I think I agree."

Again Sam's gaze drifted over Ethan's clothing. "What the
hell happened?"

Ethan explained Rachel's hallucination and told Sam what
Maren had said about monitoring Rachel's withdrawal and
her concern about Rachel going home to a family and life she
couldn't remember.

"She's worried about the strain it'll put on Rachel. She
thought it would be best for you and the others to go ahead and
smooth things out so that her homecoming would be as low-key
as possible."

"I don't like the idea of leaving you behind," Sam muttered.

"I'll stay."

Ethan and Sam looked up to see Garrett standing in the doorway.

Sam shook his head.

"You don't get to make all the decisions," Garrett said evenly. "I'll stay with Ethan and Rachel. You can take the others back. Cole, Dolphin and Steele need medical care beyond what they're getting here. You and Donovan can break the news to the family. Whenever Rachel is well enough, Ethan and I will take her home."

Ethan nodded. "I think it's best. If I call Mom and Dad, it's just going to upset them. They'll never believe I'm not delusional. They'll have time to process the news before Rachel gets home. I don't want her overwhelmed. This is going to be hard enough on her as it is."

Sam frowned. "I don't like leaving either of you behind."

"Ethan and I can handle it," Garrett said.

Sam let out his breath. "Okay," he conceded. "That's what we'll do. If Maren gives the okay to transport the injured men, we'll leave in the morning. I want a report every three hours. I'll have a chopper return for you as soon as Rachel can leave."

"And what about Maren?" Garrett asked. "I don't think we should just pack up and leave her without protection."

"She hasn't been without protection since we got her out of Africa," Sam said. "She's watched. She just doesn't know it."

Ethan nodded. And suddenly the thought of going home didn't hold the comfort it had before.

"Something wrong, Ethan?"

Ethan looked up at Garrett. His brothers always picked up on his moods. Any change or shift no matter how small. At times it was like living under a microscope.

His hands shook, betraying him as he fought to remain steady and unaffected. How was he supposed to be Rachel's rock when a good stiff wind would blow him right over?

The words stuck in his throat, refusing to roll off his tongue. He was a man who'd seen and experienced the worst the world had to offer, and he'd done it stoically and without fear.

He closed his eyes. "I'm afraid."

"You have every right to be," Sam said evenly.

Ethan shook his head. "No. It's time for me to step up to the plate. Man up and be the husband Rachel deserves. I may not have been afraid in the past, but I was a fucking coward."

His brothers looked at each other and Garrett shrugged. No, they wouldn't know what he was talking about. His marriage to Rachel was a study in secrets. Secrets she would have never divulged. She would have never gone to his family with their problems. He'd known it and taken advantage of it.

"I'm afraid she'll never remember. And then I'm afraid she will," he said quietly.

A distinct, uncomfortable silence ensued. Ethan looked down. He'd said too much. It was harder to keep quiet now, and maybe in a twisted way, he was seeking absolution from past sins. But only Rachel could grant him that. It was her he had to make restitution to.

Garrett cleared his throat. "The best thing you can do, man, is to take her home and surround her with as much love and support as you can. We'll all help. You won't be doing this alone."

Sam leaned forward, his expression intense. "The important thing is, you have her back. Nothing else matters."

"You're right. I know you're right. I just feel like I'm going to wake up and be back home in our bed. Alone. And this will have all been a dream."

"I know this year hasn't been easy for you, but you've been given another chance that many would kill for. Don't waste your time borrowing trouble. Enjoy each and every moment, because you of all people know how fast it can all be snatched away."

Ethan raised his haunted gaze to his brother. "Yeah, I do. And I'm not going to let it happen again. I won't lose her. Not twice."

CHAPTER 12

THE next morning, an hour before dawn, Maren's clinic was buzzing with activity. Cole and Dolphin were propped against the wall in the waiting area as they waited for the chopper to arrive that would carry them into Mexico. Maren had given Cole a pair of crutches, but he'd promptly discarded them with a few choice words.

Sam, Donovan and Garrett met with Ethan inside Rachel's room. She was resting comfortably for the first time in hours, and they spoke in hushed tones so they wouldn't disturb her.

"Maren's right about one thing. It's better for us to go ahead and pop the surprise so that everyone has a chance to get used to the idea before Rachel comes home. It's going to be over-whelming enough as it is," Donovan murmured.

"Hell, our family intimidates *me* half the time," Garrett grumbled.

Ethan thrust his hands into his pockets. "I don't want this just thrust on Mom and Dad. They loved her like a daughter. I know they're going to be happy, but I don't know what kind of shock this is going to be for them."

"You let us worry about that," Sam said. "You just take care of Rachel and get her home as soon as possible."

He slapped his hand on Ethan's back. "This is the best news

this family has gotten in a long time. Just think about how great Christmas is going to be this year."

For a moment Ethan couldn't even speak. Christmas. Rachel was crazy about the holidays. She and his mom drove everyone nuts every year decorating, shopping, making everyone else join in on cutesy family celebrations. He hadn't realized just how much he enjoyed that time of year until last year, the first Christmas Rachel missed. It had been a solemn, gut-wrenching holiday.

He'd spent Christmas Eve alone at home with a bottle of cheap liquor. In the dark. No festive lights or Christmas music that predated his grandparents. Only the memory of Rachel's smile and the way she tore into presents on Christmas morning.

He would have given anything for just one more Christmas with her, and now his wish had been granted.

"God help us," Donovan said in amusement. "Between Rachel and Mom, no one will escape with their sanity intact."

Garrett rolled his eyes. "Or without one of those stupid Santa hats."

"Which reminds me, it's your turn to play Santa," Sam told Garrett.

They all burst out laughing at the deer in the headlights look that flashed on Garrett's face. God, it felt good to laugh again. To not feel like nothing good would ever happen.

Ethan grinned broadly as he stared at his brothers. He'd missed them as well. The last year had been painful enough without Rachel, but he'd closed himself off from his family as well. This would be a homecoming for him as much as Rachel.

"I'll let them dress me like Rudolph if it puts a smile on their faces," Garrett said after he stole a quick look at Rachel who was still sleeping soundly.

"Amen to that," Donovan muttered.

Sam's expression grew serious as he looked at Garrett and Ethan. "We need to get on out of here. You two stay in touch and be careful. Donovan and I will break the news to Mom and Dad and get things ready for Rachel to come home."

Ethan stared back at Sam and then glanced at Donovan and then Garrett.

"Thanks."

"Come on, Van. Let's go before Ethan gets mushy again," Sam said.

Ethan slugged Sam in the gut as he walked by and Sam bent over in an exaggerated grimace.

"Pussy," Garrett muttered.

Ethan turned to Garrett. "Will you hang out here in case Rachel wakes up? I want to see them out."

"Yeah sure. Go ahead. Give them a kiss for me while you're at it."

Ethan grinned and shook his head. Then he flipped up his middle finger as he walked out behind his brothers.

RACHEL stirred and sleepily opened her eyes. Then she remembered the things . . . the bugs that had crawled over her body, and she yanked her gaze down to her arms, her belly. But all she saw was bloodstained clothing.

She frowned as she struggled to remember all that had happened in her hysteria. And then as she looked beyond the bed, she saw Garrett slouched in a chair by the window.

When he saw she was awake, he immediately got up and moved to stand beside the bed. His smile was gentle, and his voice low and soothing.

"Hey, sweet pea. How you doing?"

She tried to smile, but she felt more like crying.

Garrett sat down on the edge of the bed like Ethan had done the night before. "Hey now, don't look like that."

"I'm losing my mind."

Her voice came out as a sob, and she despised it.

He touched her cheek and smoothed hair from her face. "You're not losing your mind, Rachel. You're getting it back. There's a difference. You've been through a very tough time. Most people wouldn't have survived it, but you did. Don't sell yourself short."

Tears gathered in her eyes, and he gently thumbed one away as it trickled down her cheek.

"Where's Ethan?"

"He'll be back soon. Want me to go get him?"

She shook her head. She did want him, but she hated the way she seemed to cling to him. Surely she could survive a few moments alone. But then she wasn't alone. Garrett was here, and he'd been her friend. She knew that much.

"You gave me away at my wedding," she whispered.

He smiled. "I did. It was a toss-up, really. Dad very much wanted the honor."

She cocked her head to the side. "Then why didn't he?"

"Because you asked me to," he said simply.

"Ethan said I had no family, that I was a part of his before we ever married." It was voiced as a question rather than the statement she'd intended.

"That's true. Mom taught you in school. You were always one of her favorite students. After your parents died, she pretty much adopted you into the Kelly fold."

"So Ethan and I knew each other? I mean before we got involved?" Then she frowned. "Involved" sounded so . . . impersonal.

Garrett smiled. "I'm pretty certain he always noticed you, but it wasn't until he came home on leave and discovered that our younger brother Joe had asked you out that he got his ass in gear."

Her brow furrowed in concentration. Try as she might she couldn't summon a mental picture of Joe or Nathan. "Ethan told me that Nathan and Joe were twins, but I can't remember either of them."

"Maybe when you see them it will all come back, and if it doesn't, there's no hurry," he said easily.

"Why don't I remember them? Or Sam or Donovan?" She shook her head in confusion. "I don't remember your parents either, and it sounds like I was close to your mom."

"Give it time, sweet pea. You've got all the time in the world now. You have nothing to worry about other than resting and letting us all take care of you."

"They aren't . . ." She trailed off and looked down.

"They aren't what?"

"Sam isn't mad because I can't remember him? Or Donovan?"

Garrett took her hand in his, letting her fingers lie over his much larger ones. "No one is angry with you. We all love you. Sam and Donovan too. They just want you home where you're safe and healthy."

"I want to go home. It's so hard for me to believe I have a home. I used to dream. I thought I made the memories up but now I know they really happened."

"What kinds of things?" Garrett asked.

She pursed her lips, concentrating on the haphazard images dancing in her mind. "There's a lake and a dock. I'm barefooted and wearing shorts. You're standing in front of me and Ethan is behind. I run to you thinking that you'll save me from Ethan, but you pick me up and toss me into the water."

A warm smile transformed the darkness of his features. She stared at him in fascination.

"You don't smile much."

He gave her a startled look.

"I know that," she said, "and I also know that you smile for me. I remember that. I remember that I can make you laugh and that everyone teases you about being so grouchy."

He chuckled lightly. "Yes, I'm grouchy and yes you can always make me laugh. Yes, I threw you in the water when I was supposed to be saving you from Ethan. You paid me back later, though."

"Oh?" She leaned up in the bed in her excitement. Information. Details. She craved them as much as her body craved the drugs.

"You conned Sam, Donovan, Joe and Nathan into ganging up on me and tossing me into the lake. It took all four I might add, but you got your revenge. I took two in with me," he added smugly.

She smiled, feeling the wonder of his words clear to her soul. It did sound like she had family, like they were all a family.

And then she frowned again. "Why am I so afraid of Sam? It sounds like I had a good relationship with him."

"Because you can't remember him yet. You fear the unknown. You remember me and Ethan so you feel comfortable with us. As more of your memory returns, you'll remember how comfortable you were with us all."

She nodded, grasping onto his explanation, drawing comfort from the idea that she wouldn't be this scared mouse forever. And then she had an unsettling thought. What if she had always been this timid?

Garrett laughed, and she realized she'd voiced the question aloud.

"You've always been quiet and shy, particularly around new people, but I'd never call you timid. You fit into our family as if you'd been born a Kelly, and you never took any crap off anyone. No one could survive our family for an extended period of time if they were timid. We're loud, noisy . . ."

"But we protect our own," she said as if repeating someone else's words.

"The Kelly mantra. See, you remember more than you think."

"Don't fuck with the Kellys," she said and then her eyes widened as the expletive rolled off her tongue. She slapped a hand over her mouth and stared at Garrett with shocked eyes.

He threw back his head and laughed. "Got it in one, sweet pea. I couldn't have said it better myself."

Ethan stood just outside the door, listening to Garrett and Rachel talk. Then he heard Garrett's laughter and then astonishingly Rachel's as well. The sound hit him where he lived, put a chokehold around his throat until he struggled to breathe. There wasn't a more beautiful sound than her laughter, but he hadn't been the one to coax it from her. Garrett had. Just as he always had.

He willed the bitterness, the old feelings of insecurity and jealousy to leave him. They'd never brought him anything but misery. Him and Rachel both. He couldn't, he *wouldn't* allow that back into their lives. He'd sworn on Rachel's grave that if he had a chance to do it all over again, he wouldn't give in to the jealousy that nearly ate him alive during their marriage.

"Why do I have blood on my clothes?" she asked when the laughter died away.

"Just an accident with the IV," Garrett replied. "Want me to get you something clean to wear?"

There was a brief hesitation, and Ethan couldn't stand outside any longer. He walked into the room, making sure his face didn't reflect the dark train of his thoughts.

When she looked up, he forgot all about everything else except the way she lit up when she saw him. Garrett got off the bed and turned to face Ethan.

"I'll go get her something else to wear if you want."

"Thanks, I appreciate it. Check with Maren. She said she had a clean gown she could wear when she woke."

Garrett nodded and started to move past him, but Ethan stopped him.

"Thanks, man."

Garrett didn't react, just nodded and moved past as if it were nothing. As if Rachel's laughter hadn't about put Ethan on his knees.

Ethan moved forward to take Garrett's place on the bed. "Garrett been taking good care of you?" he asked as he settled into place.

She smiled and nodded. "He said you wouldn't be long."

"I wouldn't have left, but I needed to see Sam and Donovan off."

"Off? Did they leave?"

He nodded. "They went ahead of us. Cole and Dolphin needed medical care, and Sam and Donovan are going to break the news to Mom and Dad. As soon as Maren gives the okay for you to travel, we'll go back too."

"I want to go home," she said softly. "I don't like it here."

"I know, baby. I want you home too. You can't imagine how much I want you back in our house, where I can hold you and take care of you."

She stared up at him with wide brown eyes. There was a certain amount of trepidation in her gaze, and she licked her lips as if she was struggling with what she wanted to say.

"Is there something wrong?" he asked.

She gave a short negative motion with her head. And then words, so sweet, like a cool northern breeze blowing off the lake. "You could hold me now."

It was almost his undoing.

"Ah baby."

He turned and reclined beside her until she was tucked solidly against his chest. Then he wrapped his arms around her, one sliding underneath her head as he gathered her close.

Her heart beat against his chest, fluttering like a baby bird. She gave a contented sigh that he felt all the way to his soul.

Life didn't get any better than this moment. It would never be sweeter, and he'd never hungered for something more.

Garrett walked in a second later, but when he saw them, he dropped the gown on the end of the bed and quickly retreated.

She could change later. For now Ethan was reluctant to disturb the wonder of having his wife snuggled deep in his arms.

CHAPTER 13

MARLENE had just set dinner on the table when she heard the front door open and the sweetest words filled her ears.

"Ma, we're home! Where are you?"

She turned just as Joe and Nathan rounded the corner, both grinning like idiots, with bags slung over their shoulders. They let them fall to the floor about the time her mouth did the same.

"Nathan! Joe!"

She dropped the casserole dish on the table and flew around to hug them both. Joe gathered her in his arms and swung her around, and she was promptly swept into Nathan's as soon as Joe let go.

"My boys, oh my God, what are you two doing home?"

"Hey, Dad," Nathan said as Frank got up.

Frank enfolded both the boys in a hearty embrace. When he pulled away, his eyes were suspiciously wet.

"What the hell are you two doing home? Why didn't you call us?"

"We weren't sure we were going to wrangle the leave," Joe said. "We tried to get home for . . ."

"We'd hoped to get home on the sixteenth," Nathan said quietly.

"That was good of you," Marlene said. "I'm sure Ethan would have appreciated it."

"Where is Ethan? We stopped by his house on the way in but no one was home."

Marlene exchanged a look with Frank.

Nathan and Joe didn't miss it.

"What's going on, Mom?" Nathan asked.

And then for the first time he and Joe seemed to notice Rusty, who was sitting at the table looking very much as if she'd like to sink into the floor.

"Boys, I want you to meet Rusty. She's staying here for a while."

As Marlene had expected, they both scowled and immediately looked at their father. To his credit, Frank didn't so much as flinch.

"Boys, say hello to Rusty," he said in a gruff voice.

"Hello, Rusty," Nathan said. Joe just nodded and then flashed a questioning look at his mother.

"Sit down, sit down," she urged. "You're just in time to eat. You're probably starving."

"It wouldn't matter if we weren't," Joe said with a grin. "It's been so long since we had home cooking that I'd eat even if I was about to bust a gut."

Marlene managed to get them all herded to the table, and she dished up generous portions. She gave Rusty's hand a reassuring pat as she passed her a plate. It was inevitable that she'd meet all the boys at some point. Better that it happened in stages than all at once. Marlene knew her boys were a handful, and even she was overwhelmed when they all got together.

"Now what's the story with Ethan?" Joe asked after things had settled down a bit.

"He went to work with your brothers," Frank said. "That's all."

Marlene pressed her lips together but didn't say a word.

"Uh-huh, okay, what are you about to pop a blood vessel over there about, Mom?" Nathan asked.

She sighed and glared at her youngest child. Never could fool any of them any more than they could fool her.

"I don't rightly know," she admitted. "Just something's off about the whole thing. Your father called Ethan on the morning of the sixteenth, and Ethan sounded horrible. The next thing we know, Sam, Donovan and Garrett are off on some classified mission. With Ethan."

Joe frowned. "All of them?"

Frank's brows drew together. "You know I didn't even consider that. They never all go. Sam's adamant about it."

Marlene nodded vigorously. "You see, I'm not crazy. There is something going on. I don't like it one bit."

Joe turned to Nathan. "You said Van emailed you a few days ago. Did he say anything?"

Nathan shook his head. "Just the usual bullshitting."

"Are you all a bunch of spies or something?" Rusty blurted out.

Joe and Nathan both jerked around like they'd forgotten she was there. Not difficult since she hadn't uttered a peep the entire time.

The corner of Joe's mouth turned up. "No, not spies. Military."

Rusty looked suspiciously at him. "Military spies?"

Nathan laughed. "If we told you, then we'd have to kill you."

Rusty rolled her eyes and went back to her food, muttering something under her breath.

"How long have they been gone?" Joe asked.

Frank's brow creased in concentration for a moment. "Few days. They left about a week after the sixteenth."

"Well, hell, they had to have been in the planning stages when Van emailed that they were doing absolutely nothing and that things were quiet."

"They probably didn't want to worry you," Marlene said soothingly.

"That's just it." Nathan piped up. "They've never been worried about telling us shit before. Why would they start now, ironically when Ethan crawls out of his hole?"

"I don't like it," Joe muttered. "Sam's number one rule is that all of them never go on the same mission."

Marlene yanked her worried gaze to Frank.

He reached over and put his hand over hers. "Don't worry, honey. You know our boys can handle themselves." But she didn't miss the uneasiness in his eyes.

She sighed and turned her attention to the boys she hadn't

seen in nearly a year. She wasn't going to let worry over her other boys overshadow the twins' homecoming.

"Eat," she ordered. "I swear you're both too thin. Doesn't the army feed you?"

They both grinned at her. "Not nearly as well as you, Ma," Nathan said.

"Oh, I'm so happy to see you both," she said. "You are staying here since your brothers aren't home, right?"

Joe raised his eyebrow in Rusty's direction. "You have room?"

Marlene snorted. "Room? Do you forget all six of you boys grew up in this house? Rusty's going to have to get used to the chaos sooner or later."

She saw Nathan and Joe exchange pointed looks. They were staying quiet for now, but they'd ask plenty of questions later when Rusty was out of earshot.

"So tell me what's been going on with you two," Frank said. "I know you email every week, but it's not the same as hearing it in your own words."

"Our tour is up," Joe said.

Marlene gasped. "Really? I thought you had three more months. Oh, that's wonderful!"

"We pulled out ahead of schedule."

"How long are you home for?" Frank asked.

"Ten days. Then we'll be back at Fort Campbell," Nathan said.

Marlene clapped her hands together. Tears pricked her eyelids. "That's fantastic. It'll be so nice to have you close to home again."

"Let's help your mother clear the table and then we'll go into the living room and have a beer," Frank said as he rose.

Nathan and Joe both cracked grins then stood and carried their plates over to the sink. Marlene watched them, her chest about to burst with pride. She felt that way about all her boys. It seemed over the last year that they had scattered to the winds, all going different directions. It just wasn't the same after Rachel's death.

Her heart gave a pinch, and she mentally scolded herself for allowing sadness to encroach on her time with Nathan and Joe. They were home, and she was going to enjoy every minute of it. And she was going to push her worries about her older boys right out of her mind.

Rusty stayed close to Marlene while Frank and the boys went into the living room. It didn't take a genius to figure out how intimidated Rusty was by Nathan and Joe, but at least they'd largely ignored her. It wasn't the most polite thing, but Marlene couldn't blame them. And the alternative would have put Rusty over the edge.

"Come on, dear. You'll have to face them all sometime." She gestured for Rusty to follow her into the living room, where the TV was already on and, typically, the men were arguing over sports.

Nathan and Joe patted the space between them on the couch and promptly each put an arm around Marlene when she sat down. She was treated to a big sloppy kiss from both, and she beamed and patted their cheeks in return.

Rusty took a seat in the chair next to Frank's recliner and attempted to blend in with the upholstery.

It was loud and chaotic, just the way Marlene liked it. She sighed in contentment and patted both boys on their legs. It didn't matter that they were approaching thirty. They were still her babies.

The sound of the front door slamming made her sit up straighter. Frank heard it too, because he immediately hit the mute button on the remote.

"Mom, Dad? You home?"

"Sam," Marlene breathed.

She looked up to see Sam stride into the living room, followed by Donovan. They were both a mess. Camo, boots, dirty torn shirts, and they looked like they hadn't had a bath in two days. They *never* came home like this.

A soft moan escaped her lips. Ethan and Garrett weren't with them.

CHAPTER 14

SAM halted in the doorway of the living room, stunned to see his younger brothers sitting on the couch next to his mom.

"Nathan? Joe? What the hell are you guys doing home? Is something wrong?"

"That's what we want to ask you," Nathan said as he stood. Joe also stood, and the two men looked warily at their older brothers.

"Van," Joe said with a nod in Donovan's direction.

"What's going on?" Frank barked. "You're standing around like a bunch of damn strangers and you're scaring your mother to death."

Donovan grinned hugely and strode across the room. He stopped in front of Nathan and then took him down in one swift motion. Nathan landed on the floor with a thump just as laughter burst from his chest.

"Goddamn it, Van, get off me."

Joe wrapped his beefy arms around Donovan and lifted him clear off the ground. Donovan may have had the element of surprise when he got to Nathan, but being the smallest of the Kelly brothers put him at a major disadvantage.

Sam finally managed to shake off the shock of seeing Nathan and Joe. He held his hands up and barked an order for his brothers to quiet down.

Nathan and Joe looked up in surprise. His mom and dad looked at Sam with worried eyes.

Sam crossed the room and grabbed both his youngest brothers in a rough hug. "It's damn good to have you both home."

"Where's Ethan and Garrett?" Joe asked in a steady voice as he pulled back.

It suddenly occurred to Sam what they all must have thought with him and Van bursting into the house looking like they'd both been rode hard and hung up wet and without their other two brothers.

He and Donovan exchanged quick glances.

"Tell me," Marlene demanded.

Sam held his hands up in a soothing motion. "They're fine, Mom. I promise."

"Want to tell us what's going on, son?" his dad said.

Donovan spoke up. "I think everyone should sit down. Ethan and Garrett are fine, but there's something we need to tell you."

"It's good news, Mom," Sam said quickly as he took in her stricken features.

Their worry all turned to puzzlement as they slowly took their seats. It was then Sam noticed a young girl huddled in a seat next to his dad's recliner. He raised an eyebrow in his dad's direction.

"We'll worry about that later," Frank said impatiently. "Now tell us what's on your mind before your mother bursts."

Sam scrubbed a hand through his hair. There was no easy way to explain everything that had happened. He could pussyfoot around the subject and take forever or he could just put it out there.

"Rachel's alive," Donovan broke in before Sam could get it out.

Dead silence fell over the room. No one stirred. No one said a word. Their mom's face was frozen in shock. Their dad simply looked like he hadn't heard correctly, while Nathan and Joe's faces darkened with fury.

Nathan launched himself from the couch. "What the hell, Van?"

"Nathan, sit down," Sam said.

Nathan's eyes widened at the authority in Sam's voice.

"Sam, what's going on?" his mom asked in a quivery voice.

"You better have a damn good reason for coming home and springing this sort of thing on your mother," Frank growled.

Sam sighed and sat down on the steps leading down into the living room. "Ethan got evidence on the sixteenth from someone claiming that Rachel was alive."

"And from this you come over and give your mother false hope?" Frank demanded.

"Dad, listen to him," Donovan cut in.

"He came over to the house with pictures. Of Rachel."

"Oh, Sam, how could someone do that to him?" Marlene cried. "To any of us?"

Sam leveled a look at his mother. "Mom, she's alive. I've seen her, held her. So has Donovan. Ethan is with her now, as is Garrett."

Marlene gasped. Frank went completely white. Nathan and Joe looked at Sam with open mouths.

"But how?" Marlene finally managed to get out. "My God, Sam, where has she been for a year? Did she run away? Did she leave him?"

Sam took a deep breath, knowing what he had to say wouldn't be easy for his family to hear. "The mission that we went on— that we all went on—was to rescue her. She's been held prisoner in South America for the last year."

"Oh, my God!"

The entire room erupted in a chorus of denials, of exclamations and demands for more information. Nathan and Joe stood while Marlene buried her face in her hands. Frank gripped the sides of his chair with white knuckles. Only the young girl viewed the goings-on with disinterest.

"What do you mean held prisoner?" Nathan demanded. "What the fuck is going on, Sam?"

For once, their mother didn't threaten to wash his mouth out with soap. Sam doubted she'd even heard what Nathan said. Her features were drawn in shock.

"Is she okay, Sam?" his mom asked.

"She's not, but she will be," Donovan said soothingly. "It's going to take time."

"She's very fragile," Sam said grimly. "It's why we came ahead to break the news so that hopefully things will have calmed down by the time Ethan brings her home."

"Calm down?" Marlene asked. "*Calm down?* How can I calm down? You tell me the daughter of my heart is alive after we've mourned her for the last year and I'm supposed to be calm? When is she coming home, Sam, and just how bad is she?"

"That's just it, Mom. We have to be calm. She can't stand the excitement. She's . . . she's in withdrawal. They kept her heavily medicated during her captivity. We don't know what all she endured. She's on the verge of shattering, so we absolutely cannot overwhelm her when she gets home."

"There's something else you should know," Donovan said quietly.

All eyes turned to him.

"She can't remember a lot of her life."

"What?" Marlene gasped. Tears crowded her eyes and spilled down her cheeks. "My baby can't remember us?"

"She remembers Ethan. And Garrett. Not much else. I scare her witless, and Donovan might as well be a stranger," Sam said grimly.

"Lord have mercy," Frank said shakily. "That poor child." He looked over at Sam, his eyes drawn and angry. "Why? Why did they do this to her?"

"I don't know that, Dad. But I plan to find out."

"Holy shit," Joe breathed. "This is heavy stuff." Then he looked up at Sam. "Drug cartel?"

Sam nodded.

Nathan swore. "What the hell happened? Did she see something over there she shouldn't have? And if so, why the big charade? Why not just kill her and be done with it?"

"Nathan!" his mother exclaimed in a shocked whisper.

"He's asking a valid question, Marlene," Frank said. "He's not saying they should have killed her, but it seems awfully damn weird that they sent us home her rings and told us she was on a plane that she obviously never set foot on."

"Are you sure it's Rachel?" Joe asked.

Both Donovan and Sam nodded.

"Thank God. Thank God," Marlene choked out. "It's a miracle. She's alive." For the first time, joy shone in her eyes as it finally sank in that Rachel was alive. "What a wonderful gift. Ethan must be beside himself."

Donovan blew out his breath. "This isn't going to be easy for either of them. They're going to need a lot of help from us. The biggest thing we can do is not to crowd them and to let them find their way back on their own terms."

"When are they coming back?" Marlene demanded. "I need to go over and clean the house and get everything ready for them. There's groceries to buy. She'll need new clothes."

Sam held up his hand. "One thing at a time, Mom," he said soothingly. "It'll be a few days. She's being treated, and the doctor wanted her to wait a few days before traveling. You're right, she'll need new clothes. She's thinner. Coming home to a bunch of clothes that don't fit her might be upsetting, so it would be nice if you could shop for her."

Marlene brightened. "Rusty and I can shop for her, can't we, Rusty?"

She turned to where the girl had been sitting a few moments earlier, but her chair was now empty. Marlene blinked in surprise. No one had seen her leave.

"Who is Rusty?" Donovan asked.

"Someone who will be staying here awhile," Marlene said almost belligerently.

Sam exchanged pained looks with his brothers. Their mother's defensive tone could only mean one thing. She'd taken in another stray. Only this time it was a human.

"Mom . . . ," Joe began.

"Don't you 'Mom' me, young man," she said firmly. "Rusty is a guest here, and you'll treat her like one of the family, you hear?"

Then her expression softened. "She needs us, boys. The poor thing. You can't imagine the life she's had."

Sam blew out his breath in frustration. The last thing they needed right now was a rebellious teenager who'd managed to con their softhearted mother into opening her home.

With that, Marlene stood up and clapped her hands together. The brothers looked at one another and groaned. It wasn't any wonder they'd gravitated toward the military. Their mother rivaled any drill sergeant they'd ever encountered.

"We have a lot to do and not much time to get it all done," she said firmly. She pinned Nathan and Joe with her stare. "I want you two to get over and get Ethan's yard in shape. Frank and I will tackle the inside, and then I'll go shopping for groceries and the things that Rachel will need."

Sam eyed her indulgently. "And Donovan and I?"

Her gaze softened, and she walked over and pulled him up to stand in front of her. Then she enfolded him in her arms and hugged him tightly. "I want you and Van to go home and get cleaned up and sleep for about twenty-four hours straight. You both look like hell."

He hugged her back and allowed the first strains of emotion to escape. His family had suffered multiple blows over the last year, and they had some hard issues to face, but for the first time in a long time, they were all going to be together again.

"As much as I'd love to do just that, Van and I have a lot to get done. Our mission isn't over, and we have injured to see about."

"Anything we can do, Sam?" Nathan asked.

It was a fact, he'd welcome his younger brothers' help, but he wasn't about to tear them away from their mom on their first day home.

As if knowing the direction of his thoughts, Marlene let out a snort and stepped away. "If you need them, they're yours, Sam. The sooner you get your business squared away, the sooner I can have my family together under one roof."

"Glad we're handed around so easily," Joe drawled. "This feels like the damn army."

"Well, if you're serious about the offer to help, Van and I could sure use you. I'm getting reports every three hours from Garrett, and Rio is back on the ground. Cole and Dolphin are at Fort Campbell, but I don't expect them to stay more than twenty-four hours before they demand for me to get them the hell out of there. Steele, Renshaw and Baker are itching to go back into action, and I'm leaning toward letting them because Rio is without any sort of backup."

"Nathan and I—"

"Don't even say it," Donovan broke in. "You two buttheads don't belong to us. You belong to Uncle Sam, and he gets pretty pissy when his recruits show up in foreign countries on private missions."

"The best you can do is come back to the house and help out with the communications while Van and I catch some sleep. I can't even tell you the last time we caught any shut-eye."

"I expect you all back here for lunch tomorrow," Marlene said firmly.

"Fried chicken?" Donovan asked hopefully.

Marlene patted him on the cheek and then hugged him as she'd done Sam. "For you, anything. Now go home and get some rest."

CHAPTER 15

"RACHEL. Rachel, honey, wake up."

Rachel roused herself from the deep void of sleep and rubbed a tired hand across her eyes. Then she squinted as the bright sunlight speared her vision.

The plane came to a stop and the whir of the jets cut off. Next to her, Ethan stroked gentle fingers across her cheek.

It was then she realized that they'd already landed.

She sat up, then weaved precariously as she moved too fast. Ethan caught her arms and steadied her. Across from them, Garrett unstrapped himself and went to open the hatch.

"Are you ready?" Ethan asked.

"Where are we?"

"We just landed at the Henry County airport. We're about forty minutes from home."

She let him help her up and guide her toward the exit. Garrett was there to grab her hand as she stepped down. The sandals she'd borrowed from Dr. Scofield slid up and down on her feet as she struggled to keep her footing. The clothes, like the shoes, were too big, but she was clean and comfortable, which was more than she could say she'd been for a very long time.

Sam stood a few feet away. She almost didn't recognize him in the faded jeans and white T-shirt he wore. He seemed much more approachable out of the camouflage warrior mode. Even his expression was softer, less threatening. He wasn't quite so scary.

He stood with arms crossed, watching as they got down from the jet. He leaned nonchalantly against the parked SUV, but he smiled when he saw her.

Determined to put on as brave a front as possible, she straightened her shoulders and pried herself free of Garrett's and Ethan's grasp. Each step forward, away from their support, felt like walking into a void, but she pressed on anyway, until she was just a foot away from Sam.

"Hello, Sam," she said in a low but steady voice.

His smile deepened, and he opened his arms, but made no move toward her. It was up to her to accept the gesture. Taking a deep breath, she walked into his embrace. His arms came around her as he hugged her tightly.

"Hello, sweetheart," he said against her ear. "Welcome home."

Tears pricked her eyes, and she buried her face in his neck. He smelled like Ethan. Strong and steady.

He kissed her hair and simply held her until finally she pulled away. His hand came out to tuck a strand of hair behind her ear in a tender gesture.

"How you feeling?" he asked.

"I don't know," she said honestly. "I'm . . . I'm a little scared."

Ethan's hands crept over her shoulders, and she turned instinctively into the shelter of his arms. He pressed a kiss to her temple. "There's no need to be afraid, baby. You're home now with people who love you."

"Come on. I've got the truck waiting," Sam said.

Rachel watched as he and Garrett picked up the few bags that Ethan and Garrett had brought back with them, and then they headed toward an SUV parked several feet away. Ethan gave her a squeeze and then urged her forward.

She walked almost mechanically, unable to process the bizarre feeling that this was all normal, or it should be. After months and months of fear and captivity, she was free. Back in the regular world. She'd resume her life as if it hadn't been on hold for the last year. As if the people who loved her hadn't gone on with their lives without her.

Garrett piled into the front while Ethan ushered her into the back and then crawled in beside her. Sam got into the driver's seat and pulled away from the small landing strip.

It could hardly be called an airport. It was a tiny airstrip in the middle of acres of farm ground. There were only two hangars, one larger and one much smaller, and they were just tin buildings.

Their truck kicked up a cloud of dust as they drove away. Moments later, Sam pulled onto a paved highway and sped up. Rachel looked curiously out her window, hoping something— anything—would register with her.

After several miles, she gave up. It looked like any place. She could be anywhere.

Rachel leaned into the curve of Ethan's arm, and he immediately tightened his hold on her.

"You okay?" he murmured.

She nodded. She hadn't completely shaken off the effects of her withdrawal. The last several days had been harrowing, an experience she never wanted to repeat. There was still an aching emptiness, a hollow void begging to be filled, but it was more bearable now. And she refused to give in. She wouldn't be the only weak one amid these strong warriors.

Ethan had stuck by her side—he and Garrett. They'd taken turns holding her when she screamed and cried, when she'd begged for relief. At her most desperate hour, she'd pleaded with Ethan to get her the drugs.

He'd stood with her, fully clothed, in the shower when she'd been convinced she was covered with spiders. She still shuddered at the memory of the horrible creatures—hundreds of them—scuttling across her body.

After several seemingly endless days, the worst had been over. She was exhausted, and she knew Ethan and Garrett hadn't fared much better.

"Where are we going exactly?" she asked. It was silly to ask. Ethan and Garrett had gone over the details of her homecoming numerous times, but she couldn't help the anxiety that swam rivers through her mind.

She hadn't realized that her hands were clasped together, her fingers twined so that the tips were white, until Ethan carefully pried them apart and laced her fingers with his.

"We're going home. To our house, baby."

She tried so hard to bring an image of their house to mind. Just a brief glimpse, something to tell her that she had a connection to the place she'd lived with her husband.

"I can't remember," she said in frustration.

Garrett turned in his seat, reached over to touch her knee, and as he'd done so many times over the last few days, he offered comfort with just a few well-placed words.

"You're trying too hard, sweet pea. Relax and let it come to you. Even if you don't remember now, there's nothing to say that when you walk inside your own place, that it won't all come back. And if it doesn't? So what. You have all the time in the world."

She let go of Ethan's hand and grasped Garrett's, squeezing with all her might. "Thank you. I love you."

She gasped, completely mortified as the words escaped. Ethan stiffened beside her. She dropped Garrett's hand and raised her fingers to her mouth, horrified by what she'd said.

Garrett stared back at her, no hint of emotion or judgment in his eyes. Just patient understanding and answering love. Why hadn't she said those words to Ethan? Why Garrett?

Her gaze flew to Ethan, apology etched into every surface of her face. She wanted to scream it but was too embarrassed.

There was no anger in Ethan's eyes, just a tightness as if he battled some unknown reaction. A sound from the front had her turning away. It was Sam. Laughing.

Sam glanced in the rearview mirror, a wide grin splitting his lips. "I'm seeing more and more of the Rachel we know and love all the time. You always were the most lovey, demonstrative woman I know."

Ethan chuckled and seemed to relax against her. But she was too far rooted in regret to feel as if the awkward moment had passed. She closed her eyes and turned away, for the first time denying herself the comfort of his embrace.

"Rachel."

Garrett's deep voice washed like warm water over her ears. Slowly she looked up until she locked gazes with him.

"I love you too, sweet pea. We all do."

She smiled tremulously and nodded. Ethan's hand crept back over hers, and he gave her a little squeeze. Gathering her courage, she peeked up at him, almost afraid of what she might see in his eyes.

She sucked in her breath at the shock of emotion she found. Raw, searing. She couldn't breathe.

He touched her cheek, slid his finger underneath her ear and to her nape, and then he pulled her carefully forward until her lips were just a breath away from his.

"I love you," he whispered.

"I—"

The words choked her, and before she could try again, his lips touched her cheek. Undemanding and so tender, almost as if he was afraid that the slightest pressure would make her fold.

The knot in her throat grew bigger, as did her panic. Why did the idea of saying the words that had come so naturally just a moment before instill such gut-wrenching fear?

She broke away, twisting in her seat as she gulped for air. Ethan touched her shoulder, tentative and seeking, but she flinched away. She was going to be sick.

"Sam, stop the truck," Ethan barked.

He caught her arm as Sam veered off the highway. A few seconds later, her door flew open and she surged forward. Sam caught her as her knees buckled and she sank to the ground.

"Deep breaths," Sam murmured. "Take it easy."

She shook from head to toe. She was simultaneously hot and cold. Thick sweat soaked her clothing and yet she shivered. Rapid images, harsh and unrelenting, hammered her mind.

Ethan's face harsh and drawn in anger. Shouting. Demands. Accusations. She covered her ears and shook her head, trying to shut out the ugliness.

"Rachel."

Ethan's voice, so far away.

"Rachel, what's wrong?"

Garrett this time, closer.

"He hates me," she whispered as tears slipped down her cheeks.

Two sets of arms surrounded her. Hands smoothed her hair back and eased away the tears on her face.

"No one hates you, baby."

Ethan sounded so fierce, as if he'd single-handedly chase away all her demons.

Slowly the darkness faded away. The voices stopped their assault and the coldness dissipated, leaving warmth.

She sagged, her head falling forward. Strong fingers kneaded her neck while other hands supported her shoulders.

"Let's get you back in the truck," Garrett said.

Before she could respond, Ethan picked her up and cradled her close. His chest heaved, and she opened her eyes to see such pain reflected on his face. He looked . . . tortured.

"I'm tired," she whispered as she leaned her head against his neck.

"Then sleep, baby. I'll wake you when we get home."

Ethan ducked into the back and laid her on the seat. He retreated, closing the door, and then walked around to the other side. He climbed in and picked up her head and pillowed it on his lap.

The slamming of the front doors signaled Sam and Garrett getting in, and then came the roar of the engine and the low hum underneath her back as Sam maneuvered back onto the road.

I really am losing my mind. Maybe I already lost it. Maybe I'll never get it back.

She closed her eyes as more tears gathered and spilled silently down her cheeks.

Ethan watched helplessly as silver, damp trails marked a path over her pale skin. What had she meant? Was she remembering? Was her mind tortured with memories of their marriage? Was she putting it all together so soon?

He hates me.

He wanted to puke. Who had she been talking about? God don't let it be him. Don't let her ever think he hated her. He'd die before ever letting her think that even for a moment.

I love you.

The words she'd said so easily to Garrett haunted him. He wanted so desperately to hear them from her lips. Directed at him. Wanted to go back in time to when not a day passed that she didn't tell him how much she loved him.

But a woman will only go so long putting her heart on the line without getting anything in return. If only he'd just returned them. *I love you too, baby.* Only in the beginning. Later, he'd nod or even smile. In the end, he didn't even do that. He'd felt too guilty. The words that were so sweet in the beginning became daggers that slithered insidiously between his ribs and into the vulnerable organs beneath. He'd felt like the worst sort of hypocrite, and so he'd remained silent, until finally she'd stopped saying anything at all.

That had been the worst. He lived each day hoping to hear those words again, only to get angry and resentful when they didn't come. He punished her for what was his own doing.

"Ethan."

Ethan looked up to see Sam studying him in the rearview mirror.

Sam sighed. "I wish I knew what to say, man. I know this isn't easy for you."

"This isn't about me," he gritted out. "It's about her. It's all about her. She's what's important."

Sam nodded. "I know that. But you're hurting too. You're not a machine. You can't just shut it off because you don't want to feel the pain."

"I can handle anything as long as I get her back," Ethan said in a low, desperate voice.

At that, Garrett turned, his gaze probing and thoughtful. "You have her back, man. What are you so afraid of?"

Ethan swallowed. Never would he admit to his brothers just how much of a role he'd played in Rachel getting on that plane to South America, how he'd driven her away, rejected her and her love.

How could he possibly ever tell them that what he feared most was losing her . . . again . . . after getting her back?

CHAPTER 16

"RUSTY is gone!" Marlene said as she waved her hands frantically in front of her.

"Calm down, Mom," Joe said soothingly.

She shot Joe a fierce glare. "I will not calm down. I'm tired of my sons telling me to calm down."

"What do you mean she's gone?" Nathan asked.

Marlene threw her hands up as she surveyed three of her sons as they slouched in her living room. None of them looked like he was in the least concerned that Rusty had run away. Rusty had been quiet since the news had broken of Rachel's homecoming, but Marlene hadn't expected her to disappear on the day Rachel was due to arrive.

"I sometimes wonder if all the common sense wasn't handed out long before you two came along," she muttered.

Nathan winced. "Ouch, Mom. That wasn't necessary."

Donovan cracked up. But before he could issue a snappy comeback, Marlene shut him down with a well-aimed frown.

"I want you all to get your butts up and help me find her. I can't handle this right now. Rachel is due home anytime now and Rusty is gone."

"Has it ever occurred to you that she wants to be gone?"

Donovan said carefully. "You can't make her stay, Mom. She's a troubled kid. You can't save them all."

"I don't care if she wants to be gone, not that I believe she wants to be out on her own for a minute. She needs to have her rear end back in the house. I have no idea what's happened, but unless I hear it from her own lips, we're going to treat this as a family member in need. Would you be sitting here arguing if I told you one of your brothers had disappeared? You certainly didn't waste any time going after Rachel when you learned she was in trouble."

Nathan scowled and stood up. "Now wait just a minute, Mom. You can't compare this kid to Rachel. She's just using you and Dad."

Marlene's lips tightened. "I want all three of you out looking for her. Don't you dare come back without her. I'll go find your dad and we'll take the truck. You call me the minute you find her, you hear?"

Joe sighed and rolled his eyes.

"That's enough disrespect out of you, young man," she snapped.

"Yes, ma'am," he said meekly.

They all wore disgruntled looks, but they shoved off the couch and headed out the front door.

Nathan climbed into his Dodge truck and gave his brothers a look of resigned sympathy out his window as they climbed into their vehicles. When Mom got off on one of her tangents, there was no escaping. She'd turn Stewart County upside down looking for this Rusty girl.

He backed out of the drive and headed west. He'd take the county roads that paralleled the lake, and he'd leave Dover to his brothers.

He drove a little faster than was necessary, but impatience flared in him. He was much more interested in hearing that Ethan and Rachel had gotten home, and he was eager to see Garrett and get a report. He couldn't very well do that when he was off on some fool's errand for his misguided mother.

That wasn't entirely fair, he supposed, but his irritation didn't allow for more charitable thoughts. She had the softest heart of anyone he knew. Too soft. And once she decided something, nothing and no one was going to change it.

For half an hour he took winding paths off of 232 and then doubled back as he continued farther south along the lake. He'd just crossed Leatherwood Creek when he rounded the bend and saw a lone figure walking down the side of the highway. Rusty.

He slowed and rolled down the passenger window as he came up on her. She glanced warily over at him when he pulled up alongside her, and then she stiffened when she recognized him.

"Any particular reason you're walking by yourself down the highway when my mother is about to lose her mind worrying over you?" he snapped.

She stared straight ahead and kept walking, her shoulders stiff and her jaw set.

"She doesn't care about me," Rusty muttered.

"Oh, really. I suppose that's why she took you in, fed you, clothed you, gave you a place to stay and is generally making the rest of us insane demanding that we accept you, not say a damn word to you and all get out looking for you right now when we'd rather be focused on Rachel's homecoming."

She came to an abrupt stop, her lips curling into a snarl. "Rachel. I'm so sick of hearing about Rachel. Rachel is so wonderful. 'The daughter of my heart.' Everyone loves Rachel. Marlene has no need of me now that her *real* daughter is back."

Despite his irritation, Nathan softened as he stared at the girl. She was hurting, and she was doing everything in her power not to let him see how *much* she was hurting.

"Get in," he said.

She shook her head.

"Come on. We'll go for a drive. If you don't want to go home yet, we'll just drive."

She hesitated, and her lips trembled. He reached over and opened the door, shoving it outward. She gave a deep sigh and climbed into the passenger seat.

"Seat belt," he said patiently.

She scowled but slapped the seat belt around her and clicked it into place.

He drove on down the highway, so she would know he wasn't taking her home right away.

"Now, suppose you tell me why you'd think something so wonderful as Rachel coming home to us would change the way my mom feels about you?"

"I'm nobody," she said sullenly. "Just someone your mom felt sorry for. She was feeling sad because of Rachel, and I guess she thought I could fill in."

"And she told you this?"

Rusty hesitated. "Um no."

"Maybe you overheard it."

Again she shook her head, scowling as she got where he was heading with this.

"Or maybe my mom's done something to make you think she's not very sincere and she enjoys jerking around teenage girls who are in trouble."

"You know she hasn't," Rusty muttered.

"Hmm, okay, well I'm out of guesses. Maybe you ought to just tell me. Guys can be slow."

She was silent for a long time as she studied her hands in her lap. "I just thought . . . I assumed that since Rachel was coming back that she wouldn't want me anymore."

Nathan reached over and took her hand, ignoring her flinch of surprise. "I understand why you might have felt that way. But one thing you need to understand is my mother's limitless capacity for caring. She taught school for years, and she can still tell you the names of every student who ever came through her classroom."

He gave a light chuckle. "For that matter, try being her youngest child with five older brothers. If anyone ought to feel left out and overlooked, you'd think it would be me. But somehow she manages to make every one of us feel special, like we're the only person in the world who matters to her. Don't get me wrong. She's not a pushover, and when she sets her mind to something, she's like an alligator with fresh meat."

Her lips trembled, and she pulled her hand away from his. "I'm not used to anyone giving a damn."

"Well, maybe it's time you got used to it," he said simply.

Her lips twisted again as apparently she roused her defenses. "What do you care? You and your brothers don't like me. You'd prefer I go anyway."

"This isn't about me or my brothers, so don't make it so. My mother cares about you. We don't know you. Are we concerned that you're taking advantage of our mother? Hell yeah. And you can bet we'll be watching your ass, and if you make one wrong step, we'll be on you like a duck on a June bug. But as long as you don't screw up, you don't have anything to worry about."

"Are you saying you want me to go back?" she asked suspiciously.

He sighed. "Quit twisting my words and buck up, Rusty. You're capable of making your own decisions and taking responsibility for them. If you want to go back, then quit wasting both our time and say the word. I'll take you home, no questions asked. If you don't want to go, then fine, but you're going to tell my mother that to her face instead of slinking off like an ungrateful coward."

Her mouth rounded in shock, and then unexpectedly she smiled, and it transformed her entire face. Replacing the sullen, defeated look was a young, vibrant girl who was actually quite pretty.

"I like people who don't lie and say it like it is."

Nathan chuckled. "Then you should get along with the Kelly clan just fine. Now, are we going home or not?"

A sparkle lit her eyes, and she looked . . . hopeful. Excited even. Then as suddenly as happiness had fired, the flame died and she looked apprehensively at him.

"Are you sure? I mean are you sure she wants me?"

He stared at her a long time and gave thanks that he had never had to feel unwanted in his life. "Yeah, Rusty. I'm sure."

CHAPTER 17

RACHEL eyed the house from the window of the SUV as Sam came to a stop in the circle drive. She waited for recognition to hit her, but she stared numbly as if it were someone else's house. Not her own.

It was a beautiful house, and she could certainly see it as a place she would have loved. A cypress log house with a rustic front porch complete with swing and potted ferns.

Ethan had told her that they didn't live very far from the lake.

"How long did we live here?" she whispered.

"Three years," Ethan replied. "We moved in right after our honeymoon."

She cocked her head to the side and stared curiously at him. "Where did we go on our honeymoon?"

He looked momentarily surprised and then he smiled, warmth flooding his eyes. "We went to Jamaica and spent a week on the beach. I don't think you ever wore much more than a bikini the entire time we were there."

A hot flush stole over her cheeks, and she ducked her head.

"Ready?" he asked solemnly.

She took a deep breath and nodded. He opened the door and stepped out and then reached back to offer her his hand. She slid her fingers into his, and let him pull her from the vehicle. Sam and Garrett had already gotten out and were standing in the walkway to the front door.

She didn't realize how badly she was shaking until Ethan wrapped an arm around her to steady her as they walked by his brothers.

"Do you want us to stay, Ethan?" Sam murmured.

Ethan paused at the steps to the front door and tightened his grip around her waist. "No, we'll be fine. Tell Mom I'll call her later."

"Okay, man. Let us know if you need anything." Sam slapped Ethan on the back and started back toward the truck.

Garrett hesitated a second then reached out to touch her shoulder. "Take care, sweet pea."

She wrenched away from Ethan and threw her arms around Garrett's waist. He stepped back in surprise but then curled his arms around her and returned her hug.

"You'll be back, won't you?" she whispered.

"I'll never be far," he murmured. "If you ever need me, I'll be here. Promise."

Reluctantly she freed herself from his embrace. Garrett smiled down at her and then turned to his brother.

"Holler if you need anything."

"We'll be fine," Ethan said softly.

Garrett ambled down the walk and climbed into the truck next to Sam. They both offered a wave as they drove away from the house.

"Okay?" Ethan asked as he turned to the door.

She stared up the steps, almost dreading what was inside. Why did it scare her so badly? Why was she such a coward?

"Let's do it," she said.

Ethan put the key into the lock and opened the door. Cool air blew over her face as they stepped inside. She braced herself for the surge of memories, but as she moved farther into the interior, she was only struck by the feeling of unfamiliarity.

Her hands crept up her arms and she rubbed absently as her gaze traveled the living room. It seemed so . . . quiet. Uncluttered. Still even. Calm was reflected in the decoration, from the piano catty-corner to the stone fireplace, to the framed art hanging on the walls.

How could this house be hers when every part of her mind screamed chaos?

"Baby? Are you all right?"

Ethan touched her arm, and she jerked from her perusal of the room.

"I-I'm fine."

"Anything seem familiar?"

She shook her head, precariously close to running as hard and as fast from the house as she could.

"What's bothering you?" he asked gently.

She turned in a tight circle. The walls, the furnishings seemed to close in on her and mock her. They called her a fraud and told her she didn't belong.

"Are you sure I belong here?"

"Come here," he said as he pulled her into his arms. He held her tightly, resting his chin on top of her head. "You belong wherever I am. You belong with me. Always. I know this has to be overwhelming for you, but we'll get past it. Just promise me that when something frightens you that you'll tell me so I can make it better."

She squeezed him, holding on as tight as she could. She inhaled his scent and felt the steady, reassuring beat of his heart against her cheek. They could do this. She could do this.

Finally she pulled away and then reached for his hand, lacing her fingers through his. "Show me around?"

"I'd be glad to."

As they wandered through the house, Rachel's frustration grew. She felt no kinship to this place.

"This is our bedroom and through that door is the master bath," Ethan said as they walked into a spacious room.

The furnishings seemed feminine. Even the bed was a four-poster with a frilly bedspread. It was hard for her to imagine Ethan in such a setting.

"It doesn't look like you," she said slowly.

He smiled. "I have the decorating sense of a mule."

"But it doesn't look like me either," she said helplessly.

"It's exactly you. Calm, uncluttered. Feminine and beautiful."

She shook her head, hating those words. Words she'd used to describe the living room exactly. They weren't her. She walked blindly toward the bathroom, just wanting an escape.

The bathroom was large, with a Jacuzzi tub and a separate shower. The toilet was in its own tiny closet and there were his-and-her sinks lining the wall. But her gaze locked onto the tub.

A distant memory floated by on a cloud, lazy and unhurried. The splash of water. Her sitting in the tub, the water up to her chest. Ethan. She blinked as the image came more sharply into focus.

She was in his arms, leaning against his chest as the water lapped over her breasts. His hands cupped them, his thumbs brushing over the taut peaks. A shiver stole over her body.

And then his fingers through her hair as he soaped the long tresses. Her hands automatically went to her head, to her shorn locks. Her hair had been much longer then.

"Will you take a bath with me?" she blurted.

He blinked in surprise, and for a long moment he didn't say anything. He seemed to struggle with exactly what to say, how to respond.

"You used to wash my hair. I remember you touching me."

Fire built in his eyes, sparking the blue until it resembled a storm front.

"Are you sure, baby? I don't want to do anything to make you uncomfortable."

She shrugged, hating the awkwardness of asking her husband, her *husband*, to be intimate with her again.

"I just want you to hold me."

He drew her into his arms, and to her surprise, he trembled against her. Was he as adrift as she was? In some ways this had to be even harder for him. He had memories that she didn't. He could recall how it was between them and miss what they'd lost.

"Have a seat on the bed. I'll draw the water and then we'll get undressed together, okay? Mom bought you some new clothes and left them on the bed, so you can pick out something to wear while the water is running."

She nodded and retreated to the bedroom. There were several shopping bags on the bed, and she sat down and opened one. Jeans, tops, even socks and a new pair of tennis shoes. There was also a bra and several pairs of underwear.

She glanced down self-consciously as she realized she hadn't worn a bra in longer than she could remember. Or underwear.

Unbidden the image of a man ripping her clothing and her underwear from her flashed in her mind. And then another man stepping between him and her, shoving her attacker away. She'd huddled naked on the dirt floor of the hut while they'd argued, and then her rescuer had shoved her tattered clothing back at her, minus her unsalvageable underthings.

She hadn't thought—or remembered—that instance until now. Her attacker was dead. But her savior? Who was he and why had he cared what the other man did to her?

With nervous fingers, she pulled out the lacy panties and the bra that somehow looked too large for her small breasts. How would she look in them now? Even she knew she had to be thinner. Suddenly the idea of taking a bath with Ethan didn't seem so appealing.

She clutched the clothing to her and waited with growing dread for Ethan to come out. A few moments later, he appeared in the doorway, his body language as tense as hers.

"The water's drawn. Are you ready?"

She stood and met his gaze. "Maybe I should go in first. Can . . . can you give me a few minutes to get into the tub before you come in?"

"Absolutely, baby. Take as much time as you need."

He gestured for her to go in, and when she passed him, he quietly closed the door behind her. She walked over to the sinks and laid the clothing on the counter.

When she looked up, she caught the first look of herself in the mirror. She was momentarily startled. The woman staring back at her with wide, frightened eyes didn't feel like her.

Her hair curled limply at her nape and ears. Her cheeks were thin and hollow, her bones more pronounced. Even her throat looked too small, and her shoulders were angular, not softly rounded.

Her gaze drifted down to her narrow waist and hips. Boyish. There didn't seem to be any softness about her. What could Ethan possibly see in her? Had she always looked like this?

Transfixed by the stranger in the reflection, she pulled at her clothing. Soon she was nude, and she looked with clinical detachment at her breasts. Though small, they still seemed too large for her thin frame. Too plump.

She looked for any imperfection, turning sideways to study her profile. Her butt was just there, pale, unassuming, not too big, not too small. Just a butt.

She lifted her arm and ran her fingers over the now smooth shaven skin under it. Maren had offered her the use of a razor to shave her legs and under her arms but had refused to leave while Rachel used it.

A soft laugh escaped. Number one rule of dealing with crazy people. Never leave them alone with sharp objects.

There was nothing there to inspire a man to lust, but neither was there anything to send him running for the hills. Feeling marginally better, she moved toward the bath and stepped into the steaming water.

It slid over her skin like silk, and she let out a deep sigh of pleasure as she sank down into the tub. Such a simple pleasure, but right now she wouldn't trade it for anything in the world.

She lay back, allowing the water to creep to her chin. She closed her eyes and allowed peace to wrap her in its sweet embrace.

A moment later, she heard the door open. Automatically she sat back up, and she hunched her knees forward in a puny effort to shield her body from view.

Ethan walked over and sat down, still fully clothed, on the edge of the tub.

"Tell me how you want me to do this, baby. I can get in with my shorts on if it makes you feel more comfortable, or I can leave you alone if that's what you want."

She emitted a shaky laugh. "If you get to see me naked, I get to see you naked."

He leaned forward and tucked a finger under her chin. "You can see me any way you want, whenever you want."

With that he stood and slowly pulled his T-shirt over his head. His chest and arms rippled with muscles, and she watched in fascination the dips and curves that traveled his taut skin.

He had the body of a warrior. There wasn't an inch of spare flesh on his body. Every part bulged with muscle and his skin was a study in fascinating contours.

His hands traveled to his narrow waist and hooked into his jeans. The fly popped open and then the denim slowly worked its way over his hips.

No longer able to stare so avidly, she looked down, disconcerted by the heat in her cheeks. This was her husband. Why was she embarrassed to look? She desperately wanted to reacquaint herself with every nuance of her relationship with him.

Wanted the intimacy back that he seemed to hint at. The closeness of their love.

When his jeans hit the floor, he climbed over the edge of the tub and gently pushed her forward so he could position himself behind her.

His penis brushed along her spine as he lowered himself, and she held herself rigid, not moving. She would hold it together. She would.

Finally he was situated, and then he wrapped his arms carefully around her and pulled her back against his chest. The springy hair at his groin, softened by the water, brushed the top of her buttocks, but she relaxed anyway and let him hold her.

She laid her head against his collarbone, and he kissed her temple. To her shock, she felt a shudder roll through his body about the same time she registered wetness against her skin. Tears. His tears.

She started to turn around, but he tightened his grip.

"Stay," he said in a choked voice. "Just let me hold you, baby. Just let me hold you."

She let herself relax back into his arms and nestled her head into the curve of his neck. Tremors continued to work through his body, and quiet little huffs sounded past her ears.

He held her tightly, a wealth of emotion straining in those muscles she'd admired. Instead of being reassured by the knowledge that someone loved her so deeply, she felt vulnerable. Scared. And maybe a little unworthy.

After a while, Ethan seemed to collect himself. His grip loosened and he cupped water in his hands to wet her hair. Then he squeezed shampoo onto her head and dug his fingers into her scalp, rubbing and kneading.

She moaned and closed her eyes in absolute bliss.

"Feel good?" he husked in her ear.

She wanted to cry. Such tenderness was alien. She couldn't remember this, and it hurt all the more that she couldn't bring such sensation readily to mind.

"Why can't I remember?" she asked in a choked voice. "I want to remember. I do."

His hands paused for a moment, and then he continued with gentle, loving strokes as he worked the lather. "You will, Rachel. You will."

After a moment, his hands drifted down to her shoulders,

kneading and massaging her tense muscles. They moved lower, hovering at her chest and then dipping into the water. She sucked in her breath, but he didn't cup her breasts. His fingers glided over the soft swells but went quickly past to her belly, where they stopped, content to rest there at her waist.

"Slide down so I can rinse you."

She went limp and eased down his body. He raised one hand to cup her chin and lifted so that her face stayed out of the water as her head reclined. Then he carefully rinsed her hair.

When he was done, he pressed a kiss to her forehead as she stared up at him, and then he put his hands underneath her arms and lifted until she was upright again. His fingers once again brushed across her breasts when he moved his hands, but as before, they didn't linger.

"Rachel."

Her name came out, almost an entreaty, expelled on a long, soft breath, one that bordered on an ache.

She stilled, waiting for what he wanted to ask.

"Do you remember much about your captivity?"

She stiffened, and her breathing ratcheted up. His hands smoothed over her shoulders, petting in a soothing manner.

Slowly she nodded. "Some. Not everything. The stuff . . . the drugs they gave me made things muddled."

"What can you remember? Can you tell me about it?"

She shook her head. "No. I don't want to think about it."

His hands tightened around her shoulders. "Did they hurt you?"

She wilted against him, sagging like a deflated balloon. Around her the water was cooling, and a shiver burst over her skin. Ethan cursed softly and fumbled with his foot for the drain.

"Let's get out and we'll talk in the bedroom. We could both use some rest and it would be nice to hold you for a while."

He braced himself on the sides and pushed himself upward. Water rained down all around as it spilled from his body. He stepped out and reached for a towel. This time, she stared unabashedly as he dried himself off.

When he was done, he got another towel and laid it aside. Then he reached for her hands and pulled her to stand. As she stepped out, he wrapped the towel around her and pulled her against his naked body.

He rubbed her dry from head to toe and then toweled her hair.

"I know I told you to get an outfit, but how 'bout I give you one of my shirts, and when we get up later you can dress. Or maybe we'll just stay in bed until tomorrow."

She offered a tremulous smile. "That sounds nice. I'm so tired."

He kissed her upturned lips then backed away. "Stay right there. I'll get dressed and get you a shirt."

He returned a second later wearing gym shorts and carrying a T-shirt for her. He pulled it over her head, and it fell down her body to her knees. She looked down and then back up at him.

"That shirt never looked as good on me," he said with a smile. Then he reached for her hand. "Ready?"

She slipped her fingers into his and nodded.

CHAPTER 18

A normal bed. It looked warm, soft and inviting, and she all but dove into the mound of covers. The simplest pleasures, ones that would be so easy to take for granted in everyday life, were now the sweetest. A hot bath. A comfortable bed. All the things she'd been denied for a year.

"Am I even going to be able to find you underneath all those covers?" Ethan teased as he crawled onto the bed.

"I think I'll just stay here for a week," she said wistfully.

"I could be persuaded," he said as he settled beside her.

He lay on his side and propped his head in his palm as he wedged his elbow between the pillows. She stared up at him, studying his expression, the different glints of his eyes.

"Your eyes are darker than Sam's," she mused. "You look a lot like Garrett. You think that's why I remember him?"

He blinked as if he hadn't expected the random thoughts she'd thrown his way.

Her brow crinkled as she brought Donovan's face into view. "Donovan has green eyes, but the rest of you have blue eyes."

Ethan smiled and touched her cheek. "Slow down, baby. Let me catch up."

She burrowed a little deeper into the covers and stifled a yawn as she stared up at him. She loved the contrast between the white sheets and his tanned skin. He was a beautiful thing to behold, and she ate him up with her eyes.

Had she always looked at him with such adoration? Why couldn't she remember? A spark of emotion. Anything.

Darkness crept up again, uninvited and insidious. Fear took hold. Fear of the unknown, but there was also a fear of remembering. Why? What dark secrets did this seemingly perfect house hide?

"Most of us have blue eyes. Dad has blue eyes and Mom has brown. Van ended up with green, while Nathan and Joe got Mom's brown eyes."

"I thought brown was always dominant over blue," she said with a frown.

"You're asking a dumb military grunt to explain genetics?"

"You're not dumb," she said fiercely.

He grinned and smoothed his thumb over her lips. "Still as feisty as ever when it comes to sticking up for those you love. Anyway, my granddad on my mom's side had blue eyes, so Mom obviously carries the gene or whatever you call it. Geesh, I haven't done those stupid gene squares since high school.

"And yes, I look the most like Garrett, but you and Garrett were . . . close. That's probably why you remember him."

"I don't remember your other brothers at all. Or your mother." She sighed. "How can I face them all when they'll be strangers to me?"

Ethan shifted his weight slightly, and he scooted lower into the bed until their noses were just a breath apart.

"This isn't about them. It's about you. They aren't going to be angry. Sad? Probably, but it's because they love you and they hate what happened to you. They want you to be happy. They want you to get your life back, your health and your memories."

Her breath escaped in an unsteady hiccough. "Ethan?"

He tucked a strand of hair behind her ear in a loving gesture. "Yes, baby?"

She licked her lips. "I don't remember a lot about what happened. I mean I remember pieces, like when one of the men tried . . ." She clamped her lips shut for a moment but then shook off her shame and reluctance. She had nothing to be ashamed of. Nothing. They tried to take everything from her. She did nothing to bring about their actions.

Ethan's fingers stilled on her cheek, but she felt more than saw the shudder roll up his big frame.

"What did he try?" he asked in a low voice.

"He tried to hurt me," she said vaguely. "But another man stopped him. I don't know why, but he got the man off me and gave me back my clothes."

Ethan's face was a rigid, immovable stone. Only his eyes betrayed the raw emotion burning inside.

"Did he ever try again?"

"I don't think I was raped," she whispered. She looked searchingly up at him. "Wouldn't I know? How would I be able to forget something so terrible? I remember everything else, I mean about what they did."

"What did they do?" he asked gently. His hands shook against her face, and his eyes were so intent, so focused on her that she felt . . . cherished.

She frowned as some of the memories rolled back through the shadows.

"They told me I was never going home. That I was serving a purpose. An insurance policy. What did they mean, Ethan? I don't understand."

His breath huffed out, and his fingers stilled against her cheek. "I don't know. But I'm going to find out. I swear it."

"Once when I tried to escape, they put me into this . . . cage. It was a box in the middle of the camp. The hot box they called it. One little hole at the top to let air in, but otherwise it was dark and so hot. I baked in it."

She shuddered involuntarily, and Ethan gathered her in his arms, pulling her close to his chest. His heartbeat thumped against her ear, and she could feel the rage billowing off of him.

"After that, they started with the drugs. I hated it. They frightened me so badly, but then I started needing it, and I only felt good when they gave me another injection. I hated them for that, for making me dependent on a drug for my sanity when all the while I was losing it bit by bit anyway."

"No, baby, don't," he protested.

"They used it to control me after that," she said, barging ahead, recalling the bitter hatred and the incessant need that even now still crawled through her body. "They'd withhold the drugs, knowing what it would do to me. They kept me in a constant state of withdrawal until finally I hated myself more than I hated them."

"God."

His body trembled against her. His shoulders heaved, and she thought he might be crying, but she was afraid to look up, afraid of her own tenuous grip on her emotions. If he broke in front of her, she would simply shatter.

"We're going to beat this, Rachel," he said fiercely. "You're already almost there."

She couldn't tell him that right now she wanted the needle more than she wanted to live. She couldn't tell him that she'd sell her soul for just a moment of sweet oblivion. And so she lay in his arms and said nothing and prayed that the incessant craving would somehow go away if she slept.

ETHAN snatched up the phone when it rang, hoping it wouldn't disturb Rachel. She was curled on the couch, a blanket tucked up to her chin, and she was sleeping peacefully. Perhaps the most peaceful rest she'd had in the three days since they'd gotten home.

"Hello," he said in a low voice as he walked toward the kitchen.

"You know if you'd just turn on your damn cell phone, you could put it on vibrate and not have to worry about someone waking Rachel," Sam grouched in his ear.

"Now, why would I want to make it so easy for the rest of you to get in touch with me?" Ethan drawled.

"How is she?" Sam asked, ignoring Ethan's teasing.

Ethan sobered and stole a glance in Rachel's direction.

"She's doing better. It's been rough. She hasn't been sleeping well. Between the lingering effects of withdrawal and her nightmares, neither one of us is getting much rest."

"You sound wiped," Sam said, concern bleeding into his voice.

"Nothing I can't handle."

"Mom is getting antsy. It's all I can do to keep her away."

Ethan sighed. "I know this is hard on everyone. There's nothing I'd like more than for everyone to see her again. Hell, I'm hoping she'll remember something or someone once she's reunited with the family, but she's just so fragile Sam. It's taking everything she has just to keep her feet beneath her."

"Have you taken her to the doctor here?"

"Yeah, almost the first thing I did. Got the name of a therapist in Clarksville I'm going to call as soon as Rachel feels ready. She seems willing enough to talk to me, but so far she's balked at going to anyone else."

"What does the doctor say about her physical condition?"

"Same as Maren said. She's extremely fragile. Undernourished. Her reserves are sorely depleted. He put her on a vitamin regimen and I'm feeding her three good meals a day with snacks in between."

"And the withdrawal?"

Ethan ran a hand through his hair and blew out his breath. "She's still jittery as a June bug at times. I know it eats at her a lot more than she admits. She's so stoic and I can't figure out if she's ashamed and doesn't want me to see or if she's somehow trying to protect me from the viciousness of what she's going through."

"That's a hell of a note," Sam muttered.

"Tell me about it. I'm supposed to be protecting her."

Ethan turned when a knock sounded at the front door.

"Shit, I need to go, Sam. Someone's at the door."

Sam paused. "It's probably Garrett. You had to know he'd be by to check in on you and Rachel."

"Yeah. I'll talk to you later, Sam."

Ethan hung up the phone and went to the front door. Indeed, it was Garrett, standing with his hands shoved into his pockets. He stared at Ethan and took a step forward. "Can I come in?"

Ethan opened the door wider. "Sure. Just be quiet. Rachel's sleeping on the couch."

"How are things?" Garrett asked as he followed Ethan into the house.

Ethan shrugged. "We're getting by."

"You look tired, man. Why haven't you asked any of us for help?"

The question came out gently, but to Ethan it still sounded like an accusation. Hell, he probably deserved it, but how was he supposed to explain to anyone how he felt? He'd lost her. For an entire year he existed with the knowledge that she was dead. And now by some miracle he had her back.

Garrett walked by the couch in the living room and looked down at Rachel. His gaze softened and he carefully touched her cheek. Then he glanced back up at Ethan.

"I think you should go over and see Mom and Dad. Hell, I don't even know if anyone told you that Joe and Nathan are home. They're anxious as hell to see you."

"Sam told me," Ethan said in a low voice. "I'm not going to leave her. I know everyone wants to see her. Believe me, I understand, but I have to do what's best for Rachel, and I'm worried about bombarding her with family right now."

"I wasn't suggesting you take her over yet. I agree you shouldn't overwhelm her too soon. But I think you should go over. Mom's worried sick about you. So is Dad."

"I can't leave her," Ethan said incredulously.

"I'll stay with her. She's sleeping. You need to get out, man. Get some fresh air. Breathe a little. You can't keep this up or you're going to fall apart, and then what good will you do her?"

Christ. Ethan swallowed. Garrett made all the sense in the world, but damn it, he didn't want to leave Rachel. Even for a minute. How could he explain the sheer panic he felt over the idea? What if he got over to Mom and Dad's and discovered this was all some bizarre fantasy?

Garrett walked over and put his hand on Ethan's shoulder. "Look, the way I see it you have two choices. You can get your ass in your truck and go see Mom and Dad for a couple of hours. Or, I can call Sam, Van, Nathan and Joe and have them come over and haul you out forcibly. Either way, you're getting out of this house for a while."

Ethan clenched his fingers into a tight fist. Never before had he wanted to hit someone like he wanted to hit Garrett right now. And Garrett knew it, but he just stood there, arms down, making no effort to defend himself.

"You need your family right now," Garrett said softly. "And Rachel needs you."

Ethan closed his eyes. "All right. I'll go. Swear to me you'll call if she needs me. Sometimes when she wakes up, she forgets . . . she forgets where she's at. You'll need to be right there so she doesn't panic."

Garrett cut him off before he could go any further. "Go. I can handle this. I'll watch over her for you."

Ethan took a breath and then turned away to look for his keys. When he found them, he walked over to the couch, where Rachel hadn't as much as stirred. For a moment he watched the soft rise and fall of her chest. A crease marred her forehead, and she looked worried even in sleep. He bent down and kissed away the wrinkle.

"Sleep well, baby," he whispered. "I'll be back."

CHAPTER 19

ETHAN got out of his truck, slammed the door then took a deep breath before heading to the front door of his parents' home. As much as he was looking forward to seeing Nathan and Joe, being away from Rachel, even for a few minutes, had him on edge.

The door flew open as soon as he mounted the steps, and his mother rushed out to greet him, her arms open wide. Though he swallowed her up, it was her doing most of the holding and hugging.

Tears pricked his eyelids, and he sucked in a big breath to hold them back.

"Ethan, thank God you and Rachel are home," his mom said. She leaned up, cupped his cheek and kissed him even as she wiped tears from her own cheeks.

She reached for his hands and squeezed then pulled him toward the door.

"Nathan and Joe here?" Ethan asked as he ducked inside.

She shook her head. "No, they're helping Sam and Donovan out. Come in, sit down and let me look at you."

She parked him in a chair at the kitchen table and stood staring at him, all the love of a mother shining in her eyes.

"You look like hell," she scolded. Then she sank into a chair across from him and grasped his hands in hers. "How is she?"

He swallowed the knot in his throat. "She's okay. I left her sleeping. Garrett's there."

"How is she really?" she asked softly.

He closed his eyes. "She's fragile, Ma. Those bastards . . . those bastards kept her prisoner for a year. A year. A year where she needed me, where she went through God knows what."

He choked back a sob, ashamed to be breaking down in front of his mother, for God's sake.

She rose and he was back in her arms, her arms wrapped tight around his shoulders, and he turned into her as he'd done when he was a child, his grief muffled by her shirt.

"You should have come sooner," she soothed. "This is too much for you to stand up under alone, son. There are so many of us who will help you, but you have to let us."

"She needs me," he said hoarsely. "I failed her already. I won't do it again."

"Are you failing her by taking a moment to see the mother who is worried sick over you while Garrett watches over her?"

"He called you."

"Yes, he said you were coming. And it's about time. Did you think we'd storm the castle or not understand if you couldn't bring her to us yet? We're so worried for you both, Ethan. I want to see her so bad I hurt. I want to hold her in my arms again. I want to see my daughter. But I can wait."

"Ethan, you're home."

Ethan looked up, then hastily away, as his father entered the kitchen. His emotional outburst was bad enough in front of his mom, but to break down in front of his father was more than he could stand.

That thought fled the moment his father hauled him up and crushed him in his beefy embrace. His father wept openly, his big body shaking convulsively as great sobs tore out of his chest.

"Thank God, thank God you're home. Your mother and I were so worried. And then Sam and Van came home alone. You'll never know what it was like seeing them come in the door so dirty and haggard and not seeing you and Garrett. It was as bad as the day they told us Rachel died."

"I'm sorry," Ethan said as he cupped the back of his father's head. "I never meant to scare you or Ma. But we couldn't tell you. Not until we were sure. I'd never get your hopes up like that."

"So it's really her? She's home?" his dad asked hoarsely.

"She's home," Ethan said, allowing the joy of that statement to flood his chest.

Now his mom's eyes filled with tears again, and she raised her shaking hands to her face.

"Bring her to us soon, Ethan. Dinner. Just like old times. We won't push her, I swear. Just let us see her. Everyone loves her so much."

Ethan wiped at his eyes with the back of his hand and reached for her hand. "I will, Ma. Sunday, okay? Sunday dinner just like old times. The family will be together again."

"Praise God," she breathed out. "Oh, Ethan, it's a miracle. You've been given such a precious gift."

He smiled at her, touching her damp cheek with his fingers. "I know. I won't screw it up this time."

She frowned at that, but he turned to his father before she could question his meaning.

"I'm really sorry we scared you. Things happened so fast. If it was Rachel, we had to get in there fast, and if it wasn't, we didn't want you to go through the loss all over again."

"It's okay, son. The important thing is my boys and my daughter are home again where they belong. I can't ask for more than that."

"Let me fix you something to eat," Marlene said as she bustled around the counter toward the fridge. "You can take leftovers home for Rachel."

He hedged, checking his watch. He'd already been gone half an hour.

"She'll be fine with Garrett," his mom said in a quiet, understanding voice. "You need a break, Ethan. Let me feed you. You probably haven't eaten a thing I've sent over since you've been home."

"When have I ever turned down your cooking, Ma?"

She smiled when he cracked a grin.

"That's better. Now sit. Talk to your father while I whip up supper. Garrett will call if she needs you and you can be home in less than five minutes."

THE dream was the same. Ethan was angry, his features drawn into a dark cloud. Despair washed over her in waves, and a feeling of helplessness assaulted her. More powerful than her fear of her captors. No, that was in the past. Now she faced something worse.

Was it a nightmare? Some terrible image fueled by her fears and insecurities, or was she remembering more about her life with Ethan?

She twisted, held captive to her dreams. A tortured moan escaped her over and over, and all she could think was *He doesn't love you. It's not real.*

"Rachel. Rachel. Wake up, sweet pea. You're dreaming. Come back to me."

She shrank away from the soft croon, and her eyes fluttered open. She blinked rapidly as Garrett's face came into view. Relief staggered her, and she felt sick that she was relieved it wasn't Ethan kneeling next to the couch.

She grabbed at his hand and clutched tightly, her heart threatening to beat right out of her chest.

"Hey, are you okay?"

She nodded but she kept her fingers wrapped tight around his hands as she struggled to sit up.

Garrett helped her and then slid onto the couch to sit next to her, his arm hung loosely around her shoulders.

"Ethan's over at Mom's, but he'll be back soon. I can call him if you need him."

She shook her head. "No. I'm fine. Really."

"Can I get you something? You hungry?"

"Water."

He rose and with a concerned look in her direction walked into the kitchen. A few seconds later he returned with a glass of water. She took it from his outstretched hand and drank thirstily.

After a few moments some of the blackness of her dreams receded, and she could breathe easier. She held the glass in both palms and rested the bottom on her knee as she stared straight ahead, trying to collect her scattered thoughts.

"Rachel? Are you sure you're all right? That seemed like a really bad dream."

Her mouth lifted in a half smile. Then she glanced over at him, easing a little more at the worry in his eyes.

"Tell me about Ethan," she said softly.

Garrett's brows came together in confusion.

"About me and Ethan," she corrected. "Were we happy? Did he . . . did he love me?"

Garrett sucked in a deep breath and then he leaned back on the couch. He held out his arms to her. "Come here."

She went willingly, seeking his comfort, wanting the truth but also hoping it eased her mind.

When she was settled in the crook of his arm, he nudged her head until it was pillowed on his shoulder.

"Ethan is a stubborn son of a bitch. There was never a doubt about that. He's butted heads with every one of us. You included. But he loved—loves—you. Don't ever doubt that. You were just right for him. No other way to put it. You were calm when he had the tendency to get all worked up over things. You centered him."

"My nightmare was about us," she admitted. "In it he was angry. Really angry. I don't know about what. But I was so . . . afraid. Scared. Not that he'd hurt me but that he didn't love me, that he didn't want me. Why would I dream something like that?"

He tightened his hold on her and kissed the top of her head. "You're scared, sweet pea. We're a bunch of strangers to you. You're suddenly thrust back into a world you can't remember. I can only imagine how frightening that has to be. I'd be amazed if you weren't having nightmares about all of us."

She sighed, her chest caving a little in relief. He made so much sense.

"But there's something you need to know," he continued. "Ethan was devastated when he lost you. Not a day has passed that he hasn't mourned for you. He damn sure didn't stop loving you. He's scared too, Rachel. Scared out of his mind that he'll do or say the wrong thing, that he'll hurt you or that, God forbid, he'll lose you again."

"I'm not the only one hurting," she murmured.

"No," he agreed.

"Thank you," she said simply. "I'll remember that. I'm glad he went to see his mom. She must be worried about him."

"We all are. We're worried about you both."

Her hands shook, and she clasped them tighter around her water glass to control her nerves.

"Will you take me to him?" she asked.

Garrett hesitated. "I'm not sure that's a good idea. He won't be long. I can call him to come back. He's just five minutes away."

She gave him a perplexed look. Her brows scrunched together as she studied him. "Why not?"

"We don't want to overburden you too fast. Ethan has a big family. There are a lot of us," he said tactfully. "It can be overwhelming."

"I'm okay," she insisted. "I want . . . I want to see them. Maybe I'll remember something. Besides I don't want to keep Ethan from his family because he worries I'm going to freak out. I can only imagine how worried everyone has been for him."

"And you, sweet pea," Garrett said gently. "We're most worried about you."

"Will you take me to him?"

He inhaled through his nose, his big chest puffing outward, and then he released his breath in a long exhale, his chest sinking.

"Okay. I'll drive you over. Ethan might kick my ass over it."

She eyed him doubtfully. "You're bigger than Ethan."

His teeth flashed as he grinned. "But Ethan's meaner."

She raised her hand to her lips as laughter spilled out. Then her eyes widened in surprise to hear the sound.

"Ahh, sweet pea, that sure does sound good. Come on. Mom and Dad will be so glad to see you. If we're lucky, the rest of the clan is still over at my place, so you won't be subject to everyone at once."

CHAPTER 20

THEY weren't so lucky.

Garrett sighed when he pulled into his mom and dad's driveway to see that the yard resembled a used truck lot. Not only were Nathan and Joe back, but it appeared they'd brought Sam and Donovan with them.

He glanced over at Rachel, who sat quiet and pale in the passenger seat. Her fingers were balled tight in her lap, and she stared at the front door as if she expected it to explode. And hell, maybe it would.

After pulling to a stop behind Ethan's truck, Garrett cut the engine then reached over to take Rachel's fist. Carefully he pried her fingers open until he stroked the length of her hand reassuringly. He wasn't even sure she noticed.

"I can turn around and take you back home," he offered.

Finally she turned to look at him, her eyes deep and haunted. "No. I can do this. Maybe I'll remember something."

He had to admire her courage. His family was enough to make him run screaming like a girl on a good day. Facing them when they were complete strangers? Brave.

Theatrically he sucked in a breath and made a show of squaring his shoulders. "Ready?"

A smile wavered on her lips. "Ready."

He opened his door and walked around as she was getting out of the truck. He reached for her hand and she tucked it trustingly into his.

As they neared the door, he paused and squeezed her fingers. "Just remember they love you."

She smiled bravely and he opened the door.

Cool air washed over him as he stepped into the foyer. In the distance he could hear the TV and the murmur of voices. Everyone was in the living room.

As much as he savored the idea of reintroducing Rachel to her family, he knew it should be Ethan's decision. His brother was going to be pissed. But then Ethan hadn't been the one faced with Rachel's pleading expression. Garrett had never been able to tell her no, an affliction he was sure Ethan shared.

He stopped in the dining room, just a short distance away from the steps leading down into the living room. Rachel bumped against him and he felt her tremble. He squeezed her hand one more time but kept her solidly behind him as he started forward again.

At the top of the steps, he stopped again and softly cleared his throat.

All eyes turned in his direction. Ethan was first to react. He stood straight up, his face a thundercloud. His mom cocked an eyebrow and then frowned. He recognized that look. A reprimand was about to fly. He almost grinned. The woman could make him feel five years old again with one stare.

Nathan and Joe looked up with only mild interest. Sam frowned and Donovan just looked. But then that was Van. Calm and nonjudgmental.

"You're supposed to be with Rachel," Ethan exploded. "Goddamn it."

"Ethan," his mom scolded. "Watch your mouth."

In response, and because at the moment he wanted to survive with his hide intact, he pulled Rachel out from behind him. She was stiff as a board, and her eyes looked wild.

The room erupted in chaos. He held up a hand to shut it down before Rachel bolted.

"Quiet!" he shouted above the din.

Ethan stalked over, his eyes never leaving Rachel. His worry was evident because he didn't even threaten to kick Garrett's ass. He didn't even look at Garrett.

"Rachel, baby," Ethan said softly. "Are you all right? I'm sorry I wasn't there when you woke up. I shouldn't have left."

Behind Ethan, Nathan and Joe stood, their gazes locked on Rachel, utter disbelief etched in their expressions. Garrett couldn't blame them. Until he'd actually seen Rachel, he'd doubted her existence. Stuff like this only happened in the movies. She'd died—or so they all thought—and now she was back.

His mom held both hands to her mouth, tears flowing unchecked down her cheeks. Even his big ole burly chested dad looked pale and shaken.

As was her habit when the family was together, Rusty sat away, her gaze flickering dispassionately over the hubbub. Once it rested on Rachel, and her eyes narrowed before she quickly looked away. Garrett frowned. The last thing Rachel needed was a lone dissenter. Especially someone who didn't belong. When Rusty glanced up at Garrett, he scowled at her, letting the full force of his disapproval bleed into his expression. Rusty blanched and looked down at her hands, refusing to pick her head back up.

"I wanted to come," Rachel said in a quiet, shaky voice. "I asked Garrett to bring me. Don't be angry with him."

Ethan touched her cheek. "I'm not angry. Just worried about you."

She offered a tremulous smile. Garrett moved slowly away, leaving her standing there with Ethan. He shot his mom and dad warning looks, and his mom scowled as if to say she wasn't an idiot.

Rachel peeked around Ethan and nervously scanned the occupants of the room. She recognized Donovan and Sam, of course. The older couple had to be Ethan's mom and dad, which left the other two men to be Nathan and Joe. There was a young girl sitting away from the rest, and Rachel searched her memory for any mention of a female member of the Kelly family. But it was all a blank.

Disappointment surged over her. She didn't recognize them. Tears brimmed at her eyelids, but she bit her lip to keep them at bay. She was damn tired of being so weepy.

"Rachel?"

Ethan's mom crossed the room to stand beside Ethan. Rachel swallowed the ache in her throat. She could see the hope in this woman's eyes. The love. And Rachel could remember nothing. Couldn't conjure the same memory of love and affection.

"My baby," his mom crooned, and she gently enfolded Rachel in her embrace.

Rachel gulped in steadying breaths, but God she wanted to break down and sob like a baby. Was there anything better than the love of a mother? This wasn't her mother. She didn't have one, but if Ethan and Garrett were to be believed, Marlene Kelly was as much a mother to her as she was to her own children.

"Thank God you're home with us," Marlene murmured against her hair.

She drew away and then kissed Rachel's cheek. Her hand stroked down her hair, and she gave Rachel a watery smile.

"You've monopolized her enough, Marlene. Let her breathe a minute so I can hug my daughter."

The gruff voice made her jump, but she immediately relaxed when she saw Frank Kelly step to Marlene's side. She smiled tentatively up at the big man, and to her surprise his face crumbled and big tears rolled down his wrinkled cheeks.

She stared in shock as he put his arms out to her. He didn't move to her as Marlene had done, and maybe he was worried she'd reject him or was afraid.

As anxious as she was, she wanted to comfort *him*.

After only a brief hesitation she walked into his hug and wrapped her arms around his waist. His admonishment to Marlene to let her breathe made her smile. He was squeezing her so tight she could barely pull air into her lungs.

She closed her eyes and inhaled his scent. Old Spice aftershave. Made her think of grandpas. Leather and the overwhelming smell of comfort. Home.

"Hey, no hogging."

Rachel opened her eyes to see a grinning face close to Frank's shoulder.

"Which one are you?" she asked.

His teeth flashed in a wider smile. "I'm Joe. The good-looking one."

Unable to resist, she smiled back just as Frank released her. Joe tugged her into his arms and lifted her up.

"Hey, knock it off, dumbass," Ethan growled.

Joe ignored him and twirled her around. As she stared into his eyes, a memory as dizzy as he was currently making her skittered through her mind. Just a brief glance. But it was Joe, standing nervously in front of her. He was younger. Same short haircut, but he was in uniform. Army fatigues. Boots.

Her brow furrowed as she sought to hang on. Joe carefully eased her down, and she blinked as he stared at her in concern.

"Hey, you okay? Sorry, didn't mean to get carried away."

"You asked me out," she blurted.

Joe cast a nervous glance over at Ethan then grinned at her. "Yeah. Well not lately."

Sam stepped forward, and she willed herself not to flinch.

"You remember him, Rachel?" Sam asked.

She raised a hand to her brow and pressed over her right eye, suddenly aware of the slight throb. Ethan's hand slid over her shoulders and he massaged, a silent message of support. Reminding her of his presence. She sank back against him, tired but unafraid. She may not remember these people, but she couldn't refute the love in their eyes.

She stared up at Joe again, searching the vague images for something that made sense.

"You were standing in front of me. You had your uniform on. And you were nervous."

Joe smiled. "Hell yeah. I was asking a gorgeous woman out."

She tilted her head. "Did I accept?"

Joe adopted an exaggerated crestfallen expression. "No. You let me down easy, though." He clutched his heart and staggered back a step. "I recovered. Eventually."

She chuckled at his antics. Then her gaze flittered to the man she now assumed had to be Nathan. He stood back, a slight smile curving his lips.

"You don't look alike," she said.

"Thank God," Nathan muttered.

"Yeah, I got all the looks. He got . . . Well he didn't get much," Joe said.

Nathan rolled his eyes then shoved by Joe. "Got a hug for me?"

She went willingly, her unease gone. His body shook with emotion, and she realized that despite his and Joe's back-and-forth, they were as affected as the rest of the family.

When he let her go, she stepped back, putting enough distance between her and the rest so that she could study their faces.

"I really do have a family," she said in wonder.

Pain flashed in Ethan's eyes. She hadn't meant to hurt him. Why had her words hurt him?

"Yes, sweet pea," Garrett said. "You have a family. You have all of us. Warts and all."

Ethan moved to her again. His hand slid over the side of her neck and then up to cup her jaw. His thumb grazed restlessly over her cheek, and she tilted her chin so she could look into his eyes.

"Are you okay, baby?"

Everyone else seemed to disappear. His face lowered precariously close to hers. He hadn't kissed her yet. Not as a husband. He'd been so careful with her. Understanding.

She licked her lips at the same time she realized she wanted him to kiss her. Here. And then her gaze skated sideways to his family all standing there. Watching.

She ducked her head and took a step back, Ethan's hand falling away. But she reached out to catch it, wanting to maintain some semblance of contact with him.

He smiled and laced his fingers with hers then pulled her against his side.

"Are you hungry?" Marlene asked.

Ethan chuckled. "Ma's answer to everything. Food."

Marlene harrumphed, but her eyes twinkled. "You didn't turn down a hot meal."

"I'm no idiot."

Donovan spoke up. "Hey, if she's not hungry, I am."

Rachel turned in the direction of his voice. He smiled and nodded, but he kept his distance almost as if he knew how overwhelmed she was.

"You're the quiet one, aren't you?"

Donovan's eyes widened a little, but his cheeks colored slightly.

"If you're asking if I'm an obnoxious loudmouth like all my other siblings, the answer is no."

"I danced with you at my wedding," she said, as the music danced in her head just as they had done. "I teased you and said you were the only one of your brothers who hadn't bruised my toes."

His smile lit up his face. "Yeah. I always said they were uncouth mammoths."

Laughter rang out over the room, and she realized that it was a sound she'd heard often in her past. She stared from face to face, her heart swelling and aching with the irrefutable truth. She was home. She had family. She was loved.

CHAPTER 21

IT had taken a while for Rachel to become accustomed not only to sleeping in the wondrous luxury of a bed, but also to sleeping with Ethan. Not that she'd had any difficulty making the transition. In fact, she was usually so glued to him by the middle of the night that she was surprised he didn't shove her away. But he seemed as content as she was to sleep so melded together.

The part she'd had to grow accustomed to was not living with the fear of him being gone when she woke up. He never left the bed before she did and always made sure he was there, holding her, when she woke up.

Some mornings they'd lie there lazily, limbs entwined, and he'd rub a hand up and down her arm as the sun rose higher, filling their bedroom with light.

This morning was no exception. She'd actually woken before Ethan, and she lay there watching him sleep. He looked almost vulnerable in this unguarded state, and she found the contrast fascinating. He was so hard and tough, so very protective of her, and yet right now she wanted to touch him, ease the worry she often saw in his eyes.

She wondered what he'd do if she kissed him. Though he was affectionate with her, and touched her frequently, he hadn't made any effort to kiss her—really kiss her. There were light kisses to her forehead. A peck on the lips. Sometimes a brush across her cheek. But he hadn't kissed her like a lover.

Part of her was curious to see if she'd remember the passion that once existed between them, but the other part of her was scared to death. What if she didn't react appropriately? What if she couldn't remember her feelings for him. Worse, what if she felt nothing if they tried to make love?

She frowned. No, that couldn't be possible. She was too physically aware of him.

She snuggled a little closer to him, until her mouth was hovering just an inch from his. Her pulse pounded, and she chided herself for being so ridiculously nervous. It was just a kiss. They'd kissed any number of times before.

She licked her lips and then carefully pressed her mouth to his. The kiss was so light and yet it gave her a giddy thrill. She pulled quickly away, worried she'd woke him. But he hadn't moved.

Encouraged by the warm sensation all the way down to her toes, she moved forward again. This time she kissed just the corner of his mouth and enjoyed the scratchy sensation of his morning shadow against her cheek.

Gaining courage and confidence, she slid her mouth fully over his and kissed him again. His lips parted, and she gasped in surprise. She pulled away to see him watching her through half-lidded eyes.

"Good morning," he murmured.

Fire lit her cheeks. She felt like an errant teenager stealing her first kiss.

"G-good morning."

He smiled and ran his finger down her nose. "I like your way of saying good morning."

Her cheeks tightened and she ducked her head.

"Hey," he said softly. "I liked it. Do you know how many nights I've dreamed of waking this way? You in my arms, your lips on mine."

She smiled shyly. "I feel so silly. We've kissed so many times, but to me this feels like the first."

He slid his hand behind her neck and cradled her head in his palm. "Then let's make it perfect." He lowered his mouth to hers and pressed warm and sweet against hers.

Her heart fluttered and turned over like someone had set a jar full of butterflies free in her chest.

He was exquisitely tender. So reverent that it brought tears to her eyes. He kissed her lips and then started at one corner of her mouth and kissed his way to the other side.

His tongue slid sensuously over her top and then bottom lip and then gently slipped between to open her to his advances. With a sigh, she acquiesced, and their tongues met, tasting each other, exploring. Advancing and then retreating.

They performed a delicate dance, their tongues dueling, slowly at first and then faster. Their breath came faster and was swallowed up, given and then taken back. They shared each puff of air, savored it before demanding more.

Had she really thought she wouldn't respond to him? She ached for him. All she wanted was to lose herself in him. Curl so tightly into him that she'd never be without his strength—his *love*.

The thought shook her to the bone. How could he love her when she'd forgotten their past? How could he love her when he'd thought her dead for the last year? And how could she hope to love him when all she had were bits and pieces of their life together?

Why couldn't she remember?

Ethan drew away and moved his hand from her nape down her back to cradle her behind.

"What are you thinking?"

She smiled tremulously, her lips swollen from his kisses. "I wish I could remember. I want to remember how it was. Was it always like this? Was it as sweet? Was it better?"

"I think it gets better each day we spend together," he said. "I think twenty years from now, we'll look back and laugh at the idea that it couldn't get better or that somehow we'd reached a standstill. Isn't that the way it should be?"

She nestled back into his arms and laid her cheek against his broad chest. "I hope you're right."

"I am this time," he murmured.

She leaned back, puzzled by his response, but he kissed her again, and she forgot about everything but the heat of his lips on hers.

"I had an idea for something to do today," he said when he drew away again.

She raised an inquiring eyebrow.

"I thought we could go to Sam's to swim off the dock. You've remembered several instances of being there, and I thought it might help to be in a place you remember being happy."

Excitement bubbled up. Random snippets peppered her mind, crowding in until they overwhelmed her.

"I'd love that. When can we go?"

He smiled at her enthusiasm. "As soon as we get our lazy butts up and get out there."

"Sam won't mind?" she asked anxiously.

Ethan laughed. "You, my darling wife, have all my brothers wrapped around your little finger. You may not remember it, but that doesn't change the fact. They won't mind a bit if we come over."

Her brow crinkled. "Oh, that's right. I'd forgotten you told me that Garrett and Donovan live there too."

"Don't get all worried on me. It'll be fine. You'll be fine."

He squeezed her hand for emphasis, and she leaned forward to give him a quick kiss, delighted that she could be spontaneously affectionate with him without awkwardness. It was a start.

RACHEL looked eagerly out of her window when they pulled into Sam's gravel drive. The house was beautiful, and the lot was huge. A separate building, larger than the house, was situated to the right, and she focused on it intensely, but there was no flash of recognition.

"What's there?" she asked, pointing at the building.

It was odd in that it didn't look like a house. It couldn't remotely be considered home-like. It was a square, gray stone building with what looked like steel doors. It reminded her of a bomb shelter or what she'd assume they looked like.

"That is the current KGI headquarters. Sam's working on a much bigger place. He has this idea in his head that the entire Kelly family will live under lockdown in a compound that serves as the headquarters. Whatever you do, don't ask him about it. He'll talk your head off about it."

She laughed. "Really? The entire family?"

Ethan sighed. "Yeah. He makes a good argument, don't get me wrong. KGI has made enemies, and that won't stop. It'll only get worse. He wants several hundred acres so that he doesn't have to rely on any outside sources for transportation or supplies. If and when he gets it up and running, it'll have its own landing strip, helicopter pad and training camp for the teams."

Her eyes widened. "I knew . . . I mean I saw the soldiers who were with you when you came for me, but . . . Well I don't know what I thought. Are all those KGI?"

He nodded. "And more. I don't think you saw Rio or his team. Sam's looking to add more teams, but it takes time and training. He's very selective, and he wants the recruits trained by Steele or Rio. In order for that to happen, he needs more manpower and more assets."

It was growing warm now that Ethan had cut the engine, so Rachel opened her door to let in the breeze. Still, she was curious about KGI and why Ethan didn't work with them. What had he done when he quit the SEALs? For that matter, why had he quit?

"Seems like all that would take a lot of money," she said doubtfully when Ethan came around to get her.

The corner of Ethan's mouth lifted. "Sam's made a lot of money since he got out of the army. He's worked like a dog for it, and it all goes back into KGI. Garrett and Donovan are equal partners, and they pour all their take back into the company too, hence the reason they're all still living together in the same house."

He took her hand and pulled her into the hot sun. She'd sworn that if she ever had the chance she'd never live where it was hot. It was a vow she'd made during the long, unbearable days in the hot box in her prison. But this was different. She wasn't baking in a dark hole. She was in the sunshine, the golden rays spreading as far as the eye could see. She was free.

For a moment she stood there, pulling taut against his hold as she turned her face into the sun and closed her eyes. Never had freedom felt as sweet as it did right now.

When she opened her eyes, she looked down at the bikini top, cutoff shorts with strings hanging from the hem and the pair of flip-flops. She was barely wearing more than she had during captivity, but this was her own life and it brought her comfort. How many times must she have worn these clothes to swim from Sam's dock?

If she closed her eyes again, she knew she could recall the horseplay. Garrett throwing her into the water. Her coming up with a mouth full of lake water and shrieking in indignation and finally helpless laughter.

Ethan diving in after her. Them racing from the dock toward the middle of the lake, where the current was stronger. The many barbeques on the worn wooden deck. Watching the sun go down after long summer days.

"Rachel, are you all right?"

Ethan's voice drifted through the hazy memories, and for a moment she resented the intrusion. Then she smiled and looked at him.

"I was remembering. This place makes me happy. There are a lot of happy memories here. It's nice to be able to grab onto a few of them, to know they're real and not some fantasy I've conjured in a hallucinogenic state."

He drew her to him, cupping his hand behind her neck as he tilted her up to meet his kiss. He didn't act as reserved as he had before. Not since she'd kissed him this morning in bed. Maybe he'd been waiting for her to make the first move.

"I'm glad you have happy memories. How about let's go make some new ones? I'll even let you throw me in."

She grinned and then darted around him, instinctively going down the stone path that led around the house to the back. She'd wanted to ask him why he'd quit the SEALs and why he wasn't working for KGI, but now she was loath to ruin the lighthearted mood they found themselves in.

When she rounded the corner and bounded onto the deck, she stopped in her tracks at the gorgeous sight before her. No wonder she'd loved it here so much. The water sparkled like a million diamonds under the veil of sunshine. Rich blue with a fringe of white on the tops of the gentle swells. It looked inviting, and suddenly she couldn't wait to get in.

She glanced over at Ethan and bit her lip to keep the mischievous smile at bay. She eased from her flip-flops and then bolted down the ramp toward the dock.

"Last one in is a rotten egg!"

She couldn't remember the exact depth of the water from the dock, only that she'd been thrown in more times than she could count, so she sailed off the end feet first and landed with a splash several feet away.

The cold exhilarated her and stunned her. She came up gasping for air and shrieked at the chill.

"Serves you right," Ethan called from the dock.

She looked up to see him removing his tennis shoes. She gave a little shiver and then started back to the dock. He stripped off his shirt, and she caught a glimpse of his chest silhouetted against the sunlight.

He was, in a word, magnificent.

Then he executed a perfect dive into the water beside her. Barely a ripple disturbed the surface. He came up several yards away and shook the droplets from his short hair. White teeth flashed in a broad grin. He ducked underneath again, and the next thing she knew, she was being lifted in the air.

She laughed as he held her high out of the water while treading water.

"How on earth are you able to do that?"

He dropped her with a splash, and when she came up, he gathered her close.

"I'm a SEAL, remember? We do the impossible, and we do it in the water."

She rolled her eyes and then her question came back to her. Cocking her head to the side to let the water drain out of her ear, she peeked at him from under her lashes. "Why did you quit the SEALs? I don't think you've ever said. I mean I'm sure you did," she added hastily. "I just can't remember."

Darkness flickered in his eyes, momentarily chasing away the sun's rays. "You needed me. I needed to be here."

"Why didn't you go to work with KGI? Is that why you quit, so you could go to work with your brothers?"

He shook his head and then dove beneath the surface. She watched the swirl of water that signaled his presence underwater and followed it a good distance from the dock.

Somehow she'd stumbled onto unwelcome territory. Either he was unhappy with his decision to quit or there was some other reason she didn't know. More than ever her lack of memory frustrated her. How was she supposed to forge a future when the past lay silent?

Determined that the day wouldn't be ruined by things beyond her control, she swam after Ethan, colliding with him midway in a tangle of arms and legs.

Laughing around mouthfuls of water, she beat at his shoulders. "You planned that!"

"You two having fun?"

Rachel looked toward the dock to see Sam standing there at the end, watching them with amused eyes. Today she couldn't remember why she was so guarded around him, and she let her good mood take over.

"Come in," she said with a wave. "The water's not *too* cold."

"I know exactly how damn cold—"

He was cut off midsentence when he pitched forward into the water. Rachel stared in shock as Garrett doubled over laughing from the end of the dock where he'd shoved Sam over.

Sam came up sputtering, and he turned with a shout in Garrett's direction. "You son of a bitch! I'll get you for this. Kelly motto number two. Don't get mad, get even."

Garrett just howled louder. Donovan ambled behind him and gave both brothers a curious look.

"Dude, it's better to wear swimming trunks. Getting wet jeans off is a bitch."

"Oh fuck you, Van," Sam grumbled.

Rachel couldn't control herself any longer. Laughter bubbled up and spilled over. She laughed so hard, she had to reach down to grab her sides and then sputtered when her head sank below the surface.

Ethan yanked her back up and held her by the arm as she laughed and spit simultaneously.

Garrett grinned down at Sam. "There. That had to be worth the unexpected swim."

Sam smiled good-naturedly. "Yeah, you got me there. Just, next time? *You* can make her laugh by going in."

This she could remember. Lots of laughing and joking. Good times in the summer. Them all swimming until late in the evening. Having a beer on the dock with their feet dangling in the water. Watching the spawning bream in late spring.

Here, happiness didn't seem so far away. It wasn't some distant point she couldn't see ever reaching. It was present. It was everywhere. Hope was alive inside her. She didn't want today to ever end.

"It doesn't have to," Ethan murmured.

She realized she'd said the last aloud.

"We can do this over and over. You'll see, Rachel. We can have our life back. It just takes time."

She twined her arms around his neck, momentarily forgetting his brothers as they argued and joked loudly in the distance.

"Do you really think so, Ethan? Sometimes I worry we can never get back the past. Other times like today I'm more hopeful. I hate not remembering. I hate it."

He looked at her so seriously that she went silent. "The past . . . is the past, Rachel. All we can do is go forward. The past doesn't matter. Just here and now and today and tomorrow. You'll remember the past. You get back more with each passing day, but what's important to us is tomorrow."

She smiled and hugged him to her, pushing them both down toward the surface. He laughed and grappled for a moment as he fought to keep them afloat.

"Trying to drown me, woman?"

"You can't drown a SEAL," she taunted. "How embarrassing would that be?"

"God yes," he muttered. "Shoot me, hang me, let me die of infection from a hangnail, but don't let me die in the water. They'd send me to hell on principle."

"You two want something to eat?" Garrett hollered from the dock.

Ethan waved him away. "Go away. I'm about to kiss my wife."

And then he lowered his head and did just that.

CHAPTER 22

"**ARE** you sure you feel up to this? We can always skip it and stay home tonight."

Rachel glanced up to look at Ethan's reflection in the mirror then laid her brush down.

"No, I want to go," she said in an even voice. She understood Ethan's concern. She even found it endearing, but her frustration grew with each passing day.

He looked doubtfully at her, but to his credit he didn't argue.

"Okay, but I want you to promise me that if it gets to be too much you'll tell me immediately."

She nodded and smiled. "I will. But Ethan, I can't keep hiding in this house."

The walls were closing in on her, and what she didn't tell him was that if she didn't get out, she was going to go as crazy as everyone probably already thought she was.

Marlene had planned a welcome home party, though from Ethan's muttered remarks, Rachel guessed the event had escalated beyond a simple family gathering. In her more morbid musings, Rachel thought it should be a welcome back from the dead party.

It still baffled her that everyone had thought she was dead for the entire year she was gone. In a lot of ways, she supposed it was the kindest thing they could have thought. They mourned. They moved on. Knowing she was alive and in captivity would have made them suffer. Like she'd suffered.

Her fingers trembled as she tried to grasp the brush again, and she fumbled clumsily at it to keep from dropping it.

The cravings hit her at the oddest times. Sometimes she could go days and forget about the poison that had surged through her veins with clockwork regularity. Other times she wanted it more than she wanted her next breath. But she'd never tell Ethan that. How could she?

He worried enough without her adding more to it.

Strong hands slid over her bare shoulders and squeezed. She glanced up to see him standing behind her at the mirror.

There was such warmth in his touch. A comfort that she needed as much as she'd once needed the drugs.

She sighed and leaned back into him, looking up as she did. His fingers glided up her neck to the slender column of her throat and to her jaw. Then he leaned down and kissed her forehead. Just one, brief, gentle kiss.

She made a sound of frustration when he pulled away, and he frowned.

"Something wrong?"

She stood and turned, tilting her neck so she could look up at him.

"I want you to kiss me, Ethan. A *real* kiss. I want it so much that it overwhelms me. I want to feel like a real wife, not some fraud you aren't sure of. You haven't kissed me again since that morning when I kissed you."

As she spoke, she put her hands on his chest and emphasized her words with a firm push. He caught her hands and held them still over his heart.

"God, Rachel, I want it too. I want it so much I hurt. But I'm afraid, damn it. I'm afraid of saying or doing the wrong thing. I'm afraid of frightening you just because I want to touch you more than I want my next breath."

She trembled, but not in fear. An odd sensation raced up her spine, spreading in a warm glow that made her muscles tighten and her nipples pucker. It was then she realized that what she felt was desire, and she almost laughed.

She'd forgotten what it felt like to feel such pleasure, to

experience the anticipation of her husband's touch. It had been a long time since her pulse quickened with a simple glance. She missed it. God, she missed it.

The stirrings of desire had begun the morning she'd kissed him awake. She'd felt the unmistakable ache of awareness, but this, this was so intense that she thought she might go mad if the ache wasn't assuaged.

"Kiss me," she begged in a soft voice that was nearly inaudible.

With a groan, he pulled her close until her chest was crushed again his. His hands—he had such wonderful, strong hands—slid up her arms and then up her neck until he cupped her face.

Then he lowered his mouth to hers. Just before their lips touched, she heard his swift intake of breath, and he held it.

The warm shock of his mouth on hers was the most pleasurable sensation she'd felt in her scattered incomplete memories. Had it always been like this? Had she lived for such intimacies when they'd been married or had she taken them for granted the way most married couples do?

Never again. She'd savor each moment and hold it close. She knew firsthand how fast things could change, how easily a life could be shattered.

Eager to be an active participant in the kiss, she brushed her tongue across his, and sighed as he tenderly probed into her mouth in return.

Soft and so gentle, he deepened the kiss, his fingers thrusting upward into her hair, tangling as he pulled her even closer.

He shook against her, his chest throbbing with tightly held emotion. It overwhelmed her that this man felt so deeply, that he was as moved as she was and seemingly just as desperate for her touch as she was for his.

She reached up and tentatively stroked her fingers over the side of his neck and then over his clean-shaven jaw. She wanted to touch all of him, to relearn all the contours of his body. She wanted to see and touch, to explore and reclaim what was hers.

It was on the tip of her tongue to tell him she didn't want to go to his parents' after all.

With a ragged gasp he pulled away and then returned, pressing quick, breathless kisses to her mouth, to the corner of her lips and then her jaw.

"Tell me what you need, Rachel. I swear I'll give it to you. Anything."

It took all her courage to say what it was she most wanted. He'd made all the sacrifices so far. He'd been patient, understanding. He deserved this much. He deserved her courage.

"Will you make love to me? Tonight?"

Fire blazed in his eyes, turning them a brilliant shade of blue. He opened his mouth and just as quickly closed it. His nostrils flared with the effort of his breathing, and when he finally did speak, his voice was hoarse.

"I'll make love to you, baby. I'll do anything you want."

She brushed her hand over his cheek, the need to touch him a living, breathing thing.

"Do you want me? I mean as a wife."

The words came out rushed, and she stammered over the last. She didn't realize she was holding her breath until it escaped in a jerky explosion.

He caught her hand and tucked his mouth into her palm. The kiss sent a shiver over her skin, raising chill bumps in its wake.

"Want you? I want you so much I hurt. There isn't a time when I don't want you. But I want you to feel safe and protected more. I'd never do anything to frighten you, but I worry that I'll do it unintentionally. I can't stand the thought of screwing up and hurting you."

His face twisted in pain, and her heart surged, fluttering so wildly she had a hard time catching her breath.

"Ethan."

It was all she could say. Her throat ached.

She rose up on tiptoe and kissed him. Hard, with all the passion she'd been afraid to show. It bubbled out, rising sharply until she thought she might well explode.

There was no finesse, certainly none of the skill of a practiced seduction. Her hands stabbed clumsily at his face and finally ended up clasped around his neck, her fingers toying with the short hairs at his nape.

When her starved lungs demanded she pull away, they were both gasping and pulling in big mouthfuls of air.

"You won't hurt me, Ethan. I *do* feel safe with you. I knew the moment you showed up in my hut that I was saved. I dreamed of you. You were all I remembered of my life before. I held on to you when everything else fell away."

He lowered his head until his forehead rested against hers. Their lips were so close that she could feel each of his breaths.

"I'm just sorry I wasn't there sooner," he said painfully.

She smiled and tilted her chin just enough that her lips brushed his again.

"You came. That's all that matters."

He sighed and pulled away. "Are you sure you want to go to Mom's? I can always cancel."

She shook her head. "No, she's been planning this for days. I don't want to disappoint her. Nathan and Joe are home for the night, and she seemed so thrilled to have everyone together at the same time. I gather this is somewhat of an unusual occurrence."

He grinned. "Apart from Christmas, and even then it's not always possible, it is hard to get everyone together. We've all served in the military, and all getting leave at the same time is pretty much impossible. It got a little easier when Sam and Garrett formed KGI. That only left Nathan and Joe enlisted."

"Maybe we can all be together this Christmas," she said. And she realized she really looked forward to Christmas trees, holiday music and big family get-togethers. The idea filled her with such longing that she knew it was something she must have loved.

With reluctance she turned back to check her hair again. There wasn't much to do for it given its length, but she'd used a curling iron to give a little lift to the ends and it looked an intentional style now instead of the butcher job done to it by her captors.

"You look beautiful," Ethan said.

She smiled brilliantly at him. "You always know what to say and when to say it. I admit I was feeling a bit sorry for myself. I've only to look at pictures to see that my hair used to be much longer and that I'm much thinner now than I was."

"Your hair will grow, and if Mom has her way, you'll gain your weight back in no time."

She had to chuckle at that. Marlene did take her role seriously in that regard. Not a day had gone by that she hadn't sent someone over with food or just demanded Rachel and Ethan's presence for meals at her house.

"Okay, let's go before I lose all nerve."

Ethan took her hand and squeezed. "You're going to do great."

THE party was a real drag, but then she hadn't expected the Kellys to bust out with a real party. Rusty sat in the corner and observed the goings-on with ill-suppressed boredom.

What they needed was some good music and decent alcohol, not the pussy light beer some of the men were drinking. She'd give her right arm for a cigarette right now. She'd given serious consideration to sneaking a pack, but Marlene would have a cow if she found out, and despite how hung up she was on the rules, Rusty liked her. And she didn't want to mess up the first decent home she'd had.

So she sat there like a good girl, with her good-girl clothes and her good-girl haircut.

"Are you one of the family members?"

She whirled and scowled at the man who'd snuck up on her. "What's it to you?"

He lifted an eyebrow and amusement brightened his eyes. "Just wanted to ask a few questions about Rachel's homecoming, but I wanted to ask a direct family member."

A peculiar feeling settled in the pit of her stomach. To her surprise the idea that she was family or could even be regarded as such sent a surge of pleasure through her veins.

"I'm as direct as they get," she said airily. "I live here after all." She waved her hand at some of the Kelly brothers gathered in a bunch across the room. "None of them do anymore."

"Ah, good, then you're just the person I want to speak to. Mind if I sit?"

CHAPTER 23

RACHEL gripped her glass and stood with a smile frozen in place. She didn't even know what was in the glass, and she hadn't tasted it.

Who were all these people? She knew all of the Kellys, or at least what was considered the immediate family of Ethan's brothers and parents. But the room was crammed full of people she'd never seen before in her life.

She grimaced. Of course she'd seen them. She just didn't remember them. It was hard to smile and pretend when so many spoke to her as though they'd known her forever. Several even cited specific instances that she had no recollection of whatsoever.

But she nodded at appropriate times and smiled until her teeth ached. After the sixth person had approached her, she lost track of names and faces.

Ethan had remained at her elbow the entire night, but she felt the need to escape for just a few minutes, so she turned and pasted a reassuring smile on her lips.

"I need to go to the bathroom. I'll be back in a minute, okay?"

He nodded and she broke away, threading her way through the crowded room. Instead of going to the bathroom, she slipped through the kitchen, hoping that Marlene was otherwise occupied. She signed in relief when she saw that the coast was clear.

She opened the sliding glass door that led into the back garden and stepped into the night air. Her lungs filled with the fragrance of dozens of different flowers, all planted in boxes and brick planters lining the walkway.

Marlene had told her that the two of them had spent hours designing the perfect garden and then they'd turned their attention to Rachel and Ethan's house.

Not wanting to go far in case anyone got to looking for her, she took a seat on the wooden bench that overlooked the birdbath and she concentrated on each breath. In and out. After a few minutes, the tightness in her chest eased and she began to relax.

Her fingers uncurled, and she placed her palms on the smooth finish of the bench. Frank had made it. That memory popped into her head, and she smiled, welcoming the information like an old friend. She searched her memory for more, and little tidbits filtered through in scattered blips.

Frank owned a hardware store. She knew that from the present. But he was also good with his hands. Loved tools. When Marlene had despaired of him ever building her the bench she wanted, she'd gone to Walmart across the lake, in Paris, and bought a simple garden bench.

Frank had taken immediate exception and presented her with a sturdily constructed bench in three days' time. Marlene had smugly told Rachel that she'd saved the receipt and had never taken the bench out of the garage. Her husband was predictable if nothing else.

Rachel smiled at the memory and hugged it close, savoring those pieces of information that told her where she came from and where she belonged.

She was so ensconced in her memories that she didn't realize she was no longer alone until someone to the left cleared his throat.

Startled, she sat forward, her head jerking warily around to confront her company.

A man stepped from the shadows, and she spied his uniform and the gun on his hip.

"Sorry if I startled you."

His soft drawl was more pronounced than that of Ethan or the other Kellys. He had a hint of the Deep South. He also looked young, but not too young. Maybe midtwenties.

She hadn't met him, but she assumed he was the sheriff's deputy the Kellys were so fond of.

"You're Sean?"

Then she realized her mistake. If he was Sean, no doubt she'd met him before. She didn't know how much Marlene had told everyone. For all she knew everyone knew she was stark-raving mad and had no memory of her life before.

He smiled and stepped farther into the glow of the outside lamp. He had kindness in his eyes, which surprised her given his profession. He had muddy blond hair cut short, a lot like the military cuts the Kellys wore. But he sported a goatee that framed his mouth and gave him the appearance of age despite what she knew his to be.

"That's me," he said. "Had enough of the inside?"

She sighed and decided not to lie. "It's a bit over-whelming."

Sean gestured to the spot next to her. "Mind if I sit?"

She scooted all the way over in response, and he settled next to her.

"I'm not much of a crowd person myself, but Marlene would nail my hide to the wall if I missed one of her get-togethers. Like you, I'm pretty much a Kelly adoptee. She may not have given birth to me, but that hasn't stopped her from arranging my life, mothering me endlessly and adding me to every family gathering on record."

Rachel laughed. "She's quite something, isn't she?"

"She's the best," he said in a sincere voice. "But I'm more comfortable with the people I meet on the job. I don't have to pretend to be social when I'm arresting someone, and I don't have to worry about meaningless chitchat and how-do-you-dos."

The grimace on his face had her giggling again. "You poor thing. These things must be hell for you."

"Let's just say I was glad to see I wasn't the only one running for cover. Now, if asked, I can blame my absence on you."

"Oh nice," she said dryly.

He laughed. "So how are you doing? Had any problems with red tape I can help with?"

She twisted her mouth into a rueful grimace. "It's a lot easier to stay dead than it is to come back from the dead. Ethan's tried to do everything quietly. The last thing we want is for some human interest story to be run. The driver's license wasn't too hard to arrange, but the social security issue is a bit more difficult."

Sean patted her on the knee. "You'll get it all sorted out. In the meantime if there's anything I can do, just let me know. I've known you since I was in high school. You graduated two years ahead of me."

She winced. "Sorry I don't remember."

"Hey, don't worry about it. You'll get it back. And when you do, you'll remember you owe me five bucks."

Startled, she cocked her head to the side.

Mischief gleamed in his green eyes. "You lost a bet. You bet me Tennessee would beat LSU. As if that would ever happen."

"Ahh, Louisiana then? I thought your accent sounded a little different."

"Born and raised."

He went quiet and turned sharply, a frown replacing his smile.

"Rusty, is that you?"

Rachel turned in search of the young girl Marlene had taken in. Rusty hadn't had much to say to Rachel since Rachel had arrived home, but Nathan had hinted that she felt a little threatened by Rachel's homecoming.

Rachel just wished there was something she could say or do to ease the girl's fears. Marlene had been blunt about Rusty's situation.

Rusty stepped into the garden patio area from the walkway that led to the front of the house.

"Yeah, Copper, it's me."

"Who was that you were talking to?" Sean demanded.

His voice had gone from congenial and teasing to complete and utter business. He might as well have been interrogating a suspect for all the steel in his words.

"I didn't realize I had to get permission to have a conversation around here," Rusty snapped. "Back off, donut man. I'm not drinking or smoking or otherwise taking advantage of Marlene's hospitality."

Sean cursed under his breath, and his fingers flexed at his

side. He opened his mouth to speak, but Rusty disappeared back into the house.

"I swear that girl makes me nuts," Sean muttered. "She's so belligerent. I'd love to teach her a little respect plus a few manners while I'm at it. If I ever catch her talking to Frank or Marlene like that, I'll turn her over my knee myself. Someone should have done it a long time ago."

"That age is hard," Rachel said, surprised by the need to defend Rusty. "From what Marlene said, she's had it tough. Plus I've never heard her be anything but respectful with Frank and Marlene. Everyone else, though . . ."

"Yeah, tell me about it. She really loves me since I'm a cop, and I get the impression she's been a round or two with the police before. Marlene told me she had a record but forbade me—in true mom fashion—from running her. She doesn't want me to be influenced by Rusty's past. For the love of God."

Rachel grinned at the disgust in Sean's voice. And then she realized how long they'd been outside.

"I should probably go back in. I told Ethan I was going to the bathroom."

"Ah, there's the search party now," Sean drawled as Garrett stepped outside.

"Everything okay, sweet pea?" Garrett asked as he walked over.

"Yep. Just talking to Sean and getting some fresh air."

Garrett shoved his hands into his pockets. "You mean you're hiding out here with this pussy who's here for the same reason."

Sean grunted. "Yeah, the exact same reason you've run outside like a damn girl."

Garrett grinned. "Too many damned people. Ma eats that shit up, but I swear it makes the rest of us crazy."

"So at what point is she going to figure out we've fled the premises?" Rachel asked. The last thing she wanted was to hurt Marlene's feelings.

"Not to worry. Mom is well used to having to round us up. She usually gives us ten minutes or so to get the crazed look from our eyes, and then she'll come out all sweet-like but with a glint in her eyes you know better than to ignore."

"And at that point, she drags us back inside by our ears," Sean finished.

"Sam should be making his appearance soon," Garrett said. "He got snagged on his way out. We all left Ethan on his own fielding questions. Poor bastard."

"Oh," Rachel said. "Maybe I should go back in. I didn't intend for him to get stuck answering questions about me all night."

Garrett shook his head. "Not to worry. He deserves it for the time he sicced Aunt Edna on me at Thanksgiving. The woman talked my ear off for damn near an hour while Ethan made his escape. The rest of the bastards stood outside the window and laughed their asses off at me."

Laughter bubbled up and spilled from her lips. She could so picture it in her mind, and the more she imagined it, the harder she laughed.

"So this is where you assholes are," Sam growled as he shut the patio door behind him. "Although I don't think we're far enough away from the house to do us much good. Mom will only let it go for as long as she's preoccupied. The minute she notices we're gone, we're toast."

Rachel edged a little closer to Sean and then realized what she'd done. Why the hell did Sam still intimidate her? By all rights Garrett should scare the life out of her. Sam wasn't near as big or as scary-looking as Garrett, but something akin to panic gripped her every time Sam got close. Maybe it was because he'd been the first one into her hut that night, and she'd been so convinced he was there to kill her.

No matter how stupid that seemed now, she couldn't rid herself of the memory of him standing over her, big and menacing, holding a gun.

To his credit, Sam seemed very aware of her fear, and he always made a point of being cautious around her. Even now, his eyes softened and he didn't seem hurt by her overt unease.

As if realizing her sudden stiffness, Sean casually rested his hand on her knee. He gave it a gentle squeeze and never looked away from Garrett and Sam.

"It's hard to run away from Ma in her own house," Garrett said in resignation. "She'll just hunt us down and give us the look."

Sam chuckled. "Damn shame when grown men are reduced to a bunch of pussies by their mother."

The patio door jerked open and Ethan stuck his head out, his expression grim.

"Hey have you guys seen Rachel?"

"I'm looking at her," Sam said.

Ethan stepped out, and relief settled over his face. He stopped beside Garrett and glanced between Rachel and Sean and then at the others.

"You okay?" he asked.

She smiled, not wanting him to worry. "I'm fine. I stepped out for some fresh air not realizing this was a time-honored tradition of escaping Marlene's get-togethers."

Ethan relaxed and stuck his thumbs in his belt loops. "Yeah, it's become something that rivals war games. He who survives the longest without being hauled back in by Mom wins."

As he stared at her, she knew he was thinking of their earlier conversation, of when they kissed and what she'd asked him to do. His gaze settled over her skin, warm and electrifying.

She shivered, and she wasn't the least bit cold. The late summer air was humid and warm to the point of discomfort, but all she could feel was the heat of his stare, and the promise in his eyes.

"Do you think your mom would mind if we left?"

Her voice sounded husky, and she swallowed the butterflies that danced in her stomach and surged upward as if chasing an escape route.

"If you leave now, she won't know until it's too late," Garrett smirked.

"Good point," Sean said.

Ethan shook his head and reached for Rachel's hand. "They're right. We can sneak around front, and if no one's blocked us in, we can be gone before anyone sounds the alarm. And they will. Sound the alarm that is. I'm sure Garrett hasn't forgotten the Aunt Edna incident."

"If it weren't for the fact that Rachel wants to go, I'd have already blown the whistle on your ass," Garrett said in disgust.

Ethan pulled her up to stand beside him and chucked her chin. "I suggest we go now before he changes his mind."

She turned and leaned down to kiss Sean on the cheek. "It was very nice re-meeting you. Thank you for keeping me company."

He seemed surprised and then pleased by the gesture. Then she turned to Garrett and gave him a quick hug. Determined to not act like a ninny, she awkwardly moved toward Sam.

"Good night, Sam," she said almost formally.

He opened his arms and simply waited. Taking a quick breath, she went forward and hugged him. He let her do most of the touching and only loosely returned her hug. She stepped away and gave him a genuine smile.

Anyone who was this solicitous of her feelings was certainly not the bad guy.

He returned her smile and briefly touched her cheek. "See you later, Rachel."

With a small wave, she followed Ethan from the garden and to the path that led up to the front yard. As they walked toward Ethan's truck, he slipped an arm around her and pulled her close to his side.

Her pulse could chop a cinder block. She was looking forward to making love with Ethan. She was as nervous as hell, maybe more nervous than she'd ever been about being with him, but she wasn't about to let that hold her back.

It was high time to reclaim her marriage and her husband.

CHAPTER 24

ETHAN gripped the steering wheel as he pulled to a stop outside the house. For a long moment, he stared straight ahead, and then he realized he was holding his breath like a teenager on his first date. In some ways it was. His first date. With his wife. God. He still couldn't get over the idea that he had Rachel back. That he'd been granted a second chance.

His pulse pounding in his ears, he cut the engine and turned to look at Rachel. She looked as nervous as he felt. His chest caved in just a bit at the brave set of her lips.

"Rachel. Baby? Do you still want me to make love to you?"

His palms went clammy and slid over the steering wheel. Before he asked, he'd had no idea just how afraid he was that she'd back out. He'd understand. He'd wait forever if that's what it took, but he wanted to be able to touch her again more than he'd ever wanted anything else.

She turned, and her eyes glowed softly in the dim light cast from the porch lights. There was much reflected in the pools. Fear, hesitancy, hope and desire. Determination.

"Come inside with me, Ethan."

Her husky voice sent a shock wave over his skin. His groin tightened until he shifted to alleviate the discomfort. She reached for his hand, her fingers trembling against his.

He laced his fingers with hers, twining them tightly and squeezing reassuringly. Finally he raised her hand to his lips to kiss each knuckle.

"Let's go," he whispered.

They both opened their doors and hurried for the porch. When he fumbled clumsily at the doorknob, Rachel leaned against the entryway and dissolved into giggles.

Surprised to hear the joyful sound, he stopped with the door cracked open. Her eyes twinkled merrily and she gasped for breath as she held her stomach.

"What a pair we are. Is this how we acted when we dated? Nervous as two cats and so eager to get to bed that we trip over ourselves on the way in?"

Ethan grinned, and then a chuckle escaped, followed by outright laughter. The tension evaporated, and he leaned against the door as he wiped at his eyes.

"I guess we do seem a little desperate. Well, I do. Leave it to a man to get all antsy when sex is mentioned."

She grinned again and shoved her hair away from her face. "Well, I'm glad you're a normal guy. Would be hard to seduce you if you never had sex on the brain."

Unable to resist her any longer, he pulled her into his arms and tucked her head under his chin. She just felt . . . right. If only he'd seen that before.

He closed his eyes and chased those memories away. Not tonight. Not when everything could be so perfect again.

Shoving with his shoulder, he opened the door and tugged her along behind him. Cognizant of her unease with the dark, he immediately reached for the switch, flooding the living room with light.

He touched her again, more to reassure himself than her. His fingertips grazed her cheekbone and then cupped her jaw.

"Wait here. I'll come for you in a few minutes. I want this to be perfect for you."

She cocked her head to the side and looked at him in confusion.

He smiled and leaned in to kiss her nose. "Indulge me. Let me try my hand at romance and all the stuff women are supposed to love."

The trust in her dark eyes humbled him. Made him want to be better. To be worthy. Not to let her down, damn it.

He turned and hurried into the bedroom. He stopped in the middle of the floor and turned in several circles, looking, not sure what he wanted or where to find it.

Candles. Rachel loved candles. She always had several scattered over the house.

Where the hell were they now? He hadn't thrown anything away, but Ma had come over and boxed a lot of stuff up. No way he wanted to be rummaging around in the garage when Rachel was waiting for him.

The closet.

He yanked open the door and flicked the light on. Several boxes were piled in the back. Hoping the candles were in one of them, he dragged the top one down and pried open the top.

He huffed in frustration when he found assorted knick-knacks, then he opened the second box. A light floral scent wafted up as soon as the lid flapped over. Inside were several candles in varying sizes. Perfect.

He grabbed as many as he could carry, then went back into the bedroom and placed them strategically around the room. Satisfied with the placement, he went back to the kitchen for matches.

A couple of minutes later, the bedroom was alight in the warm glow of a dozen candles. It wasn't the most perfect setup, but it would do.

Now to get Rachel.

Dragging a hand over his hair and then down the front of his shirt, he sucked in a breath to steady his bounding pulse and walked back into the living room, where Rachel stood at the glass doors looking into the night.

He came up behind her and slid his hands up her arms and over her shoulders. Her hair fluttered and caught the light. He stared for a moment and then leaned down, nudging her hair aside with his mouth as he nuzzled the side of her neck.

Her soft sigh of contentment sent a wave of satisfaction over him. He loved the softness of her neck and the silky short hairs at her nape. And her smell. So feminine and light. He inhaled deeply and kissed the area just behind her ear, enjoying her betraying twitch.

"Come into the bedroom with me?"

She turned and twined her arms around his neck, leaning up on tiptoe so her mouth was close to his.

"I'm so nervous," she admitted. "I want you to know that. I'm not afraid. I know you won't hurt me. I'm not even sure why I'm so anxious. I want this so much, but my stomach is fluttering like crazy."

He stroked her cheek, tracing the lines of her jaw and then her lips.

"I'm nervous too, baby. We'll be nervous together. This matters. We both want it so much. We just need to relax and take it slow. Take it together."

"Oh, I like that," she breathed. "Together. Make love to me, Ethan."

He took her hand and pulled her toward the bedroom. When he led her in, she stopped and turned in a circle, her eyes wide at all the flickering candles.

He bent to nuzzle her ear. "I take it you approve."

She sighed and leaned into his touch. "You didn't have to do all of this."

"But I wanted to. I want this to be perfect."

Rachel turned and slid her hands up his chest to his shoulders. She loved the hard contours of his body, the slight dips, the ridges. Perfect. How could it be anything else? This was what she had waited for.

"It will be, Ethan."

He lowered his head. She tilted hers to the side. Their mouths were just an inch apart. The first touch of his lips sent a shiver down her spine.

Soft. Exquisitely tender. She curled her hands behind his neck and pulled him closer. It was she who deepened the kiss, she who demanded more.

She felt deliciously wanton, and for the first time in longer than she could remember, she felt beautiful and desirable.

Ethan's hands ran down her back, then lower, until he palmed her behind. He squeezed lightly, rolling and kneading the cheeks.

She loved how he tasted. It was hard to put a label on it. Part of it was smell. Strong and masculine. She kissed a line along his jaw then pulled his head lower so she could sample the column of his neck.

When she found his earlobe, he let out a long hiss. With a smile, she sucked the lobe between her teeth and teased it with her tongue.

"You realize I'm supposed to be seducing you," he growled.

She laughed and simply let the joy of the moment wash over her.

"How about we seduce each other?"

He captured her lips again. "I can work with that."

Their kisses became hotter, more breathless, less teasing. Deep in her belly, desire curled, tighter and tighter, spreading outward in waves.

"First rule of seduction. At least one of us has to get naked. Preferably you," he murmured.

Nervous apprehension replaced some of the excitement. It was silly. He'd seen her naked. Many times. They'd made love before. But for her it was like the first time all over again.

"Hey," he said softly. He drew away and tucked a finger under her chin, prompting her to look up at him. "We'll take this as slow as you need. If I could make love to you with you fully clothed, I'd do it, but I think we both know that's not an option."

She giggled and felt some of her unease leave her.

"Let's not take it too slow or we'll both be old and decrepit before we ever make love."

"Mmm, I plan to make love to you until they put me in the grave. That's what they make Viagra for."

She leaned into him and hugged him fiercely as another laugh escaped.

"Make you a deal. We undress together. Last one naked is a rotten egg."

She yanked away as she said the last and immediately began peeling her clothes off.

"Oh hell no," he sputtered. "Maybe you don't remember what a competitive family you married into."

"While you're talking, I'm getting naked," she taunted.

A wicked glint sparked in his eyes. "I fail to see how I lose either way."

To her utter shock, he was out of his clothing before she managed to get her jeans off.

All her breath left her body as she stared, transfixed, at the lean contours of his muscular body. Narrow hips, broad shoulders, a hard chest. At his groin, a dark nest of hair surrounded his jutting erection.

Her mouth fell open and she stared with unabashed fascination.

"Hell, Rachel, you've seen me before," he muttered.

She swallowed and glanced back up at him. To her surprise there was a hint of awkwardness in his eyes. She smiled.

"How on earth did you get out of your clothes so fast? I got a head start for Pete's sake."

He grinned, his shoulders relaxing. "You forget I was in the Navy. You have to be able to shuck and jive pretty damn fast."

"More like you don't have all the crap we women have to wear," she grumbled.

"I'd be more than happy to help," he said innocently.

She gestured down her body at her bra and panties. "Be my guest."

He closed in on her, and she stared down once more at his cock. She wanted to touch it so bad, and then she realized there was no good reason she couldn't.

As he pressed against her, she reached down and circled his girth with her fingers.

He groaned. "You don't play fair."

Fascinated by the dual sensations of hard and soft, she stroked, amazed when he grew even harder in her grasp.

"Do you like that?" she asked.

"Hell yes."

"I'm still clothed," she reminded him.

"Not for long."

He backed her toward the bed, his hands gliding down her sides and to her hips. His thumbs hooked into the band of her underwear and he tugged.

One hand slipped around to the small of her back and then delved lower to where the panties had covered the spot just above the cleft of her behind. He stroked and then slid his fingers lower, along the seam, and she shivered with pleasure.

He obviously knew all her sweet spots. In truth, she was looking forward to discovering them again with him. How odd it felt to make love to a man who remembered her pleasure points, when she herself didn't.

"I love your ass. I'd be a happy man if you never covered it."

She flushed at his statement, but a surge of pleasure at his approval rushed heatedly through her veins.

"I could arrange to uncover it for you on a regular basis," she offered.

"Mmm, you're on."

Her underwear fell down her legs and pooled at her feet. His mouth found her neck, and she tilted to the side to give him better access. As he kissed a line down to her shoulder, he moved his hands up to her bra straps and pulled them down her arms.

Hot and warm, his mouth worked lower, just above the swell of her breasts. His fingers fumbled with the clasp of her bra and finally it fell away, baring her breasts to his mouth.

She sucked in her breath and held it when his lips hovered precariously close to her nipple. She strained upward, wanting that intimate contact. Her nipples puckered and formed stiff, sensitive points.

And then his mouth closed around one straining peak.

Her knees buckled, and she clutched desperately at his shoulders in her effort to remain standing. He sucked strongly and laved the bud with his tongue.

Pleasure streaked sharply through her groin. Her pelvis tightened unbearably, and her clit swelled and twitched. She wanted him to touch her there, to relieve the unbearable pressure that grew with each swipe of his tongue.

For a moment, she lost her sense of time and place. Feeling, sensation, things she'd long been void of, came rushing at her from all directions. It frightened and thrilled her in equal parts. For too long the only things she'd felt were fear and loathing. How much more powerful were sensations of being loved and cherished?

And then he gently enfolded her in his arms, almost as if he knew how quickly she'd spiraled out of control. He was an anchor in a violent storm. Her rock. Her protection. She melted into him, holding on to him with what she could only deem desperation.

He picked her up. Her feet left the floor, and he carried her back until the mattress clipped the backs of her calves. Then he lowered her ever so carefully. His eyes bore into her. His expression was a study in fierce concentration. And determination.

Her back met the plush softness of the sheets. She shivered when for a moment he left her. Immediately she felt bereft of his warmth.

But he returned, crawling onto the bed. He loomed over her, his gaze so intent that she felt the heat to her toes.

"I wonder if you even know how beautiful you are to me," he whispered as he straddled her body.

Sudden tears swam in her eyes, and she smiled up at him. She reached up to touch his face, her fingers shaking with the force of her emotions.

"Right now I *feel* beautiful."

He captured her hand and pressed her palm to his lips. "I don't want a day to ever go by where you don't feel as beautiful as you do right now then. I'll consider it my job to remind you at every opportunity."

Her heart melted.

He took her hands and slowly lowered them to the mattress. He slid them high, just above her head, until he stared down at her, and she lay underneath him, completely vulnerable.

The thought should scare her. Logically. But she'd never felt safer. She smiled and arched her body invitingly.

With a tortured groan, he kissed her hungrily, loosing some of his tightly held control. He didn't just kiss her, he ravaged her mouth.

Hot. Deep. So breathless she could never catch up. His tongue slid over hers, tasting, delving until all she could taste was him. All she could feel was him.

His body came down over hers, his hardness melding to her softer curves. His erection prodded impatiently at the juncture of her thighs, but he didn't press forward. She cradled his hardness, the delicious sensation of him sliding over her most tender flesh, so erotic, so immensely pleasurable.

She opened her legs, and his cock jumped, bumping against her swollen, throbbing clitoris. She moaned softly and twisted restlessly underneath him. He swallowed up the sounds she made. Devoured them and her with his hungry mouth.

The past year slipped from her mind. There was only now. Only the indescribable feeling of being back in her husband's arms. He moved over her, big and urgent. She felt small underneath him but so very protected and cherished.

He swallowed her. No part of her was left untouched. His hands slid down her waist to her hips. His fingers curled underneath her buttocks, and he held her as he inserted his thigh between hers to spread her farther.

Then he slipped a hand between them and tenderly pushed his finger between her folds. The tip fluttered across her clitoris, and she reacted immediately, arching up. A whimper escaped her mouth.

He propped himself up with one hand while he carefully explored the delicate tissues of her femininity. He eased one finger inside her, testing her readiness.

It was almost enough to send her completely over the edge. She clamped down around his finger, her body so tight that she feared bursting.

He worked his thumb over the taut nub hidden within her folds, as he slid another finger inside her.

"Ethan, please."

It didn't sound like her. This needy, mindless woman wasn't her, was it? She wanted to beg. Wanted to force him to thrust inside her. She wanted him more than she imagined ever wanting anything else.

As if sensing how far gone she already was, he shifted his body back over again and reached to position his cock at her opening. He took the time to stroke her with his fingers once more before moving his hand up to lace his fingers with hers.

"Tell me if I hurt you," he said hoarsely. "I want you with me all the way, baby. If anything I do scares you, tell me. I'll stop."

In response she lifted her hips, wanting him to slide inside.

He closed his eyes, as if fighting for control, and inched forward. She gasped at the sensation of him opening her, of her body stretching to accommodate him. It was the most magnificent, overwhelming sensation.

Her eyes went wide, and her breath caught in her throat when he probed deeper.

He stopped and looked down at her, his eyes worried.

"Okay?"

She nodded, too wired and senseless to form a coherent response. Her nails dug into his shoulders as she silently urged him on.

Finally he moved. In one hard thrust, he went deep. Her mouth opened in a silent exclamation. Her vision blurred. She shivered uncontrollably and held onto him for dear life. She wasn't going to last. It was too much. It had been too long.

"Please," she begged.

She arched, she twisted, she writhed. He cupped her to him and began thrusting hard and fast. Oh God, yes. Finally.

He had been tender. He wanted to be tender, but right now she needed him to be strong. Hard. Fierce. To remind her of all she'd missed.

Her protector. Her warrior.

She threw back her head, squeezed her eyes shut and gripped his shoulders so tight she was sure she'd leave marks.

The friction was so wonderfully torturous that it was almost too much to bear. He was swollen and hard. So hard. He filled her again and again, his body driving relentlessly into her.

Tension built. They both gasped and squeezed.

"Come with me," Ethan whispered. "Be with me. Love me."

The gentle words were a balm to her soul. She closed her eyes, gathered him close and simply let go.

His hips powered against hers. He tensed against her and gripped her as hard as she held him. Their bodies were meshed so tightly that there wasn't a centimeter between them. Their limbs were entwined as their hips undulated in frantic rhythm.

He buried his face in her neck and whispered her name. "Rachel."

She flew. It was the only word to describe it. She soared. Euphoric, so light. She could almost feel the rush of the wind in her face. She lifted her face to the sun and felt the warmth on her skin after so long in the dark.

And then she floated down, and Ethan was there to catch her. She drifted lazily, finding home in his arms. Home. Finally home.

His lips found hers. He kissed her long and sweet. Hot tears slipped down her cheeks, mingled on their tongues.

"Are you all right?" he asked.

She kissed him again, too overcome to say anything. She wasn't sure she had words for what she was feeling. So she said nothing and nodded.

"I love you, baby. Never doubt that."

She touched his face, stroking his firm jaw. "I won't."

Carefully, he withdrew from her body and rolled to the side. He gathered her close, so close she could feel every beat of his heart.

"Thank you," she whispered.

He stiffened slightly in surprise. His eyes were puzzled when he looked at her. "For what?"

"For making me feel love again."

He leaned his forehead against hers and drew his fingers through the strands of her hair.

"You'll never know anything else again," he vowed.

CHAPTER 25

THE dream was dark and ugly. It hit her on a deep emotional level that frightened her. Ethan was there, but he wasn't her comforter or the warrior she'd imagined for so long. He was furious with her.

The desperation that gripped her was born of the knowledge that whatever they were once to each other, it was long gone, buried under broken trust.

She faced him, frightened, knowing this was it. The end of their marriage, of their love. She wasn't strong enough to face him, but he gave her no choice. He wanted her to know. Why was he so adamant?

The eyes she so loved were not filled with warmth and support. They were hard and resolved.

"No," she whispered. She didn't want to see him this way. It was just a dream. A nightmare. It wasn't real. Was it?

You're a fraud. Your marriage is a fraud. He doesn't love you.

The voice whispered into the most vulnerable part of her soul. It twisted and turned through the paths, spreading despair in its wake.

"No. *No!*"

"Rachel. Rachel, wake up, baby. It's just a dream. Come back to me."

Gentle hands caressed her face, wiping away the tears on her cheeks. Her eyes fluttered open and she blinked to adjust to the darkness.

"Hey," Ethan said softly. "It's okay. You're safe, Rachel."

He gathered her in his arms and hugged her to his chest. Her heart drummed relentlessly against his chest, and she struggled against the panic still on the fringes of her consciousness.

Why was she having this dream? It was growing stronger, not weaker. Shouldn't her panic be going away the more time elapsed after her captivity? And why was she dreaming about Ethan this way?

A therapist would probably feed her a line about her unconscious fears rearing their ugly head when she was most vulnerable.

She snuggled closer to Ethan, holding on as tight as she could, as if by sheer will she could point and say, *See? He doesn't hate me. He's here. He loves me.*

He kissed the top of her head and stroked over her chilled skin. She wore nothing after their lovemaking, and his hands should have felt like magic on her flesh. Instead she tensed, dread filling her.

Maybe she really was crazy.

"Baby, talk to me," Ethan murmured. "What's got you so scared? Can you tell me about the dream?"

She closed her eyes again. What could she say? *Gee, Ethan, I dreamed you were a real bastard and that you hated me.* That would certainly make him feel good.

But she had to tell someone.

The idea of going to the therapist Ethan had gotten information on scared her. It made her feel out of control and helpless. But maybe it was time. Maybe she couldn't do this alone.

"WHAT the ever-loving fuck?"

Sam stopped shoveling cereal into his mouth long enough to cast a suspicious eyeball at Garrett, who was reading the paper.

Garrett slapped the newspaper down on the counter with enough force to slosh milk over the side of Sam's bowl.

"Chill out, dude. What's got your panties in a knot this morning?"

Garrett scowled back at Sam, his eyebrows drawn into angry thunderclouds. Oh yeah, Garrett was pissed. This went beyond his usual grumpy-ass demeanor.

Garrett drew in several steadying breaths. Worried now, Sam shoved the bowl aside and reached for the paper.

"Spill for God's sake."

"Page three," Garrett seethed.

Sam thumbed over to the page in question and quickly scanned the contents. He stopped when he saw the Kelly name splashed predominately across the headline.

"Whoa."

"Yeah," Garrett said in disgust. "Read it."

Sam read through the article touting Rachel's miraculous return from the dead. When he got to the part about the role KGI had played, his fingers tightened until the edges of the paper crumpled in his fists.

"God damn."

"Keep reading," Garrett said grimly.

Nothing was left to chance. Rachel's drug addiction was mentioned, but nowhere did it say the drugs were forced on her. Just that she battled the effects of cocaine and heroin addiction. It was even suggested that her memory loss wasn't real, that it was a ruse to incite sympathy.

Sam couldn't think beyond the rage building. "Who the fuck told them all this crap?"

Garrett snatched the paper and then stabbed a finger at part of the article. "Read!"

The words wobbled back and forth until Sam grabbed Garrett's wrist to steady the paper. There in the article it cited a close family member as the source.

"That's bullshit," Sam exploded. "No fucking way. There is no goddamn way one of us sold Rachel out like that."

He got up, knocking the stool over, and paced back and forth in the kitchen, so furious he wanted to break something. He yanked his gaze back to Garrett, who didn't look any happier.

"Who do you think did this?"

"It wasn't me. It sure as hell wasn't you. It wasn't Ma or Dad. It damn sure wasn't Van, Nathan or Joe. Who does that leave?

No one knows this kind of shit. How the fuck would they know that much about KGI?"

"Sean does," Sam muttered.

The two brothers exchanged looks and both reached the same conclusion.

"No way he did it either," Garrett said. "He loves Ma and Dad. He's practically one of the family."

Sam stared at Garrett as sudden realization swept over him. "Rusty."

"Son of a bitch," Garrett swore. "I'll kill her. Mom can't save her ass this time."

"This'll hurt Ma," Sam said.

"What did the little bitch think she was doing?"

Sam sighed. "Rusty has seen Rachel as a threat from the beginning. She's young and messed up and she resented the attention Rachel got when she came home. I guess this is her way of taking her down a notch or two."

"She goes," Garrett said coldly. "No one betrays the family like this. I don't care what Ma says. Once Dad finds out, he'll agree. Rachel will be devastated when she sees this."

"I need to call Ethan. He'll need to know, and he'll want to confront Rusty with us."

Garrett nodded, his lips still a tight line of fury.

"Morning," Donovan called as he sauntered into the kitchen.

He eyed Sam and Garrett suspiciously as he opened the fridge and took out the orange juice.

"If I interrupted violence, by all means I'll step back. Always nice to see bloodshed first thing in the a.m."

"Rusty sold Rachel out," Sam said bluntly. "It's all over the paper."

Donovan frowned, shut the fridge and walked over to pick up the paper. As he read, his frown deepened.

"Son of a bitch."

"Yeah," Garrett said.

"What's that you're holding?" Sam asked Donovan, noticing for the first time the papers in Donovan's left hand.

Donovan glanced down as if he'd forgotten them.

"An email I printed off. Possible job. I know we said we were laying off for a while, until things are good here with Rachel, and Cole and Dolphin have had time to heal."

"But?" Sam asked. "I hear a definite but in there."

Donovan flushed guiltily. "I might have told them we'd take it anyway."

"What the fuck?" Garrett's face went red and his cheeks puffed out as if it was all he could do not to explode. "Am I the only dumbass who still thinks this is a partnership around here?"

Sam held up a hand before Garrett went completely apeshit. Guilt ate at him. Garrett would have a coronary if he knew what Sam had ordered Rio to do and that Sam would be going back to South America.

"Okay, tell us, Van. What's the gig and why did you already agree to it?"

"It's a kid," Donovan said painfully. "An abduction case. Parents are frantic. No ransom demand. Cops have exhausted all leads. Wife is convinced it's her ex-husband, an avenue the cops have pursued but hit a dead-end. The ex lives out of the country, so she wants someone to whom that wouldn't pose a problem."

Sam blew his breath out in a long exhale as he and Garrett exchanged resigned looks. If it involved a kid, Donovan was a goner. No way he would have turned it down.

"Okay Van, you need to give us details and then you need to tell me how the hell we're going to swing this."

Donovan leaned against the counter and folded his arms over his chest, the papers still held tight in his hand. "Rio is free. He hasn't pulled a mission in a while if you don't count the pussy recon mission we sent him on. Steele's still giving him shit over that."

Sam shook his head. "Rio and his team can't do this."

Garrett swung around. "Why the hell not?"

Sam ignored him. "Half of Steele's team is out of commission for the next little while, and I still don't think it's a good idea for us all to leave when Ethan and Rachel are going to need all the support they can get, particularly after this morning's little news story."

Donovan plopped down on the stool across the bar and put his elbows up on the counter.

"Okay, I can take P.J., Renshaw and Baker. You and Garrett can stay here and look in on Cole and Dolphin."

Sam looked at Garrett, who didn't look entirely happy with the setup, but then that was Garrett. He didn't like anything he hadn't been in on and planned from the start. And Garrett was still staring holes through Sam, which told him they weren't done with the Rio issue.

"Let me see the email," Garrett grunted.

The corner of Donovan's lip curled, but he kept the grin off his face, which was good since it just would have pissed Garrett off more.

As Garrett read, he let out a curse. "Christ, the kid's only four years old. You neglected to mention that the ex is a convicted child molester."

Donovan shrugged. "Whether he is or isn't, I'd still want to go in after the kid. The mother is out of her mind. Her current husband adopted the daughter. He's raised her since she was an infant. He's destroyed by the fact no one can help them. We're their last resort. I couldn't tell them no."

"You know where he's holed up, Van?" Sam asked.

"I have a good idea. Did some digging. Hacked into his finances. He's living it up in some shithole in Mexico. We can go in. He'll never know what hit him. I figure we can get the kid and be back in forty-eight hours tops."

"Looks like you better give Steele a call and let him know what's going down. He'll want to go. Make it clear he's out of commission for a while. It'll piss him off that you're taking his team, but he'll get over it. You'll need time to get geared up, get the intel you need and get your men together. You don't go in blind, Van. You wait until we have all the information and then you go."

"Yeah, yeah, I got it. If you two are finished mothering me, I'll go make some calls while you go over and tear a strip off of Rusty's hide. Just sorry I'll miss it."

Sam watched his brother walk out of the kitchen, the papers clenched tightly in his hand.

"Van."

Donovan stopped and turned, his eyebrow lifted in question.

"Put it away, okay? I'll pull the plug on this in a nanosecond if I think your head's not on straight."

Donovan's lip curled in distrust. "I don't tell you how to deal with your shit, Sam. Back off. Steele and I can handle this in our sleep."

"Fair enough."

Sam turned to Garrett after Donovan had left. "You going to call Ethan or am I?"

"Neither of us is calling him yet. Not until you tell me what the fuck is going on with Rio," Garrett said.

"He's busy," Sam said shortly.

"Yeah? With what?"

Sam blew out his breath. "Goddamn it, Garrett."

"Don't bullshit me," Garrett snapped. "What the hell is it with you and Van making unilateral decisions around here?"

"I sent him back into Colombia," Sam said tightly. "I'm meeting him in a couple of days and we're going in after those bastards. I want information, and I don't care how we get it."

Garrett's eyes glittered with anger. "You sent him back. Without telling me. You're going back. Without me. Anything else you're doing without me, Sam?"

"Cut the crap, Garrett. This is precisely why I didn't tell you. You'd get all pissed off and you'd want to go in with us."

"Goddamn right I would!"

Garrett stood and slapped his hands on the table.

"This isn't just your family, Sam. You aren't the lone patriarch of the clan. I get it. You want to protect everyone and take responsibility like a good soldier. Well guess what? That's not the way it works. We're a team. Remember? We live and die by the team. Your words. Not mine. Or do you think those rules only apply to everyone else but not you?"

"I made a decision. I stick by it."

"I don't give a fuck *what* you decided. If you think I'm going to let you go on some half-cocked revenge mission, you're out of your mind."

Sam also stood and he got into Garrett's face. "We need information, Garrett. We need to know why the hell they kept Rachel a goddamn prisoner and treated her like an animal for a year!"

Garrett snarled and didn't back down. They stood nose to nose, each glaring holes in the other.

"I don't dispute we need information. You like to throw around that word without giving any yourself. Think, Sam. Use your goddamn head for a minute. You go off to South America and don't tell us shit. You get blown to shit. What the hell am I supposed to tell Mom and Dad? What the hell am I supposed to do when I don't even know where to look for you? This is stupid and you know it or you wouldn't be hiding it from me."

"It's revenge. It's messy. It's not honorable, and *I can't ask you or anyone else in this family to do what I have to do,*" Sam seethed.

"Always Captain fucking America," Garrett said mockingly. "What about Ethan and what he has to do? Rachel is his wife. Why are you fighting his battles for him?"

"Because he's my brother."

Garrett stared into his eyes. He wasn't backing down, but there was understanding there where before there had just been anger.

"You're not going alone."

"You're not going, Garrett."

"Try and stop me."

Sam ground his teeth in frustration. "Goddamn it, Garrett."

"I'm going or I'll pull Rio out right now."

Sam raised a hand to his head. "Pull him out? When we need the intel? Are you crazy? We have to find out why they targeted Rachel. There's a threat out there to my family."

"*Our* family," Garrett corrected. He punched his finger in Sam's chest to punctuate his statement. "Our family."

The intensity in Garrett's expression took some of the wind out of Sam's sails. He knew if the situations were reversed, he'd be every bit as pissed and determined as Garrett. It didn't make it any easier to give in.

"Son of a bitch," Sam swore. He bit out a few more colorful phrases before Garrett rocked backed on his heels, a flare of triumph on his face.

"Gotcha."

"Okay, okay. Don't fucking rub it in."

Garrett shrugged. "Now, you going to call Ethan or am I?"

CHAPTER 26

AS a matter of habit, Geron Castle had an array of local newspapers from across the state of Tennessee delivered to his office every morning. It was his practice to drink two cups of coffee as he browsed the human interest stories.

Ever the politician, he looked for any angle to exploit, and he pompously considered that it kept him in touch with his constituents.

He browsed through Knoxville, Nashville and Memphis first. Then he focused on the smaller publications and yawned his way through small-town bullshit. These people had no lives. Cattle, horses, hunting and fishing. It was all they seemed to live for. It was a wonder the suicide rate wasn't higher in this godforsaken state.

He consoled himself with the fact that these uneducated, backwoods louts were the ones who put him in the Senate, and they would indirectly be responsible for him shaking the dirt of Polk County from his feet when he made the jump to the White House.

He was sipping at his second cup and idly contemplating his upcoming vacation when his gaze lighted on the article about a Stewart County resident declared dead who had miraculously returned after surviving a supposed plane crash in a South American jungle.

He choked on his coffee and sloshed it all over his lap when he read the woman's name. Rachel Kelly.

He leapt to his feet, slapping at his pants as the heat scorched the more tender portions of his anatomy. He let out a string of curses that would have had his mother washing his mouth out with soap. She was a devout, churchgoing woman, and she had no tolerance for ungodly behavior.

Half his life had been spent following her dictates and example. The other half had been spent veering as far from the path of righteousness as a man could.

He wasn't proud of his sins, but he didn't regret them either.

And now it looked like his sins were coming back to haunt him.

He tossed the cup aside, ignoring the stain on the carpet and the line of liquid on his desk. He snatched the paper back up and read the article in its entirety.

This was a disaster. Not just a disaster but the end of his career. The end of his presidency before it ever began.

How the hell was the little bitch alive?

The fucking drug cartel had screwed him over. What possible motivation they'd had for reneging on their end of the deal he didn't know, but they wouldn't get away with it.

He grabbed his phone and started to dial and then slammed it back down, shaking his head at his stupidity. This wasn't a safe place to make such an important call. He couldn't use his cell phone either.

Impatience and panic vied for equal attention. He flung his chair back and all but ran from his office, past his startled secretary, who probably saw the mess he'd made of his clothing.

Then he forced himself to calm down. Nothing good would come of him drawing unwanted attention. He forced a smile at his secretary and told her he was going home to change. A slight mishap, he said with a fake smile.

He drove out of town, giving thanks he hadn't been in D.C. when the newspaper article was released. He didn't always get the papers at his residence or his office there. What would have happened if he'd missed it?

At the first gas station with a pay phone he came to, he pulled off and made sure no one was close enough to overhear his call. Then he placed a phone call. His instructions were clear.

The cartel had fucked up. He needed no witnesses. Anyone who could connect him to drug trafficking had to die.

And Rachel Kelly needed to return to the grave.

CHAPTER 27

RACHEL hung up the phone with shaking hands, and then she turned to Ethan, praying she didn't look as sick as she felt. Her stomach churned, and she was eternally grateful she'd refused breakfast.

"She'll see me right away," she said in a low voice.

Ethan closed the distance between them and pulled her into his arms. She clung to him, her anchor, the only thing in her world that made sense right now.

"Do you want me to go?"

She hesitated, because more than anything she wanted him to go with her. She was scared to death and didn't want to do this alone. But worse than her fear of being without Ethan was her fear of him finding out why she was finally agreeing to go to the therapist in the first place. How could she face him and relate the horrible things she dreamed about at night when he'd been so absolutely wonderful to her?

"No, I need to do this on my own."

Her lips trembled so bad she could barely get the words out without the urge to puke. The thought of going to some stranger and laying out her soul terrified her.

He leaned in and brushed his lips across hers. Then he deepened the kiss, seeking and exploring her mouth.

When he pulled away, they were both breathing hard, and her lips were swollen and tingling.

He reached into his pocket and took out a cell phone, and placed it on the counter next to her.

"This is yours. I've programmed my number as well as everyone else's in the family. Sean, the sheriff, and all the deputies. Anyone I could think of that you might ever need. If you change your mind, you call me. I'll be there as soon as I can."

She smiled and leaned into him, circling his waist with her arms. She gave him a squeeze, pleased that she could feel and act so affectionate with him after the terror of her dreams the night before. In the daylight they faded and made her feel silly and reactionary.

The phone rang, startling her. They rarely got calls, and she was sure it was because Ethan's family was respecting their privacy.

Tentatively she reached to pick it up, remembering that this was her house too. She actually smiled as she brought the phone to her ear. Her home. Her phone.

"Hello?"

There was a short pause and then Sam's voice sounded in her ear.

"Hey, Rachel, how are you?"

His tone was gentle as it always was, and remembering how abrupt and foulmouthed he was with his brothers, she grinned. For once the thought of the big man didn't intimidate her.

"Hi, Sam. I'm good."

"That's great, honey. Is Ethan around? I need to speak to him for just a minute."

"Sure. He's right here."

She turned and handed the phone to him.

He gave her a quick kiss and then took it.

"Hello?"

Rachel moved away to give him space, but even across the room she felt the sudden anger emanate from him.

"What the hell? You're shitting me."

She winced and turned in concern to see Ethan's face clouded in fury.

"You'll have to come by to get me. I need a ride. Rachel's taking the truck. I still haven't gotten her new wheels."

He glanced up at her as he spoke and made an effort to ease his expression.

"Yeah, give me half an hour, okay? Don't you fucking go over there without me."

He hung up the phone and curled his fist into a tight ball. He looked for the world like he wanted to smash something, but he stood there, breathing in and out, instead.

"Ethan?" she asked cautiously.

He slowly relaxed his fist and looked back at her. He even tried to smile. "It's okay, baby. Just some stupid stunt Rusty has pulled. Sam wants to go over and give her hell. It's time Mom came to her senses. This girl is trouble, and this time she's gone too far."

Rachel frowned unhappily. "Oh, that's too bad. Try not to be too hard on her or your mom. Rusty has had such a bad time. She just seems so fragile."

To her surprise, Ethan smiled, so much that it lit up his entire face. He crossed the room and took her shoulders in his hands.

"God, you sound just like yourself. So tenderhearted and always looking out for the underdog."

"I'm trying, Ethan. I really am. I want to be the Rachel everyone knows. I just have to remember her first."

"I know, baby. I know. You should get on the road. I want you to be careful, and if anything freaks you out or if you just get there and change your mind, you call me. I'll come immediately."

She rose up on tiptoe to kiss him. "I will. I promise."

RUSTY sat on the edge of her bed staring down at the fingers that had lost feeling five minutes ago. Her knuckles were white, but she didn't lessen her grip on them.

Even with her door closed she could hear the raised voices drifting up the stairs from the living room. Sam, Garrett and Ethan were there along with Nathan and Joe, Marlene and Frank. A regular family meeting. The only people missing were Donovan and Rachel.

Rusty frowned unhappily. She'd fucked up this time. And the pisser was she hadn't meant to. They'd never believe her, though. They'd want her out on her ass because nobody would allow anything to upset poor, pitiful Rachel.

She should start packing, but then she hadn't come here with anything. Everything she owned had been bought by Marlene and it just didn't feel right to take it.

The knot grew bigger in her stomach. Stupid, stupid, stupid. It wasn't the first time she'd been taken in by a friendly face. When was she going to learn that no one was ever nice to her without an ulterior motive? Except Marlene. Rusty hadn't yet figured out any reason the woman had been so nice to her other than that she wanted to.

She liked the Kelly brothers because they didn't pretend. They didn't like her, they didn't approve of her, and they didn't make a secret of it. She could take that kind of bluntness. Truth was, she wasn't that crazy about any of them either even if she did admire them in a twisted sort of way.

She admired all the Kellys. They were fiercely loyal to each other. She wanted that. Wanted to be part of something that big and larger than life.

"Dream on," she muttered. After today she'd be back on the street trying to figure out where her next meal was going to come from.

Heavy footsteps on the stairs made her flinch. She squeezed her hands harder, determined not to let anyone see their betraying tremble.

No knock. No doubt she'd lost any privileges she may have earned in this house. The door swung open, and Nathan stood there, his expression solemn. Well at least his eyes weren't sparking hatred. She knew she'd run into that just as soon as she faced Rachel's little protective brigade.

"Mom wants to see you downstairs, Rusty."

She flashed a resentful glare in his direction. "Don't you mean your brothers want to yell at me?"

Nathan leaned against the door frame and studied her with that disturbing, probing stare that told her he saw way too much. "You don't think they have reason?"

She started to pop off some smart-ass remark, but she closed her mouth. She had no defense, and they both knew it. With a resigned sigh, she rose from her perch on the bed. Better to just get it over with.

"Take me down to face the firing squad," she muttered.

Worse than Nathan taking her to task, he remained silent. He just looked at her with those eyes that saw too much. She'd much rather he snarl at her or tell her what a fuckup she was.

Injecting steel in her suddenly jellified spine, she went stiffly down the stairs, dreading the bottom with every step. They were all gathered in the living room. Just great.

She tromped down the steps, not looking at anyone. Still, she could feel their heated stares, feel the anger coming off them in waves. Worse, she could sense the deep disappointment coming from Marlene's direction.

She chanced a look at Frank, and her heart sank when she saw not anger, but sadness.

Forgoing a seat near any of them, she perched on the brick hearth instead. She could hear the intake of breath as they prepared to launch into a diatribe about how evil she was.

"Look," she blurted. "I didn't mean to do it. I know you all hate me. I get it. I fucked up."

"Watch your mouth, young lady," Marlene said in her snippy motherly tone that Rusty loved so much. Maybe because her own mother had never spoken to her in such a way. Like a real mom.

"I just want to know why you did it," Ethan demanded.

Rusty glanced up and wished she hadn't. Ethan stood between Sam and Garrett, and they all scared the bejesus out of her. They were pissed. Okay, she got that. They even had the right to be.

Her throat swelled and she swallowed angrily. Damn if they'd make her cry. No one could make her cry. Not her crazy-ass mother. Not her mother's stupid husband who called himself Rusty's stepfather. They could all go straight to hell.

Surprisingly, Nathan came to her rescue.

"Cut the interrogation," he said to his brothers. "Let her tell us what happened. You've already tried and convicted her." Then he turned to Rusty. "Okay, let's hear it."

Something in his expression made her want to explain. It made her want to fight for her place in this family where before she'd been prepared to say fuck you all and hit the road again. She didn't have any experience with seeing it when people looked at her, but she could swear it was . . . trust.

She glanced over to where Marlene and Frank sat. Marlene's face was drawn into a pained expression. Shit, it looked like she'd been crying. Frank . . . he just looked disappointed. Rusty would rather stick an ice pick through her eye than put that look on his face.

Then she turned back to Ethan, Sam and Garrett, and she finally realized why she hated them so much. They were pissed beyond reason because Rusty had done something that hurt Rachel. Rachel, Rachel, Rachel. Rusty didn't hate her, but she envied her so much it was like poison in her blood. She wanted someone to feel as strongly about her. She wanted brothers—a family—to love her and want to protect her from all the bad shit in the world. Just like what they were doing for Rachel. Rachel who'd been through hell and didn't deserve any of Rusty's vitriol.

"I just wanted to be . . . one of you," she choked out.

A tear rolled down her cheek, and she slapped the back of her hand against it, mortified that anyone would see her crying like a baby.

Sam's eyes flickered, and his arms lowered from their position over his chest.

"Care to explain that? How does you doing a hatchet job on Rachel and shoving KGI into the spotlight make us believe you'd want to be part of this family?"

"I didn't know he was a reporter," she said miserably. "He was at the party so I assumed he was someone you all knew or trusted. He was nice and funny and he seemed genuinely interested in what I had to say. He wanted to talk to a member of the family and it felt so good, for just a minute, to pretend that I was."

"Oh, honey," Marlene whispered.

"But why would you say those things about Rachel?" Ethan demanded. "Do you have any idea what this will do to her when she sees it? She's at the therapist this morning, Rusty. She's there because she's about to break. She has nightmares. She's afraid she's losing her sanity, and her family is the one safe harbor she should have above all else. Why would you try to ruin that?"

Rusty hung her head, no longer trying to hide the hot tears that splashed onto her hands.

"I don't hate her. I didn't mean to hurt her, I swear. It just all came out. I envied the way everyone seems to rally around her. I was afraid now that she's back that Marlene wouldn't want me to stay anymore. I thought maybe I was some lame replacement for Rachel."

"Rusty."

She whipped her head around at Frank's gravelly voice. Even the others stopped whatever it was they were going to say.

It was obvious they respected their father. They loved him and he held sway over his sons.

"Come here," he directed as he shoved forward in his recliner.

On trembling legs she pushed up from the hearth and took the few steps to where he sat. Oh God, if he denounced her in front of everyone, it would kill her.

She couldn't look at him. Couldn't stand to see the judgment in his eyes.

Instead he took her hand in his much larger one, one that was wrinkled and weathered by age. He squeezed comfortingly, and her astonished gaze swung to meet his.

"You were never a replacement for Rachel. Marlene, bless her heart, has decreed that you're part of the Kelly clan. God help you. That means for better or worse you're family. Now, not everyone has to like it. I can't shield you from that. You have to earn your stripes in this family. You don't automatically get respect or privilege. You earn it."

Her mouth fell open. She had no response, no defense for the acceptance and forgiveness she saw in his eyes. She didn't deserve it, but she wanted it. Oh God, she wanted it so badly she could taste it.

She heard a strangled protest behind her, but a disapproving look from Frank silenced it immediately.

"You owe Rachel an apology," he said sternly. "You also owe my boys an apology for bandying their business about."

"Y-yes, sir."

He nodded approvingly. Then his gaze softened until the lines at the corners of his eyes wrinkled and spread out.

"This won't be the last time you screw up. Just don't make a habit of it. Around here, we take responsibility for our mistakes. We don't hide from them. Understand?"

"Yes, sir," she said again, stronger this time.

CHAPTER 28

RACHEL stumbled out of the therapist's office, inhaling the smell of new paint, new drywall. The entire neat little building was sparkly new. It was a gorgeous office. The kind you didn't mind sitting in while waiting forever for your appointment. Only she couldn't wait to get out. The walls were closing in around her and so was her panic.

"Rachel."

The therapist's voice slithered like barbwire over her nerves. Kate . . . Kate Waldruff. Or something like that. Perfectly nice. Understanding. Professional. Appropriately sympathetic. It was all Rachel could do not to childishly put her hands over her ears.

Instead she stopped and turned around to face the worried expression of the therapist. Rachel's heart thudded so painfully against her breast that she put one palm over her chest as if to hold it in.

"I wish you'd let me call someone for you at least. You're upset."

Rachel tried to smile. "I'm okay. Really. I just want to go home. Thank you for trying to help."

Kate sighed. "I can't work miracles in one session, Rachel. Give it some thought. Call me back when you're ready. I'll fit you in no matter what."

Rachel nodded and fled the sterile office building, out into the bright sunlight that nearly blinded her. She got into Ethan's SUV before she gave in to the horrible itching.

Her flesh felt alive. Ants. Bugs. Thousands of them. They'd invaded her bloodstream, and there was only one thing she knew that would make them go away.

She licked her lips. Right now she'd give anything for a needle. Anything at all. It shamed her, but desperation made up for a lot of shame.

The session had sliced her open. Made her feel so bare and vulnerable and *helpless*. God, she hated the helplessness above all else. Intellectually she knew, she *knew* that one session wasn't a cure-all. But somehow she'd hoped that by some miracle the therapist could listen to her rattle on about absolutely nothing and then offer a pat solution. Then she could go home, get on with her life and live happily ever after.

Need, harsh and edgy, rose until she thought she might go mad with it. She gripped the steering wheel and stared over the parking lot to the small grocery store across the highway. There was a teenage boy doing stunts on his skateboard.

Would he know how to score what she so desperately needed? How did she even broach such a subject. *Hey, kid, know where I can get drugs?*

Her door was open and her legs swung down so her feet met the pavement before she realized what she was doing. She stood, shielded by the window, staring in horror at the boy. Just a kid. Someone she had been perfectly willing to ask to break the law.

She pressed a fist to her mouth to stifle the sob working from the depths of her soul. What was she thinking? Had she honestly gotten out of the truck with the intention of buying drugs?

She'd like to tell herself no way in hell, but she knew differently. If he was closer, if she had more courage, if she wasn't afraid of ruining what was left of her life, she'd be over there in a heartbeat, braving everything for temporary relief from the clawing pain so deep she might never be able to assuage it.

Before she could do something incredibly stupid, she threw herself back into the truck and started the ignition. With jerky movements, she thrust the truck into gear and roared out of the parking lot and onto the highway toward home.

She shook from head to toe, her hands rattling against the steering wheel. Tears streamed from her eyes until she could barely make out the road in front of her.

Had her life come to this? Had she finally come home—a place she'd convinced herself didn't really exist in those long, harrowing days in captivity—only to piss away any chance she had of a normal life?

What was it about her that she was trying to destroy her life? She was doing her best to think the worst of her marriage, of a man who'd risked everything for her. She had a family who loved her and supported her unconditionally, and she was prepared to ruin not only her life, but the life of some kid she didn't even know, and to destroy the people who loved her.

Maybe she was as crazy as she secretly feared. Maybe the bastards who'd held her had destroyed her after all.

She felt completely and utterly broken.

She had no idea of the miles she'd traveled, only that she was driving too fast and too recklessly. Something deep within crumbled and she felt precariously light. The sound of a horn blaring wrenched her from her desolation long enough for her to swerve back into her lane.

She pulled to the shoulder and cut the engine, knowing she couldn't drive another mile. She gripped the steering wheel at the top and buried her face against the backs of her wrists and wept.

SEAN Cameron topped the hill and automatically slowed when he saw the SUV pulled to the shoulder. No flashers were on even though he could see someone in the driver's seat. He frowned. It looked a lot like Ethan's vehicle. But the driver was too small to be Ethan. It looked more like a woman. Or a really short man.

As he neared, he radioed plates and pulled behind the vehicle. He didn't have to wait for the dispatcher to come back. It was definitely Ethan's truck.

Checking back for oncoming traffic, he got out and cautiously approached. In the sideview mirror he caught the image of a woman bent over the steering wheel. Rachel.

He dropped his hand from his holster and hurried forward. He could see her shoulders shaking through the window, but she never even registered his presence.

Not wanting to frighten her, he carefully tapped on the glass. She reacted violently, yanking herself up, her ravaged, tearstained face staring back at him. Her pupils dilated—in fear? His chest tightened at the idea that he'd inadvertently scared her.

"Open the door, Rachel," he said, loud enough so she could hear through the glass.

For a moment he thought she'd refuse, and then her eyes dulled in resignation, and she hesitantly opened the door a crack.

He pried the door from her fingers and then went down on one knee. "What's wrong, Rachel? Are you okay? Did you have an accident?"

He couldn't see any damage to the vehicle, but he hadn't been around it for a full inspection.

A low sob welled from her throat and more tears trickled down her cheeks.

"You should arrest me, Sean."

Of all the things he'd thought she might say, that wasn't one of them. He rocked back, completely poleaxed by her statement.

He eyed passing traffic with concern. This wasn't the best place to hash out whatever Rachel thought he should arrest her for, and it was obvious this wasn't something that would be solved in one or two minutes.

He rose and reached gently for her elbow. "Come sit in my car with me. I'd feel better if we were farther out of the line of traffic. Then you can tell me what's bothering you."

She looked so damn forlorn that it discomfited him. Hell, he dealt with women in various forms of distress all the time through his job. He arrested them, gave them bad news, took reports from the abused, but he didn't know any of them.

She stared ahead, biting her lower lip as if she couldn't decide what she should do.

"Come on, honey," he said a little more forcefully. "Let's go talk about it and then I'll get you home."

She turned her gaze to him and her eyes filled with tears again. "I can't go home, Sean."

Hell. What was he supposed to say to that? And where the hell was Ethan?

He lifted her arm, hoping she wouldn't fight him. He reached down to unclasp her seat belt and urged her from her seat. She stumbled as she got out, and he wrapped an arm around her waist to support her as they walked toward his squad car.

"No, not in the back," he said when she went in that direction.

He walked around to the front passenger seat and ushered her inside. Then he hurried around to the driver's side and slid in next to her.

He tapped his thumbs on the steering wheel for a moment and then broached the subject head-on.

"Why on earth do you think I should take you to jail?"

She raised a trembling hand to her forehead and closed her eyes. He could see the deep pain grooved on her forehead.

"God, Sean. Do you know what I almost did? I came out of the therapist's office." She broke off and laughed, a harsh, brittle sound. "I ran out of the office more like. All I could think was what a mess my life is and how I wanted the needle more than I wanted to live. I looked over and saw this kid riding his skateboard in the parking lot of the grocery store. A *kid*, Sean. And I wondered if he'd know how to score a hit. I got out of the truck before I even realized what I was doing."

She wilted in the seat, all the fight completely gone. There was such despair in her eyes that it made him want to cry like a damn baby.

"Ah shit, Rachel. You should have called me. Or Ethan. Or anyone else."

She jerked her head around, her eyes red-rimmed, exhaustion and self-recrimination stark in her features.

"What was I supposed to say? That I'm the world's biggest screwup? That I'm trying my best to mess up my life as soon as I get it back? Do you have any idea how much I hate myself?"

Sean pulled her into his arms and stroked her hair. "Give yourself a break. You didn't do it. Do you hear me? You didn't do it. You may have wanted to but nothing you could ever say will convince me that you would have gone through with it. And I sure as hell can't arrest someone for wanting to commit a crime for God's sake. If that was the case, the whole damn world would be in jail, including yours truly."

Her muffled laughter sounded pitiful, but at least she'd stopped crying.

"I'm about to go out of my mind," she said against his shirt.

He could feel the light shudders of her body and knew she was suffering. How she'd endured this far was a mystery to him.

"I'm not sure I have a mind left," she added.

He held her for a minute and absently ran his hand through her hair.

"You're doing fine. You probably insisted on going alone this morning when you should have been willing to ask for help. You're surrounded by people who'd drop things at a moment's notice if you needed them. You need to be willing to use that. We're your family. That's what families do. It's what you used to do for everyone else. Now it's our turn to repay that. Do you understand that? You don't have to make it on your own. It doesn't make you weak to need help. You don't remember, but when I first came on the job, I was shot because I did a really stupid thing. I was a rookie. Second week on the job and I thought I knew it all. Went into a situation without backup because I was confident I didn't need anyone's help. I'm lucky I didn't get killed.

"During my recovery you and Marlene took turns cooking for me. You cleaned my house. Did my grocery shopping. Made sure all my bills were paid. And you lectured me endlessly about making damn sure I never did something so stupid again.

"Now, you tell me how that's any different than what's going on with you. You need help. You've got a family who's all dying to pamper you and spoil you endlessly. Not everyone is as lucky to have a family like yours."

She pulled away and stared up at him, a mystified look on her face.

"I guess I am being pretty stupid. I just feel so ashamed. It kills me that I can't just turn off the need. Most days I'm okay, but then days like today I need it so much I feel like I'm going to die without it."

"Those are the days you need your family the most," he said gently.

She blew out a long breath and sagged against the seat.

"I'll drive you home. Ethan can have one of his brothers come back to get the truck. You shouldn't be driving right now. You're damn lucky you didn't wrap yourself around a telephone pole."

She reached over and hugged him so tight he couldn't catch his breath.

"Thank you," she breathed. "Just thank you."

He pulled her away long enough to level a hard stare at her. "Promise me something, Rachel. Promise me if you ever find yourself in that situation again, you'll call me immediately. Don't make me respond to a call because you've gotten involved with the wrong person and I have to be the one to tell Ethan you're dead."

She shivered and her eyes went wide, but he didn't regret for a minute scaring her this time.

"I promise," she said in a low voice.

"Okay then, let's get you home."

CHAPTER 29

"**LEAVE** it to Dad to make us all feel like shit," Ethan grumbled.

Sam chuckled and Garrett just scowled.

The brothers stood outside with Nathan and Joe, while inside their mom was busy mopping up Rusty's tears and laying down the law. Again.

"It was a stupid stunt. She should have known better," Garrett growled.

"She's a kid," Nathan said in her defense. "A scared, strung-out kid who's never had anyone give a damn about her. Cut her some slack. We all did some pretty stupid shit when we were her age."

"Speak for yourself," Joe said mockingly. "I was an angel."

Snorts abounded.

"Where's Van today anyway?" Nathan asked. "I wanted to see him before Joe and I head back to Fort Campbell."

Sam and Garrett exchanged glances, and Ethan leaned forward in interest. So did Nathan and Joe.

"Researching a mission he's taken on," Sam said.

Joe's brow went up. "He's taken on? I take it you don't approve?"

Garrett made a rude noise. "He's heading the job with part of Steele's team. Sam and I just don't happen to be going along."

Nathan made an exaggerated expression of shock. "You? Mr. Have to Be Involved in Everything? Not going?"

Garrett held up his middle finger. "Fuck you."

Ethan's cell phone rang, and he quickly dug into his pocket. Everyone who'd have any business calling him was with him. Except for Rachel.

He glanced at the LCD and frowned. Sean? He flipped the phone open and stuck it to his ear.

"Hey, man."

"Ethan, hey. Look, I'm driving Rachel home, but I need one of your brothers to go pick up your truck. It's on the shoulder of 79 just outside of town."

Ethan motioned for his brothers to be quiet.

"What the hell? What happened? Why is Rachel with you?"

"She's fine, Ethan. Relax. I don't want to get into it on the phone. I'm on my way. We'll be at your house in about ten. I just wanted to be sure you'd be there."

Ethan held the phone away in shock when the call was disconnected. What the fuck? Blood pounded in his ears. Why hadn't she called him, and why the hell was his truck on the side of the highway? He was going to kick Sean's ass for this.

"What's up?" Sam demanded.

Ethan shoved the phone back into his pocket. "Look, can one of you go get my truck? Sean said it's parked on 79 just outside town. He's driving Rachel home."

"Shit," Garrett swore. "Is Rachel okay?"

"Sean said she was but wouldn't say anything else. I need a ride home. He said he'd be there in ten."

"Come on," Sam said in his usual take-charge manner. "Garrett and I'll drive you home. Nathan? Can you take Joe to get Ethan's truck and drive it back to his house?"

"Yeah sure. No problem." Nathan looked in Ethan's direction. "Hope everything's okay, man."

Ethan wasn't paying attention. He was already climbing into Sam's truck.

The ride home was silent, which was just as well. Ethan had no desire to talk or speculate. Worry was eating a hole in his gut. He should have never let Rachel go alone, no matter what she said. Had she been in an accident? Had the appointment with the therapist been too much?

"Stop beating yourself up," Garrett said in a low voice. "You don't even know what, if anything, happened. Save it."

Ethan blew out his breath in frustration and didn't respond.

When they pulled into the driveway, Sean's patrol car was already parked in front. No one was in it, and as soon as Sam pulled up beside it, Ethan hopped out and hurried to the front door.

"Rachel?" he called as soon as he got inside. "Baby, where are you?"

He burst into the living room to see Rachel sitting on the couch, her face pale and drawn, her eyes red-rimmed and swollen from crying. Sean sat beside her, and relief flashed over his face when he looked up to see Ethan. He stood and moved forward to meet Ethan.

Ethan's stomach dropped as he locked onto Rachel. He walked past Sean, ignoring everything but the look on Rachel's face. She looked . . . lost.

Sean stepped back to the couch and briefly leaned down where Rachel could hear him.

"Remember your promise. And tell Ethan everything. It'll be okay, I swear it."

She nodded but looked away, as if trying to hold on to her rapidly deteriorating composure.

Sean touched Ethan on the shoulder and then walked across the living room to where Sam and Garrett now stood. Ethan turned long enough to see Sean motion Ethan's brothers outside, and then he and Rachel were left alone.

Something in Rachel's expression kept him from going to her and taking her in his arms. There was something dark and terrible in her eyes, and for the first time since she'd come home, he felt real, tangible fear. Of what he wasn't sure.

Oh, there were plenty of things he was afraid of. But he could put a name to those. He was scared shitless she'd remember what a dick he'd been, that he'd asked for a divorce, that he'd made terrible accusations and that he'd done everything in his power to drive her away.

But this. This was different and that fear paralyzed him.

"Rachel."

Her name came out a croak, and he cleared his throat, shamed that he couldn't be stronger for her.

"Sean says I should be better about leaning on my family,"

she said, surprising him. "That I shouldn't be ashamed to ask for help or to tell you when things are . . . bad."

Ethan sat down beside her, still afraid to touch her. There was such a wounded look in her eyes. Had she remembered things about their past? Their marriage? What an utter bastard he was?

"He's right. That's what we're here for. We love you."

She smiled tremulously. "I told him he should have arrested me."

Ethan stiffened from head to toe. "What the hell?"

"I was such a mess after meeting the therapist," she said, her voice thready with emotion. "I don't know what I expected. Well, I do, but it was stupid and unrealistic. I wanted her to wave a magic wand and fix me. I felt so helpless and angry. God, I was so angry. I thought I might explode with it. And then I left and I needed . . . I wanted a needle so bad it was all I could focus on."

She looked away, her eyes going down as they crowded with shame. "I almost asked a kid if he knew how to get drugs, Ethan. A kid. Dear God, what have I become? I was a teacher. And I was willing to ruin a kid's life by dragging him into my addiction. I was willing to ruin my life, what's left of it."

Sudden rage suffused her face, turning it red as her eyes sparked.

"God, I sound so pathetic. Damn it, Ethan, I'm tired of sounding so pitiful. 'What's left of my life.' Enough. Enough, enough, enough," she chanted. "I'm so lucky. I have a second chance and I tried to screw it up. How unforgiveable is that? I have a husband and a great family who loves me, and I was willing to throw all of that away because some woman asking me questions made me feel helpless and inferior."

She stood, agitated, her hands curling into tight fists at her sides.

"Well, I'm done with that," she said fiercely. "Do you hear me, Ethan? I'm done. This need inside me is killing me, but I won't let it. Do you hear me? I won't let it. I might be crazy, but I'm not going to let you or my family down. I'm not going to let myself down."

Her shoulders heaved, and by God, she was magnificent. Her eyes were puffy and swollen, red-tinged, and her breaths came out in short, erratic rasps, but it was the most animated, the *strongest* he'd seen her since she'd come back to him.

"Come here," he whispered, barely able to get the words out around the huge knot in his throat.

Never in his life had he been more unworthy of her. If he had courage, he'd tell her everything. He'd tell her the bald truth and beg her forgiveness. Beg her for the chance to make things right.

But all he could do was fold her into his arms and hold her so tight. She shook against him, and he realized it was rage rolling through her veins. Not tears.

It was funny. He knew what to do with the fragile, tearful Rachel. He could hold her, comfort her, let her lean on him when she didn't have the strength to stand on her own. But with her angry and resolved, he was clueless. So all he could do was hold tight.

"Never be afraid to tell me anything," he whispered against her hair. "No matter how ashamed you might feel. I'll never judge you, Rachel. I love you."

His words echoed in his ears. Harsh. Everything he told her was true and it made him the worst hypocrite. What he expected from her he was himself unwilling to give. The truth.

He closed his eyes and buried his face in her hair. He was on borrowed time. She'd remember. It wasn't a matter of if but when. Every day more came back. Little snippets. Memories that pushed to the surface. How much longer could he hope to keep the truth from her?

"I'm sorry, Ethan," she said.

She drew away and leaned back into his embrace, coiling her arms around his neck.

"I went a little crazy. I hate the way I felt," she whispered. "How much longer will I live with the addiction? Hasn't it been long enough? I'm fine and then bam, out of the blue my skin is crawling and I want relief so bad I think I'll do anything to get it."

"I'll take you back to the doctor. We'll work it out, Rachel. I swear it. If you don't want to go back to the therapist, we'll figure out something else. Together we can do this."

She smiled then, and it took his breath away. Hope shone in her eyes for the first time since he'd walked in the door to see her so devastated.

"You're right. Sean's right. We can do this together. I'll do better, Ethan. I just want things back the way they were before," she said wistfully.

The way they were before. God. If she only knew. It was the last thing he wanted. He wanted things to be different. He never wanted to go back to the way things had been before she left, before he thought she'd died.

He wanted a new beginning for them both. But in order to have that new beginning, they were going to have to face the past.

CHAPTER 30

ETHAN shot a glance over at Rachel to see how she was handling the crowded living room. The family had gathered for Nathan's and Joe's last night home for a while. They were leaving on a training mission in two days, and it wasn't as if their mom ever needed an excuse to get her brood together.

The night may have belonged to Nathan and Joe, but Rusty had taken center stage with a very subdued apology. Rachel's reaction had been hard to guage. Ethan hadn't even wanted her to know what Rusty had done, but it had been impossible to keep it from her as a result of his father's demand for Rusty's public apology. Rachel had remained quiet and as subdued as Rusty through it all.

The thing was, Rusty had seemed sincere. Even now the girl stood to the side, pale, lines of worry around her young face. Hell, all she should be worrying about was boys and curfews, right?

Ethan sighed and briefly closed his eyes. He was bone weary and worrying about whether or not Rusty was going to shape up wasn't on his list of priorities.

"Hey, you okay, man?"

Ethan opened his eyes to see Donovan standing over him, a frown on his face.

"Yeah, I'm good. Thought you were heading off on assignment?"

Donovan nodded. "Tomorrow a.m. Had to see Nathan and Joe off."

"You sure you don't need any help?"

Not that Ethan wanted to leave Rachel even for a minute, but he wasn't comfortable with the idea of Sam and Garrett staying behind, especially when he was sure they were sticking around because of him.

"Nah, I'm good. Piece of cake. The asshole will never know what hit him. Besides, Rachel needs you. Your only concern is to make sure she's taken care of."

Ethan stole another glance over at Rachel, who stood quietly next to Marlene as she hugged Nathan and Joe. Suddenly he found himself dragged upward as Donovan gripped Ethan's arm.

"What the hell?"

Donovan didn't say much. He just hauled Ethan toward the back door, which was pretty laughable given that Ethan had at least thirty pounds and two inches on his older brother.

Still, he didn't fight. Whatever bug was up Van's ass, Ethan figured it needed to be routed before he left the next morning.

"Okay, spill it," Donovan said grimly when they were outside.

"Spill what?"

Donovan sighed and punched a finger into Ethan's chest. "Whatever the hell is bugging you. Dude, you look like shit. You probably haven't slept in days. You keep staring at Rachel with this sick puppy dog look."

"Christ," Ethan muttered. He damn sure hadn't realized he'd been so fucking obvious.

"What the hell's going on?" Donovan asked quietly.

Ethan rubbed a tired hand over his face. He didn't want to get into this with his brother. He didn't want to get into it with anyone. He opened his mouth to say, *Nothing*, but caught Donovan's fierce scowl directed at him. Van didn't get worked up about too many things. The man was a study in being laid back. Right now he looked as determined as a pit bull clamped down on a prime piece of ass. Ethan almost rubbed his own behind at the image.

He looked around to make sure he and Donovan were the only ones outside. Just because he was spilling his guts to his brother didn't mean he wanted it broadcast for the world to hear. One was bad enough.

"You remember things were tough when I came home. After Rachel's miscarriage."

"Yeah, you'd resigned your commission. It was a huge adjustment for you. For both of you."

He smiled at Van's show of loyalty. He didn't really deserve it, but it felt damn good.

"I was an ass," Ethan admitted. "I did everything I could to drive Rachel away. Hell, I don't know why she stayed with me as long as she did."

Donovan frowned, his brows coming together in confusion. And then his eyes widened as if he was finally understanding that there was a lot that the rest of the family didn't know.

"Does Rachel remember any of that?"

Ethan winced at the direct hit. Then he shook his head.

Donovan blew out his breath and shoved his hands in his pockets. "How bad are we talking here, Ethan?"

"I told her I wanted a divorce right before she left on her mercy mission."

"What? You told her *what*?" Donovan stared at him in utter shock.

"I knew the moment she left that it wasn't what I wanted," Ethan said wearily. As if that was a defense for the things he'd said. "I had these grand plans of sweeping her off her feet the moment she got home. Telling her I was sorry and begging for another chance. God, I never got the chance."

"Holy shit, man. I never knew. I mean what the hell are you going to do now? I mean . . ." He stared at Ethan for a long moment as if he grappled with what he was about to ask. "Do you feel stuck? I mean do you want *out*?"

For a moment all Ethan could do was stare. It was a fair question in light of what he'd just told Donovan, but the mere thought of getting out of the relationship sent a cold chill down his spine.

"No. No! God no. I'm worried, Van. I'm worried about the day she remembers what a bastard I was to her. I . . . I love her."

"Have you told anyone else this?"

Ethan shook his head. "I was too ashamed. I fucked up. Really fucked up."

His brother's hand came down on his shoulder. Donovan squeezed, and sympathy shone bright in his eyes.

"You made mistakes, Ethan. We all have. What matters now is how you go forward. Have you talked to her about it?"

Talked. If it was only that easy. He closed his eyes and swallowed against the helpless rage burning in his gut.

"She's on the edge, Van," he said in a quiet voice. "I can't push her that much closer. Right now the only thing she knows is that I love her. I can't make her doubt that even for a moment."

"Shit," Donovan breathed. "I'm sorry. I don't know what to say."

"Nothing to say. I made my bed and now I have to lie in it and hope to hell I don't lose her after I got her back again."

"Do you plan to say anything?"

Ethan shook his head. "No, and I'd prefer to keep it that way."

"You'll work it out." There was worry in Donovan's eyes and maybe a little doubt. It hit Ethan hard in the belly. "It's obvious you love her."

"I haven't ever not loved her," Ethan said quietly. "But I'm worried that when she gets her memory back, she's going to realize she stopped loving me a long time ago."

Donovan's lips tightened into an adamant line. "No way I believe that. She loves you. I'd bet my life on it. Memory or no memory. That kind of love doesn't just go away because you were a bastard."

A harsh laugh cracked through Ethan's lips. "Thanks. I think. I'm glad one of us is confident."

"If there's anything I can do . . ."

Ethan nodded. "I know, man. And I appreciate it. More than you'll ever know."

He held out his fist and Donovan balled his own to knock it against Ethan's.

"Good luck tomorrow," Ethan said. "And be careful. Garrett's about to have a kitten at the thought of you going alone."

Donovan snorted. "He's just pissed because he's out of action. It'll be good for him to have to sit and cool his heels. Man works too damn much. He'll have an ulcer before he's forty. If he lives that long."

"Shi-it. Don't tell Ma that. She'd henpeck him to death."

Both men stopped and stared at each other in realization. Slow grins spread across their faces and they burst into laughter.

"Oh hell. Garrett'll kill us for this, but it'll be worth it," Donovan chortled.

"You wanna tell her or should I?" Ethan asked as his shoulders shook.

Their mother on a mission was a scary sight to behold. Any hint that one of her chicks wasn't as he should be would bring immediate action.

"Nah, I'll tell her on my way out. It'll distract her from the lecture she's sure to give me."

Ethan slapped Donovan on the back. It was good to be back among his brothers even when they annoyed the holy hell out of him. Already he felt better. Some of the heavy cloak of doom had lifted and he didn't feel as weighed down by fear and anxiety.

"Be careful, okay? I want you back in one piece."

Donovan rolled his eyes. "Okay, Mom."

"Ethan?"

Both men turned at the soft voice floating from the back door. Rachel stood half-in, half-out, looking at them with a guarded expression. Ethan would have given anything to be able to remove the uncertainty in her beautiful eyes.

"Hey, sweetness," Donovan said easily.

She smiled, and it chased away the shadows, brightening her eyes.

"Hi, Donovan. I heard you were leaving tomorrow. I hope you'll be careful."

"Always. I'll be back before you know it."

"Did you need something, baby?" Ethan asked.

She frowned for a moment and tugged on her bottom lip with her teeth, as if searching her memory for what she'd come out for.

Then she raised her gaze again, her eyes lighting with recognition. "Nathan and Joe are about to leave. You should come in and say good-bye."

Ethan and Donovan both headed toward the back door where Rachel stood. Ethan couldn't resist dropping a kiss on her upturned lips. She smiled under his mouth and he ate it up, taking that smile as deep as he could. He lived for her smiles. He hadn't enjoyed them in longer than he cared to remember.

She tucked her hand into his and they walked back into the living room, where Nathan and Joe were both being bear hugged by their dad.

"Hey, there y'all are," Joe said as he looked up. "Thought maybe you and Van had flown the coop already."

"If I thought Ma would let us get away with it . . ." Ethan began.

Nathan snorted and promptly enfolded Ethan in a hug. They pounded each other on the back and hurled a few insults. Yep, life was good again.

"You be careful," Ethan warned. "Get your ass back here in one piece."

"Always."

Ethan moved to Joe while Van and Nathan did their mutual insult fest.

"You take care of our girl," Joe said in a serious voice as he pulled away from Ethan's embrace.

"Always," Ethan said, echoing Nathan's vow.

"Okay, man," Nathan called to Joe. "Let's get on the road."

The two men held up their hands and waved as they headed out the front door. The family followed behind, crowding into the front yard as the twins piled into their trucks.

Ethan looped his arm over Rachel's shoulders as they watched them drive away.

"Anyone up for a barbeque tonight?" Sam asked. "I'll volunteer Garrett's cooking."

"Nice, asshole," Garrett muttered.

Donovan chuckled. "I'm in. I could use a big nasty steak. Have to keep my strength up."

"I'll get the meat if you and Ethan will make the beer run," Sam said to Donovan. "Mom? Dad? You guys want to come over?"

Marlene reached over and patted Sam on the cheek. "That's nice of you to ask, but I think I'm going to put up my feet and rest awhile. Rusty said she'd cook dinner tonight and I aim to take her up on it."

Ethan glanced over to see Rusty's face turn bright red. She wasn't pleased that Marlene had spread that little tidbit around. Tough kid. Not an ounce of softness in her. At least not where anyone could readily see it.

He wrapped his arm tighter around Rachel and smiled down at her. "What do you say? Wanna go on a beer run with me and Van?"

She smiled as she looked between him and all his brothers. "Are you sure you want me along? This seems like one of those male bonding things. I could head home and let you guys do your thing."

Sam and Garrett both looked affronted.

"Well hell, Rachel. Stick a dagger in our hearts. You always used to come hang out with us. Too much testosterone otherwise," Sam said.

Her smile broadened. "A steak really does sound good." She glanced up at Ethan. "Do you care if I run home to change?"

He touched her cheek. "Not at all. You want me to come?"

"No. You go with Donovan. I won't be long."

He fished the keys out of his pocket and dangled them off the end of his fingers. She reached for them and warmth spread up his arm as her hand closed around his. It surprised him that even after so long she affected him with something as simple as her touch.

Uncaring that his brothers were standing around watching, he bent to kiss her, capturing her mouth with his. She tasted small and feminine. Perfect. It was a taste he'd dreamed about at night when he lay in their bed alone, aching.

She pulled away as breathless as he was, her eyes slightly glazed. It was then he realized that she didn't look at him like she had before her disappearance. Then she'd been guarded with him, never allowing him to see what she was thinking. It was a self-protective measure he'd forced on her with his coldness. Now she looked at him with warmth. With love. She hadn't said the words, but he felt more at ease, more confident of her affection now than he had in a long, long time.

"Get a room," Garrett smirked.

Ethan held up his middle finger behind Rachel's back. Sam and Donovan laughed while Ethan kissed Rachel again.

"Better go now, baby," he murmured. "Otherwise I'm coming home with you."

Her cheeks bloomed pink as she pulled away, but her eyes laughed up at him. Man, he'd missed that.

"I love you," he whispered, more for himself than for her.

She smiled, her teeth flashing, her eyes shining with happiness. It took every bit of his breath away.

"I won't be long," she promised.

Then she leaned up on tiptoe to offer him a kiss.

CHAPTER 31

EXCITEMENT curled in Rachel's stomach as she slid back into Ethan's truck. Comfortable now in cutoff jeans and a T-shirt, she was eager to get to Sam's house on the lake.

Her old clothes fit her better now. The shorts were still loose in the waist and her T-shirt hung over her shoulders and gathered around her breasts. Thanks to countless meals Marlene had brought over and Ethan's relentless nagging to eat more and better, she was putting on weight. Her color was better. Her eyes were brighter. Even her hair had regained its sheen.

Now if only she could get rid of the lingering effects of the drugs and regain complete memory of her past. It was the only missing piece to the puzzle.

She started up the bridge over Kentucky Lake. The water shimmered and sprawled for miles on either side of her. It was a calm day, and the sun still shone bright overhead. Perfect day for a barbeque.

Reflexively, she slowed as she reached the top, where the concrete guardrail had been knocked out a week before by a tractor-trailer wreck. Orange cones sat strategically on the edge, but there was no protection between the road and the drop-off.

The right lane was closed and traffic rerouted to the left lane so no one ventured into danger. As she neared, she accelerated, only wanting to be beyond the scary spot.

A sharp impact sent her forward into the steering wheel. Her seat belt clamped down in reaction and yanked her back against the seat. Someone had hit her from behind! Worse, they'd struck her left fender, spinning her so she faced the gaping hole in the side of the bridge.

She whirled in her seat to see behind her when she was struck again. The sickening sound of metal crunching assaulted her ears. The truck lurched forward, and she cried out as she rocketed toward the edge.

Her foot slammed onto the brake, and she put all her weight on it as if sheer will alone would keep her from plummeting over the side.

Her neck snapped forward as, once again, she was struck from behind. She screamed when the front end of the truck dipped as it left the surface of the bridge. She closed her eyes, prepared to feel the impact of the water and the cold surrounding her.

After several seconds, she cautiously opened her eyes again to see the sunlight still streaming through her windshield. A windshield that was bobbing precariously up and down.

Oh God. She was hanging over the edge, rocking softly up and down. Any movement could send her over.

She didn't move. Was afraid to breathe. Only her eyes moved, rapidly, side to side, as she tried to figure out how she was going to get out. Her hands curled around the steering wheel, holding so tightly her knuckles were white. Her seat belt was still fastened, and she didn't dare release the steering wheel to unbuckle it.

And so she sat, terrified, as the truck did a gentle seesaw motion in the breeze. Around her, she heard voices shouting to her, but she couldn't even turn her head. She stared ahead and wondered if she'd survive the drop from the bridge.

Ethan was trained in water. He lived in the water during his years with the SEALs. She frantically searched her memories for anything that could help her now. A hysterical laugh escaped. Escaping a submerged vehicle hadn't come up in any of their conversations. She was sure of it.

The voices were closer now. Surely they wouldn't try to pull her out. Panic exploded in her stomach. Slowly and carefully she turned just so she could see out her window from the corner of her eye.

Two men were standing a few feet away shouting at her. What were they saying? If the buzzing in her ears would abate long enough, maybe she'd know.

She sucked in several steadying breaths and forced herself to relax.

Don't move. Stay there.

Yeah, she heard that. Not to worry. She wasn't going anywhere. Except maybe down.

A moment later she heard the wail of sirens. Her chest caved in relief. Surely they'd know how to get her out of this.

Anxiety was making her sick. Nausea welled in her stomach until she was sure she would vomit. The only thing keeping it down was the knowledge that if she allowed herself to be sick, she'd likely roll right over the edge.

"Rachel! Rachel!"

Relief swamped her. Sean. She tried to turn her head to see him.

"No! Don't move, honey. Sit tight, okay? I just want you to know we're here. We'll get you out of this, okay? Just don't move, for God's sake."

The worry in his voice did nothing to soothe her ragged nerves. Calm, unflappable Sean had an edge to his voice that sounded like panic.

A low moan escaped before she could clamp her lips around it. It was stifling inside the truck. Sweat rolled down her neck and between her breasts. Her breathing was shallow and rapid, and it made her light-headed.

Memories of that hated hot box slammed back into her mind. The days had bled into one another. The only way she knew it was night was because the temperature went from unbearable to slightly less so. And then it began all over again.

Her hands shook despite her best efforts to remain calm. She couldn't go back there. She wouldn't. She closed her eyes against the memories because now it all seemed too real. Maybe she'd dreamt everything. A hallucination brought on by withdrawal and days baking in the heat in the hated prison.

Her hand left the steering wheel and flailed at the window. Air. She needed air.

The truck rocked precariously, and the window slid down, letting in a blast of fresh air.

"Rachel, no! Goddamn it, don't move!"

She had to get out. She didn't want to die.

"Goddamn it, hurry up and get it secure!" Sean yelled.

She let out a low whimper. Her throat tightened until she couldn't breathe. She could hear Sean talking to her, his voice low and soothing. She could hear the noise around her, the men hurrying to secure the back end of the truck so they could pull her back.

"Okay, Rachel, listen to me."

She turned just enough that she could lock onto him. He stood just a foot away from the truck. Close enough to touch, but neither he nor she made any move to do so. His features were tight and worried, but his lips were set in a determined line. He wasn't going to let her die.

Some of her panic abated. No, Sean wouldn't let anything happen to her. His determination bled into her, and she grabbed hold with both hands. She was equally determined that she wouldn't survive a year in hell, only to come home and let some asshole force her off a bridge.

Sean stepped closer, until he was inches from the truck. He leaned down so they were at eye level.

"We're going to pull the truck back, okay? I need you to stay calm. Let us do our job. We'll get you out safe. We won't let you go. I need you to trust me, Rachel."

She gave one slow nod to let him know she heard and understood. There was a slight bump from the rear, and she grabbed the steering wheel again as her heart accelerated damn near out of her chest.

"Easy!" Sean barked. Then he turned back to Rachel. "Okay, honey, stay with me here. We're going to do this."

Again she nodded. She swallowed the panic back. Sean was here. He wouldn't let anything happen to her. But she wanted Ethan. She needed him here.

"Ethan," she whispered hoarsely

"He's coming, Rachel. He'll be here any minute, okay? Promise."

The metal of the truck creaked and groaned in protest. It lurched back, popping her neck forward. There was a protesting shriek and then she saw the hood start to shift over the edge.

Then there was a loud crack and a bang and the truck dipped forward. She screamed and then her door flew open. Sean reached in, yanked at her seat belt, then hauled her roughly from the seat.

They fell to the ground, her sprawled over him. She looked back just in time to see the truck plunge over the bridge. Horrified, she heard the explosion of water and felt the spray as it lifted into the air and blew back over them.

"Son of a bitch," Sean muttered underneath her.

Numbly she stared at the empty spot where Ethan's truck had rested just moments before. She couldn't wrap her brain around it. There were people everywhere. Fire trucks, ambulances, police cars. They'd roped off the entire area, and rescue personnel raced to the edge and stood looking over with expressions of awe. Then they looked back at her.

She began to shake. No matter how hard she tried to control it, every muscle in her body jittered. It was worse than withdrawal.

Sean sat up, his arms closing around her.

"Are you okay?" he asked gently.

She couldn't even answer. Her teeth chattered together painfully. She raised a hand to her mouth, but even her fingers trembled violently.

They sat on the hard surface of the road, her sprawled over his legs as he held her. All she could do was stare at the empty space on the bridge.

"Oh my God," she finally said. "Ethan's truck."

"Don't worry about the truck. Ethan will only be glad you're alive," Sean soothed.

"Rachel!"

She turned in the direction of Ethan's voice, and a moment later, he burst through the crowd, shaking off hands that tried to hold him back.

Finally his gaze lighted on her, and the relief she saw was staggering. He ran over and dropped to his knees beside her and Sean. Then he hauled her into his arms, his hold so tight she couldn't breathe.

"Oh God, baby. You scared me. Holy hell, never do that to me again. Are you all right? Are you hurt?"

As he rambled, he pulled her back and ran his hands over her body.

"I'm okay," she croaked. "Sean saved me."

"Thank God, thank God," he said over and over as he rocked her in his arms.

"Your truck," she blurted. "It's gone. I'm sorry."

He framed her face in both hands and stared fiercely at her. "I don't give a fuck. You're all that matters to me."

Garrett, Sam and Donovan all came running up and staggered to a halt where she, Ethan and Sean were still sprawled on the ground. Sam ventured toward the edge where so many others were standing and peered over.

"Jesus," he muttered as he came away again.

Rachel turned to Sean, who was still pale and breathing erratically.

"Thank you. You risked your life to save me when the truck was going over."

"Was glad to do it, but Rachel? Can we never do that again?"

She mustered a smile and reached over to squeeze his hand. "I promise."

Sam and Donovan reached down to haul Sean to his feet. Garrett bent down and gently helped Rachel up while Ethan also got up.

"You okay, sweet pea?" Garrett asked.

She nodded. "Thanks to Sean."

She glanced down at the hands that wouldn't quit shaking. She sagged tiredly against Ethan and clutched at his waist.

"Can we go home?"

Ethan looked toward Sean, whose lips twisted in regret.

"Are you up to answering some questions for me, Rachel? I need to know what happened here."

Cold fear snaked up her spine as her mind flashed to that moment before impact. It was odd just how clear it all was in her mind. That brief glimpse in the rearview mirror. The feeling of impact. And the second. She frowned.

"Someone tried to run me off the bridge," she blurted.

Ethan stiffened beside her. Garrett's face drew into a storm cloud while Sam and Donovan raised their brows in confusion.

Sean frowned, then gestured toward a waiting ambulance. "Why don't you have a seat in the back and let the paramedic look you over. We can talk while he's taking a look at you."

She looked down. She wasn't hurt. Then she looked around at all the faces staring back at her. Deep concern was etched into their expressions. Sure, she was shaking like a leaf, but did she look that bad?

Ethan guided her over to where a paramedic waited. The first thing he did was wrap a blanket around her shoulders, and then Ethan lifted her to sit in the back of the ambulance.

Dutifully, she listened to the medic's instructions, and she frowned when she shook even harder. "Shock," she heard someone murmur. Well duh. She'd nearly fallen off a bridge.

"Now, tell me what happened," Sean said in an even voice.

She shrugged. "I don't really know. One minute I was glancing over where the last accident had taken place and then he hit me from behind."

"He?"

Her brows scrunched together. "Well I suppose it could have been a she. I didn't see. It was just a supposition."

"I see. What happened then?"

"He hit me on the left so that I spun toward the part of the bridge that was missing. Then he hit me dead-on. It pushed me closer. I practically stood up on the brakes, but he hit me a third time, and that was what pushed me over the edge."

Sean exchanged glances with Ethan and his brothers. She couldn't tell if he was concerned over the idea that someone would try to push her off a bridge or if he was worried she was losing her mind.

"I'm not crazy," she said softly.

Ethan curled his hand around hers. "Shhh, baby. Of course you're not."

"Any witnesses, Sean?" Garrett asked.

"They're being questioned now. No sign of the other vehicle. We're looking. No plates, not even a partial. Likely the guy panicked and fled the scene. We'll find him. He couldn't have gotten far. There has to be substantial damage to his front end."

"Can I take her home now?" Ethan asked over her head.

"Yeah sure. I'll follow up with more later, but yeah, get her home. She looks done for."

"Come on, I'll give you a ride," Garrett said. "Sam, you need to get Donovan back home so he can head out."

Ethan helped Rachel down as the paramedic smiled encouragingly at her. Though Ethan took a wide berth around the gaping hole in the side of the bridge, she knew what was down there, and she couldn't shake the uneasy feeling that whoever had hit her had done it with a single purpose in mind. Her death.

CHAPTER 32

ETHAN lay back on the couch and rubbed his fingers up and down in a soothing pattern on Rachels' arm. She was huddled close to him, her body warm and sweet against his.

Both of them had their shoes kicked off, and she had her legs entwined with his and her feet tucked between his. They were wrapped up like mating love bugs, and it was hard for him to remember a time when he'd been more content.

"I could stay like this forever," she murmured.

Had he been so transparent? He was thinking the exact same thing. It did odd things to him that she seemed as content as he did.

He continued stroking her arm, simply enjoying the sensation of touching her. She snuggled a little deeper into his embrace, and he smiled as her hair fell over his lips and nose.

"Feeling better now?" he asked.

"Still a little jittery, but yes, much better now that I'm here with you."

A surge of pleasure shot through his chest. He didn't tell her, but his insides were pretty much toast. He was amazed he could even lie here so calmly and hold her when he was still screaming *what the fuck* in his head.

Never did he want to relive the terrible moment of Sean calling him to say Rachel was in danger of going over the bridge. Never. And to know that only Sean's quick actions of jerking her out of the truck saved her still had the power to drive him to his knees.

She shifted and elevated herself so that she could look down at him. Her hair had grown some in the last weeks, and thanks to a trip to the stylist with his mom, the ends had been trimmed and layers had been added.

Her small hands spread out over his chest and she smoothed them upward to his shoulders.

"Ethan?"

He looked at her, knowing that in this moment she could ask him for damn near anything and he'd tell her yes.

"Would you mind too terribly if I made love to you?"

He swallowed and swallowed again. Here was this beautiful woman, a woman he loved more than anything. The woman he'd married and lost. Now she was here, like a dream, asking him so sweetly if she could make love to him.

Dear God, yes. Yes. Yes. Yes.

"I'd love nothing more," he managed to croak out. It sounded better than *oh hell yeah*, even if that was what his cock was screaming.

She smiled, and her eyes turned sultry. The fear and anxiety was replaced by a warm, earthy glow that sent shivers down his spine.

He used to love it when she took the initiative in bed, but that had stopped when he'd started pushing her away. It didn't take too many times of getting shot down before she stopped making the effort.

His body reacted, leaping to life at the promise of seduction in her gaze. He let his hands linger on her arms as she shifted more so she could straddle him on the couch.

Some of the wounded bruising so prevalent in her eyes had been replaced by an almost playful light. He could drown in that look.

"I want to touch you," she whispered.

"Oh God, baby. I want you to touch me too."

"Will you undress for me?"

There was a shyness now to her gaze, and she dropped it slightly, refusing to meet his eyes. He picked up her hands and brought then to his mouth. He kissed each finger and then carefully shifted from underneath her.

He rolled, putting his feet down to get up from the couch.

Then he turned back to her and reached for the fly of his jeans. There was a spark of curiosity in her eyes, coupled with desire.

He was so aroused by her open perusal that he had a hard time prying the jeans down over his erection. When it sprang free, he sighed an audible sound of relief.

Her eyes widened in appreciation, and he hardened further, until his cock stretched painfully upward toward his navel. Forgoing the idea of being playful and teasing, he ripped his T-shirt over his head and tossed it aside. Then he stood before her nude, wanting her so damn much it was all he could do not to toss her down on the couch and ride her long and hard.

She looked uncertain and nervous.

"Tell me what you want me to do, baby," he encouraged.

Instead of directing him, she scooted forward on the couch, the T-shirt she'd changed into hanging around her knees. She glanced up at him once and then reached hesitantly until her fingers circled him.

He let out a groan as the tips danced over his erection, stroking, petting lightly. Sweat broke out on his forehead when she cupped his balls, squeezing with just enough pressure to drive him insane.

He wasn't going to survive this. He was trying to be good. Patient and understanding when every instinct screamed at him to take his woman and make love to her until she forgot both their names.

Then her lips found him and *he* forgot everything but her. It was just a light kiss. And then a playful lick. She grew bolder and he grew harder.

His fingers curled into tight fists at his sides. He clenched and unclenched until he lost all the feeling around his knuckles.

"You taste good," she murmured.

Ah hell.

She licked a circle around the head, paying particular attention to the crease at the back and to the slit at the top. She was making him crazy. Absolutely stone cold nuts.

"Rachel, baby, God . . ."

Teasingly she slid her tongue up the shaft and then underneath so she could suck gently at his sac. His toes curled into the carpet and he strained upward, wanting more of that delectable mouth.

She gripped him tight with her hand and rolled outward, following her lips back up to the tip. Once again she licked delicately, and then without warning, she sucked him into her mouth, taking him deep.

"Ahhhh!"

He sank into the hot velvet clasp of her mouth. Her tongue rasped along the underside, the friction delicious and unbearable. When he reached his depth, she sucked gently and then with more force.

His fingers stuttered clumsily through her hair until he gripped the top of her head. He rocked up on his toes and then forward, thrusting deeper. He was about to crawl out of his skin. It was itchy, alive, and the most exquisite, torturous pleasure he'd ever experienced in his life.

"Baby, you need to stop," he groaned. "I'm going to come. I can't hold out any longer."

She pulled carefully away and leaned back, eyeing him as she licked her lips like a satisfied cat. Jesus, it was all he could do not to shoot his wad here and now. He reached down and pinched the head of his cock between his fingers and tried to chase away the erotic images that floated in his head.

"If you come now, are you done for the night?" she asked curiously.

"Baby, the way you're looking at me, I think I'd be hard again in about five minutes."

It probably wasn't true, but damn if he didn't believe it as excited as he was.

"Then I definitely want you to come now."

The husky timbre of her voice washed over him. His cock jumped in his hand, as if to tell him to get the fuck away and let the woman do the handling. And he was only too willing to let her.

Her hand replaced his, cool and soft. For a moment she fondled, exploring the lines, tracing a path to his balls and then back again.

He needed her mouth. He was going to come soon, and he wanted in her mouth, wanted to be deep with her lips circling the base, his balls resting on her chin.

As soon as she parted her lips to take him inside, he thrust hard and deep. She sighed around him, a sweet, breathy sound of satisfaction that sent shards of pleasure all the way to his toes.

It should be him making love to her. It should be him laying her down and kissing every inch of her body. But God, he needed her so bad. He'd missed this, missed their openness.

He'd never appreciated her until it was too late, and now he was determined to live every moment and never take her for granted again.

Fire started low in his pelvis. His balls tightened and his cock swelled until it felt like he'd split open at the seams. She was so in tune with his body. He loved that. She instinctively tightened her grip, giving him that extra pressure he needed.

Up and down she worked with her hand, hard and tight. She sucked him deep, hollowing her cheeks.

The world around him blurred. All he could process was the sensation of her hot, moist mouth wrapped all around his dick. It was heaven and hell all rolled into one.

"I'm going to come, baby," he warned. He even tried to pull away so he wouldn't spill into her mouth, but she wouldn't allow it.

She held him at the back of her throat and swallowed. It was all he could stand.

With a hoarse shout, he began coming. The first jet exploded from his cock, painful, nearly excruciating in intensity.

She swallowed rapidly and sucked him deeper, working her hand up and down.

He pulsed a second and a third time and then again. He threw back his head and closed his eyes as he strained forward. Both hands tangled in her hair, pulling her closer until he felt his balls brush over her chin.

He'd never come so hard and so much in his life.

When he regained his senses, he glanced down to see his hands buried in her hair. He immediately let go, worried he'd been too rough, but she remained where she was, perched on the edge of the couch, her mouth gently working him down from the most intense orgasm he'd ever experienced.

"That was amazing," he said breathlessly.

She pulled away, her hand still cupping him, and looked up at him, her eyes glowing with desire. Hell, maybe he hadn't lied about being able to get it up again so soon. If she kept looking at him with those temptress eyes, he'd be sporting wood the size of a tree trunk.

"Come here," he muttered as he reached down to hook his hands underneath her arms.

He pulled her up and into his arms. She hastily licked her lips, removing his semen from her mouth just before he crushed his lips to hers.

"It's my turn," he rasped as he nibbled at her plump lips.

Her entire mouth was cherry red and delectably swollen from the attention she'd given him. He was determined to give her every bit as much pleasure as she'd given him. He wanted her screaming his name when she came.

He reached down and slid his hands underneath the T-shirt, yanking impatiently. She stepped back and allowed him to pull it over her head.

All the air left his lungs when she stood before him in only a pair of plain white panties. How could she make a slip of cotton look so darn erotic?

His gaze traveled to her full breasts, and he couldn't resist the urge to palm them both, measuring the weight and size in his hands.

They were perfect. Like her. Soft and incredibly silky against his fingers. He brushed the pads of his thumbs over the swollen crests and watched in fascination as they puckered into taut peaks.

"Tell me you want me, Rachel. Tell me you need me," he begged softly.

She circled his neck with her arms and leaned into his body, her face upturned, her eyes shining with desire.

"I do need you, Ethan. So much. Love me, please."

He hugged her to him and let his hands glide down to the curve of her bottom. He loved touching her, loved how she reacted to the simplest of caresses.

He fondled the shapely globes then traced one finger up the cleft to the small of her back and chuckled when she shivered.

"You used to love it when I went all he-man and carried you off to my cave."

She made a soft humming sound that told him she wasn't at all opposed to the idea.

He nibbled at her ear and tongued the shell, knowing he'd get another full-body shiver out of her. She sagged against him and he grinned as he tasted the softness of her neck.

Reaching down, he hooked his arm underneath her knees and hoisted her up against his chest. She settled against him. A perfect fit. Like she'd never left. Like he'd never made her leave.

Hope beat so hard in his chest that he could feel each painful burst. Let this be it for them. He couldn't lose her again.

Laughter spilled from her lips, carefree and beautiful as he strode to the bedroom. When he got to the bed, he spun around with her in his arms, simply enjoying the joy in her eyes.

When they were both dizzy, he dropped her onto the bed, and she sprawled on her back, her eyes still laughing up at him.

"Ditch the underwear," he growled.

Giggling, she reached down with her thumbs but then stopped and stared mutinously up at him.

"If you want them off, you do it."

He raised one eyebrow and stood back, hands on his hips. "Getting saucy on me, wench?"

She stifled her laughter with one hand, but her shoulders shook and her breasts jiggled enticingly.

He crawled onto the bed and loomed over her on hands and knees. He planted one palm next to her side and reached with his other hand to slip his fingers into the waistband of her panties.

His patience gone, he pulled, working the delicate material over her hips until the soft flesh of her pussy filled his vision. He let her kick free of the underwear, and then he ran his fingers up the inside of her leg until the downy tuft of hair whispered over the tips.

With the pad of his thumb, he stroked over the plump folds. Her liquid heat surrounded his fingers as he delved beyond the soft lips. She arched and moaned, such a needy sound that sent a bolt of lightning straight up his dick.

Going up on his knees, he nudged her legs farther apart until the pink flesh glistened in the low light. He swallowed hard then lowered himself so he could lose himself in her sweetness.

"Ethan," she whispered as his mouth found her.

He lazily tongued her, taking his time and eliciting delicate little shivers with each lick. Her clit puckered and swelled against his lips. He circled it, leaving a wet trail as he worked it into a quivering, tight bud.

He hadn't forgotten how to pleasure her. He knew her body better than his own. He hadn't always been a selfish bastard, and now he reveled in reacquainting himself with all his favorite ways to please her.

One finger slipped inside her entrance. She gripped it, her muscles convulsing wetly. He withdrew, sucked the moisture from his finger and then probed her opening with his tongue.

She came off the bed, gasping his name. Her hips bucked upward, and her fingers curled into the sheets. Her chest heaved with each breath and her nipples were beaded into tight little knots.

"Come in my mouth just like I came in yours," he said hoarsely.

Her eyes glittered and her face was flushed with excitement and arousal. He lowered his head again and gently sucked her clit into his mouth. He held it between his lips and feathered his tongue over the tip with just enough force to make her squirm wildly.

Her legs trembled uncontrollably. She arched, all her muscles tensing against him. She was close, so close.

He sucked harder at her clit, taking care not to cross that delicate line between pain and pleasure. When she let out a cry, he quickly moved down, covered her opening with his mouth and sucked hard.

Her taste exploded on his tongue as her orgasm rolled like a force of nature through her body. She twisted and writhed underneath him, but he held her hips firmly as he drank every bit of her essence.

Silky and sweet like honeysuckle.

Before she completely came down, he spread her wider then moved up her body until his straining cock pressed urgently where his lips had just left.

He slipped inside, taking care not to hurt her. She took him with ease, and he glided over her swollen tissues, absorbing the sensation of her hot and wet around him.

Liquid heat. Velvet. Heaven.

Her legs came up and wrapped around him, holding him deep. He lowered himself over her, coming down like a blanket. She cradled him, taking his weight, and he lay there for a long moment just enjoying their connection.

Her hands traveled over his back, up to his shoulders and then to his neck, and cupped his jaw. She raised her mouth and crushed it to his.

Hot. Wild. Incredibly sweet. She held so much power, and he doubted she even realized it. He was hers. He belonged completely and utterly to her.

Lifting himself slightly off her, he adjusted his position and settled more comfortably between her thighs. She lifted her hips and he went deeper.

With a groan he withdrew and then thrust forward again.

She reached up and wrapped her arms around him. Her entire body was wrapped tightly around him. He sheltered her. It was just the way it should be.

"Ethan," she whispered again.

He'd never tire of hearing his name on her lips.

He drove into her, his senses blurring. She was here. In his arms. Safe.

Faster. Harder. She took everything he gave. Her fingers dug into his shoulders and her legs trembled around him.

She was so tight, so swollen around him. Liquidy satin. He was mindless.

"Rachel. Baby."

The words slipped from his lips as every muscle in his body went tense. His orgasm flashed, much faster and more intense than before. There was no long buildup, just an instant explosion, so vivid that he lost himself for several moments.

When he regained at least a semblance of consciousness, he looked down to see Rachel staring up at him with her heart in her eyes. His breath caught in his throat. Then she said it.

"I love you, Ethan."

Tears blurred his vision, sharp and stinging. He didn't have words. He couldn't have spoken if he'd wanted to. The knot in his throat threatened to choke him. He tried to breathe around it and found himself closed off.

"Oh God, baby. I love you too. So damn much."

He dropped his forehead to hers, and both their chests heaved against each other as they tried to catch up.

After several seconds, he wondered if he'd dreamed it, if his need to hear it had manifested itself in fantasy.

"Say it again," he choked out.

Her eyes went soft, and she framed his face with her hands. For a moment she idly stroked the contours of his jaw and stared up at him with so much emotion reflected in her gaze.

"I love you. I love you so much, Ethan. I may not remember everything, but if feels right. We feel right. I'm as sure of this as I am of anything."

A tear splashed onto her cheek. He hadn't even felt it fall. His breath simmered in and out as he tried to hold in the emotion. It was like a dam breaking, though. He simply gathered her in his arms, their bodies still joined, and held on for dear life.

CHAPTER 33

THE stench of death lay heavy in the air. Rio eased his hand up to halt his men and then signaled them to fan out and circle. His gut was screaming that this wasn't right. Any of it.

The air smelled of blood. Fresh blood. His nostrils flared and quivered as he took position in a dense snarl of plants. He blended seamlessly into his environment, more of a chameleon than a human. With slow, careful movements, he sighted his rifle on the encampment below and did a sweep.

He mentally crossed himself. Sweet Jesus, Mary and Joseph but it was a brutal sight, and he'd pretty much seen all there was to see when it came to death and murder.

What he saw wasn't an efficient kill zone. It was a message. A bloody one. Bodies were spread out over the area like litter at a campsite.

Whoever had performed the massacre had been gone at least twelve hours. Rio could detect no movement, no sign of life from the silent village. But he wouldn't take any chances with his men until they knew for certain the area was clear.

Patiently he waited and watched. Even the carrion hadn't found the fresh bodies yet, and in the jungle, scavenging was sometimes the difference between life and death.

He carefully moved from his cover and let out a low call to

his men to converge on the camp. They came in a tight circumference, their rifles up, their gazes cautiously skirting left and right for the slightest warning they weren't alone.

Dead men didn't make any sounds, and all that was left here was the dead.

Rio stepped over two bodies on the edge of the clearing where the huts began and the jungle gave way to the encampment. Rachel Kelly had been held for a year in just such a place as this. Anger blazed through his veins. It was no place for a woman. There was no telling what the animals had done to her.

He noted with grim satisfaction that the assholes had been spared no quarter. Poor bastards probably never knew what hit them. Whoever had performed the hit had come in with firepower to rival an army.

Terrence stepped into the center of the village and looked toward Rio. Then he signaled the all clear. One by one, his men pushed out of the jungle, their expressions hard as they studied the carnage.

"Somebody did our work for us, I see," Terrence said as Rio approached him.

"Dead men don't talk, though," Rio said in disgust.

Terrence nodded. "Could be why they were killed."

"It's highly coincidental that within days of our guys here setting up a new camp after the old one was destroyed in Rachel's rescue, someone comes through here and takes out the entire village, and I don't believe in coincidence."

"Yep, too convenient if you ask me," Terrence agreed. "Whoever did this didn't want any loose ends, that's for damn sure."

Rio scowled. Sam wasn't going to be happy. Hell, *he* wasn't happy. He'd been looking forward to kicking some cartel ass. Using women in war was for pantywaists. It would have been fun to see if the assholes would feel so tough when they weren't up against a defenseless woman.

He glanced around as his men carefully picked their way through the field of bodies. What the hell was being covered up here? Rachel's "death" had been carefully orchestrated. She'd been cut off from her family and held in a godforsaken shit-hole just like this one. Why? None of it made sense, and now someone had gone to a hell of a lot of trouble to make sure no questions were answered.

"So what now?" Terrence asked as he looked around at the bodies strewn left and right.

"I sure as hell ain't burying them," Rio muttered. "And I sure ain't saying any Hail Marys. Let them burn in hell."

He broke off when a low sound carried on the wind from just a few feet away. Rio and Terrence hauled their rifles up and pointed in the direction of one of the "dead" men. Only he wasn't dead.

"He's still breathing," Terrence muttered.

Rio rushed over, and after making sure he wasn't walking into a suicide trap, he lowered to one knee beside the grievously injured man.

"Habla Español?" Rio demanded.

The man's eyes opened to narrow slits. "English," he whispered. "I speak English."

Rio and Terrence exchanged glances. What the fuck was an American doing mixed up in the Colombian drug cartel?

The man coughed, and a stream of blood spattered out of his mouth. He focused his glassy gaze on Rio. "I don't have much time." Each word seemed pulled from him with excruciating precision. His breathing was so labored that his chest rose and fell dramatically. "I tried to help her. I protected her as much as I could. Can't choose one person over the good of the mission. You know that. You're a soldier."

"What the fuck are you saying?" Rio snarled. "You're some kind of goddamn government agent and you sat by while Rachel Kelly was tortured and held captive for a year?"

The man closed his eyes and more blood trickled from the corner of his mouth. "Had no choice. I did what I could. Drugging her was the kindest thing they could do to her. I sent information to her family in hopes they'd come for her."

"Yeah, well, they did," Rio bit out. "You picked the wrong woman to fuck with." His gaze swept over the destroyed village and at all the bodies on the ground. "Who did this? It wasn't us."

The man shook his head. "He knows. Has to know by now. He wouldn't have allowed anyone he struck the bargain with to live." He closed his eyes and made a peculiar choking sound.

"Who knows?" Rio demanded. He shook the man's shoulder to get him back to consciousness "Who was behind all of this?"

The man's eyes flickered open once more. "She isn't safe. He'll go after her next."

Then his eyes went blank and his head lolled to the side, his gaze fixed in death.

"Shit," Terrence bit out. "That told us absolutely nothing."

Rio rose to his feet and frowned. He didn't like any of this. "Let's get the fuck out of here so I can report back to Sam."

"Steele will be disappointed," Terrence said with a wry grin. "It already pissed him off that we wouldn't wait for him to go in."

"Fuck Steele. He doesn't run my team. He needs to take care of his injured instead of worrying about what we're doing."

"Do we tell him now so he doesn't make the trip, or do we let him get over here before we let him know the mission is an abort?"

Rio grinned as he and Terrence exchanged sly looks. Pissing Steele off was about the most amusement they got these days.

"Gather everyone up and let's make tracks. I don't want to be here in case whoever bloodied the jungle decides to come back."

Terrence's hand went into the air, but he wore a slight smile. Nothing had been decided about Steele, but they both knew they'd let him come in hot and then take the wind out of his sails.

They took their fun where they could get it.

CHAPTER 34

THE dream tormented her. It was more vivid this time. More real. Even though she was still ensconced in the scene unrolling before her, she fought, not wanting to relive the nightmare all over again.

Ethan stood in their living room. His face was drawn into harsh, angry lines. He was shouting and she stood, stunned, all the fight gone.

Then he turned to the bookshelf. Her bookshelf that housed countless volumes of literature, her teaching manuals, her romance novels that she so loved. He pulled a sheaf of papers from between two of the books and shoved them at her.

They had significance, but what?

She could feel herself breaking. Could feel the despair that swamped her.

She roused herself from sleep and sat up in bed, her heart beating wildly. She glanced down to see Ethan still sleeping solidly beside her, and she put her hand on his arm to reassure herself.

Still, the sick feeling inside her festered. Why was she having these dreams? Was she so insecure that her fears of losing him had inserted themselves into her subconscious?

Or were they memories?

The thought slammed into her with painful intensity. Sure, she remembered more of her life every day. Little things. Bits and pieces that eventually formed the whole puzzle.

She rolled out of bed, nausea forming in her belly. Ethan loved her. She loved him. He hadn't given her any reason to believe differently.

Chill bumps raced up her bare legs, and she hastily pulled on a pair of sweatpants and grabbed another of Ethan's T-shirts from his drawer.

The bookshelf. Surely that would prove whether or not this was all some bad nightmare or if it was in fact an elusive memory.

God, maybe she really was cracking up. She could blame it on the stress of her accident. She was having paranoid delusions. First someone was out to kill her, and now her husband was hiding mysterious documents in between books.

She walked into the dark living room and stared fearfully at the bookshelves. How on earth was she supposed to know where, between what books? She had six bookcases and more books than she could shake a stick at.

She switched on the lamp at the desk and then stared at the books. She closed her eyes and tried to recall the dream. He was standing between two and in front of one, so the one in the middle. Which side?

Encyclopedias. Shoulder level for him so a bit taller for her.

She crossed the room and rose up on tiptoe to pull out one of the encyclopedias. Surprise, surprise, nothing there. She went down the row, feeling more like an idiot with each volume she pulled out.

She was ready to give up when she got to the third from the last and a set of folded papers fell onto the floor when she yanked the book out.

Her heart plummeted and she stared down at then like they were some hideous creature about to take her leg off.

Carefully, she reshelved the encyclopedia and stepped back, still staring down. Squatting down, she picked up the papers and walked back over to the desk so she could see in the lamplight.

She unfolded the papers, and at first couldn't make sense of what they were. They were legal documents, that much she knew. It wasn't until she'd read the first page three times that it sunk in.

Shock hit her with the force of a speeding train. Divorce. Ethan had filed for divorce.

She put one hand over her stomach as nausea bubbled and boiled deep in her belly. Oh God.

She closed her eyes as bits and pieces of that awful day came back to her. So much of it was still fuzzy, but she couldn't get Ethan's furious face out of her head.

He hated her. He wanted out of their marriage. God, some of the things he accused her of.

Her hand flew to her mouth. He'd accused her of having an affair with Garrett. Was any of it true? God, she couldn't remember!

She sank into the chair at the desk and buried her face in her hands as more of that day bombarded her. Ethan said he was tired of living this way. He hadn't wanted her to go on her mercy mission to South America. He'd told her there was plenty to fix right here at home so why was she going off to some shit-hole on some do-gooder mission?

It was more than that. His kind of unhappiness didn't happen overnight, and she could remember her own misery, the feeling that no matter what she did, she'd never make it right. That there was no hope for their marriage. And yet it destroyed her when he pulled out those papers.

He hated her. He didn't love her anymore. And then she'd died. Had he been glad? Why the big farce now? Did he feel guilty?

His family didn't know. The thought popped into her head. She remembered how trapped she felt because she didn't feel like she could go to his family; she'd die before allowing them to know the extent of her marital problems. Ethan wouldn't have gone to them either, so they wouldn't have known how awful things were.

Oh God, so was that why he was now acting like she was the love of his life? Why? God, *why*?

There was too much she didn't know, that she needed to know. She had to get out of this house before she screamed the walls down.

Garrett. He'd always been there for her. Always. But had they betrayed Ethan? No. It wasn't possible. She'd loved Ethan. Had been devastated when he asked for a divorce—no, *demanded* a divorce.

But Garrett would know. He'd have some of the answers. The time for her to be silent and keep everything to herself was over. She had no one else. Only Ethan, and now she knew she didn't even have him.

She choked back a sob as she got up. Garrett had left keys to his truck on the kitchen table. Sam had come to pick him up so she and Ethan would have transportation until they replaced Ethan's truck.

It was impossibly dark outside when she hurried out to Garrett's truck. She hadn't bothered to check the time, and now as she drove toward the same bridge she'd nearly gone off of earlier, panic gripped her.

Her palms were slick with sweat, and her breathing was so shallow she felt light-headed. As she approached, she slowed and almost pulled over to the side. She had a cell phone. Garrett's number was programmed. He could come get her.

With a snarl of disgust, she stepped on the accelerator and barreled over the bridge. She kept to the far inside lane and didn't spare a glance at all the police tape and the barricades erected around the gaping hole.

"No one can save you now but you," she chanted to herself. Maybe if she said it often enough it would sink in.

Ten minutes later, she pulled into the gravel drive of Sam's lake house and parked Garrett's truck beside Sam's. With Donovan taking off so late—or early—they probably hadn't gotten much sleep—if any—and now she was barging in.

She searched her tattered memories for some idea that she was mistaken about her relationship with Garrett, but all she could come up with was the sense of a close friendship.

At the door, she hesitated and spent several long seconds working up her courage. She rubbed damp palms down her sweatpants and mentally chided herself for being such a wimp.

With shaking hands, she knocked and then rolled her eyes. Like they'd hear that? She pressed the doorbell several times instead and waited, anxiety eating a hole in her stomach.

The door yanked open, and she instinctively took a step back as she stared warily at Sam. He wore gym shorts, no shirt, and he had a scowl that made her swallow.

The scowl disappeared when he stared back at her. Worry instantly replaced his irritation, and he too took a step back as if to not seem more threatening.

"Rachel? Honey, is everything okay?"

She would not cry. Would. Not. Cry. She made painful facial contortions to maintain her composure as she stared back at him.

"I need to see Garrett," she said haltingly.

Sam opened the door wider then reached for her arm. "I'll get him. Come in and have a seat. Where's Ethan? Is there something wrong?"

Again the threat of tears nearly undid her. She expelled her breath in halting jerks, and she bit into her bottom lip as she followed him inside.

"Ethan is at home," she said softly. "He's fine."

Sam's sharp gaze flickered over her, and it was obvious he didn't miss that she'd left herself out of the "okay" equation. He motioned for her to sit on the couch, but she couldn't. She'd go crazy.

He left the room, and just a few moments later, Garrett came barreling into the living room, his hair mussed, concern creasing his forehead. Sam followed behind now wearing a shirt and a pair of jeans.

No longer able to control the tide of emotion, she launched herself at Garrett and buried her face in his chest. Tears seeped into his shirt and she held on as all the anguish she'd tried so hard to keep in spilled out.

"Hey, what's wrong, sweet pea?"

He wrapped his arms around her and held her as he stroked a hand through her hair. After his first question, he didn't say anything. He just waited as she wept all over him.

When she finally got control of herself and the sobbing had been reduced to sniffles, he carefully pulled her away and tilted her chin up so she looked at him.

"What's wrong, Rachel? Can you sit down and tell me about it? Where the hell is Ethan?"

At Ethan's name, she closed her eyes and blinked back more tears.

"Ah shit," Sam muttered from behind them. "Tell me that bonehead hasn't done something stupid."

She let Garrett guide her over to the couch and sit her down. He settled beside her, perched on the edge and turned in her direction. She gripped his hands, afraid to let go, afraid that she'd break down again and she'd never get any of her questions answered.

"Do you want something to drink?" Garrett asked.

She shook her head and licked her lips, wondering how on earth she was going to broach this subject with him. She took a deep breath and raised her gaze to meet Garrett's.

"I need to ask you something," she asked painfully. "I need the truth."

He brushed his hand over her cheek and then tucked a strand of hair behind her ear. "Anything."

She swallowed and then put it out there. "Did we—did you and I—ever have an . . . affair?"

Garrett's eyes went wide with shock. Sam made an exclamation, but she focused solely on Garrett. If his reaction was any indication, she was way, way off base, and now she felt like the worst sort of idiot.

"God no," he exclaimed. "Why on earth would you ask a question like that? Sweet pea, tell me you haven't been torturing yourself thinking that you betrayed Ethan or that we betrayed him. Hell. You haven't, have you?"

"He thought we did," she whispered.

"Who?"

"Ethan."

Garrett's mouth dropped open. He and Sam exchanged bewildered looks. Sam flopped onto the recliner catty-corner to the couch.

"Okay, you have to back up, sweet pea. Because I'm not getting any of this. Ethan thinks you and I had an affair?"

"He wanted a divorce. He demanded one," she said painfully.

"Holy fuck," Garrett hissed. "Has he lost his goddamn mind? He said all this tonight? After you almost went over a fucking bridge?"

Garrett's face was getting redder by the minute. He looked like he was about to explode, and she rushed to diffuse the situation.

"I'm explaining this badly. No, not tonight. Oh God, Garrett. I think I'm losing my mind."

Sam leaned forward, his voice soft and even. "Take your time, honey. Back up and tell us everything."

She dragged a hand through her hair. She was so tired. Just hours before she'd felt like she could conquer the world. She'd been happy. She'd been secure in Ethan's love. Finally she'd thought her life was back on track, and now everything was so messed up.

"Were we happy?" she asked. "Did you think Ethan and I were happy? I mean before I died."

Neither answered, and maybe they thought it was a rhetorical question. She sighed and continued on.

"I've been having these dreams. Nightmares really. In all of them Ethan is angry. So angry. He's shouting. I'm bewildered and feel helpless. I wondered if my insecurities were just manifesting themselves in my dreams because Ethan has been so perfect since he rescued me. Everything has been so . . . perfect. I've wanted to tell him I love him, but the thought always terrified me. Something always held me back. Tonight, though, I finally told him, and he was so overcome. And then I went to sleep and had the most horrible nightmare again."

"What is your nightmare?" Sam asked gently.

"More shouting. More anger. The knowledge that he hates me. He was shoving these papers at me."

Remembering that she'd stuck them into the waistband of her sweatpants, she pulled them out now and held them in trembling hands.

"I got up to look for them because in the dream it felt like my world was coming to an end when I saw them. Now I know why."

"What are they?" Garrett asked quietly.

Tentatively she held them out and he took them from her. Sam got up to switch on the lamp, and she blinked at the sudden wash of light.

Garrett stared at the papers in disbelief while Sam read over his shoulder with a similar look of incredulity.

Garrett looked back up at her. "These are dated before . . . before you left. What the hell?"

"Am I living a lie, Garrett? He said some terrible things before I left. I don't remember everything. God, I wish I did. I only have bits and pieces, but he was so angry. He wanted out. He accused me of having an affair with *you*."

"Holy fuck," Sam muttered.

Garrett was still gaping at her like he couldn't wrap his brain around the accusation.

"Jesus, no. We never had an affair, Rachel. I swear it. It wasn't even a thought. Shit, you're like my little sister. And it was always Ethan for you. Since the day you two met there was never anyone else for you. It was the same for him, or at least I thought so."

"I don't know what to do." She hated the miserable, helpless feeling those words evoked. "He threw those papers at me the day I left for South America. I left with the knowledge that my marriage was over. And now a year later he loves me? None of that ever happened? How am I supposed to reconcile the two versions of our marriage?"

Sam sat down on the other side of her and put his palms against his temples.

"Obviously there is a lot I didn't know—that we all didn't know—about what was going on with you and Ethan before you left, but honey, it nearly destroyed him when he thought you died. That was not a man who didn't love you anymore and who wanted out of his marriage. He grieved the entire year you were gone. The only sign of life we saw from him was the day he got that package telling him you were alive. You were his sole focus after that. Getting you back."

She held her hands up in confusion. "I don't know what to do. I know now that I never went to any of his family with our problems. I wouldn't have done that. I shouldn't be here now, but I had to know if I'd somehow betrayed him."

Garrett's hand closed around hers. "You can always, *always* come to me, sweet pea. Ethan is my brother. I love him. But you're family too. He doesn't get a free pass just because he's a Kelly. I don't want you to ever feel like you're alone."

She smiled tremulously and then silently cursed when more tears slid down her cheeks.

The phone rang, startling her. Sam reached over to answer it, and she could hear Ethan's worried demand even from a few feet away.

Sam looked over at her.

"She's here, Ethan. She's fine. Just upset. No, I don't think it's a good idea if you come over just yet. We'll bring her home if that's what she wants later."

Sam held the phone away from his ear and shook his head.

"He hung up already. Guess he'll figure out a way over here."

Rachel gripped Garrett's hand tighter.

"You don't have to talk to him right now," Garrett said.

"Sam and I can toss him out and make him go back home. You get to call the shots here, sweet pea. Okay? You don't have to do anything you're not comfortable with."

"No, I need to know. I can't go on like this. I need to reconcile the here and now with the past. Everything I've thought about my marriage since coming home is a lie."

She closed her eyes to the pain those words sent through her heart. The idea that she truly was alone frightened her. The idea that the husband she'd come to love all over again was nothing more than a façade had the power to kill her when a year in captivity hadn't. Had she survived the impossible only to come home and die a slow death as she watched her hopes and dreams wither?

Garrett pulled her into his arms and held her tight. He kissed the top of her head and murmured words she couldn't decipher close to her ear.

"Hell of a day," Sam muttered.

"All I can wonder now is whether it was a relief for him when he thought I died," she whispered against Garrett's chest.

"Shhh, sweet pea. That's crazy talk. I was there when they told him. I was there for your funeral. I've watched him become a shell of himself for the last year. And I watched him when he held you again for the first time. I don't know what happened before, but he loves you. He loves you."

"I often wondered what went through his head when he came home after your miscarriage and found Garrett staying at the house with you. At the time I thought he was dealing with guilt over not being here with you, but now I wonder if it wasn't jealousy. Or maybe it was a combination of both."

Rachel stiffened and drew away from Garrett to stare at Sam. "I lost a baby?"

Sam closed his eyes and cursed. "Christ, I'm sorry. I forget that you haven't remembered everything. I'm so sorry, honey. I wouldn't hurt you for anything."

Her mind was frighteningly numb and blank. To her it certainly appeared her life before her "death" was a complete and utter mess. Was it any wonder she'd blocked the entire thing from her mind? Oh, she knew she had the drugs to blame and that hers wasn't a case of hysterical amnesia in the clinical sense, but now in the face of the truth, any sane person would have wanted to forget.

She almost laughed. But she wasn't sane, was she? She felt precariously on the edge, much like being on that bridge just hours ago. Teetering, about to fall over, and with the sickening knowledge there was nothing she could do about it.

"Tell me," she said faintly.

"You miscarried while Ethan was away on a mission," Garrett said gruffly. "You were pretty sick afterward so I stayed with you at the house when you got out of the hospital. Ethan got home a week later. Soon after that he resigned his commission."

She managed a dry laugh. It was either that or sob hysterically. How much more pitiful could her life get? She'd imagined she had the perfect life and perfect marriage. Perfect family. Perfect everything. She couldn't have been further from the truth.

"I don't know what to do," she whispered.

A loud knock at the front door precluded any further discussion of her life or lack thereof, which was just as well. She was having the discussion with the wrong people.

Fear gripped her as she stared nervously at Sam and Garrett. Ethan was here. How could she face him knowing the truth? She wasn't sure she could bear to look at the love that always softened his features and know that none of it was real.

"You don't have to talk to him now," Sam said gently. "He won't get in here unless I let him. He can stay as long as you like. You can go back home. Just tell us what you want. We'll make it happen."

She smiled faintly. "I don't know why I was so afraid of you in the beginning. You've been nothing but kind to me."

He smiled back and reached over to squeeze her hand.

Garrett touched her hair, and she turned to see concern in his blue eyes. "What's it going to be, sweet pea? You want to talk to Ethan or you want us to make him go away?"

CHAPTER 35

ETHAN stood at his brother's front door simmering with impatience. It was locked or he'd already be inside, and if Sam didn't hurry the fuck up, Ethan was going to break it down.

He raised his fist to pound again when the door opened and Sam stood on the other side, his expression almost accusing.

"Where is she?" Ethan demanded as he shouldered past his brother.

"She's in the living room," Sam said stiffly. "With Garrett."

Sam seemed to be studying him as he spoke, but Ethan didn't care. He was frantic with worry over Rachel. As he walked by Sam, it looked like Sam wanted to say something to Ethan, but again, Ethan ignored his brother and focused on finding Rachel.

When he entered the living room, he saw Rachel huddled on the couch next to Garrett. It was obvious she was upset, and Garrett raised his head and sent Ethan a look that would have made a lesser man piss in his pants.

Jesus, what the hell was going on?

He dropped to his knee in front of Rachel and pried her hands away from Garrett's.

"Baby, what's wrong?" he asked softly. "What happened? I woke and you were gone. Do you have any idea how scared

I was? The truck was gone. You were gone. I had to call Sean and ask him to drive me over here."

She flinched away from him, withdrawing like she couldn't bear to touch him. He stared at her in shock.

Garrett got up and backed away until he stood close to Sam.

"Do you want us to stay, Rachel?" Garrett asked in a quiet voice.

Ethan looked between them, more confused than ever. Something was going on here that he himself was clueless over. A sick feeling settled into his stomach. Had she remembered everything?

Rachel shook her head. "No. But thank you."

"We'll be in the basement if you need anything," Sam said as he and Garrett turned to walk out of the living room.

"Rachel?" Ethan asked when they were alone.

The knot in his belly was growing larger with each passing second.

"I found this," she said as she thrust rumpled papers toward him.

He knew without looking what they were. He couldn't even bring himself to look into her eyes.

"Oh God."

Her hands shook as she continued to hold out the papers. "I kept having these dreams about you being angry, that you hated me."

"Shhh." He pressed a finger to her lips and shook his head. "God no. Never hated you, baby. Never."

She shook him off and stared down at the papers. "These say you did. Or at least that you didn't love me anymore. That you thought our marriage was over and you wanted out. God, you didn't even try to get rid of them. You left them in the same place I saw them before I left a year ago."

What could he say? He had no defense for all the pain he'd put her through.

"I left them there because I wanted to be able to tear them up in front of you. To beg you for another chance. A chance I never got."

"Talk to me, Ethan," she begged. "I need to know. More than the divorce papers. This isn't the sole source of our problems. I don't remember everything. Just pieces here and there.

I didn't even know I'd lost a baby until Sam told me tonight. Or that you quit the SEALs right after. I need to understand what happened."

He staggered back, his gut boiling. He wasn't prepared. He'd lived with the knowledge every second of every day that she'd eventually remember and that he'd have to explain, but he still wasn't ready. He wasn't ready to face the prospect of losing her when he'd only just gotten her back.

He took a deep breath to steady his fried nerves. This was important. This was his life. He couldn't—wouldn't—lie to her no matter how bad it made him look.

"You were so excited when you found out you were pregnant," he said, smiling as he remembered just *how* excited she'd been. "I was gone a lot, and I worried I wouldn't be there when you gave birth. Garrett said he'd step in, no problem. I should have been grateful, but I was jealous and resentful.

"And then you miscarried while I was in parts unknown. I didn't even know about it until my team surfaced. Sam had been trying to reach me. I felt so guilty because I knew how much you wanted our child. I felt guilty because I wasn't there when you needed me the most, that you had to go through it alone."

He glanced back at Rachel, who still sat on the couch, her arms clutched around her slim waist. Her eyes haunted him. There was so much pain—and confusion—as she tried to filter through what she could remember versus what he was telling her.

"So I came home and there was Garrett. Garrett the rock. Garrett who'd been with you the entire time. I was furious—mostly with myself—and insanely jealous. I was also angry and grieving for our baby, and I lashed out at you. God, if I could take it all back."

He ran a hand through his hair and gripped the back of his neck as he turned away from her again.

"I resigned my commission because I knew I'd failed you. You never asked me to. You never would have. You knew how much the Navy meant to me. But I quit anyway and I hated it. Hated being home. Hated not knowing what the hell I was going to do with the rest of my life. Hated looking like a failure to my family and my wife.

"I resented you even though I knew, I knew deep down that it wasn't your fault. It wasn't your choice. It was mine, but I resented the hell out of you, and I started to blame you. I was my own worst enemy and I was destroying our marriage and your love, and that only made me angrier."

A sound of pain escaped Rachel's tightly pressed lips. She looked as though he'd struck her. He wanted none of it to be true. He wanted never to have hurt her, but he wouldn't lie to her now. It was like poison in the very heart of his soul, and he had to get rid of it. All of it.

"I shot you down at every opportunity. You tried. God, you tried. You loved me and I shit on it because I was eaten alive inside with resentment and my own personal unhappiness. I didn't want to hear *I love you* from your lips, but the moment you stopped saying it, I resented you even more. I was the worst sort of ass, and I finally decided that the least I could do for you was to set you free. Noble, huh?"

He threw up his hands in disgust and turned back around. The agony on her face made him want to puke. He wanted to touch her, to hold her, but he was afraid to, because if she rejected him now, he was lost.

"I was too much of a coward to just man up and tell you that I was unhappy with my decision. You would have supported me. I know you would have. So I made you miserable and then threw the divorce papers at you. I'll never forget the look on your face, Rachel. It's eaten me up for the last year. You walked away thinking I hated you and that I wanted out of our marriage, and I never got to make things right between us."

She stood shakily, her hand going down to the edge of the couch to steady herself on the way up. Her face was pale, her eyes huge. She looked . . . devastated.

She licked her lips and briefly looked away as if gathering her courage. Ironic, since she was the only one between them who had the strength and courage of a warrior.

When she looked back at him, the emotion in her gaze hit him square in the gut. Tears swam over her dark brown eyes and slid silently down her cheeks.

"Do you want out, Ethan? Is that guilt that's eating you why you're with me now? Because you feel responsible for what happened and that the last words you said to me were about wanting a divorce? Did you *want* me to find those papers?"

No longer able to stand apart from her, he crossed the room and gathered her in his arms.

"No, baby. God, no. Never. I didn't want out then. I don't want out now. I love you. I made mistakes. Mistakes that cost me everything. The moment you walked out that door, I knew I'd made the biggest mistake of my life. I spent the entire week you were gone planning the right things to say to you when you got back home. I was prepared to beg. To do whatever I had to do to make you stay and to show you I loved you.

"And then I got the news that you'd died."

His voice cracked, and he couldn't go on anymore. Even saying the words brought back the reality of that day. Of feeling like the entire world had dropped from beneath him. He never wanted to go back there.

"I'm so sorry, baby. I'm so sorry I hurt you. I'm sorry I couldn't be the man you needed then or now. At first I kept the papers because I wanted to tear them up when you got back. But then when I was told you died, I kept them as a reminder of all I'd lost and that the fault was mine and mine alone. When I discovered you were alive, they were the very last thing on my mind. I totally forgot I'd left them there."

He slowly drew away, needing to see her. He touched her face, smoothing the red tear blotches against her pale skin.

"I love you," he whispered.

Hot tears spilled over his fingertips, and he whisked them away, his soul hurting with each one that slithered down her cheek.

"I need to know that you're with me now because you love me and not because you feel obligated to right some past wrong," she choked out. "I can't live thinking you feel trapped because your dead wife came back from the grave. I can't live thinking I've been given everything I've prayed for the last year when it's not real. It's hell and not heaven."

He kissed her forehead and then her nose. Then both of her eyelids. He kissed the damp trails away from her cheeks and finally pressed a gentle kiss to her quivering mouth.

"The day I learned you were alive was the single greatest day of my life. For whatever reason, God gave me a second chance. He gave *us* a second chance. I don't deserve it, but I want it more than I want to live. I want to spend the rest of my life proving to you that you can trust me this time, Rachel."

She looked at him with such hope and devastation that it broke his heart.

He grasped both her hands and brought them up to his chest to lie over his heart.

"I don't expect us to have it all worked out in a day or even a month. You have a lot to remember. I have a lot of trust to rebuild between us. Will you at least come home with me so we can talk about this some more? Please, Rachel. Come home with me. Give me this much. I know I don't deserve it, but at this point I'm begging."

She hesitated, staring back at him with tortured eyes. He'd sworn he never wanted to see such anguish in her face again, like the day she walked away when he'd told he wanted a divorce. And yet now, it was ten times worse. She was infinitely fragile and so utterly destroyed that he feared she may never trust him again. What if he lost her? What if after the miracle of getting her back, he lost her after all?

"I'm scared," she said in a hoarse, heart-wrenching voice. "I'm sick at heart."

She pulled her hands away from his chest and turned away from him. The seeming rejection knotted his stomach. This was how she felt. The day he told her it was over. This was how she had to have felt. Like the world was coming down around her and there wasn't a damn thing she could do.

It hurt him that he'd hurt her—had hurt her for so long. If he could protect her from those memories, he'd do it in a heartbeat, but God, he couldn't. His time was up.

He reached out to touch her hair and then let his hand drift down to her shoulder. She flinched but he didn't draw away. He couldn't. He didn't want any distance between them. He couldn't accept that he could possibly lose her after getting back everything he'd ever wanted.

"Rachel," he whispered. "Look at me please."

For a long moment, she hesitated, and then she finally turned, her eyes lowered at first. He rubbed his thumb over her jaw and to her chin until she raised her gaze to meet his.

"I love you. I want you. I want us."

She swallowed and raised a shaking hand to wipe at the corner of her eye. "I want that too, Ethan. But only if it's real."

"Then come home with me."

She stared back at him, her heart so vibrant in her eyes. Finally she nodded her agreement, and his chest caved in with relief. At least she wasn't refusing to speak to him.

"Let me tell Sam and Garrett that I'm taking you home, so they won't worry." He raised one of her hands to his mouth and kissed her open palm. "Be right back, baby."

Ethan hurried down to the basement and stuck his head in the door. He didn't want a confrontation with his brothers, especially Garrett. It was bad enough Van knew about Ethan's fuck-ups, but now that Sam and Garrett also knew, it made Ethan feel like an even bigger ass.

Sam and Garrett both put away the files they were studying and surveyed Ethan with open curiosity.

"Just wanted to tell you that I'm taking Rachel back to the house."

Garrett frowned. "Does she want to go?"

Ethan sucked in a breath through his nose. He had no right to get angry when Garrett was just looking out for Rachel. Just like he always had, but Ethan had been too stupid and insecure to know it.

"Yeah. We need to talk. Things have changed. I fucked up." He looked directly at his brothers. "I can't lose her."

Sympathy simmered in Sam's expression, and Garrett might have softened an iota. It was hard to tell around his scowl.

"Good luck, man," Sam said.

Ethan backed out of the basement and hurried up to where Rachel waited. He held out his hand to her and waited for her to take it.

Tentatively she slid her fingers over his palm. For a moment he savored that small amount of trust, and he silently swore never to abuse that trust again.

It was still pitch-black outside, and he checked his watch. Two in the morning. Hell, they should both still be in bed, him wrapped as tight around her as he could go.

He ushered her into the truck and then got in. Quiet descended as he drove away from Sam's house, and he was loath to disrupt the silence. He much preferred any conversation to take place at home when he could hold her in his arms.

The winding road that paralleled the lake was dark as hell at night. He slowed when he saw a car stopped at the intersection ahead. As they started to drive past, Ethan reached over and slid his fingers through Rachel's.

Headlights seared through his periphery. What the hell?

Jerk was bright-lighting them. Then he saw the lights coming directly at them.

Ethan slammed on the brakes and jerked the wheel in an effort to avoid the SUV, but it slammed into the driver's side and shoved Garrett's truck all the way across the road into the ditch.

Pain exploded in his head, and he vaguely registered the smell of blood before all went black.

CHAPTER 36

THE impact nearly jarred Rachel's teeth loose. She slammed against her door and cried out as pain lanced up her arm. The truck rocked to a halt, and she sat trying to make sense of it all.

Ethan.

She turned in the seat and cried out again when her arm screamed in protest.

"Ethan," she said hoarsely. "Ethan!"

He didn't move. He was slumped against the steering wheel, shoved over by the side impact air bag. Blood ran down his forehead, and she stared in horror when he didn't stir.

"Ethan, wake up. Oh my God, Ethan."

The sound of creaking metal jerked her around in her seat just as her door was peeled open.

"Oh thank God! My husband is hurt. We need an ambulance."

The man leaned in, grabbed her by the hair and hauled her out of the truck.

She screamed when he slammed her against his body, trapping her injured arm between them.

"What are you doing?" she yelled as he pulled her toward the road.

"You're a hard bitch to kill," he bit out.

Her brain short-circuited. It was too much shock for her to process. She looked frantically back at the smashed truck where Ethan was unconscious.

"Let me go!"

She kicked back and struggled, ignoring the searing pain that sliced through her body.

He reared back and slapped her hard across the face, knocking her to the ground. Then he yanked her up by her good arm and dragged her to a waiting vehicle.

Her face throbbed, and she struggled to comprehend what had happened, and why. He'd said she was hard to kill.

The bridge accident hadn't been an accident. She *knew* it hadn't been. But why? Why would someone want her dead?

The man threw her into the backseat, where another man sat waiting, and then he climbed into the driver's seat and roared down the highway.

"Who are you?" she demanded as she tried to shake the grip of the second man. "What do you want?"

The driver ignored her and picked up his cell phone. He punched a few buttons and then barked into the receiver.

"I've got her. Yeah, no mistakes this time. I'll make sure she never talks. No, I can't make it look like an accident this time. I tried that already. Bitch wouldn't die. I'll kill her and dispose of the body. No one will ever find her. It'll just be one of those unsolved crimes. Castle will be happy, and Tony and I will disappear to Mexico."

Castle. Castle. She knew that name. She cursed her shattered mind. Where did she know that name from?

Her arm screamed in pain and her head was about to explode. She raised her good hand to her temple and massaged, willing herself to remember. Beside her, goon number two kept close watch on her and finally grasped her wrist and wrenched her arm down to the seat.

"Let me go," she begged softly. "I won't say anything, I swear it. My husband's family can pay you. They can even fly you to Mexico. Just please let me go. This will kill them. They thought I was dead."

She knew she was babbling, but she was desperate. And scared out of her mind.

The driver laughed. "Yeah, you have a way of staying alive. I'm convinced you're a cat with nine lives. You should have died a year ago. You should have died on the bridge. I'd hoped to make it look like an accident, but a bullet is more expedient."

She was going to vomit. Between the pain and the panic, she was barely able to think.

"Why?" she croaked. "I've never done anything to anyone."

"Castle wants it. I don't question. He pays the bills so I do what he tells me."

The two men laughed as the car continued to barrel down the winding road she'd just driven down an hour earlier. They were going back by Sam's house. Had they followed her? How else would they have known where to find her?

She closed her eyes as despair fell over her. In the year she'd been held captive she'd never once accepted her death. She'd waited for Ethan, knowing that somehow, someway he'd find her. Now she had no such hope. There was no way for him to know what had happened to her. He might not even be alive.

A sense of calm descended, washing away the paralyzing fear and panic. Before, she'd waited for someone to save her. Now it was up to her to save herself.

No one can save you now but you.

Her own words drifted back to her. Said such a short time ago. How prophetic they'd turned out to be.

Ethan couldn't help her now. She had only herself.

She gathered the memories of Donovan and Garrett teaching her self-defense. How they'd despaired of her being too girly to ever learn anything. She'd shown them when she'd tossed them on their asses in a rage.

They'd laughed and called her too easy, and she'd refused to speak to them for a week. They'd eventually sucked up to her with chocolate and books.

She'd made them keep teaching her. With Ethan gone so much, she'd felt it important to be able to defend herself.

Hysterical laughter bubbled in her throat, and by sheer force of will, she kept it down and recovered the eerie calm of a moment ago.

She studied both men, the one in the front and the one with a bruising grip on her uninjured wrist. She was worried her right arm was broken, but what was a broken arm compared to a bullet in the head?

Suck it up, Rachel. It's not going to be easy, and it'll hurt like hell, but you're not going down without a fight.

The driver was short but very stocky in build. The asshole sitting beside her was tall, much taller than her, but he wasn't as bulky. She'd probably have more success at knocking him on his ass, but then the driver was the one wielding the gun.

Oh well, she'd die if she did nothing, so if she died trying to escape, the outcome was still the same. It amazed her how accepting she could be of her own death. Maybe it was because for the last year, she'd been dead.

They pulled onto a gravel road that led away from the lake, and the driver turned off the headlights, plunging the world around them into darkness. The moon wasn't even out and the overcast sky blotted out the stars.

What was she going to do? She needed a plan. Plan? Her only plan was to survive, however she could make that happen.

Again the driver pulled off the road they were on, this time onto a path that led back into the woods. She stifled a groan. Even if she managed to escape, she wouldn't have a clue where she was.

The car ground to a halt, and she braced herself for the agonizing pain that would come as soon as she moved. And the jackass wasn't gentle about hauling her out of the car.

She clamped her jaw shut, but an agonized groan still escaped when his hand circled her broken arm and yanked.

"Let's make this quick," the driver muttered. "Sooner we get the hell out of here, the better."

She saw the dull metal finish of the gun as he pulled it from his pocket. She only had seconds to act.

She was crazy, right? It was time to see just how crazy she was.

As soon as tall guy wrapped his hand around her arm to haul her into the trees, she cut loose with a yell to rival a banshee's. She kneed him in the groin, and ignoring the agony ripping through her arm, she stabbed him in the eyes. He rolled away shrieking like a girl, and she was careful to keep him between her and the guy with the gun.

Her foot hit a large rock, and she hit the ground, her hand grabbing at the dirt until she wrapped her fingers around the rock. The man aimed his gun at her and she let it fly. She hadn't played softball for eight years for nothing.

It hit him right in the head with deadly accuracy. He folded like a puppet, and she scrambled up, not wasting a second before fleeing into the woods.

The sound of bullets hitting the trees beside her spurred her on. Bastard was using a silencer so she had no idea how far back he was. It didn't matter. If he caught her, she was dead.

"ETHAN. Ethan!"

Ethan came awake in an instant, every instinct screaming at him that something was terribly wrong. He glanced around to see Sean shining a light in his face. He raised a hand to shield his eyes from the glare, and Sean lowered the light.

"Christ, you scared ten years off me. What the hell happened?" Sean demanded.

Rachel.

The realization slammed into him with the force of a freight train. He reached down and yanked at his seat belt. Sean grabbed him, yelling at him to stop.

"Goddamn it, Ethan, you need to wait for the ambulance. You shouldn't move. Don't know if you damaged your spine. Come on, cooperate with me."

"Rachel," Ethan rasped. "They have her."

He threw off Sean's arms and managed to get out of the seat belt. Christ, how was he going to get out? His entire side of the truck was caved in. The window was busted out, and Sean leaned through with his flashlight.

Ethan turned in the direction of the passenger seat. Where Rachel had been. The door was still open, but her seat was eerily empty.

Heaving himself up, he crawled across the center console and all but fell out of the passenger seat and onto the ground. Sean was around the truck in an instant, that damn flashlight beam bouncing across Ethan's face again.

"What about Rachel?" Sean demanded. "Was she with you?"

Ethan hauled himself to his feet and grabbed onto Sean's shoulder when he bobbled. Fuck. He didn't need this.

"Yeah. She was with me. Bastards took her. She was right, damn it. The accident on the bridge. Wasn't an accident. Those assholes were waiting for us when we left Sam's. They rammed us and took her."

"Holy mother of God," Sean whispered.

He immediately began barking orders into his radio. He broke off at one point and stared hard at Ethan.

"Tell me every thing you remember, Ethan. We need a starting point."

"I don't know," Ethan bit out. "It was dark. I saw them parked at the intersection of the highway. They turned on their brights and rammed us when we got close. The rest is fuzzy, but I remember Rachel screaming while some guy yanked her out of the truck by her hair."

"God help us," Sean muttered. "Okay, we're going to have to organize a wide search. They have a head start on us. I'll radio for the highways and secondary roads to be roadblocked. I'll contact the Henry Country Sheriff's Department and get them out looking."

"Give me a phone so I can call Sam and Garrett."

Sean tossed him a cell phone and he dialed Sam's number. His gut was churning like a volcano. Fear had him by the balls. Sean was talking fast in the background, his radio going off like a bullhorn. Ethan had to hand it to the younger man, he knew his shit, and right now he was glad as hell to have him to help find Rachel.

He closed his eyes as he waited for Sam to answer.

I'm coming, baby. Hold on. I'll get to you, I swear it. Just hang on. For me. For us.

Please God, don't take her now.

Someone wanted her dead. Her life depended on him and his brothers figuring it out yesterday. And God help the fuckers when Ethan found them.

SAM rubbed his hand wearily over his face. What a goddamn mess. He'd never suspected. Oh sure, he'd known Ethan could be a rigid son of a bitch, but he'd never dreamed his marriage to Rachel had been in so much trouble.

He stared over at Garrett, who wore a look of equal bafflement. Garrett looked up and simply shook his head.

"Me. And Rachel."

He shook his head again, as if he couldn't wrap his brain around the idea that someone had thought he was having an affair with his brother's wife.

"That's messed up," Garrett said.

Sam glanced at his watch. It was almost time for Rio to check in. No sense going back to bed now. He gestured at Garrett.

"Come on. Let's head to the war room. Rio will be checking

in soon, and you and I need to plan our trip over. Steele's probably already on his way. Against my wishes, I might add. Never can tell that son of a bitch anything. I don't know how he ever got through basic training. He doesn't take orders for shit."

"He got through because he's a goddamn machine," Garrett muttered.

He got up to follow Sam, and the two walked out the side door and trudged across the grass in the dark.

"You ever consider how ridiculous it is to carry the sat phone from the house to the war room in the middle of the night?" Garrett asked in an amused tone as Sam punched in the security codes to the door.

Sam glanced down and shrugged. They kept the phone on them at all times when their men were pulling a mission, but he'd prefer to take report here where he had access to all their equipment.

A few seconds later, the fluorescent tubes along the ceiling lit up and flooded the interior with light. Sam checked his watch again as he took a seat behind the computer.

Donovan would be landing in Texas in another half hour and would check in once he met his team. From there they'd take the short hop into Mexico for what was supposed to be a quick in-and-out extrication.

Sam yawned. "Might as well stay up for Van."

Garrett nodded as he studied the information Donovan had left behind.

"I should have pushed to go with him," Garrett said.

Sam leaned back in his chair and lifted an eyebrow in Garrett's direction. "Like you pushed to go with me into South America?"

"I gave in to Van because he could handle that mission with both hands tied behind his back. Your trip to South America with Rio is a whole other ball game, and you damn well know it."

Sam held his hands up in surrender. Garrett was getting all lathered up again, not that it took much.

The sat phone beeped, signaling an incoming call. Sam reached for the receiver.

"Sam here. Go ahead."

There was interference on the line that made Sam frown. Damn bad time to be out of position.

"Bad news, bossman," Rio drawled. "Someone got here behind us."

"What do you mean behind you?" Sam demanded.

"We tagged your boys, set up surveillance, did a recon several miles to the north to set up an entry point for you. When we returned, the entire village had been wiped. It was professional and it was bloody. Message sent, I'm thinking."

Sam's blood went cold. It was too pat. The timing too close to Rachel's accident on the bridge.

"Son of a bitch," he breathed as he sat forward in his seat. "Pull out and get your asses back home. Immediately."

"There's more. We found one guy alive. Said he tried to help Rachel. Protected her while she was in captivity."

"Protected her my ass," Sam snarled.

"He was working undercover. No sacrificing the mission for the good of one and all that bullshit. He was the one who sent Ethan all the info, hoping her family would mount a rescue."

"You'll pardon me if I don't offer him hero status," Sam said nastily.

"Wouldn't expect you to. Just relaying our findings. And, Sam, he said to be careful that he'd be after her next."

"Who?" Sam demanded.

Rio made a sound of disgust. "Bastard had the bad manners to die before we were through talking to him. Just wanted you to be aware of a possible threat to Rachel that still exists."

"Yeah, we know that now. Get your team the hell out of there. I don't want you in any cross fire or some fucking war between the cartel."

"You're the boss."

"And Rio . . . be careful."

Rio didn't answer and the line went dead.

"What the hell is going on?" Garrett demanded. The veins in his neck bulged, and his jaw was so tight Sam thought his teeth might pop out.

He briefly explained Rio's findings and then added his own suspicions about Rachel's accident.

Garrett leapt to his feet. "We have to go after her and Ethan. Son of a bitch, Sam, she said she'd been run off the bridge. She told us that and we blew her off."

Sick fear welled in Sam's stomach.

"I'll grab the keys."

They ran back to the house, and when they entered, the phone was ringing. And Sam knew . . . he knew it wasn't good news.

CHAPTER 37

HOLDING her broken arm tight to her chest to immobilize it, Rachel concentrated on making a wide circle through the woods. She was on the wrong side of the highway. She needed to head to the lake. No one would expect her to go for the dead end, right?

Her head spun, she wanted to stop and puke. Her sides were on fire and vicious pain shot through her arm with every step she took.

She blocked it all out. She pictured the lake and how wonderful it would feel. The coolness of the water. The soothing ripples. Escape. She had to make it to the lake.

Her feet pounded the ground. She tripped over countless rocks and roots, but she kept her footing. If she went down, she was a goner. That thought alone kept her on her feet and running.

Was she even running in the right direction? She wanted to stop to catch her breath, just for a moment, but she didn't dare. They could be right behind her.

No more shots had been fired, but how did she know they weren't stalking her, waiting for her to make a mistake?

After an hour of agonizing pain, losing one shoe and batter-

ing her one bare foot, she plunged out of the woods and fell over
the riverbank and down into the water below.

The cold was a shock, and she barely called back the scream
of pain when her broken arm took the brunt of the impact.
Water filled her nose and mouth, and she picked her head up
from the gurgling stream.

For a moment she lay gasping for breath. Then she heard
voices over the gentle lap of water. They were close. Oh God.

She heaved herself toward the steep bank, crawling desperately for the shelter of the overhang. It was her only chance to
remain out of sight, and she had to pray they didn't come down
to the water.

She huddled against the damp soil and mud and curled herself into the tightest, most inconspicuous ball she could. The
voices came closer now, and she heard the driver shout to the
other one to spread out.

Her breath caught and held when dirt rained down the bank
just in front of her. He was here. *Right above her.*

Sweat rolled down her neck. Her nose twitched uncontrollably. Every muscle in her body ached. She needed to move, to
shift, something, *anything.*

"Bitch must have doubled back. She couldn't have made it
across the water," the driver yelled to his partner.

Still she waited, frozen in fear, her heart pounding so hard
she worried it would give her away. For an eternity she sat there,
pain washing over her in waves.

Just as she started to cautiously shift her position, there was a
slight noise and a trickle of dirt spilled over the bank again. She
stared in horror, paralyzed by the mistake she'd almost made.
He'd been waiting for her. He suspected she was out there, he
just didn't know where. He'd laid the trap, and she'd damn near
fallen into it headfirst.

She closed her eyes, determined to outlast him. She wouldn't
move. She wouldn't breathe. Her life depended on it.

After an agonizing, interminable amount of time, she
stretched her legs, uncurling herself with extreme care. Her arm
was stiff and swollen, and she could barely move it.

No way did she want to go back into the woods. They were
waiting for her. They had the advantage.

The creek. All she had to do was go into the water and follow it to the lake. Hopefully she wasn't too far. The water was shallow here, but she knew there were deeper pools in places.

She crawled from beneath the protective overhang and carefully made her way back to the water's edge. Her instincts screamed at her to run, to barge into the water and wade as fast as she could downstream.

Instead she mustered all her strength and quietly slipped into the water. She waded to the middle, where it was deeper, and sank down, knowing it would be easier if she could let the current carry her. She was bone tired and in so much pain, she couldn't walk much farther.

Rocks slapped her and cut into her knees and feet. She bounced along the bottom and it took everything she had not to scream every time her arm was jostled.

In places, it shallowed so much that the water was only ankle deep, and she walked over the gravel bottom, too afraid of leaving prints if she got onto the muddy bank.

How long had she been gone? It seemed like hours, but the sky was still pitch-black, no sign of dawn to the east. The water got deeper again and she sank tiredly down, only too willing to float for a while.

She rounded a sharp corner and sucked in her breath when she saw the inky black expanse of the lake spread out before her.

It freaked her out, the idea of going into the lake in the dead of night. The river channel ran quite deep, more than thirty feet in the coves, and out in the middle of the main drag, it reached depths of more than fifty feet.

Still, it beat the alternative. Anything beat being shot because *Castle* wanted her dead. A man who nagged at her memory but remained cloaked in shadows.

Tiredly she pushed on, rolling to her back and kicking her feet to propel her farther into the lake.

She was fast coming off the adrenaline rush, and shock was setting in. She needed to get to a safe place fast before she passed out.

Turning over, she struck out with one arm, holding the other close to her body. She kicked strongly, but she knew she looked like a crippled tadpole moving erratically through the water.

She focused single-mindedly on the main stretch of lake, determined to make it, to put as much distance between her and her pursuers as possible.

Numb to her toes, staggered by exhaustion, she made her way out of the cove to where she could finally see down the lake. In the distance, the lights on the bridge twinkled at her, mocking her. She had to laugh. That damn bridge, the one that had nearly killed her, now marked an impossible distance for her to travel.

Sam's house was before that bridge. His property backed to the water's edge. Would she recognize his dock in the dark? How far from the bridge was his house? The bridge seemed an interminable distance.

Two inlets? Three? For that matter, which was she in now?

Water lapped up over her face, and she struggled to keep her head above water. She was holding on by a whisper-thin thread. It would be so much easier to just roll over and let the water take her.

Insidious voices whispered in her ear. Some of them mocked her, told her to give up like a wimp. Others told her to buck up. Her family had gone through much worse. Ethan and all his brothers had been shot, injured, defied impossible odds, and here she couldn't even manage a swim with a broken arm.

Ethan's SEAL brothers would laugh their asses off at her.

She needed a SEAL—or three—right now. Or at least she needed to channel one. This would be a walk in the park to them.

Oh God, she was getting delirious.

It bolstered her spirits to realize that while she'd been carrying on a ridiculous dialogue with herself she'd made good progress. At least one thing was working in her favor. She was moving with the current.

Her first plan of action would be to find Sam's house. Or any house. If that failed, she'd go for the bridge and pray she'd make it that far.

Too tired to attempt the motions of swimming, she turned on her back again and let the current take her along.

She kept her face turned toward the bank and scanned the shore, looking for anything that looked familiar. Lights beckoned in the distance. A house? Houses?

Clumsily she struck out toward the shore. As she got closer, the shape of a dock loomed in the darkness. Excitement took a little of her pain away. There weren't many docks because of TVA regulations on new construction. Sam had owned his house for years and had purchased it from someone who had been on the lake for two decades.

Her toes dragged along the bottom and she dug them in, straining to get closer to shore.

Two docks. Did Sam live next to someone who also had a dock?

She shook her head. It didn't matter if it was Sam's place or not. She only hoped whoever lived here was home.

She slipped below the surface when she tripped over a rock. Every single movement sent tears of agony coursing down her cheeks. Finally she gave up on standing and crawled through the shallower water toward the dock. With her good hand, she reached up to circle her arm around one of the wooden posts supporting the dock.

For several minutes, she leaned her forehead against the wood and sucked in painful, sharp breaths. Her broken arm sagged against her. It hurt with each movement, and she wanted to scream in pain and frustration.

Using the dock for support, she edged along the side until finally she was only ankle-deep in water. Each step took a ridiculous amount of will. Animal sounds of pain whispered past her lips. She hadn't realized it until the sounds grew louder.

She stopped at the bottom of the incline and looked up, straining to see in the darkness. This wasn't Sam's house, and there wasn't a single light on, inside or outside, to suggest anyone was home.

As she moved up the incline, her legs buckled and she went to her knees. Nausea rose sharp, swelling hard in her stomach until she gagged and heaved. Struggling to keep what little composure she had left, she planted her fist into the dirt and forced herself back to her feet.

She went to the back door and pounded with her uninjured hand. After a long wait, silence still abounded. No lights came on.

Giving up on that avenue, she trudged around the side of the house to the front door. She rang the bell and jiggled the handle. At this point she didn't care if anyone was home or not. She just needed a phone and a safe place to hide.

When the lock didn't budge and no one came to answer, she turned around, her eyes searching the dark. Mailbox. At least it would tell her where she was.

As fast as she was able, she walked to the end of the short driveway and peered at the side of the mailbox. Her heart accelerated. If the numbers were accurate, these were Sam's neighbors. His house was a half mile down the road.

With renewed vigor, she nearly ran down the shoddily paved road. Rocks and pieces of asphalt pierced the soles of her feet, but she ignored the discomfort. Next to the agony shooting down her arm, the rest was negligible.

When she reached Sam's mailbox, she nearly fainted on the spot. For a moment she leaned her hand on the metal box and gasped for breath. Tears stung her eyelids, and she closed her eyes as she struggled to find the strength to go on.

Lights were on in every room, it seemed. Were they home? She hurried to the front door and nearly wept in relief when she found it open.

"Sam! Garrett!" she yelled as she slammed the door shut.

Silence greeted her exclamation.

She went from room to room but found them empty. She had no idea how long it had been since she and Ethan had been forced off the road. Sam and Garrett were probably with him. Or looking for her.

Fear swamped her as she realized the men who'd hit them had obviously known where she and Ethan were. They'd followed them to Sam's and waited for them to leave. Which meant they could be back.

Panic billowing through her like a flash fire, she ran from room to room, turning off every light until the entire house was plunged into darkness.

A phone. She needed a phone.

In the kitchen she yanked the cordless phone off the charger and headed for the basement. There were lots of places she could hide that would buy her time if the men trying to kill her did come back.

When she found the darkest, smallest corner in the tiny closet that housed the hot water heater, she sank to the floor and dialed 911.

CHAPTER 38

THEY'D been through all the possible scenarios. Ethan, Sam and Garrett had coordinated with the local and state authorities, and then they'd broken away to fill the cracks. If there was anything at all the police were missing, the Kellys would find it.

The call came in an hour before dawn. An abandoned SUV with the front end caved in parked off one of the gravel roads off 232.

They converged on it from all directions, but it was obvious no one had been in it for a good while. The engine was completely cold, the doors open, and footprints led away into the woods.

Ethan swore and pounded his fist into the side of the truck. Garrett gripped his hand and pulled him away.

"Save it, man. Rachel needs you."

"It's time to go hunting," Sam murmured as he bent and shone his flashlight at the mishmash of footprints. "See this one? It's smaller than the others. I think she got away from them. They lead into the woods."

"What you got?" Sean asked as he approached after his survey of the area.

Sam pointed and related his theory. Sean nodded.

"I'll have my men spread out." He looked up at Ethan and eyed him with a steady gaze. "We won't give up until we find her."

Ethan nodded. "Thank you."

The brothers followed the footprints into the woods. At times they lost the trail, when the way became too rocky to register the imprint of a shoe. Then they'd pick it up several yards later. About a quarter mile from the SUV, they found a tennis shoe lying among the leaves and dirt.

Adrenaline surged in Ethan's veins. "It's Rachel's," he said hoarsely. He scraped the dirt from the sides and the sole with shaking hands. It was definitely hers. His mom had bought them on one of her many shopping trips for Rachel.

"She kept going," Garrett said.

Sam directed the flashlight beam along the path where the imprint of one tennis shoe and one bare foot led farther into the woods.

"Atta girl," Sam murmured.

They hurried forward, keeping the flashlights aimed at the ground as they followed the footprints.

Eventually they came to a stop at a riverbank. The soil was disturbed like someone had fallen, and the incline was eaten away.

Ethan slid down the embankment to study the area closer to the river's edge. There were distinct footprints, and closer to the overhang, there was a hollowed-out area that looked very much like someone had huddled there.

Rachel's prints ended here, but the larger boot prints circled and overlapped before finally paralleling the shore west.

His brothers scanned the area beside him with frowns on their faces.

"What do you make of it, Sam?" Garrett asked.

Sam stared at Ethan, and it infuriated him that Sam was holding back.

"Just say it," Ethan bit out. "We're wasting time."

"There are two possibilities," Sam said slowly. "The smaller prints lead here and none lead away. The boot prints arrive here and they leave again in the other direction. Either Rachel lost them here or they caught up to her here and she didn't leave on her own."

Ethan sucked in his breath. He might be looking at where

Rachel had died. He shook his head. Fuck no. He refused to believe that. If Rachel got away the first time, she could do it again. She was smart, and she was a fighter.

Garrett turned to survey the river.

"She could have gone into the water. She's listened in on enough of our powwows to have picked up any number of evasion tactics. Hell, we used to sit around drinking beer and telling combat stories. It's not out of the realm of possibility that she hit the water and stayed there so she wouldn't leave tracks."

Excitement curled in Ethan's stomach. He had to believe that. The alternative didn't bear thinking about.

"So we split up," Sam said. "I'll go upriver. You two head down. If she headed downriver, she would have hit the lake. I'll radio Sean and have a search party scour the riverbanks upriver and also search the lake for any sign of her. If she's out here, we'll find her."

Their radios crackled, and Sean's voice bled into the night air.

"Sam, you read me?"

Sam picked up his radio. Ethan gripped his, but held back the urge to demand if Sean had news.

"Yeah, I read you, go ahead," Sam replied.

"We just got a 911 call . . . from your house. Woman. Terrified. Babbling about men trying to kill her. Dispatch didn't get her name before the line went dead, but I'm betting it's Rachel. I'm on my way over now."

No longer able to keep silent, Ethan keyed the mic and stuck the radio to his mouth.

"We're on our way."

Before his brothers could react, Ethan whirled and sprinted back the way they'd come. His brothers followed close behind. They crashed through underbrush like a herd of elephants. Limbs and bushes slapped Ethan in the face, but he batted them aside and kept going.

When they got back to the wrecked SUV, there was no sign of Sean. Ethan wasn't waiting around. He jumped into Sam's truck and cranked the engine. He was already backing down the trail when his brothers jumped into the backseat.

"Son of a bitch, Ethan, are you trying to kill us?" Garrett yelled.

Sam leaned up over the front seat, and Ethan heard the click of a gun clip. "Calm your ass down and get us there in one piece. We won't do Rachel any good if we're wrapped around another goddamn tree."

"How the hell did she get back to your house?" Ethan demanded as he careened back onto the highway. "We found her footprints on the riverbank. They ended there."

"I'd say our girl got smart and headed downriver to the lake," Garrett said with a note of pride.

Ethan gripped the steering wheel and ignored the pounding in his head. Sean had slapped a haphazard bandage over his brow to stop the bleeding, and it currently felt like someone had taken a sledgehammer to his skull.

They made the drive in ten minutes, and probably set a new land speed record in the process. Ethan turned into the driveway damn near on two wheels and skidded to a halt, throwing gravel in all directions.

Sam opened his door and stumbled out. "Shit. House is completely dark. When we left after Sean called about your accident, we were in a hurry and damn near every light in the house was on."

Garrett slapped a Glock in against Ethan's stomach and gripped a second one in his hand as they hurried toward the front door.

"We do this smart," Sam warned. "No one goes in like a dumbass and gets himself shot. For all we know this is one big trap and those assholes are lying in wait. They might have even forced Rachel to make the call if they caught up to her and she didn't go into the water like we thought."

"Cut the chitchat and let's go," Ethan seethed. "I get it. We go in and clear the house."

"I'll go around back," Garrett said. "Wait fifteen seconds and we'll go in together. Stay low and quiet until we know what the fuck we're dealing with."

Sam held a finger to his lips then gestured for Ethan to move in as Garrett disappeared around the side of the house.

After what seemed like an interminable wait, Sam held up three fingers then reduced to two and finally one. Ethan reached for the knob and quietly turned it before easing the door open.

He went in, gun up, his eyes scanning the dark interior. Sam slipped in beside him and went to the left, leaving the right to Ethan.

Methodically they worked their way through the upper level. After the last bedroom had been searched, they met in the living room and crept toward the basement.

Ethan's pulse was about to thump out of his skin. He could feel every heartbeat. Each breath sounded like an explosion in the quiet room.

What the fuck?

He looked up at his brothers, who were positioned at two other points in the basement.

Nothing. No Rachel. No one.

A light sound came from the far corner. Light, almost like a small animal brushing against something.

The men tensed. Sam held up a finger to his lips and raised his gun with the other. He made a swinging motion for Ethan and Garrett to converge with him.

They crept, guns up, toward the noise. Ethan was closest to the light switch. He waited for Garrett to motion beside him and then he flipped the switch on.

Light flooded the room. To Ethan's shock, Rachel was huddled in the corner, behind the hot water heater, wet, barefoot and bedraggled. She threw up her arm to shield herself from the sudden light even as she scooted farther into the corner.

Relief staggered Ethan. His knees gave out and he damn near hit the floor. He shoved the pistol into his waistband and bolted toward her. Garrett beat him there and dropped to his knees in front of her.

"Rachel," Ethan called hoarsely.

He stopped behind Garrett and stared in utter shock. Oh God, he couldn't take much more of this. How much longer would he live in fear of losing her?

"Ethan?" she called weakly. "He's here? I thought . . . I wasn't sure how badly he was hurt in the wreck."

"He's here, sweet pea," Garrett soothed.

He moved to the side so Ethan could crowd in beside him. Ethan stared, too overwhelmed to say anything. He knew if he tried, he'd just break down and cry like a baby.

She glanced nervously up at him and then her gaze skittered sideways. He swallowed. The caution was there. She was remembering what had happened before the accident. Before she'd been terrorized. His throat ached so damn bad.

"Are you okay?" Garrett asked. As if realizing he was shouting, he lowered his voice. "What the hell happened, sweet pea?"

She shifted, and a gasp of pain escaped in a loud rush. She tried to lift the arm that was clutched against her chest, and it was then that Ethan saw how swollen and misshapen it was.

"Oh shit."

"My arm," she said haltingly. "I broke it when the car hit us."

"Holy fuck!" Sam exclaimed. "Rachel, how the hell did you manage to escape with a broken arm and run through the damn woods and down a river to the lake. I assume that's what you did, hit the lake and take a ride down the shore until you got here?"

She smiled, but it was obvious she was hanging on by the barest thread. Her breathing was erratic and shallow, and she looked pale and shocky.

"Those self-defense moves Garrett and Donovan taught me when Ethan was away so much."

"You're shitting me!" Garrett said. "Hell, and to think we teased you for being such a girl."

"That'll learn you," she said faintly. "I did good. Just like you taught me."

Her words were slurring now, and her eyes slid closed, then opened again like she was battling to stay conscious.

Garrett reached out to touch her hair. "You did just fine, sweet pea. Just fine."

Behind Ethan, Sam was on the phone demanding an ambulance for Rachel.

"Baby, I need you to stay awake for a little while. Can you do that?" Ethan asked in a gentle voice.

He wanted to touch her. God, he wanted to hold her, but he was afraid to move her, afraid he'd hurt her more, but most of all he was scared to death she'd reject him.

She nodded slowly. "I'm tired. I hurt."

Garrett stroked her hair, and he glanced over at Ethan, sympathy bright in his eyes.

"I know you hurt, baby. Just hold on a little while longer, okay? Can you tell me if you're hurt anywhere else?"

She touched her face with trembling fingers. "Jaw aches where the jerk hit me. I kneed him in the balls."

Sam laughed, but it came out weak and shaky like he was

battling the same emotion so raw on Garrett's face and so agonizing in Ethan's soul.

"I'm okay otherwise. I think. Hard to tell. Arm hurts so
bad."

She was whispering now, and her head slid to one side.

"We need to get you out of this corner," Garrett said. "It'll
hurt, sweet pea. God, I'd do anything not to hurt you, but I
don't know how to do it otherwise. Sam's called an ambulance,
but it'll be easier if they don't have to cart a stretcher down the
stairs."

"S'okay," she slurred. "I'm just so glad y'all are here. I was
so scared."

Ethan closed his eyes and bowed his head. Garrett laid a
hand on his shoulder and squeezed comfortingly.

"You try to get behind her as much as you can," Garrett said
in a quiet voice. "I'll get her legs. We'll lift her out and get her
upstairs."

"I'll get some blankets and pillows," Sam said.

For just a moment, Ethan's and Rachel's gazes met and held
for a long moment. Beyond the physical pain, Ethan could see
wounded uncertainty, nervousness and deep sadness. He'd give
anything in the world not to have been the cause of her sudden
hesitation with him. Even if he understood it completely.

"I'll try not to hurt you," Ethan whispered as he slid his
hands underneath her arms.

As careful as he and Garrett were, he felt her cry of pain to
his soul. He gathered her against his chest, and Garrett carefully positioned her arm down her body.

Ethan inched up the stairs, turning sideways so he didn't
bump her into the wall. Sam had gone ahead, turned on the
lights and placed a blanket on the couch.

Ethan eased down, holding her carefully. Sam tucked the
blanket around her and they settled down to wait.

Sam's cell phone went off, startling Rachel. She flinched
and let out a low moan.

Sam yanked the phone to his ear. "Sam here."

Ethan watched closely as Sam's eyebrow went up.

"Yes, we found her. We're waiting for an ambulance. She's
hurt, but I think she'll be okay."

Another pause.

"No, that's fine. Go where you're needed. Nail those sons of bitches to the wall for me. We'll be at the hospital waiting for a full report. Check in when you can, okay?"

Sam shoved the phone back into his pocket.

"What the hell was that about?" Garrett demanded.

"That was Sean. They've arrested two men in the vicinity of the wrecked SUV. They think they're our guys. He's hauling them in for questioning now."

Ethan's nostrils flared. It took everything he had not to react, but he didn't want to disturb Rachel.

"I want those bastards," Ethan said in a low voice.

"Tell Sean . . . one was a tall skinny guy. Dark hair. Mustache. Other . . . he drove . . . was one with gun. Shorter and stocky. He shot at me."

"Son of a bitch," Garrett muttered.

Rachel was fading. Her eyelids fluttered and slowly closed, only to jerk back open again.

Garrett sat on the other side of the couch and said in an overly loud voice, "Is there anything else you can tell us, sweet pea?"

She stirred lightly against Ethan as she fought the veil of sleep. Ethan rested his cheek against her head and tried by sheer force of will to infuse his strength into her.

She opened her mouth as if to speak, and then her brow crinkled in pain. With a barely audible sigh, she lost the battle and slid into unconsciousness.

CHAPTER 39

ETHAN paced back and forth outside Rachel's hospital room. Other members of his family had gathered in the hallway, and they all looked at him with deep concern in their eyes.

Sam and Garrett leaned against the wall closest to the door while Marlene and Frank stood against the opposite wall. Marlene's eyes were red-rimmed and swollen. Rusty stood a few feet away, hands shoved into her pockets. She looked uncomfortable, but her usual belligerent scowl was absent.

"How long does it take?" Ethan spit out as he glanced at the closed door again. "Why won't they let me inside?"

His mom laid a hand on his arm and squeezed reassuringly. "They need to get her settled in without all of us looming over them. Especially you. You probably scare the nurses half to death."

Ethan spun around and paced back down the hall. He was going to go crazy. After hours in the emergency room, Rachel had finally been transported to a private room. She'd only woken up intermittently, and she'd seemed confused and shaky the few times she was conscious.

Her arm was set and casted, her other wounds and scrapes tended to. The doctor assured him she'd make a full recovery. But Ethan needed to see her. He was going to go out of his mind.

The door opened, and they all converged on the nurse as she left the room. She held up a hand with a pained expression.

"She's resting comfortably now. I gave her something for pain. Try not to overexcite her. If you could limit the number of visitors she has at one time, that would help."

Ethan swallowed and nodded. He didn't care who beyond himself got in as long as he got to see his wife. He pushed by the nurse and ducked into the room.

His chest tightened when he got his first look at Rachel lying on the bed. Her casted arm was placed carefully over her waist, and she was huddled in the sheets like she was still trying to protect herself.

A bruise darkened her cheek, and Ethan closed his eyes to the murderous rage that billowed over him.

As he crept closer, he noticed the dark shadows under her eyes. Her lashes rested on her cheeks, giving her already fragile appearance an even more delicate air. The nurse had cleaned her hair, and now it was brushed soft over the pillow and lay around her face in waves.

The flimsy hospital gown did little to modestly cover her, and he vowed at the first opportunity he'd get her something more comfortable to wear.

He reached out to touch her, but his hand shook so badly he pulled it back in an effort to control the tide of emotion soaring through his body.

She'd been through so much. Had he lost her? Had he finally lost her? She'd survived insurmountable odds, not once but twice, and yet the look in her eyes when she'd discovered the truth about their marriage had seemed to break her when nothing else had.

He bent down and pressed his lips to her forehead. The baby-fine hairs at her temple felt like silk under his mouth. Her skin was so soft, so satiny. He inhaled her scent and held it there, just wanting to savor the fact that she was okay. She was alive.

"I love you," he whispered. "I need you to believe that, baby. I need you to believe that above all else."

"Ethan."

Ethan glanced up to see Garrett standing a few feet away, his expression pained. Sam was just behind him.

"Look, man, I know there's a lot I obviously don't know about your situation. I'm not butting into your business."

Ethan stared dully at Garrett, waiting for the hammer to fall.

"She loves you. There's no doubt in my mind she loves you. She's always loved you. What happened last night . . . it pulled the rug out from under her. But she loves you. Hold on to that, okay? Things will be okay. You have to believe that."

Ethan let out a long breath. "Thanks, Garrett. After the accusations I made . . ."

Garrett moved closer and gripped Ethan's shoulder. "It's forgotten."

Ethan grabbed his older brother in a bear hug and held on for all he was worth. Garrett squeezed back and then pounded him painfully on the back.

"Okay, girls, enough," Sam said in a quiet voice. "Mom and Dad are outside like two mother hens. They'll want to peek in on Rachel, and Garrett and I need to talk to you, Ethan."

Ethan glanced up sharply at Sam. "Talk about what?"

"Let me call Mom in to watch over Rachel. I don't want her left alone."

Ethan didn't like the concern in Sam's voice. It went beyond worry over Rachel's condition. He nodded and waited tensely as Sam ducked out of the room.

Seconds later he returned, and then Marlene stuck her head in the door and shot her sons a worried look. Then her gaze rested on Rachel, and tears filled her eyes.

"My baby," she whispered.

Frank came in behind her and placed both hands comfortingly on her shoulders.

Marlene put a fist to her mouth. "I just had to see her. I won't stay, but I had to see that she was okay."

Sam touched her arm. "She will be, Ma. She will be. Garrett and I need to talk to Ethan. Can you and Dad stay with her for a minute?"

"Of course," Frank said gruffly. "You boys go do what you need to do. Marlene and I will call you if she wakes up."

As Ethan headed to the door with his brothers, his mom walked over and hugged him close. "We'll stay as long as you need us, son. If you need anything, you let me know, okay?"

Ethan kissed her on the cheek. "I will, Ma. Don't worry."

Ethan followed Sam and Garrett into the hall and noticed a uniformed officer standing guard by the door. He glanced up at

Sam for explanation, but Sam just motioned him farther down the hall.

Midway down they stopped in front of a set of windows and Sam and Garrett flanked him, almost protectively. How like his older brothers to hover. It was like he was twelve again.

"Rachel was right. Someone tried to run her off the bridge," Sam said bluntly.

Ethan nodded. It wasn't something he hadn't already figured out. "What makes you say so, though? Other than the obvious?"

"Right after you and Rachel left the house, Rio checked in." Sam's eyes flickered for a moment before he plunged ahead. "I sent him back into Colombia to do some recon. Garrett and I were going to meet him and go in after the sons of bitches who held Rachel prisoner. My plan was to make them talk no matter what I had to do."

Anger tightened Ethan's jaw. "Why am I only just hearing about this?"

"It's obvious," Garrett snapped. "Rachel needed you here, not down getting revenge."

Ethan controlled his temper—just barely. Now wasn't the place to tell Garrett what he thought about his assertion that he shouldn't be the one to exact vengeance for his wife.

"Rio tagged the new location of their camp, did some recon, cut out to scout a place for Steele to come in and then Garrett and me, but when he got back, the village had been wasted. Same day Rachel is forced off the bridge."

"Fuck," Ethan whispered. He closed his eyes and gripped the back of his neck, massaging the aching muscles. "What the hell happened over there, Sam? She had to have seen something she shouldn't have. It's the only thing that makes sense."

"But why the hell did they keep her alive?" Garrett asked.

It was a question they'd asked repeatedly, and they were no closer to getting the answers they needed. Out of a team of eight volunteers, Rachel was the only survivor. Everyone else had perished on the plane coming back to the States. And someone had gone to great lengths to make Ethan believe his wife had been included.

"We need to dig deeper into the relief effort. There has to be something we've missed. It was a small organization, and the majority of their team died in the airplane crash. They ceased operations after that. Everything we've looked into has checked out. Nothing suspicious."

Garrett nodded his agreement and looked toward Sam for his input.

"Until we find out what the hell is going on, this family is in lockdown," Sam said grimly. "No one is safe. I'm going to call in Rio and his team as well as Steele."

The brothers looked at one another as they realized at the same moment . . .

"Donovan. Goddamn it," Sam said. "Son of a bitch. I missed check-in."

"You had a good reason," Garrett said. "Donovan can handle himself. He has the best. We can't pull him out now. He'll be home in a day, and we can pull in P.J., Baker and Renshaw to help out here."

Ethan swallowed as the reality set in. War had been declared. First on his family, and now they were fighting back.

"We'll do what we have to in order to keep this family safe," Sam said in a low voice. "I know you want in, Ethan, but Rachel needs you, and your first priority has to be her and patching things up between you. We'll keep you in the loop, I swear it."

Ethan knew Sam was right. He wanted to go after the bastards himself. He wanted their blood for daring to touch Rachel. But Rachel needed him. He needed Rachel.

"Okay," he said quietly.

Sam put his hand on Ethan's shoulder and squeezed. "I'm going to head over to see what Sean can tell me, if anything yet. Then I need to try and raise Van and let him know what the hell is going on. Garrett is going to take Mom, Dad and Rusty home, and Sean is going to provide deputies for their protection. I don't want anyone in this family alone and unguarded. You go back down with Rachel. I'll come check in later."

Ethan nodded, and without waiting for them to go, he turned and hurried back down the hall. He sized up the policeman outside Rachel's door and then walked back in.

His mom looked up from Rachel's bed and then hurried over.

"Has she woken up yet?" he asked her.

Marlene shook her head. "The nurse came by to check her vitals. They gave her pain medication before they transferred her to her room so she'll likely sleep for a while."

Frank walked over and put his arm around Ethan's shoulders. "You okay, son?"

Ethan nodded. "Garrett is going to take you home so you can get some rest. I'm going to stay with Rachel."

His mom frowned. "I'll go home long enough to get you something to eat, but I'm not staying. I need to be here for you and Rachel. If anyone needs rest, it's you."

Ethan glanced at his father. "Listen, Ma. I need you to go home and stay there. Sean's going to post a few deputies for your protection. The best thing you can do for me right now is to be safe. Until we eliminate the threat to Rachel—to this family—no one goes anywhere. I'll be fine, and I'll call you with updates. I promise."

His mom's lips pursed, and she was ready to argue, but his dad put an arm around her and squeezed. "He's right, Marlene. The best thing we can do is go home and stay out of the way so they have less to worry over."

She sighed but nodded. Then she reached up and cupped Ethan's cheek. "You tell her we love her and that we'll be back to see her as soon as you'll let us."

Ethan smiled and dropped a kiss on her cheek. "Thanks, Ma. I love you."

It was with relief that Ethan closed the door behind his departing parents. Finally he was alone. He needed the time with Rachel. He needed to collect his scattered thoughts.

He pulled a chair as close to Rachel's bed as he could go and sat down, leaning forward to watch her while she slept. He took her hand and curled his fingers around hers. His thumb brushed over her palm, and he contented himself with the feel of her skin, warm on his.

How long he'd dreaded facing her when she knew the truth. As overjoyed as he'd been to have her back, each day had been spent on borrowed time. Now he faced the hardest task of his life. Making her believe in *them* again.

She stirred restlessly, her brow furrowed. He picked his head up, eagerly looking for any sign she was regaining consciousness.

Gradually her distress eased and she slipped back under, her sleep seemingly more peaceful now.

So he waited. And as he waited he replayed all their happiest memories. He focused on those, refusing to dwell on the bad.

He must have fallen asleep, because he woke to someone shaking his shoulder. He looked up through bleary eyes to see Sam standing beside him.

Ethan glanced back at Rachel, to see her still resting peacefully, and then he looked back at his brother.

"How long has it been?" he asked groggily.

"Few hours. We just came back from seeing Sean." He broke off and glanced over at Rachel. "Why don't we go down to the nurses' station and grab a cup of coffee. You look like you could use a jolt of caffeine."

Ethan hesitated for a moment then rose, disentangling his fingers from Rachel's. "Yeah, sure, just for a minute. I want to be here when she wakes up."

He followed Sam from the room and nodded at the guard, who was still sitting right next to the door.

"I'm going to leave the door cracked. If you hear her, holler at me, okay? I'll be just down the hall."

The guard gave him a short salute, and Ethan turned to follow Sam toward the coffee room.

THE soft sound of an opening door roused Rachel to consciousness. Through narrow slits, she saw the male nurse come in and draw a syringe from the breast pocket of his scrubs.

Her breath caught, and she kept her eyes barely open, not wanting him to know she was awake. Unease skittered up her spine, but she didn't understand why.

As he moved closer to the bed, he glanced almost nervously behind him, and the hard line of his profile triggered a memory of another time and place.

Castle. Senator Castle. Expected presidential nominee for his party in the next election. Then, it had been two years away. Now it would be one?

Panic made her mind race, and she scrambled to put the pieces together. Castle, this man, two others. She remembered fear of discovery. Of trying to back away. Of this man who was in her hospital room right now turning and seeing her.

His gaze had been rock hard, and she'd seen her death in those eyes. She'd heard Castle order her death.

But she'd been kept alive.

Why?

Her breath was swelling in her chest, threatening to explode from her throat. It took everything she had to lie there quietly while she gathered her courage.

Her fingers twitched ever so slightly. The man uncapped the syringe and picked up her IV line, thumbing the port. Whatever was in the syringe meant her death.

The needle slid into the port.

She erupted from the bed. She slammed her cast down onto the IV line and quickly wrapped the tubing around the stiff mold. Then she yanked as hard as she could.

The catheter jerked painfully from her hand, tape coming free as she screamed at the top of her lungs. She rolled away from the man, climbing frantically over the railing.

She landed hard on the floor and glanced up to see the shock and fury in the man's eyes. Then he turned and fled out of the door.

ETHAN quickly poured a cup of coffee and offered it to Sam and then poured another for himself. He was impatient to hear what if anything Sam had learned from Sean, but he was also in a hurry to get back down to Rachel.

"Let's head back down the hall. You can fill me in on the way," Ethan said.

Sam nodded. "Then you need to get some sleep, Ethan. You're not going to be worth a damn to Rachel in your current condition. Garrett and I can take turns staying with Rachel while you catch a few winks."

Ethan made a rude noise of disagreement and sucked down a mouthful of the hot coffee.

They stepped out of the small family room where refreshments were stored and headed down the long hallway toward Rachel's room.

They'd only taken a few steps when a shrill scream split the air. Ethan dropped his coffee and broke into a run.

The guard posted outside Rachel's door leapt to his feet just as a man dressed in hospital scrubs bolted from Rachel's room and ran straight into the policeman.

They both went down and rolled. The assailant landed a punch and scrambled up just as Ethan hit him hard, sending them both to the floor.

"I got this," Sam said harshly as he pried Ethan away. "You see to Rachel."

Only the fear of what had happened to her kept Ethan from killing the man right there in the hallway. He backed away and ran into the room.

Her bed was empty, and he glanced wildly from side to side until he located her on the floor, huddled in a corner holding her casted arm to her chest.

Her hair was tangled, her eyes wild with a heavy glaze of fear. He wasn't sure she had any idea where she was.

"Rachel," he said softly.

He knelt on the floor beside her and carefully gathered her in his arms. She let out a shudder and started trembling violently.

"Baby, are you okay? Did he hurt you? I need you to tell me what happened."

He never got an answer. The door flew open and a flood of medical personnel rushed into the room.

She went rigid in his arms, and as soon as the nurses got close, she all but crawled behind him.

He held up a hand to ward them all off and shot them his most menacing glare.

"No one touches her until you've been cleared," he snarled.

Sam strode into the door, his gaze going to the floor where Ethan sat with Rachel.

"He's in custody. Sean's on his way. Is Rachel okay?"

"Clear the room," Ethan ordered. "No one comes near her until we know what the hell is going on here."

"Sir, we need to examine her. We need to reattach her IV," one of the nurses protested.

Ethan opened his mouth, but Sam stepped between him and the nurse and put a hand up.

"One of your nurses just tried to kill Rachel. No one is going to touch her until they've cleared security. *Our* security."

The nurse blanched and backed away.

"The IV," Rachel said in a faint voice.

Ethan looked down and touched her cheek. "What about it, baby?"

"The syringe. It's still sticking in the port. He tried to inject something into the line."

Sam stalked over to the line dangling from the pole and

picked up the tubing. A syringe dangled from the port, the needle inserted, the plunger still all the way back.

He and Ethan exchanged horrified glances. Whatever was in that needle had come awfully damn close to being in Rachel's vein.

"You got a glove?" Sam demanded.

The nurse who'd confronted Ethan gestured toward a box on the wall. Sam yanked one down and then gestured for the nurses to leave. As they headed toward the door, the police officer who'd been on guard duty came in.

"Hospital security is crawling all over the hallway. I told them to stay out, but they aren't happy. Sean's got an ETA of five minutes."

Sam nodded. "Keep them out until he gets here. He can deal with them."

Sam slipped on the glove and carefully withdrew the needle from the port.

"Somehow I don't think I want to stick myself with this," he murmured.

Rachel shuddered against Ethan's chest, and her fingers curled tightly into his shirt.

"I don't want to stay here."

"I know, baby. I'll take you home."

He waited for her to refuse, to tell him she wanted someone else to take her away, but she remained quiet and still against him.

He looked up at Sam, who still stood staring at the syringe.

"I'm going to take her to Mom and Dad's. I'll have Mom call Doc Campbell to see if he can come over to see about Rachel. I don't want her here until we know who the hell we can trust."

"I'll stay here until Sean shows. He'll want to come out later to get the story from Rachel. I'll turn this over to him so they can have the lab run it. The assholes are piling up around here."

"Castle," Rachel murmured. "It's Castle."

Ethan looked down in confusion. "What's that, baby?"

"Senator Castle," she said in a clearer voice. She pushed away from Ethan and stared at him with wide, scared eyes. "He'll never let me live knowing what I know."

CHAPTER 40

SHE couldn't get the scene out of her head. It played over and over, the conversation as clear as it had been the day she heard it.

She was confused. She was scared out of her mind. But she was sure of one thing. The conversation she'd overheard a year ago was the reason for all the hell she'd endured since.

Her head ached. Her arm hurt so bad she wanted to die. Sean and several other police officers had descended on the hospital while Ethan and Sam had immediately taken her to their mother's house.

As a result, Marlene's living room had been turned into an outpost of medical and police personnel.

Another pulse of nauseating pain rolled through her body, but she was deathly afraid to take anything after what happened in the hospital. Her fear was probably irrational, but too bad. She wasn't exactly in the most rational state of mind.

"Rachel, you need to let me give you something to make you more comfortable," the older doctor said kindly.

She blinked to bring him back into focus. The pain was making her shocky, and she'd already zoned out more times than she could count during the doctor's visit.

He had a nice face. Older, lined with age. He was probably

someone she'd seen countless times, as he was a Kelly family friend.

But nice didn't mean he wasn't trying to kill her.

He sat on the couch next to her, perched on the edge as he examined her cast, took her pulse, looked over the cuts and bruises that had already been tended to in the hospital. He'd bandaged the small wound from the ripped-out catheter, and now he was offering her innocuous white pills. White pills that could be anything.

She closed her eyes. She couldn't be called paranoid if there were actually people after her, right? And now she knew why. She was at risk. Her family was at risk.

She sought out Ethan, her anxiety rising when she saw him standing just a few feet away. In the midst of hell, she remembered the gut-wrenching discovery of the divorce papers: Ethan's anger, his accusations, and the knowledge that her marriage was over.

What was he thinking? There was so much unresolved between them, but somehow it didn't seem so important now. Did he love her? Did he really want things to be different between them?

She wished she had the answers, but she was too exhausted to pick apart her feelings and her emotions. Way too tired to try to guess what Ethan might be feeling.

She looked up and caught his gaze. His eyes were a raw storm. She flinched at the pain she saw there. Unable to maintain the contact, she ducked her head and looked away again. It was a rejection. She knew it, and she hated that she couldn't do more than just sit there so helplessly. She squeezed her eyes shut and prayed that she didn't completely crack open for all to see.

"Rachel?"

The doctor's voice shook her from her thoughts, and she turned back to see him holding out those innocent little pills in his palm.

Panic leapt into her throat.

Garrett was there in an instant. Ethan started forward but then hesitated.

"Let me have them, Doc," Garrett said. "I'll make sure she takes them in a little while."

She looked gratefully at him. He understood.

The doctor reluctantly stood and held out the pills to Garrett.

"If you need me for anything, just have Marlene call. I'll come right over no matter what time."

Ethan shook his hand as he started out. "Thank you for coming so quickly."

The buzz of activity overwhelmed her. Everywhere she looked, people stood. No one paid her any attention except Ethan and Garrett. They were all busy processing information.

She leaned back against the cushions and propped her cast on her chest. She'd never felt so tired in her life. So completely and utterly beat down. Only fear kept her from succumbing to the deep need for sleep.

"Can you talk to us now?" Garrett asked.

Behind him, Sean and Sam both closed in. Sean motioned for the other officers to stand back. Sam stood off to the side, and for the first time, she made an overt invitation to him. She looked up and then held out her hand.

His eyes widened slightly in surprise, and then he came forward and sat beside her on the couch. Ethan eased down on her other side.

Sam reached for her fingers and squeezed. "You know we're not going to let anything happen to you, right?"

It seemed like an absurd statement in light of all that *had* happened to her, but she still took comfort in the quietly spoken vow. And she believed him. Believed them all. Now that they knew—or they would know—the threat, they would do whatever was necessary to protect her.

"Can you tell us what happened, Rachel?" Sean asked.

She slipped her hand from Sam's, raised it to her temple and massaged deeply as she sorted through the barrage of information pouring through her mind.

"I recognized him," she said simply. "When he came into my hospital room. I saw him a year ago in South America. He was talking to Senator Castle and two other men."

None of them looked surprised by her statement. Maybe they'd already figured out a connection between her supposed death and the most recent events.

"Do you remember what they were talking about?" Garrett asked.

She nodded. "Drugs. Senator Castle outlined a trade-off of sorts. The drug cartel would 'give' him a few victories. He'd take his 'tough on drugs' campaign to the heart of Colombia, score a few huge victories in preparation for his bid for the presidency. In return, he'd open up the drug lanes into the U.S. The cartel also sold out a few of their competitors. It was a win-win situation. Castle looked good and the cartel got unfettered inroads into America and a monopoly on the drug trade."

"And you overheard all this," Sean said.

"Yes. I had left the tent where we were administering shots to the children, to get one of the little girls who had wandered off. Castle and the other men were behind the child's family's hut. I recognized him. I remember being so shocked to see him there. He had been a supporter of the organization I traveled over with, and now I knew why. It was a perfect cover for him.

"I ducked behind one of the water cisterns when I figured out what they were talking about, but it was too late. The man who came into my hospital room saw me before I could slip away. Castle told the cartel to get rid of me. Make it look like a tragic accident."

"Jesus Christ," Ethan muttered.

"But they didn't kill you," Garrett said. "Do you know why?"

She swallowed and let her gaze skitter away as painful memories of her captivity flooded her mind.

"I was their insurance policy. The cartel's. They staged my death to satisfy Castle, but they kept me alive so that if Castle ever reneged on their bargain, they could pull me out and say, *Hey, remember her? Look what we've got.* It was the ultimate blackmail plot."

"Holy fuck," Garrett breathed. "Pretty damn good plan."

The corner of her mouth lifted into a half smile. "They didn't count on KGI."

Ethan tucked his hand behind her neck and gently squeezed her nape. She started and turned her head to stare at him. He held her gaze, and this time she didn't look away. There was so much she wanted to ask, so much she needed to know, but now wasn't the time. She wasn't entirely sure there would ever be a time. The idea that her marriage might well and truly be over hurt more than the broken arm, and medication couldn't fix that kind of pain.

Finally she turned back to the others.

"What now?" she asked, including each of the men standing in front of her in her questioning gaze.

"Now that I have the full story, I can use the leverage against the assholes in custody," Sean said. "Chances are one or all will sing rather than go down for Castle. We're going to need their testimony. A defense attorney would shred Rachel on the stand."

Ethan's grip tightened on her neck. "I don't want her to have to go through that."

Sean grimaced. "It's inevitable she'll have some part in his prosecution. It'll be up to the D.A. as to how large a part. If he can put his case together without her testimony, you can be sure he'd prefer to go that route."

"First you have to make the assholes talk," Garrett pointed out.

"You let me worry about that. In a couple of hours, it'll probably be out of my hands anyway. I'll have the feds and the state police crawling so far up my ass I'll need an enema to remove them."

A series of chuckles lightened the tense atmosphere.

Ethan leaned over to take the medicine from Garrett. Then he turned to Rachel, his expression guarded.

"You need to take the pills, baby. You're hurting."

She hesitated for a moment and then finally nodded. Seconds later, Garrett thrust a glass of water into her hand while Ethan slipped the pills between her lips.

She swallowed them down and then sagged against the couch. She wanted Ethan to hold her. She wanted to go back just two days, to when she hadn't found those damn divorce papers and remembered that her marriage was over.

She watched the goings-on around her with idle curiosity until finally the medicine kicked in and things went a little fuzzy. Sean left, but the Kellys stayed behind. They seemed to take turns casting concerned looks in her direction.

This was home. This was her family.

She wanted to fight. She didn't want to give them up.

"Sleep, baby," Ethan murmured close to her ear. "I'll watch over you."

The quietly given promise was a balm to her tattered soul. There was conviction in his voice. There was love.

Was it enough? She searched his face for something she could hold on to. She'd always considered herself a person with a deep belief in good. Optimistic even. Right now she struggled to find some of that faith. Worry and fear overwhelmed her.

She had every confidence in the Kellys and Sean, the police department. They'd unravel the story and put the pieces of the puzzle together. She'd be safe in time. She could go on with her life.

But would it ever be the same? Would she face a future without the one man she'd always known she'd grow old with? How could she face overcoming so much only to return home and see her life disintegrate before her eyes?

CHAPTER 41

RACHEL awoke disoriented and unsure of where she was. For a moment, panic billowed up her spine, but she felt steady, reassuring warmth around her body, and she relaxed.

She blinked to adjust to the low light in the room. It was one of Marlene's bedrooms. Ethan's old bedroom. It was nearly dark outside—had she slept the entire day?

Her shoulder ached from the awkward position of the heavy cast, and she tried to turn but ran into a hard chest.

Ethan.

She sucked in her breath as she came face-to-face with the man who'd made such sweet love to her—was it only last night?

The stared at each other, neither attempting to speak. Finally the crooked position of her neck forced her to turn back. Damn the cast. Damn the fact she couldn't move worth a damn.

She was spooned against Ethan and his arms hung over her waist, holding her close against his chest. Slowly, he moved his arm. The bed dipped, and to her disappointment he got up.

Again she tried to roll over, but she came up short when she saw he was simply going to the other side of the bed.

He climbed onto the mattress and lay back down. This time they faced each other, and she saw the horrible uncertainty in his eyes.

For some reason it comforted her. She could take uncertainty—God knew she was riddled with it. What she couldn't take was seeing the loss of hope.

He finally broke the silence. "How are you feeling? Is your arm hurting? I have more pain medication for you."

She glanced down at her arm. It did hurt, but she didn't want to zone out on medication again. There was too much that needed to be addressed.

"Has Sean found out anything?"

She could start there, avoid the topic of her marriage for just a little while. The mere thought of going back there squeezed her chest so tight it was hard to breathe.

"Quite a bit," Ethan said. "The FBI is arresting Senator Castle as we speak."

Her mouth fell open, and her eyes went wide. "Just based on what I said?"

Ethan grimaced. "No, baby. You aren't the most credible witness because of the holes in your memory. The men Sean had in custody rolled on him. They're arresting him for conspiracy to commit murder. Your murder. The drug trafficking, the deal with the cartel, his hand in your disappearance . . . that will have to come later as they build a case against him.

"The three assassins all want to cut deals, so they're spilling their guts. The important thing is Castle will be in jail."

"So it's over," she murmured. "After a year, it's finally over."

He thumbed away a strand of hair that had fallen over her forehead.

"Yeah, baby. It's over."

She swallowed hard, gathered her courage and looked him directly in the eyes. "And what about us? Are we over?"

His gaze looked so haunted. There were deep shadows under his eyes. The bandage on his head had been removed, and it looked like there were stitches in the cut at his hairline.

He touched her cheek, and his fingers shook against her skin. His breath stuttered erratically from his chest, and she realized just how hard he was trying to keep it all together.

"I've been the driving force in our relationship for way too long. I push, you give. I destroy and you suffer. I alone decided the course of our marriage a year ago when I shoved those papers at you and watched you fall apart. It's time that you decided what is best for you."

He swallowed, his Adam's apple bobbing up and down in his throat. He sucked in a deep breath through flared nostrils, and his eyes went shiny with unshed tears.

"I love you, Rachel. More now than ever. I want another chance. God, I want it so bad. I'd do anything for it, but I won't force you into a bad decision. I want us to be together. I want us to laugh and love for the next fifty years. I want a marriage like my mom and dad's. I want to wake up every single morning with you in my arms. I don't want *us* to go away."

"What about the SEALs? You weren't happy leaving."

"No," he admitted. "I wasn't. I quit because I thought it was what I needed to do."

"Can you go back?"

He smiled and traced a line around her mouth. "Sam wants me to work for KGI. He's wanted me to ever since I resigned my commission, but I was too damn stubborn and I was too busy being pissed off at the world. You and I need to talk about what that means, but I like the idea. My brothers are pains in the ass, but there's no one I'd trust more with my back. Or yours."

She lay there for a moment, imagining what their future might be like. Their issues wouldn't be solved overnight. It would take a lot of hard work and patience. She wasn't 100 percent yet. Maybe she'd never be.

"I could go see that therapist again," she blurted. "She wasn't too bad."

"We have all the time in the world to make things right with you and with us," Ethan said gently.

Hearing it put that way, some of her anxiety melted away. The tension so embedded in her shoulders lessened, and she relaxed into the pillows.

They did have time. No one said everything had to be perfect tomorrow or even the next day. They could take it one day at a time. Together.

Together.

Never had she imagined her life without Ethan. She didn't want to. They'd both made mistakes, and they deserved a second chance. He was right. God had given them—their marriage—a second chance. It was a wonderful gift and one she intended to cherish.

Feeling at peace with her decision, she snuggled farther

into Ethan's embrace. She turned her face into his neck and whispered, "I love you."

He stiffened, every muscle in his body so tight she could feel the tension emanating from him. Then a great shudder rolled through him, and he pressed his lips to her hair.

"I love you too, baby. God, I love you. I thought I'd lost you. I thought this time I wouldn't get you back."

He shook against her, and she closed her eyes against the tears stinging her lids.

"We can work it out, Rachel. Just give me a chance. I'll make you happy this time."

She pulled away and stared up into a face that was harsh with emotion, his eyes red, his cheeks tear-ravaged. She touched his damp skin, and her heart squeezed with love.

"I want both of us to be happy this time," she whispered.

He leaned down. His lips met hers in a warm, sweet rush. It was a seeking kiss. That of two lovers finding their way back to each other after a long, winding road apart.

She could see the two separate paths converging into one. Though she couldn't foresee the many inevitable bumps and curves that lay ahead, she was sure of one thing. They'd make the journey together.

CHAPTER 42

"I can't wait to get this cast off," Rachel complained. "It's about to drive me crazy."

Ethan smiled as he poured them each a cup of coffee. He glanced over to see his wife sitting at the table that overlooked their backyard, newspaper spread out in front of her. But it wasn't the paper that held her attention. She'd unbent a metal clothes hanger and was trying to insert the end up her cast to ease her itch.

His wife.

He'd never get tired of using the word. Of hearing it. Of thinking it.

"You're going to stab a hole in your arm with that," he said mildly as he set her coffee in front of her. "You'll probably get lead poisoning too. Or maybe lockjaw. Is it rusty?"

She glared at him for a moment and then laughed as she tossed the hanger aside.

"It itches and I can't make it stop."

He leaned forward and kissed her, savoring the brief, casual contact. It felt so normal and so old fogie, the kind of kiss couples share after being together for so long. He loved that sensation of comfort with her even if they hadn't hurdled all their obstacles yet. They were getting there, and that was the important part.

"You only have a few more hours until your appointment, and if all goes well and the X-rays are good, the cast comes off."

She sipped at her coffee and sank back in her chair with a sigh. "I can't wait."

She set her coffee down and pushed the paper toward him. "Did you see the headlines? Looks like our pal Castle is going away for a very long time."

Ethan scowled and crumpled the edge of the newspaper in his fist as he scanned over the article. He wanted the bastard to die for what he did, but in typical fashion the former senator had cut a deal. Not that it was going to do him much good. He'd still be in prison a very long time.

Ethan harbored some pretty vicious fantasies in which Castle got stuck with a bunch of inmates who rated politicians on the same scale as child molesters and acted accordingly.

Rachel continued to drink her coffee, her gaze focused on the landscape she'd supervised over the last several weeks. Ethan had worked tirelessly to turn the yard around. Between Rachel and his mother, he swore he'd worked less in the military.

Amusement twinkled in Rachel's eyes, and he wondered what she was thinking. Her memory still wasn't 100 percent. Far from it, but she seemed to regain more of it with each passing day. The more she regained her health and ridded herself of the residual effects of the drugs she'd been dependent on for so long, the more she seemed to remember.

"So who was Santa last year at Christmas?" she asked.

He blinked at the off-the-wall question. "What?"

"Christmas. You know, Santa?"

He frowned and tried to shake off the shadow that fell over his heart. "Last Christmas wasn't that great, baby. I doubt anyone was. I spent it alone. Here."

Her features fell, and she reached over with her good hand to squeeze his. "I'm sorry. That was thoughtless of me."

He smiled. "No, you had forgotten what happened, and that's a good thing. We thought we'd lost you, but we haven't, so we never have to go back to that place again. Why do you ask about Santa?"

She regained her smile, and her eyes sparkled like twin diamonds. "Well, if no one was Santa last year, that means it's Garrett's turn."

Ethan threw back his head and laughed. "We've already

reminded him, actually. I don't think he was too thrilled, but for you and Ma, he'll do it."

"We could make Rusty his helper. Between the two of them, they'd do a great rendition of the Grinch Who Stole Christmas."

Ethan winced. "Ouch. It's probably not a good idea to put those two together and expect merriment. Besides, you're assuming that Rusty will still be around at Christmas."

A thoughtful look entered Rachel's eyes. "Oh, I think she'll be here. She loves Marlene and Frank. It's the rest of you she isn't so sold on yet."

"Yeah, well, the feeling is mutual," Ethan said. "The girl is a pain."

"Just like little sisters should be," Rachel said softly.

Ethan groaned. "You're worse than Ma."

"Give her a chance, Ethan. She's young and mixed up and she's had a hard life. We all deserve second chances."

She had him there. Boy, did she have him there. He of all people should know the value of second chances. Gripped by emotion—gratitude for just such a second chance—he pulled her across the chair to sit in his lap.

She snuggled into his chest and laid her clunky cast on the table out of the way.

"I love you," she said as she kissed his neck.

"I love you too, baby. We're a study in second chances, you know?"

She turned her head up to stare into his eyes. Her bottom lip pouted invitingly, and he couldn't resist the temptation to nibble on it.

"Sometimes second chances are the very best chances," she whispered. "Because this time we'll get it right."

TURN THE PAGE FOR A SPECIAL PREVIEW OF
MAYA BANKS'S NEXT KGI NOVEL

NO PLACE TO RUN

NOW AVAILABLE
FROM BERKLEY SENSATION!

SOPHIE throttled back and the boat slowed, coming to a near standstill in Kentucky Lake. Darkness shrouded her. The sky was overcast. New moon. Only one or two stars poked through the cloud cover. She was running with no lights and keeping to the middle of the lake until she was sure she was close enough to her destination to move quickly to shore.

She studied the small handheld GPS and then lifted her gaze up the shoreline to the north. According to her coordinates, her destination was another mile down the lake.

She swallowed her fear and nervousness and automatically put her hand on her belly in a soothing motion. Would Sam even be there? How would he react to seeing her again? What would he say when he knew the truth about her?

She glanced nervously over her shoulder into the darkness. The lake was a slosh of midnight ink. The only sound she could hear was the low chop against the hull of her boat.

Her nerves were shot. She knew she was taking a risk, but she was out of options. Her uncle's cronies were closing in on her. She could smell them. She could feel them in every part of her body. There'd been too many close calls in the last weeks.

A smart woman recognized when she could no longer do things on her own. She considered herself a smart woman, which was why she was here. In a damn boat on a damn lake trying to find the father of her baby so hopefully he could protect them both.

After five months of running, the idea of being in such a vulnerable place scared her witless. True, it wasn't as if she drove boldly into Dover, asked where to find Sam Kelly and then parked in front of his house. She had that much sense. Sam would be the first place her uncle expected her to run. Which was why she stayed away for so long.

And then there was the fact that neither she nor Sam had been honest with the other. Both had been other people. The only real thing between them had been the intense desire. She'd fallen fast and she'd fallen hard.

For a man who'd despise her once he learned the truth.

She eased the boat forward, following the line on her GPS. With any luck, she'd dock right in Sam's backyard and hope to hell she didn't get shot for trespassing.

A noise ahead and to the left alerted her. Her head rose and she stared, her nostrils flaring as she sucked in the chilly night air.

A sudden blast of light blinded her. She threw up her arm to shield her face, but it was no use.

The roar of an engine accelerating kicked her self-preservation into gear. Without hesitation, she dove overboard. She smacked into the cold water and felt the shock to her toes.

The larger boat hit hers with a resounding crack. Debris flew into the air and pelted the water all around her. A huge chunk hit the surface in front of her and blew water over her head.

Her mouth filled with water, and she pushed it out before rolling to swim toward shore. She hadn't gotten a full breath, and already her lungs were tight with the need for air.

She surfaced and sucked in a huge breath. Pain exploded in her arm, and she inhaled another mouthful of water. Shock splintered with needle-like awareness. She touched her arm and felt warmth. Liquid warmth.

Blood.

Son of a bitch had shot her! Terror hit her like a sledgehammer. She fought to keep her panic at bay. She had to hold it together. Why the hell had he shot her?

Her hair went straight upward, and her neck popped back as a hand yanked her out of the water. She banged over the side of a boat, and she had the presence of mind to wrap her arms protectively around her middle.

Her baby. She had to protect her baby.

She landed with a crash on the deck of the boat and squinched her eyes shut against the beam of light shining into her face.

"Get up."

She cracked open one eye and stared up at the man looming over her. She glanced around and saw no one else.

"Go fuck yourself."

He kicked her in the arm and agony ricocheted through her body. Then he reached down, curled his hand in her hair and hauled her upright.

If he hadn't still been holding her, she would have went down. Her legs refused to cooperate. Her arm was on fire and hung loosely at her side.

"Where is the key, Sophie?"

"Look, I don't even know you," she spit out. "You don't get to call me by my first name. Or at all. Do you think I'm stupid enough to carry it around with me?"

A flash of silver caught her gaze. Her eyes widened when she saw the wicked curve of a very sharp blade. Then she raised her gaze higher and saw cold determination in the face of the assassin.

Forcing bravado into her voice, she said, "If you kill me, you get squat."

"A fact you're counting on, I'm sure," he said in a flat tone. "My orders are to make you talk. Any way that has to happen. Trust me, you'll talk."

She swallowed and sucked in air through her nostrils. God, what was she going to do? She'd been so close to Sam. So damn close.

All these months, all this time, she'd stayed to the shadows, always one step ahead of her father's grasp. Even dead, he held her by the throat. Her uncle would carry on his legacy of selling death. There was always someone willing to take up the reins.

But without access to her father's wealth and resources, Tomas was crippled. She planned to keep him that way.

The man hauled her close, his breath blowing hot across her face. She felt the edge of the knife against her belly and bile rose sharp in her throat.

"You won't die. Not at first. But your baby will. Tell me what

I want to know or I'll slice you open and let your child spill out of your belly."

Her stomach revolted and she gagged, the knot so big that she choked. Tears stung her eyes, and then rage blew hot like the first wave of a blast.

"You son of a bitch," she bit out.

She'd had enough. The fact that she was constantly underestimated usually worked in her favor, but this guy seemed smarter than the other assholes her father employed. Indeed, he was smarter than her father, who hadn't believed she'd shoot her own flesh and blood.

This bastard wasn't going to give her any easy passes because she was cute and blond and innocent looking. Which meant she had to rely on sheer grit and determination if she was going to keep her baby alive.

"All right, I'll tell you," she gasped out. "Put the knife away."

"I like it just where it is."

He wasn't going to make this easy.

She was careful not to glance down, not to even twitch. No advance warning when she made her move. She waited until she nearly jittered out of her skin. There. The knife eased just a bit and no longer bit as hard into her skin.

She rammed her knee into his balls and crashed her elbow down onto his wrist. The knife clattered to the deck and she kicked it hard, sending it spiraling across the boat.

He grabbed her by the neck, his fingers digging deep into her skin despite the fact he was hunched over, holding his balls with his free hand.

His hand squeezed mercilessly, cutting off her air supply.

She was going to die.

Here on a boat probably not far from where Sam lived. On the lake to make the disposal of her body easier. At the hands of an asshole who talked about murder like he would the weather.

Rage. Red-hot and searing. It splintered through her veins like volcanic fury.

Faking surrender, she let every muscle in her body go limp. Maybe it caught him off guard, or maybe he expected her to fight because his grip eased.

Harnessing her anger, she bolted forward, throwing herself

against the asshole. Forearms across his chest, she shoved, putting every ounce of her strength behind her movements.

He staggered backward, his feet stumbling to catch up with the rest of him. His hands flew up, and he tried to grab the railing.

She jumped on him, and they both went over the side.

The cold water hit her like a ton of bricks.

Down she went into the darkness. She fought off panic and struck out, swimming away from the boat. Several yards out, she broke the surface, gasping for breath.

He was out there. Probably close. But it would take him precious time to get back into the boat to look for her. Time she could use to her advantage.

This time she took a deeper breath as she dove back under, and she forced herself to stay under until shadows grew around her consciousness. She broke the surface and kept her head down as she hungrily sucked in air.

She glanced back to see the spotlight from the boat dancing across the water.

She inhaled quickly and ducked beneath the water again. Ignoring the agonizing pain in her arm, she swam deep and hard. Eventually, her body grew numb from the cold, and the pain receded. She gave a quick murmur of thanks and pushed herself onward.

For how long she repeated the endless cycle of surfacing, taking a breath and going back below, she didn't know. It felt like hours. She wasn't cognizant of anything but the need to survive.

When her strength finally gave out and the adrenaline fled her system, she broke the surface and looked back. To her immense relief, she didn't see the boat. No lights, just murky darkness.

The lake water lapped gently at her chin as she treaded water. And suddenly the pain came rushing back with the force of a car crash.

Barely conscious, she feebly struck out for shore, but it seemed to be a mile away. The current tugged at her legs, sucking her back and down the river channel instead of allowing her to move toward the bank.

Exhausted, she stopped fighting and turned on her back to float the best she could. She had to get out of the water. He'd be looking for her.

Her head cracked against something hard, and she let out a startled cry. She briefly fell underneath the water in panic. When she surfaced, she jerked around to see a large log bobbing in front of her.

Grateful for something to hold on to, she hauled her body up and draped herself over the trunk. The wet bark abraded her cheek, but she was too exhausted to give a damn.

She reached with her good arm and placed her hand over her belly. Her baby had to be okay. She had to be. She closed her eyes as she waited for some response from within. Just a tiny kick. Even a bump just to let Sophie know her baby was safe.

Nothing.

She ran her hand up her arm, feeling for how bad the bullet wound was. In the water, it was impossible to tell. She whispered a fervent prayer that the night's events hadn't harmed her baby.

Again she lowered her palm, feeling for movement.

She fought back the panic. It was common for a baby to be still after Mama suffered a shock. She'd read that somewhere in one of those pregnancy books.

She'd become an expert at self-treatment because she hadn't dared seek medical help. Tomas would have found her instantly. So she devoured every book she could lay her hands on. She took over-the-counter vitamins, drank her milk and exercised so she'd remain on alert. For just such an occasion as when her father's men caught up to her.

There was one star overhead. Just one, and it looked blurry and distant. It bobbed up and down, and she didn't know if it was because she shook so violently or if the lake was rough.

Her arm wrapped tighter around the log, and she pressed her cheek against the wet bark. She could ride it for a while, and maybe it would drift out of the faster current toward the calmer waters of the lake.

Her eyelids fluttered even as she fought to stay conscious. Something warm and wet ran down her arm. Blood. It smelled like blood.

Sam.

His image rose vividly to mind. Her last coherent thought was that she had to get to Sam.